PRAISE FOR VERONICA G. HENRY

"Henry skillfully layers historical realism with fantastic elements to explore the way times of desperation test the ethics of oppressed communities. Henry is a writer to watch."

—*Publishers Weekly*

"Henry's debut draws on a rich history of folklore from various African traditions, as well as African history and Black American history, and almost the entire main cast is Black. The carnival setting works perfectly for bringing together various strange and magical people who aren't at home anywhere else . . . Come one, come all, this magical carnival has all the delightful dangers a reader could wish for."

—*Kirkus Reviews*

"[*Bacchanal* is] gorgeous while somehow never losing sight of the need to unsettle. It captures a sense of wonder and reminds you that too much curiosity can lead to danger. And most importantly, it's Black and never lets you forget it. If you want endearing characters, a charming setting, and characters that refuse to bend to the world's injustices, then *Bacchanal* is the book for you."

—*FIYAH Magazine*

"Set in the Depression-era South and featuring a mysterious traveling carnival, it's a novel of Black history and magic that makes for a terrific read."

—*Washington Post*

"Beautifully descriptive prose that fully captures the places, people, and time period."

—*Booklist*

"Think of a Southern Gothic version of *The Midnight Circus* with a touch of *Lovecraft Country* . . . nail-biting scenes of tension."

—*Lightspeed Magazine*

"Filled with magic, danger, and dynamic characters."

—*Woman's World*

"With a powerful voice that grips you from its very first pages, *Bacchanal* casts a spell on readers . . . Eliza is a wonderful character . . . Not a traditional superhero, Eliza's special power is a highlight of this work, and readers will root for the young conjurer and for Henry as she explores the limits of her gifts."

—Sheree Renée Thomas, editor of *The Magazine of Fantasy & Science Fiction*, award-winning author of *Nine Bar Blues*, and featured author in *Black Panther: Tales of Wakanda*

"Writer Veronica Henry pulls on a mix of African folklore, Black histories, and carnival culture to weave a story of mesmerizing, bizarre, and dangerous magic. With a heroine of unique powers and a cast as colorful as any sideshow, this story offers up its share of delights, adventure, and frights! Welcome to *Bacchanal*. Enjoy the sights. Hope you make it out alive!"

—P. Djèlí Clark, author of *Ring Shout*, *The Haunting of Tram Car 015*, and *The Black God's Drums*

"Readers won't want their travels with the seductive and dangerous Bacchanal Carnival to end. If you took *The Night Circus* and viewed it through the gaze of a young Black woman in the Great Depression, you might get Veronica Henry's *Bacchanal*. Demons, lies, and secrets."

—Mary Robinette Kowal, Hugo Award–winning author of *The Calculating Stars*

THE CANOPY KEEPERS

ALSO BY VERONICA G. HENRY

Bacchanal

The Mambo Reina Series

The Quarter Storm

The Foreign Exchange

THE CANOPY KEEPERS

VERONICA G. HENRY

Published by 47North, Seattle

www.apub.com

ISBN-13: 9781662503801 (paperback)
ISBN-13: 9781662503795 (digital)

Cover design by Lesley Worrell

Cover images: © kaisorn, N.Petrosyan, Max_Lockwood, Christos Georghiou / Shutterstock; © Patrick Lienin / ArcAngel; © Vanessa Stührmann / Unsplash

Printed in the United States of America

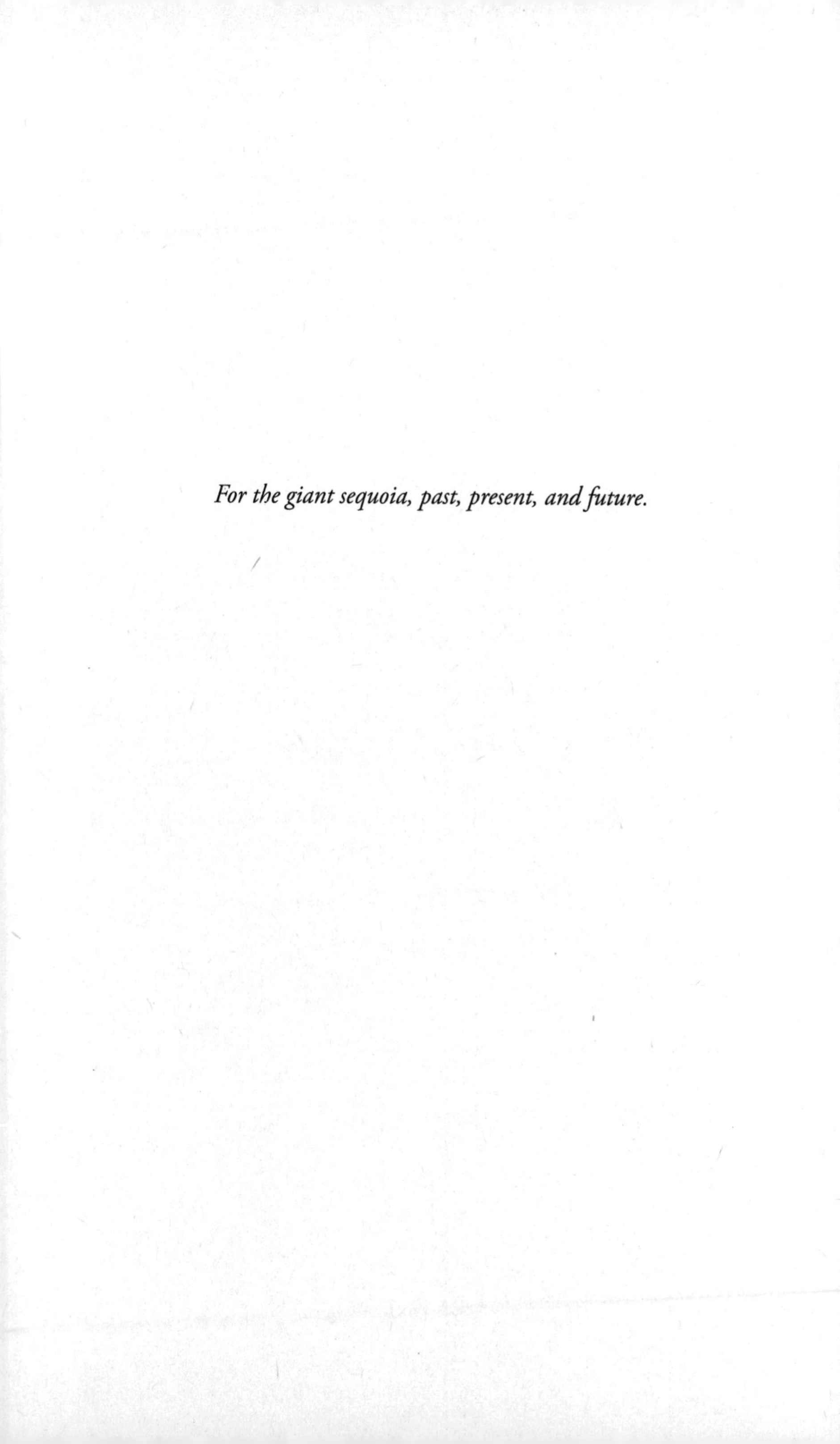

For the giant sequoia, past, present, and future.

The natives and the Rhiza once roamed this vast land

With harmony, balance, and reverence their guide, they lived for spans

But the natives, in trust, welcomed the curious rush

The Rhiza were wary, retreated and hushed

The patient natives tried to explain

But the newcomers only had disdain

For the earth, for the great horned Buffalo, for the wind and sun and moon

They only sought to tame

They bent and broke, thinned and razed

Never received their due

Now the animals gone, the Giants are few

Rhiza is shrinking, what, then, will we do?

—*A Rhiza children's tale*

Chapter One

Sequoia National Park
Middle Fork Dorst Creek Campground
September 2014

Syrah Williams doesn't always dream, but when she does, she dreams of trees.

Here's the way it would go: Soon after Daddy tucks her in for the night, she's fast asleep. And then they call. She hears the sound. No, that's not quite right. She feels it. Like a lawn mower, or maybe old Mr. Brooks's leaf blower. Feels it deep down in her chest.

Behind the place where Daddy says her heart lives.

The trees are the superhumongous ones.

Her favorites.

The Giants.

Her arms don't reach very far when she wraps them around the trunk. Cheek and ear pressed against bark that is warm and spongy. She listens to the Giant's song, a drumbeat that goes on and on. And it smells sweet, like cinnamon sprinkled on apple pie.

Branches, thin and wiry like her legs, curl down from the very top, what she knows is the canopy. They form a basket just big enough for her to sit in with her knees tucked into her chest.

Lifting up, up, up.

She closes her eyes so she won't be scared, but she still is. She's learned not to look down, not yet. Syrah lifts her face, finding comfort in the gentle breeze tickling her skin, fluttering her long lashes.

The Giant sets her atop its shoulders, and they walk through the forest. Her forest. Birds greet them with their chirpy little songs. Squirrels leap into Syrah's lap and flick their fluffy tails, tickling her nose. All the animals speak to Her, to the Giant. And also to Syrah, even if she doesn't understand them.

On those nights when she dreams of the Giants, their walk always ends at the top of that mountain—Moro Rock, at home with the clouds.

But tonight she doesn't want to dream. She's here.

Syrah figures she's just about the proudest four-year-old who ever lived. She and her big brother, Oakly, have a tent all by themselves. He earned the nickname because he couldn't stop blabbing about the blue oak tree he'd read about in school. Made their father take him to see one the very first time they came to the park, back when she was too little to remember.

Mama and Daddy are snoring like baby bears in the other tent. Mama says Oakly sleeps the sleep of the dead. Syrah isn't sure what that means but figures the dead must be a pretty quiet bunch, because her brother always is.

At home, when she crawls into his bed to protect him from the monsters that live in the closet in the corner of his room, he is so still she puts her palm over his nose to make sure his stinky breath is coming out. He only swats her hand away and raises his arm so she can nestle there in the crook made just for her.

Here in the forest, there are coyotes and deer and all kinds of animals, but no monsters. With a couple of sloppy wet kisses to the forehead, but no story, Mama zipped them up for the night. By Syrah's best guess, she has dozed once or twice. Or maybe it was more. That doesn't matter, though, 'cause she's awake now. She's outlasted them all.

And so Syrah hatches a plan.

It's always daytime when she visits in her dreams. But what about after dark? Nighttime in the forest is just cookie jar full with untold treats. The sights and sounds play out in her mind like scenes from her favorite cartoon, *Dora and Friends*.

Leaves shivering in the wind, noisy like the crinkling notebook paper she practices her letters on. An owl, probably that great horned one Daddy pointed out earlier, hooting for all it is worth. Shadows, a gazillion creepy dark shadows, and whatever hides inside them. The screech-shriek, screech-shriek of a California condor. Mama said they were all gone, but Syrah knows there must be at least one left. That skittering along the ground, probably the mouse or toad or squirrel it hunts.

The crazy-weird twisting and churning beneath her outie belly button isn't fear, though. Okay, she's a little afraid. Mostly, she's excited.

After what happened at the river last time with Oakly, where she rolled right off the log he said wouldn't sink and almost drowned—'course that wasn't her fault—Mama had flipped! She'd leaned in, so close Syrah could see the lines on her forehead, and given her that squinty-eyed look. Told her that if she tried something like that again, she'd never bring her back to the park. And Mama knew the forest was her most favoritest of places.

The way Syrah sees it, she just has a certain curiosity about the world. And hadn't Daddy said that was a good thing?

Syrah *had* had a bunch of other plans. Some of them had turned out better than others. There was that time she'd begged Oakly to ride his bike to the top of Greenleaf Hill and race down with her on the handlebars. Hadn't that been epic in its success? And over the summer, she'd made it nearly to the top of the neighbor's palm tree before she got scared and sat there crying like a baby until they found her. But the most recent—the ill-fated socked-feet slip-and-slide adventure through the house—had ended with her having a broken arm. That little stunt had put off their last trip to the park.

Which was why they might not be able to visit again before next year.

Decision made. Syrah opens her eyes. It is dark, late night with cracked streetlights dark. She blinks a few times and uses the nail on her pinkie finger to pluck away the itchy crud from the corners of her eyes. The inside of the tent begins to take shape. There's a little rip at the top. She and Oakly had whined and pouted until their parents gave in and let them pitch their tent all by themselves. Daddy had corrected them only a time or two—after the rip. Mama had stood beside him, hands on her big round hips, and warned, "If it falls down on your heads, it'll be your own doing."

Syrah turns over and squints. She can just make out Oakly's shape on top of the air mattress beside hers, his sleeping bag probably kicked aside. Their food for the weekend is locked away in that metal box the park set up for such stuff. It's supposed to help keep the bears away.

Slowly, so as not to make too much noise, she unzips her sleeping bag just enough to wriggle free. When she puts her hand down to steady herself, her fingers brush against something. Soft. Squishy. Poking right up through the tent.

Syrah feels it again, the drumbeat.

It's Her. She knows it.

It's okay, the hum tells her.

Syrah's stomach gurgles in response. She grabs the bunch and pops them in her mouth. They taste the way mushrooms do before Mama cooks them up on the stove with the eggs.

But Syrah smirks when she makes out a candy wrapper beside her brother's outstretched, likely chocolate-coated, fingers.

She nudges her brother once and he doesn't budge. The second time he flops over, facing the outside edge of the tent. Syrah crawls over him, gets the flashlight out of the tent's storage pocket, and gets right up in his face. This time, when she shakes his shoulder, she flips on the light.

His eyes get that wary look to them. It's the recognition that he'll once again be drawn into what Mama calls her mischief.

He immediately sits up. "No," he says. "I'm not—"

"Shh," Syrah shushes him.

"What do you want?" he says, lower this time. His bottom lip is poking out.

"Not me," Syrah says. "*We* want to get out there and have a look around."

He swats her away. "Your breath stinks."

"And your armpits smell like toe jam."

"Ma and Dad said not to move a muscle until they unzipped us in the morning. Not even to pee."

With the flashlight on, Syrah can see the candy wrapper more clearly. A Snickers bar that he didn't think to share with her. She tosses it in his lap. "They also said no food or snacks in the tent, right?"

Her brother huffs, like he does when he is annoyed with her. This moment has played out before. Each of the last few trips to the park, she's tried to coax him out after dark. And every time, like the scaredy-cat he is, he's turned her down. Syrah thinks she's got him this time, though. She senses his squirming, pictures him chewing the inside of his lip, trying to guess whether she'd really rat him out. She won't say anything. Won't push. She's seen Mama do the same thing to Daddy before when she wants something, and it usually works.

Instead, Syrah lays the flashlight down and crawls over to grab their backpacks. She rummages around until she finds their matching red kangaroo-pocket hoodies. She scurries back over, tries to hand Oakly his. He doesn't take it.

"You don't tattle-tell and I won't," she says.

He sighs, snatches the sweatshirt, and when she struggles to poke her head through her own, he helps her. They pull on their socks and sneakers, then slip outside.

Is it really darker outside than in the tent? For a second Syrah wonders if this is such a good idea. She looks up. The moon is there, just like it should be, but clouds are bunched up in front of it. Soon her eyes adjust.

No other families are nearby, which suits her just fine. Mama said that September was really a late time to visit. Syrah had eavesdropped on her parents and Daddy's best friend, her uncle Dane. He works at the park, and that means he gets to stay here all the time! He warned them about fires and stuff, and Mama tried to back out, but he promised to let them know if there was any sign of the tiniest spark before they came. Syrah had begged and pleaded until her parents gave in.

Syrah glances over at the much bigger and stronger-looking tent her parents share. She holds her breath. Luckily Mama doesn't sneak up on them like a ghost, ready to hustle them back to bed.

Syrah slips her hand into Oakly's, and they make a beeline for the closest path. The ground is mostly clear, except for some branches, but even with her sneakers on, their steps sound as loud as if she were clomping around the house in Mama's three-inch heels.

They run until there is nothing but trees and quiet and dark. It's like every other thing in the park is holding its breath and watching to see what she and Oakly are up to. She doesn't like the feeling that millions of tiny little eyes are watching them, but she doesn't want to turn back.

Syrah doesn't know what she hopes to see, but ain't that the whole point? Something occurs to her and she wavers. She looks up at her brother and whispers, "What about snakes?"

Oakly repeats the words Uncle Dane has told them a bunch of times before: "Stay out of their way and they'll stay out of yours." He does stoop down and snatch up a branch, though. He taps the ground, letting the snakes know that they're coming.

And what had they ever done to them? When her preschool visited the zoo last year, she'd been allowed to hold and pet one. They were actually kinda pretty when you thought about it, especially the black ones shining like the night sky coated in a glossy paint. Once you got past the fact that they crawled instead of walked, there wasn't much to be scared about, not like other kids.

Syrah is amazed by what her eyes are able to pick out with so little light. She stops to lay a hand on a tree. Cool to the touch, not cold. Kind of like a juice box that has been sitting on the kitchen counter for a while. The bark is rough and prickly, like her dad's face when he needs a shave. She takes her brother's hand and lays it beneath hers. "See," she says. "Not so bad, is it?"

"I think it's a giant sequoia," Oakly says. *Wrong*. The tree is likely a fir, or maybe one of the ones that stays green all year, a sticky-needle one. But she doesn't tell him. Mama does it all the time. When and if Syrah has kids of her own, she'll never correct them.

"Let's go," he says, and they keep walking. Syrah hooks her hand in the front pocket of his hoodie, and he wraps an arm around her shoulder, keeping her close. It may have been her imagination—her mother said it was overactive—but Syrah could swear she hears something. A crackling. Have the monsters followed them from home?

A small animal darts into their path. She can just make out shiny, beady little eyes, what looks like a large tail. A squirrel? It stops, tilts its head, then scampers down the trail and up a tree. It's not until her eyes follow it upward that she notices it. A black sky lit up with puffs of orange and gold.

"Look," Oakly says at the same time.

"It's almost morning," Syrah says, worried. "We better get back."

"No it's not, dummy," he says. "Let's get a closer look."

Excited now, they dash from tree to tree until they find one they think is both tall enough to see from *and* small enough for them to climb. It's gotta be a baby Giant—she's sure of it.

Syrah considers herself an expert. Both from her climbs at home and on their previous visits to the park. According to her brother, she's still training, but she's what her teachers call a quick study. Oakly stoops down, and she scrambles onto his back. They start to climb.

Before long, she's scared. "I don't think we should go any higher."

Oakly scooches out onto a branch, straddling it. She slips down behind him. "You stay here. I'm going up," he says.

She shakes her head. "Uh-uh."

"This was all your idea," Oakly reminds her. "I'm not going back until I see."

"No," she says, a full-on wail bubbling in her throat. She wishes Mama and Daddy were here to stop him. Looking down, her stomach flips. Too high. They should go back. They'll find their way once they get down—she's not so sure, though.

"Well, move over. I want to stand up, and I need to brace myself against the trunk."

When he stands, Syrah sees him more clearly in the strange light. His eyes wide as saucers. "What is it?" she says, blinking fast. "What do you see?"

Her brother only points. Syrah turns and tries to balance herself on the branch. But she looks down again and totters. She scoots forward, hopping along the thick branch, tearing her pajama pants in the process. *Oh!*

She jockeys for position, standing and wrapping one arm around the trunk. Next to her Oakly has done the same thing. A quick look reveals angry bunches of dark clouds crowding the orangey sky. Heat dances along her skin. Smoke stings her nostrils. They both cough.

"How far away is that?" she asks, more to herself.

Her brother is scared, she can tell. He shifts over to her side.

"Move, I can't see," he says.

"You move."

A small shoving match ensues until an image of Syrah's mother, her squinty-eyed look, crowds into her mind. He shoves her once and she can't help herself. She shoves him back.

His gasp freezes her. The windmilling of his arms. Her hand, reaching out to try to grab his but missing. Wanting to take it all back.

Her eyes lock onto his. All the way down. Through the branches that smack at his ribs. The leaves that tear at his scared little face. The awful crunch as his head slams into the trunk. The dull whap when his body hits the ground.

Syrah's heart pounds so loud in her chest she can hear it. Her hands fly to her mouth, and she sits there terrified. "Oakly," she calls. He doesn't answer. She shouts his name so many times she loses count. And the fire—she knows that's what it is now, can see the flames—is coming for them.

Her brother's whimpers snap her out of it, and she shimmies down the tree, ignoring the rips and scratches.

Near the bottom, Syrah jumps down the rest of the way and lands hard on her shoulder. On all fours, she crawls over to her brother. Palm to his nose, she feels his breath. Hands on his chest, she shakes him. "Oakly, wake up, please. *Please.*"

He doesn't answer. Tears spring into her eyes and spill down her face. She goes behind him and tries to grab him beneath the armpits. She pulls and pulls but can barely move him. She's out of breath, and the sick is rising up her throat.

Thick smoke surrounds them now. Mama and Daddy. She has to go and get her parents. They can help Oakly.

Syrah pulls her brother closer to a tree, nestles his head against a large root sticking out of the ground. She takes off her hoodie and drapes it over him. Then she stands, picks a direction she isn't sure about, and runs. Runs faster than she ever has before.

Interlude—The Mother Tree

Seeing with Ancient Eyes

Peace . . . Interrupted

Just like the fauna, the humans, and the earth, the trees of the verdant forest immemorial sleep. I alone keep watch, here deep beneath the forest floor.

My children labor aboveground. Frontline warriors, enduring all as the world conspires to destroy us.

I do not sleep. I am The Mother, and mothers take little rest.

My roots stretch down to the earth's core, and upward through the cave ceiling. *Mycelium.* Filaments like light, threads that branch and rebranch. Infinite. Pulsing with life, new and old. In this way, we speak.

On this night, two things happen, one of which I know—and which I feel deep, deep within my bark—will change the course of history. For my caretakers and, ultimately, the humans. A bristling old Giant nestled high in the upper region of the forest sounds the alarm first. Our labyrinth of delicate roots, finer than a sapling's first sprout, thunder with a dispatch that is only for our ears. The pines and firs, the cedars, and the other Giants awake with a start.

What began as a whiff of smoke-fouled air is quickly ignited. The hungry flames are already consuming the forest's living things. The trees inhale and brace themselves. The stockpiling and sharing of resources begin.

Feverish flames, cones flower and spew their spores.

Some will take root where the brush is charred and cleared; most will perish.

The flames both friend and enemy.

Heat and life.

Heat and death.

A sliver of my attention remains attuned to the lattice, doom encroaching, while the other turns to a gnarled but proud blue oak tree. Not a Giant, but a relative still.

It received the perilous missive grudgingly, as if it had more important affairs to attend to than its probable end. And in a way, it does. It continuously laments the blackened areas of its pale bark, the death blow delivered by the last of the ever-hotter fires. As the blue oak nears its end, it weeps for what will become of the place that it has called home for more than two hundred years.

The oak resists the message, considers it with a bristle of its leaves before passing it along to the next in line, a fir. In this way, the trees and their fungal partners can prepare. It cannot recall the last rainfall; the tree's memory is not what it used to be. Still, it sends its roots probing, stretching deep into the loose soil, and gathers what nutrients it finds: rich sugars, minerals, water.

A stockpile for defense.

Belowground exhausted, the oak forages nearer to the surface. There is little moisture, but it gathers what there is.

Before it sends its filaments over to help another tree, it notices a trickle of fluid near one of its larger, exposed roots. An exploratory tendril samples. Coppery, metallic, some water. It has tasted human blood before.

I recognize it immediately.

The body is small, human. The oak sends a single threadlike filament up through the earth. First it sucks greedily at the liquid, pulling out the tiny traces of water and sharing a bit more with its nearby siblings.

Having fulfilled its duties, it explores. Travels over the small, thin body. Poking and prodding. The child is breathing, but the heart rate is weakened.

The tendril encircles a small hand. The child wriggles in response. Its skin—his skin—like the tree's own, has suffered breaks and wounds. The tendril continues its exploration, along the arm and over the chest. It traverses the entire length of the body before inching upward, crawling along neck, cheek, nose. There is a slash on the forehead, oozing more blood.

Unable to stop itself, going on instinct alone, the tendril plunges into the opening.

It drinks deeply, then stops. The child is sending signals of its own. Distress. Hurt. Pain. Loss. The information is fed into the lattice, and a response comes moments later.

I inform a Giant from the upper region to alert my caretakers. I also instruct the oak to sustain the child. My command has an edge to it that makes the blue oak take notice. The Giants rarely express interest in a human. But when their leader, The Mother, has spoken, all in the forest heed the call and listen.

The flow reverses. Nutrients are fed to the human child. Replenishing. Soothing. The child squirms but doesn't fully rouse.

The Keeper. The leader of the caretakers, like me, rarely sleeps. I tell her of the arduous task at hand. As swiftly as she resists, I lay my roots down, and she acquiesces. Already the caretakers work to manage the fire.

Far away, at the base of another Giant, a veil is lifted, and The Keeper and her guardian emerge into the smoke-filled forest.

Now I see through her eyes.

The sky is blazing, the color of midday at night. She stops only once to gauge the approaching fire.

Sounds of human activity are afoot. Sirens in the distance. Voices carrying on the wind, far enough away for her to do what she must. She and her companion, ever watchful, pick up their pace, twice, three times that of the humans. In minutes they are at the base of the blue oak.

I can sense their worry, their uncertainty. Their disdain. Even my trusted Keeper of the last two hundred years is not happy about this. But I have made myself clear: take the child, bring him belowground. *Yes, a human child.*

The child—a boy—is small, not yet ten human years by my assessment. The Keeper touches him gently, assessing. She believes he likely has a concussion, probably some internal injury. But his brow is smooth, his breathing even.

Mother, why? Her thoughts come to me.

I do not answer.

I do not have to.

She is, after all, mine to do with as I please.

The Keeper scoops up the child. Her centuries-old hands strong yet tender. This time she runs faster. The forest creatures going in one direction—away. She is headed toward the growing heat.

Hesitation before the veil is lifted. She takes one look back, then steps into another world, our world, Rhiza.

Our savior, our undoer. A small, unconscious smile curves at the corners of his small mouth.

Chapter Two

Three Rivers, California
April 2042

Syrah sits alone in her car, absently tracing a slender index finger over the raised edges of the insignia on her T-shirt. The symbol, expertly embroidered onto the fabric just above her heart, is the symbol of achievement.

At the last minute, a few blocks away from her destination, she cut down a side street and killed the engine. The back end of winter saps the heat from the car. Her nerves are raw and jagged, as if shorn with a pair of dull scissors.

Three surprisingly interesting but wholly unsatisfying years of college studying botany before she admitted to herself what she really wanted. To fight back. That fire chose to pick a fight with a four-year-old; all she ever wanted was to return the favor. And to be where she was most at home. Outdoors, of course. Not just any old place either.

Sequoia.

Eventually.

It had taken a couple of stints as a volunteer firefighter to know for certain. Those were some of the hardest-working people she's ever known. Tough work and even tougher love. Without that experience she'd never have had the guts to make her decision final. One station after another followed, from brand new to barely standing. Wasn't it Rumi who said that as you start to walk on the way, the way appears?

She did it all so that she can land right where she wants to be, where it all started. Not cataloging flowers and shrubs; her mother had tried to force-feed her that path. Syrah, though, she wanted to take the fight back to her destruction's doorstep. Spend her days, her life, facing down the fire. Taking from it as it took from her.

Syrah imagines her parents, Anissa and Trenton Carthan, about two hundred miles south, in Compton, sitting on that leather sofa so worn the brown has faded to beige in spots. Arguing about which one of them made the ill-fated call to tell her about her past, about the turmoil that led to her adoption. Mama was probably behind it; it was the kind of thing she'd want to do under the guise of false nobility. Daddy, as usual, was no match for her when she put her size sevens down.

Daddy, though, had been downright frothy at the mouth when Syrah told them she was going to be a firefighter. And when she told them she was coming back to Sequoia, lord, between the tears and the shouts, she thought they'd both end up on meds—for different reasons.

The one-way arguments—they weren't really interested in the why, so she'd stopped explaining it—had ended a month ago, when she began ignoring their calls. Choosing to leave voice mails only when she knew they were asleep, letting them know she was okay. That she loved them still. In this situation, space was called for, and that's the gift she gave them all.

Forest fires *were* more frequent. Ten thousand acres razed last year alone, taking half as many giant sequoia with it. They burned hotter, burned longer, and had already wiped out much of Kings Canyon and were hacking around the shrinking edges of Sequoia too. And Syrah Carthan was not only a firefighter but the new head engineer of Fire Station Ninety-Three. You didn't have to be a parent to understand the worry. She's never told them how worried she is herself. She fears if she says the words out loud, she'll put her car in gear and motor all the way back east, where things are only marginally less bleak.

Syrah wriggles her toes in her brand-new, NFPA-certified boots. They're a little snug, yet to be properly worn in, and she's pulled the parachute cord laces too tight. Her army-green slacks rough against her skin even after a few washes. Her breath coming out in little white puffs. *Wasting time,* Syrah says to herself. She jams a thumb on the ignition button and starts the car again.

Three Rivers is her kind of town, in most ways. Outside the times when the streets are clogged with tourists, there's little traffic, no chain restaurants—not a one—and the people she's met so far seem to look out for each other in a way that isn't of the nosy-neighbor variety. It's small and close, a closet of a city, and it makes her feel more at home than she has in a long time.

The ride along Sierra Drive and Generals Highway is a dream commute. Tall coniferous evergreens, open road, and the occasional car passing along the two-lane path to her new job. She's already sampled the fare at the Gateway, and though her stomach reminds her that she was too nervous to eat last night, there are too many cars in the lot already to dip in for a bite. Maybe later.

She's scouted the way before, but this time pulling up and parking is different. "Official" is the word she'd use. Two bright-white engines sit outside in the engine bay, the number E93 painted on their sides in red. Chill bumps are having a party on her forearms. This is everything she's wanted, and now she can't bring herself to open the door.

The building has a brick facade, a flat roof with the building's only windows right beneath it. One of the engine bay doors is rolled open, probably still a little too chilly. *Nothing to it but to do it,* Syrah thinks. With a deep breath, she gets out of the car and walks toward the garage.

Her heart warms as she gets closer to the fire engine. Gleaming white with red trim. She can almost hear the siren's roar. She can't wait to go out on her first call.

Moving deeper into the bay, she finds her gaze drawn to the hose racks with rolls and rolls of fire hose, and fittings are neatly arranged to her right. A workbench with a few pegboards packed with tools. Tool chests alongside it. And toward the back she spots a treadmill, a bike, and an elliptical. A bench and a few weights. Those are the only things out of order. This is a crew that cares about fitness. A good thing. Crew lockers are lined up toward the back wall, and that's where she spots Lance.

Outside of the suits at administration, he's one of two crew members she interviewed with for the job. He had peppered her with what she thought was one too many questions about her leadership experience. Aside from that, he seemed friendly enough.

Not that she is looking for a work husband or anything. Quite the contrary. She doesn't begrudge others for making friends out of colleagues. It just isn't her thing. More important to her, Lance is clearly knowledgeable and dedicated. Couldn't really ask for more than that.

She greets him with a warm smile she doesn't truly feel. Nerves? Being cut off from her parents, perhaps? Something is making what should be the best day of her life . . . well, not.

"Heeey. Look what the cat dragged in," Lance says, extending his left hand and clapping Syrah on the shoulder with the other.

All the tension bunched up in her shoulders loosens and drains away, just like that. A shame how much a friendly welcome and a flash of teeth is all she needs to feel like herself and, though she hates to admit it, like she belongs.

Belonging is a thing high up on a shelf. Each year, as she grew, grasped for a friend, reached for a playmate, that shelf stretched farther and farther away.

"Glad to be here," Syrah says, with a grin of her own. He doesn't give her the man squeeze when she takes his hand; she likes him even more.

"You all settled? What'd I tell ya about Three Rivers? Was I right or was I right?"

Syrah chuckles at the speed with which Lance rattles off the questions. "Let me take those one at a time," she says. "Settled, yes. And this town is everything you said it was. So, yeah, you were right."

"Come on inside and meet the gang," Lance says with a flick of his head.

Though Syrah practically memorized the station layout when she toured the place, she allows Lance to precede her through the common area with the worn sectional and television mounted on the wall between two narrow floor-to-ceiling windows. Pool table, check. Small kitchenette, check. Battered old wingback in a corner, a stack of dusty frayed paperbacks stacked on an iron-legged, distressed wood side table, check.

Everyone should be gathering for the morning briefing, so Lance swerves right and, at the conference room doorway, gestures for her to go ahead.

"What's green and smells like pork?" This Syrah hears from a firefighter wearing his sunglasses indoors. The deliverer of what she knows will be a crude joke looks up at her—everyone does—before his gaze slides away as if she's a walking oil slick.

"Kermit's finger," Lance blurts out from behind her.

Inwardly, Syrah cringes as most of the members of Station Ninety-Three erupt in raucous laughter. She notes the few who don't join in. Lance, though, he's surprised her with an old nice-guy-turned-asshole bait and switch. She won't let that happen again.

She's been at her new post for no less than five minutes, and already she's made to feel unwelcome. It isn't the first time and won't be the last. It's what she's come to expect. Hiding her emotions is a requirement of the job, if not life, but she's caught off guard and can imagine the scowl on her face. Lance notices.

"Looks like the new chief here don't like the way you talk, Alan." Lance pushes past her and takes a seat at the table, leaving Syrah rooted there, seething.

"Aw, come on," the jokester says from his seat, elbowing the men sitting on either side of him. "From that little write-up they gave us, she's worked in every fire station from here to the other side of the country. I know she's heard worse. The lady can take a joke. Am I right, Ms. Carthan?"

She *has* heard worse, and she's sick of it. Alan, is that his name? He doesn't address her as *Chief*, and she doesn't want to hear her first name roll off this idiot's tongue, so she doesn't take the bait on the slight. "I can," Syrah says. "Just haven't heard a funny one."

That earns a hoot from a few of the firefighters and a mean mug from the jokester. Syrah goes over, grabs a doughnut from the open box on the butcher block countertop in the back of the room before she takes her place at the head of the table.

"Don't mind them," another firefighter says. His manner is as stiff as his voice, but she reads real concern there. Lance has already fooled her, though, so she'll withhold any thoughts of him being an ally. "They're just pissed Imagine Dragons aren't touring anymore."

Syrah appreciates him for not stating the obvious. She's the only woman at the station. A Black woman. And the head engineer. She knows exactly why some of the men at this table may already have a problem with her. She's run into so many like them she's lost count. Doesn't matter. She's landed her dream job in a dream location. Be mad. Quit. She doesn't care. She'll find other people who want to be here.

"That's okay," Syrah says around a bite of her doughnut. "I'm still holding out for Blue Ivy to start touring again."

The other men at the table don't physically move away from her, but their collective energy does an about-face. Syrah quickly finishes her breakfast in silence while the others chat among themselves. Then she leans forward, elbows on the table, and steeples her fingers. "All right, everybody. Let's get the introductions out of the way. I know Lance and the amateur comedian, but I need to hear from everybody else, and then we'll get on with the national situation report."

Chapter Three

Rhiza—Crystal Cave
Beneath Sequoia National Park
September 2014

What does dirt smell like? Romelo wondered. It was something he'd tried to figure out since he'd woken up in this place. It was everywhere. Walls that should be smooth with paint. The floor, which should be wood or tile or carpet. Even the ceiling. He was trapped in a house made of the stuff.

The weird-looking lady, Taron. She had been sitting in the chair beside him when he woke up on the hard bunk bed. Her skin was all strange, deep wrinkles more on her body than her big wide face. Clothes that didn't make any sense. Her hair—thick, ropy, and long—was nice, though.

She dabbed something on the lump on his forehead and fed him nasty, watery soup. Shushed him when he winced and whimpered. She said he had been asleep for a couple of days.

Your family is dead.

His parents had warned him about bad people. The kind who lured away little kids by telling them just that. But for as long as he could remember, Romelo had gotten feelings about people. Could figure out what and who he was dealing with.

This Taron didn't give him that side-eye that people get when they're not telling the truth; however, he still didn't want to believe her. Problem was, he couldn't remember much.

When he blinked his eyes open and the shock of seeing her passed, she held his hand and told him his family was gone; he had screamed and screamed until his voice gave out. Cried enough to fill a pool. See, his body believed it before his mind did.

At times when he awoke, the angry one, Ezanna, was there. He told Romelo that he should consider himself lucky to be away from the humans. All either Taron or Ezanna would say of Romelo's parents was that the fire took them.

He tried to run. Got lost. Woke up back in the room made of earth.

Romelo didn't know how much time had passed.

He gave the whole matter a little more thought and came to the conclusion that dirt smelled like, well, dirt.

Your family is dead.

As hard as he had tried, Romelo couldn't stop hearing those words over and over again in his head. He didn't know what time it was, or even the day. But when he poked his head out of the room—he wouldn't call it *his* room—the hallway was empty. He listened for a while and then stepped out, leaving the door open behind him.

He was underground; he knew that much. No windows or doors that he could make out. No cars rumbling by. No sun or moon.

Romelo had tried to escape—at least a dozen times by now, he guessed. Waiting until everything had gone all quiet. He would slip out, tiptoeing through what he could think of only as streets. There were only two directions: left and right. But then it got complicated. Around one corner would be a dead end, and another would open up to three or four other streets. He walked. Walked until his feet hurt—they had hidden his shoes.

Each time, the lady, Taron, or Ezanna, or one of the other adults found him scared and huddled in some corner of a cave and brought him back. She told him there was nothing left for him "topside," as she called it.

But he would try again.

"Hey, half-height." Romelo kept walking. He hated the nickname as much as he hated the boy who flung it at him like a bucket of mud. Funny that it came from the smallest boy or tree thing or whatever these people were. Small, but still not as short as him. "Did The Keeper let her pet out for a walk?"

The sounds of their bare feet thudded against the dirt. Nobody in this place wore shoes. Romelo didn't try to run.

He lifted his chin, met the leader's gaze. "Romelo Thorn Williams." He spoke slowly, clearly. He didn't know how, but this eased the fear, let the anger get out ahead of it. In his mind, Romelo's chest swelled up, wide and strong like the others. It wasn't true, but the picture helped. He scanned the group, four boys in total, looked 'em all in the eye, then settled on the leader. "My name is Romelo Thorn Williams," he said again.

"Thorn?" the instigator, Ochai, said. He twisted Romelo's name, the only thing he had left of his life, into something ugly. Spit it out like he could barely tolerate the word being in his mouth. "You modern humans are so stupid. Why must you have three names? Especially one that doesn't mean anything. You have not been assigned your life's work yet, and you never will. Not here. You don't belong in Rhiza."

Hearing Ochai tell him he didn't belong only made Romelo want to prove him wrong.

"Yet here I am," Romelo said. "And if you want to show me how to get out of here, and you're half as brave as you are down here in a freaking cave, you can come to my neighborhood. See who don't belong then."

"Did you hear that? It speaks!" another boy said. It was the tall thin one with the mean eyes. The one who always marched up to him and thumped him in the still-sore spot above his left eyebrow. They were all almost as big as grown-ups. Way, way taller than him. "All we heard when he woke up was him mewling like a wounded dog."

The boy went on to try to imitate Romelo's wailing cries after Taron told him that the only life he knew, even if he couldn't remember it, was over. The others laughed and jeered. Romelo squeezed his eyes shut, trying to block out the sound.

His memory about that night had spots as big and wide as some of the caves he'd explored. The faces of his family were clear, though: Mama, Dad, Syrah. When he pictured them, he felt warm all over. It didn't last, though. As hard as he tried to hold on to their pictures, they seemed to fade more every day.

Human, outsider, half-height, weak. All these things had lured him into fights he'd lost. But he did learn a few things too.

"You dumb topsider." Romelo felt the sting of the insult like a slap but did nothing. He didn't cry, and for that he was immensely proud of himself.

Ochai turned his back to Romelo and spoke to his loyal followers. "It was abandoned in the forest," he repeated. Already Romelo was tired of hearing the lie. The instigator had the bulk of a teenager but the squeaky voice of someone Romelo's age. "His parents were losers who start forest fires."

A rage that had been slowly building, stoked by every insult, burned in Romelo's belly. They could say mean things to him; they could beat him up. Slip worms in his food when he wasn't looking. But the one thing he had from the time before he'd been constricted to being a prisoner in this place was those three people. He knew that they loved him. He wouldn't let anyone talk smack about them.

An inhuman snarl escaped Romelo's throat. Trapped like he was, it felt good to let it out. Ochai turned, a look of surprise on his face. Romelo balled his fists and launched himself at him. They toppled to the ground, and Romelo twisted himself up on top of Ochai.

He pummeled the boy's face until it was bloody. It was all over Romelo's hands, on Ochai's nose. Splattering his face.

But then Ochai laughed.

He flipped Romelo over easily and pounded him with one crushing blow after another.

Romelo's body felt like pulp. It seemed a year or two had passed before the crowd cleared and someone pulled Ochai off him. Romelo was snatched up and dragged away. Over his shoulder, he looked back at the stunned faces of his tormentors. He expected to be punished, but it would all be worth it.

Then he locked eyes with Ochai. He wasn't really hurt, maybe more shocked than anything. Even a little afraid. But if Romelo wasn't mistaken, there was a little bit of admiration too.

Romelo knew then that this had to be the last time he let them bully him. Told himself it would end here. And he believed it.

I should be dead.

But he was as alive as anyone, and the only thing he could promise himself and his dead family was that he would survive.

Chapter Four

Sequoia National Park, California
April 2042

Syrah pulls up outside the cabin. And there, standing on the porch, waving at her, is her uncle, Dane Young. A virtual relic of a park ranger, family friend, her rock. "Uncle Dane" until her twenty-fifth birthday, when he said she didn't have to call him that anymore. Seven years later, she still can't break the habit.

According to her mom, he is a bachelor through and through. Her words of choice had been "die-hard recluse, weird." Daddy had corrected her, saying that if a man chose to remain a bachelor, who were they to question it? At least the man can probably leave his underwear on the floor without somebody hassling him, he'd say.

Syrah has seen him a few times since she moved east, mostly holiday dinners at her parents' home in Compton. But more often than not, they'd had to make do with video calls. He thought the fossil fuels still in use by most of the airlines released too much CO_2 and, along with the nitrogen oxide vapor trails, made flying irresponsible. Most cars were electric, but he wasn't one for cross-country drives. She didn't think the man ever left the state of California.

Dane Young isn't a blood relative, not a former neighbor or treasured teacher. But he's family all the same.

And his Christmas presents? Legendary. New laptops every other year (her old ones donated to kids in need), the expensive telescope he sprang for when she first expressed an interest in studying flowers as a little girl, windfalls in the form of college-fund contributions. Dad had gone so far as to tell him he was doing too much. The tall man with the gentle smile and sad eyes had been a steady, welcome presence in their lives. And until now, as she climbed out of her aging car, she hadn't asked why.

The cabin sits at the center of a small rise, nestled between stands of conifers: firs and spruce and pines. A wall of jeweled pale greens intensifying into glistening emeralds. A clearing sits on either side of the winding graveled driveway. Prismatic wildflowers poke their way up through the tall grasses, swaying their thin hips in the breeze. It is the smallest house she's ever seen, but it rivals a Beverly Hills mansion in natural beauty.

"I see you made it," he says, coming down the steps and pulling her into an embrace. He is one of those rare people whose hair doesn't gray. From the fuzz on his chin and upper lip to the Afro still dented by his ranger hat, his hair is as dark as hers. Rare is the time when you find him without his uniform, but today he wears dark blue jeans, sneakers, and the University of Southern California sweatshirt she got him for Christmas of freshman year.

"One thing is clear." Syrah returns the hug and plants a peck on his smooth cheek. "You don't have to worry about anybody rolling up on you out here. You'd see them coming a mile away."

"I bet you whoever built this old house had that in mind," Dane says. "For me, it's just home." He watches her for a moment. It never makes her uncomfortable, these little breaks of his. Uncle Dane is more thinker than talker. She wonders if maybe he, like her parents, is going to lecture her. Instead, he says, "I'm really proud of you. Come on inside."

There are two people on the planet whose approval Syrah covets: her father and her uncle. These words from him are like the gift of a million stars. Her chest goes all tight, and just before she cuts it off, something inside her relaxes. Allows herself the time to feel, to let the emotion sit there unbothered. She's safe. She doesn't have to chase the feeling away. She'll always belong here.

Syrah glances over at the two antique rocking chairs on the porch. The bright-white paint looks like a recent job. If she squints just so, she can make out the streaks of red that she remembers. "Mind if we sit outside?"

In answer, Uncle Dane makes his way to the chair nearest the railing, his chair.

"Gonna hit the bathroom first," Syrah says.

Her uncle is already rocking, his gaze focused somewhere over the tree line. "I'll be out here."

Before Syrah can fully close the door, her mind is already at work, trying to knit the broken pieces of her time here back together. But her bladder urges her toward the short hallway, two doors on either side of the birch-lined walls. She's had a boyfriend or two in her time, emphasis on the "boy." Supposedly grown men who had no idea of the power of a toilet brush and a little vinegar. She needn't worry about that here. Dane's bathroom is a little aged, a rust spot here and there. But it is as clean as her daddy's kitchen.

She makes quick use of the facilities and washes her hands. After tearing off a strip of paper towel from the dispenser mounted on the inside of the cabinet door, she dries her hands. When her hand is on the front door, it hits her. Of all the things to recall, she knew where to look for the paper towels?

Back outside, Uncle Dane is sitting with an ankle crossed over his knee. Sinking into the other chair, Syrah enjoys the gentle creaking.

And then, in her special way, she sees.

Blades of grass trembling lightly, the work of a grub or worm, or another insect marching across the ground. A trail of large brown ants winding their way up the post, single file. The leader holds something aloft, an offering for the hive, for their queen. A fat bumblebee zipping from plant to plant. One yellow ring slightly more vibrant than the others.

Her gaze traverses the evergreens, the cones, and then settles back on the porch. She looks over, and her uncle is watching her again.

"What?" she says, then: "No, don't answer that, because I know what you're going to say. Just tell me, which one? Did Dad or Mama convince you to try to change my mind one last time?"

Dane's laugh sounds richer in person. Like the coffee she used to get at that diner outside Florida City when she worked at the Everglades National Park.

"One thing's for sure, nobody is going to put anything over on you." Dane regards her with an expression she is starting to grow concerned about. Is it worry for her, or is something wrong with him? And how old is he anyway? She knows that he's got a few years on her parents. Why hasn't she thought to ask? Kids are often so wrapped up in their own lives, the adults around them become fixtures, sort of like furniture. Always there for them when needed, but not worthy of much inspection. She vows to change that. To get to know who this man is, lonely now that she really looks at him.

"Why do you stay out here by yourself?"

"Let's talk about my alternatives, shall we?" he says.

"I'm listening."

"Los Angeles." Dane rocks and talks.

"You would have been able to come to my soccer games, for one," Syrah says with a chuckle.

"Smell that?" Dane lifts his face and sniffs.

Syrah does the same. There is a hint of smoke long past, but beyond that, nothing. "I don't smell anything."

"Exactly," Dane says. "That smog you grew up with? I tried to get your parents to move to Fresno a dozen times. The air down there—the air everywhere else—can't compare. There's no traffic. No smog and, most importantly, no Walmart within twenty miles."

Syrah nods. "Can't argue with that."

"I could ask you the same question."

"You already have."

"You know what you're walking into," Dane says. "It's not like I thought it would stop you from trying. And I'm not just talking about those knuckleheads you have to deal with at the station. This can be a good post, but it's dangerous. We're losing, you know. The last fire almost took out this old place."

"And somebody has to be here to help stop the next one," Syrah says, suddenly annoyed. She's so tired of fighting this battle. Why can't the adults in her life just accept her decision?

"Didn't have to be you, and that assistant engineer down there at Ninety-Three is going to remind you of that every single minute of every single day."

"I've dealt with worse, trust me." Syrah stands and leans against the porch railing. "No, I don't know why I was drawn to work here. Maybe it was so somebody could watch over you," she says. "It just feels right." She gazes out over the clearing.

"And it's weird," she adds. "It feels familiar."

Dane stops rocking. "Familiar how?"

It is the tone in his voice that makes her look down at him. She wonders at his sudden alarm, but hunches her shoulders. "I don't know. It just does. Maybe I'm just making it up. It probably looks like every other park I've worked at."

"Those didn't have the Giants." Dane seems to settle back down.

"I've seen the pictures," Syrah says.

"Those are nothing." Dane shakes his head. "You have to see them in person."

"Even more of a reason for me to be here. These trees aren't going to protect themselves."

"It's not like I haven't tried," he says. "I've added an educational component to the tours. For the people that visit, you know? Trying to get them to understand that we're the trespassers. And that if these trees die off, it won't be long before we all follow."

Syrah ponders this in silence. She hates to admit that, until now, she hasn't seen her mission as quite as lofty. The words circle, then settle on her shoulders like a fifty-pound shawl.

Interlude—The Mother Tree

Seeing with Ancient Eyes

Sadness.

In the beginning, we were only us.

Giants alone with the sun and the moon, the gentle breezes and distant ocean sprays. Nascent and fertile. Sound and smell and sight were birthed. We stood strong and nimble, saplings soaring toward the sky, branches and leaves arcing ever upward.

There was peace.

They may suggest otherwise, but the fungi were the second to colonize this earth. Vast swaths, relentless in their replication. They glimmer as parables for life itself. Their black fungal strands groping blindly until they mixed and blended with our roots. And the latticework dawned.

Next came the animals. Four legs first, then two.

For a time, there was reverence. A recognition of our preeminence. But within a century, the slaughter began.

An explosive shrieking rattled the rootcast. Protect. I birthed the first of them. It was not so unusual then. To grow a thing, a humanoid like a leaf, dangling from branches, sustained by nutrients from the fungi, the very earth.

They grew and thrived. They reproduced and burrowed beneath. Growing and gaining strength.

The onslaught continued. The intruders cut and sliced and mowed us down with a manic frenzy.

The protectors rallied. There was much blood and bad feeling born of it. I have purged much of this history, but some of it persists.

The massacre abated, but in their infinite quest for discovery, the two-legs set about destruction, ours and theirs, under the shroud of industrialization.

Now the air is too warm, as are the seas. The land is shrinking. The fires burn too bright.

The waters roil and hurricanes build, ripping us from the ground, tearing our roots.

The air that we take through our leaves, that we breathe, is tainted with poison.

We, the Giants, adapt. When the flames blacken our trunks, we drop our cones and hope that the seeds of the next generation take root, that we may begin anew. That when the parents succumb, the saplings might live on.

We are creatures made of time; we live in the present and the past and the future all at once. Enduring the fears and hopes and all the anxieties and anticipations that are the price we pay for our majestic crown. Through our latticework, we tap into our fertile memories, plotting a future despite the dim realities that await.

In cities, some plant more. But they are small and separated. The earth packed so tightly that roots have no place to grow and expand. And when they buckle their concrete and pipes, we are made to suffer for our very being, our fight to survive in their world.

All because of the Western humanoids and their bloodthirst for more, always more.

The numbers of our protectors are thinning. Gone in the fires and succumbing to sickness from pesticides they were never made to ingest. We have stood idly by for so long, content to watch our destruction like casual observers. But the trees grow angry. We have the ability to fight back, and more are determined to do so.

But this would mean war.

I have done my best to quell these thoughts of rebellion, but every year my voice grows weaker. The earth is crying.

And I fear the time for reckoning grows nigh.

Chapter Five

Sequoia National Park, California
September 2014

In the aftermath of the last of a devastating series of fires, park ranger Dane Young combed the western edge of the park with grim determination. Against the warning of the fire ops crews, he had joined them in the search. Even with the oxygen flowing through the tank, he struggled to breathe. To see. Billowy clouds of ash and smoke blurred everything around the edges.

Survivors from the foothills area campgrounds streamed past them. Those who'd made the wise decision to camp closer to the park entrances. His friends were seasoned campers, and they'd chosen one of the more remote areas of the park. The area closest to where the fire had started.

Bad weather wasn't to blame, nor were lightning strikes or excessive heat. He'd checked and checked again. Chances were, one of the people running past them had started the blaze. No matter how many signs were posted around the park. No matter how many times he'd counseled and updated the park website, people still managed to do stupid things. Things that cost them more than they understood.

His friends were out there somewhere. The Williamses and their two children. Panic flared in every cell in his body. If they didn't make it out of this . . . he wouldn't finish that thought.

"Over here," a voice called. He and a couple other firefighters surged toward the voice, and he stopped in his tracks and sank to the ground. The tent. He had helped them pitch it the day before. And he also recognized the two bodies, huddled close together. They weren't moving. They had been spared the flames, but what most people didn't understand was that the smoke was often deadlier, at least to people.

Dane let the tears flow freely. He had long since stopped caring what other people thought of him. One of the firefighters asked him, "Were these the folks you were looking for?"

He nodded. But then his eyes settled on the smaller tent next to theirs. A burst of adrenaline propelled him back to his feet, and he ran toward it. He unzipped the flap while the others ripped the sides open. The kids weren't there.

Dane—Uncle Dane to the children—spun in all directions. "The kids," he said. "Two of them. They've got to be here somewhere."

He hoped against all hope that they were out there, together and safe. The group split up so that they could cover more ground.

They walked for what felt like hours. The park was thankfully absent the animals that had no doubt gone to search out higher ground. He took in the state of some of the trees. Some untouched. Others with blackened trunks. His grief doubled.

He walked until he was exhausted, waved off suggestions that he should head back. That they could continue the search without him. It was already daybreak, and he'd been out all night, but he couldn't stop. Wouldn't. For his friends.

But by the time they made it to the line of the fire, where the damage brought fresh tears to his eyes, they hadn't found either of the kids.

They doubled back, sweeping the area again. Near midday, when they completed the circuit, the kids were still unaccounted for.

While the others continued their sweep, Dane got the idea to check the nearest visitor center—Lodgepole. In these kinds of emergencies, the centers became gathering places for both survivors and those seeking news of loved ones lost.

The fire's lingering heat spewed its hot breath across his face and hands, carrying the scent of charred wood and—he gulped—flesh. The sounds of raised voices and frantic activity battered him from all sides. Dread and fear played a macabre game of catch in his mind.

The air was a little clearer here. Swirling lights announced the presence of a couple of ambulances sitting in the parking lot, while one streaked away, siren blaring. A few blank-faced people sat on the ground in parking spaces meant for cars, blankets wrapped around their shoulders.

It was the glass littering the scene that drew his attention next. Lodgepole's entire front facade was blown out. Looters? Frightened folks seeking shelter? Probably both. Then his gaze was drawn to a group congregated off to the side of the entrance, near the park placard. Between them, a small child, a flash of Dora pajamas.

The girl, Syrah.

She locked eyes with him and ran straight into his outstretched arms. She was trembling so badly. Breathing interrupted by racking sobs. Dane struggled to hold himself together, to not dissolve right along with her. He willed the tears back. After Syrah calmed some, he asked her, "Your brother? Is your brother with you?"

She could only shake her head. "I couldn't find him," she cried. "He fell. I pushed him. I couldn't find Mama and Daddy. I left them. I left them all."

The child wailed again.

She was hysterical, and Dane didn't blame her. Her parents, her brother, missing. His friends. And he had told them it would be okay.

"Don't worry," Dane lied. It was a mercy. "We'll find them."

Just then another ambulance pulled up. Though Syrah appeared all right, he wanted her checked out. He picked her up and took her over just as the EMT stepped out. He explained to them all that she was his godchild. That her parents were gone.

He stood by while they examined her. He exhaled the breath he had been holding when they confirmed that, aside from a few cuts and scrapes, she was fine.

It fell to him to tell her about her parents.

"I have something to tell you," he said. "Your parents. You know how much they loved you—"

"They're dead," she screamed. "I know it. They're gone."

Dane's heart shattered with each convulsive sob. He didn't know what to do. He was probably all she had left, but he was in no position to care for a four-year-old girl. Where would she go to school? Sleep? He hadn't even been able to keep his houseplants alive.

His friends would want him to try, but how could he? He would have to find a way. Wasn't it his fault that they were gone? He couldn't get the image of their bodies out of his mind. The girl hadn't asked how her parents died, and he was in no hurry to tell her. He had only said they hadn't suffered. But they had. They had choked and worried about their kids with their last breaths. He was sure of it.

"We're still looking for your brother," he told her. "And we're going to find him."

Only, days later, her brother still hadn't been located, and he steeled himself to tell her so.

By that time she had stopped crying. She barely ate and slept on his small cot while he slept on the floor beside her. She spoke little. And after he told her about her brother, that he was likely also lost to the flames, she didn't speak a word again. Until.

Chapter Six

Sequoia National Park, California
December 2014

Uncle Dane slept on the bedroom floor. Syrah knew it was hard 'cause she sat there sometimes during the day, just doing nothing. He had told her he wanted to sleep there. Said she was doing his back a big favor.

Her uncle didn't think she saw how he scrunched up his face and rolled his shoulders and neck when he woke up in the mornings, but she did. Every day when he asked her if she slept well, she told him she did, even though she didn't. She didn't go walking on the Giant's shoulders in her dreams anymore.

It made him happy, this little thing about her sleep. Most of the time he was so sad, as sad as her. When she fake snored, she heard him sniffling. He cried most nights, but she couldn't.

Their days were so quiet. She watched him sometimes. Uncle Dane just stood there, looking out the big front window and sighing. He missed them too—Mama, Daddy, Oakly.

When she tried to go to that part of her mind, where she was sure the answers she wanted would be, as she got closer, it was like a bright-red stop sign popped up. Every time she tried to remember, she couldn't get past it. After a while she figured it was just easier not to try.

When her uncle attempted to talk about them, asked her if she really understood why she now lived with him instead of her parents, she only shrugged. Oakly used to say she talked too much. Now her words were all dried up.

She could remember her old house; it was bigger than Uncle Dane's. She even had her own room. She did her best to stay out of his way, but they often tripped over each other. It was like living in a log cabin. The walls, floor, and even the roof were some kind of wood. She didn't think the Giants liked that so much.

The kitchen was in one corner at the back of the cabin. It had a really tiny refrigerator and a deep sink, where she stood on a stool and washed the dishes after dinner.

There was no computer, but there were books. Only books about the park and flowers and stuff. She couldn't read all the words, but she liked to look at the pictures when the TV couldn't hold an image, which was most of the time. The bedroom was big enough for the bed and a dresser. All the art on the walls were of trees.

But she loved the front porch. Sometimes she sat in the red rocking chair, but most of the time she just sat on the top step and looked out at the park. She was sitting there when she saw the white car coming up the long drive. It drove up in front of the cabin. A lady she didn't know got out.

The lady gripped a bag on her shoulder and walked on heels like Mama's that sank into the dirt. But Syrah thought she had a kind face, so she didn't comment.

"Hello, Syrah," the lady said with a smile.

"Hi," Syrah mumbled. She didn't return the smile, though.

"Is Mr. Young here?"

Syrah looked around behind her, and then the front door opened.

"Ms. Martin," Uncle Dane said. He shook the lady's hand. "Wasn't expecting you so soon."

"Syrah," she said instead of answering him. "Would you give us a moment, please?"

Syrah looked up at her uncle, who nodded. She went inside and pushed the door to just shy of closing. Adults thought you couldn't tell when they wanted to talk about something important. Of course the lady had come to talk about her. And the way Syrah saw it, if it was about her, then she ought to know what was said firsthand. But instead of arguing, being empty of words and all, she just plopped down on the floor with her back against the door, pulled her knees up to her chest, and listened.

"How's she doing? Talking any more?" the lady, Ms. Martin, asked.

Uncle Dane paused before he spoke. "If she remembers anything, she ain't saying. Aside from some nightmares, she's physically all right."

"Physically," Ms. Martin repeated. "How long has it been? A couple months? Almost three? And not a word about any of it? Maybe we need to get her in front of the doctor again?"

Her uncle blew out one of his tired breaths. "I can't tell you how to do your job, but you ask me? Maybe it's best if she doesn't remember."

"I can understand why you'd say that," Ms. Martin said. "Truth is, I kind of feel the same way. I mean, what she's been through. It's awful."

Syrah thought about that. She inched her way toward that spot in her mind, the place with the big flashing stop sign, and decided to back away. Maybe, for once, the adults were right.

"Look, I love that kid. I loved that family. Everything in me wants to keep her here. Keep her safe and do right by my friends. But I've got to be honest. The other part of me knows I'm in no position to raise a kid out here."

So quit this job and let's move somewhere else, Syrah thought.

"There's school," Ms. Martin added. "Friends, socialization."

"The only friends she'll have out here are bears and squirrels."

"I'm glad you're seeing things my way," Ms. Martin said. Syrah heard some papers shuffle. "I think I've found a suitable adoptive family."

"So soon?" Uncle Dane said.

Syrah leaned too hard on the door at that, and they must have heard her, because someone closed the door all the way shut. It was much harder to hear, but Syrah pressed her ear against the door.

"Not soon enough for them," Ms. Martin said. "They've been waiting to adopt for two years. They're really good people. Completely vetted. Financially stable. Married twelve years, no children."

"And they're okay with adopting a four-year-old?" Uncle Dane asked. "One that's been through some trauma?"

"I've advised them of the circumstances of Syrah's accident and what happened to her family."

I don't want a new family, Syrah thought.

"You know," her uncle said, "I was about to ask you why they didn't have any kids, and I stopped myself. I get the same question all the time, and I hate it."

"I can understand why," Ms. Martin said. "I get the opposite. People ask me all the time why I have three children and still work this kind of job."

"It's because it suits you," Uncle Dane said.

"Exactly," Ms. Martin agreed.

"Okay, tell me more about these people." A pause, then: "The Carthans?"

"Anissa and Trenton Carthan." Ms. Martin sounded all excited. "Aside from what I told you, it's all there, and I'll leave that with you to review. Mr. Carthan is a math teacher. High school. Mrs. Carthan is a physical therapist."

"What about them personally?" Uncle Dane asked. "And the marriage? On solid ground?" He waited again, and Syrah held her breath. "As solid as any marriage can be, anyway?"

"They've actually just completed two years of marriage counseling. According to them, best decision they've ever made."

"Wait a minute," Uncle Dane said. "This says Compton. That's hours from here. I thought we talked about Visalia or Fresno even. I want to be able to stay in contact with her."

"It's not easy to find someone willing to adopt a child her age. The Los Angeles area was the best I could do. At least it's still in the state. They really are the best family I could find. The others I didn't even present to you."

Syrah didn't understand exactly what marriage counseling was, but it sounded like a good thing. She tuned out after that, though. Because one thing was clear. She was happy here with her uncle, only he didn't want her anymore. She was going to have to go live with these new people. The Carthans. Part of her didn't want to leave this place. It was beautiful. But somewhere deep inside, it felt like it would be good for her to leave. She was old enough to see that her being here made Uncle Dane sad.

When she heard the car driving away, on the other side of the door, Uncle Dane said, "Back up, I'm coming inside now." She did as told, and he walked in and asked her to join him at their two-seater dining room table.

"Knowing you like I do, I'd say you heard most if not all of that. Am I right?"

Syrah nodded.

"If I could, I would keep you here and raise you myself, but I hope you understand why I can't. Would you be willing to look at this file with me? Learn a bit more about these people?"

Syrah nodded again.

Uncle Dane touched her chin before he opened the folder. "Know that no matter what, I'll be here for you. I'll visit. I'll stay in touch."

He flipped through the contents and read out loud. "Anissa and Trenton Carthan. Early thirties, close to my age." Then he showed her the pictures. They were almost of equal height. In one picture they stood side by side, holding hands. She recognized it as a pose, something she and Oakly did all the time for their parents. But it was the second picture that made Syrah smile.

It was one of the ones people take without you knowing. Where Mama said showed your true personality. The two of them were in a store of some sort. They each had toy lightsabers and were waving them around.

Uncle Dane told her they had a small but well-kept two-bedroom home, and she would have a room all by herself. A nice public school within walking distance.

"They look like good people," Uncle Dane said to a still-silent Syrah.

She looked up at him, lip trembling with the threat of tears. "But they aren't you."

Chapter Seven

Sequoia National Park, California
June 2042

There was a television show once, or was it a movie? Syrah had seen the firefighter, suited up, fearless as an ill wind bearing down on a dead leaf, race into a building that was more flame than whatever structure it had been. While the other firefighters and onlookers shook their heads at what they were sure would be the end of the woman, even a young Syrah guessed they were wrong.

Sure enough, commercial-break quick, the lady rushed out of the building carrying a squat, trembling bulldog, just before the whole thing went up in a fiery whoosh and collapsed behind her. Ma and Daddy had sucked their teeth and walked off, but Syrah had decided then and there what she'd do with her life. She, too, would become a firefighter.

She chuckles now, thinking about how ridiculous that imagery was, even if it did plant the seed. As the droughts worsened, shows like that one had sprung up on every television network. Some did a more serviceable job than others, but most barely scratched the surface of what it really meant to be a wildland firefighter. It's exhilarating. "Hiking to the top of Mount Everest"– or "crossing the one-hundred-yard-dash finish line ahead of the pack"–level stuff.

And it's mentally and physically exhausting. Fires don't spin up between the comfy corporate hours of nine to five, then neatly extinguish themselves at the end of a scorching shift.

No, ma'am, they burn hot and heavy for hours, days, sometimes weeks. Endurance is what it takes to battle the flames—Olympic-gymnast, pro-footballer, long-distance-runner kind of shape.

It's not hard, then, to understand why when firefighters aren't out battling a blaze, preening over a fire truck and other equipment, or engaging in some continuing education, they are training. Always . . . freaking . . . training.

Syrah is the last one outside—intentionally. She doesn't show it, but Lance's little stunts have begun to grate on her last nerve. She hasn't told her family, choosing to confide only in Uncle Dane. With him she won't have to hear Dad's I-told-you-so's or Mama's bullish hints that she should go back to school and finish that botany degree. Blind, the both of them. Can't they see that if somebody isn't here to fight the fires, the few plant species in the park that haven't already died out will be gone right along with the Giants and everything else?

The effects of losing those most senior, most vital of Sequoia's citizens? She can't afford to even think it, afraid her fears will one day manifest into the most devastating of finales.

Keeping up her "work face" has grown more difficult with each day. And this is only two months in. How is she supposed to make it a year? If there's one positive out of this whole mess, it's that she's got two allies so far, a few others likely waiting to see if she's got what it takes to stick it out, both the job and the harassment.

Most of the crew haven't been buddy-buddy, but fair and at least cordial. Then there's Alvaro Reyes. Dark eyes, long lashes that stir up a tidal wave of butterflies in her gut every time he bats them at her. He calls himself her Afro-Cubano right hand. He's always checking the ringleaders, Lance and Alan, and generally having her back.

Feelings can be so underhanded. She hasn't been remotely interested in anyone since that last breakup more than a year ago. And now she's getting all doe-eyed over a man who works for her. *Don't shit where you eat.* Mama's advice for once is spot-on. But someone needs to tell that to the butterflies.

The breakup. Her mother had liked this boyfriend; that should have been the first sign. But he had been a good guy. A Georgia Gullah Geechee and military veteran with a fierce love for his parents and huge extended family. Syrah had never told him, but as an only child without so much as a play cousin, it made her jealous. He was a little much with neatness and prone to let that family of his use him as their personal bank. But this was a man who made dinner, massaged her shoulders, and rubbed her feet when she'd been out in the field for twenty hours straight, instead of telling her she needed a more suitable job.

The roses in front of her apartment complex had gone through two seasons of triumphant blooms when she'd broken it off. It had been all his fault. He'd driven her down an unpaved road and over a rotting bridge to her personal edge. Four words of fuel, delivered one quiet, perfect evening: *Move in with me.*

The crew is milling around waiting, and with effort Syrah leaves the hurt for now, knowing she'll revisit it another day.

It is Alvaro she nods at when she walks up. She wishes it were different, but traditionally the assistant engineer leads the exercises. If she were to go outside protocol and change it, Lance would put up a stink about it. She gestures for him to get started, and he gives her the barest of chin lifts in response.

"Finally," Lance says and claps his hands together. "For today's physical festivities, we'll do a nice easy hike up to Alta Peak. Seven miles there, seven back. Some rough terrain but views that you'd cough up half your paycheck for. Any questions?"

When there are none, the crew files into the fire trucks. As pump operator, even if not on a call, Alvaro is in the driver's seat. Syrah, as captain, sits in the front right seat. She looks at the radio, blessedly silent. Just to spite her, Lance piles into the seat right behind her. The rest of the crew hops into the other truck, and they are off.

They drive through the town, passing homes small and large, nestled in the trees. Everything is quiet at this early hour, no movement besides a deer or two gearing up for a day of foraging. Highway 198 is a real shit show of a drive in a car. In a fire truck the size of a small yacht, it's downright scary. Two narrow lanes winding ever upward and, in spots, only a low railing separating you from the steep drop-off. But Syrah keeps her breathing easy and her hands clasped not too tightly in her lap. Lance's presence fills the truck; he's like a boil on her behind, making it difficult to get comfortable. She feels a quick brush against her hand—Alvaro. She doesn't look down but can't deny how much the gesture settles her.

She's here. The park and the post she's fought so hard for. Once she gets outside, she can let it all go. Lose herself in the crisp, clean air and be in the presence of the Giants. Let the physical activity give her something else to focus on.

Soon they pull into the Wolverton parking lot that services Alta Peak. Everyone files out of the trucks. The crew fall into their individual preparations: stretches, neck rolls, deep breaths. After a few minutes, Lance calls everyone to attention.

"All right, guys and gal"—he stops to wink at Syrah—"let's move out."

Lance takes off at a sprint toward the Wolverton trailhead. Syrah charges out behind him, and the rest of the crew falls in, single file. The first two miles are a piece of cake. Her body falls into a natural rhythm with the pace that Lance sets. Her lungs blissfully expanding and contracting. She's lost in the beauty of the surrounding landscape. She's heard that spring is the time to visit. And she knows she did so when she was much younger, with her birth parents, but those memories are smudged. Only hints and suggestions remain, like words fading from aged paper.

Greens of every hue; massive red firs (deeply furrowed purple bark and bottlebrush needles), white firs, a few sugar pines. On the right side of the trail, the narrow ravine that houses Wolverton Creek. Wildflowers in a profusion of color that the almost botanist in her hopes to peruse in more detail one day. By the fourth mile, the trail takes a few steep switchbacks before you come huffing and puffing upon an open space that reveals views south over Kaweah Canyon and the Castle Rocks formation.

This is Panther Gap, where the path junctions with the Alta Trail that runs between the Giant Forest Museum and the summit of Alta Peak.

Lance speeds up. And the terrain is steeper and higher. Soon the tightness in her calves and the burn in her thighs confirm it—running anyplace else is not running in the Sequoia National Park.

But as she passes the General Sherman tree, it is the Giant that really takes her breath away. There are more images online of Sequoia's Giant groves than of any other tree in any national park. Uncle Dane had told her, and he couldn't have been more right: nothing prepares you for seeing one in person. You'd think with such reverence, people would care more about protecting them.

Bark the color of cinnamon sticks. Trunk wide as five Baltimore row houses. She has to crane her neck to see the top, stretching nearly half as tall as Los Angeles's Wilshire Grand Center. The thick canopy like a leafy green cap. So taken is she that she stumbles over her own two feet.

"All right back there, Chief?" Lance calls over his shoulder.

"Never better," Syrah snaps, annoyed at herself for giving him the chance to see her misstep.

She rights herself and the run continues. The air is still morning cool, but sweat trickles freely down her back and pools uncomfortably around the snug band of her sports bra. Nearing a bend in the pathway, Syrah is distracted again, this time by the scenic view from an overpass. From the corner of her eye, she notices Lance dodge left.

Her head swivels back just in time to see a massive branch directly in her path. She can't stop herself and trips over it. Syrah curses and stumbles off the path and slams into a gnarled old blue oak tree. She falls, tearing through her pants leg and nicking her knee.

She glances over her shoulder and sees the entire line has stopped. Lance, of course, is the first one at her side.

"We get this fallout all the time," he says, offering a hand to help her up. "Storms toss these branches everywhere."

Syrah looks at his hand like it's a dangerous animal and comes to her feet on her own, brushing the dirt and blood from her knee. She lays a palm against the blue oak's trunk to steady herself, and her breath catches. Not because of the pain. It's the vibration, like the feel of a motor. The tremor pulses through her body, straight up to the base of her skull. Something about the sound tickles a space in her memory, but it's out of reach.

"I called out, you know," Lance says, waving a hand in front of her face. "Over my shoulder. 'Branch!' Didn't you hear me?"

"Bullshit." Syrah rounds on him. "You didn't say anything, you son of a bitch, and you know it."

Lance screws up his face. "You calling me a liar?"

"I'm calling you an asshole *and* a liar."

"Whoa, whoa." Alvaro steps in between them. "Let's just keep our cool. Officially, if you look at the brochures, when you interview, even that sappy-ass video on the website says that hazing is a thing of the past. That don't mean anything to old Lance here. He cooks up something different for everybody; you never know when it's coming. Guess he's determined to keep the old traditions alive. Ain't cha, Lance?"

Lance blinks. The rest of the crew seems caught between wanting to nod and wanting to look away. And then Lance laughs.

"It's just a little good-natured ribbing," he says. "I see you, Chief." He gestures at her pants leg. "Guess you'll be wanting to head back and tend to that knee."

In response, Syrah takes off at a fast run. She doesn't have to turn around to know the crew is behind her. The sounds of their feet pounding on the path let her know. She doesn't care if Lance is with them or not, but she vows to never let him lead again. Protocol be damned.

Syrah has never run this path, but she checks her watch and notes the time. She'll run for another half hour, then turn and circle back the way they came. She resolves to run every single trail in the park in her downtime so that Lance never has the chance to blindside her again.

After a time she finds herself lost in the run again. She wanted this job more than anything. A bear may get her. She might take a fall off Moro Rock. The flames and the smoke are always threats. All these potential hazards may take her away. But no self-assured, misogynistic loser is going to. She eats insecure men like him for breakfast.

She is the only woman in the crew. That doesn't bother her. She was the only one on her flag football team, the only Black woman in the advanced physics class her father made her take in high school. What bothers her is the suggestion that she is less. That she can't and never will stand for. It is something her father has prepared her for, though. That speech he gave her at every precipitous turn: "You'll have to be twice as good, work twice as hard." And that even then, there would be those who will find her very existence a threat.

Fear, though, makes people do strange things.

Her knee hurts. Her feathers are not only ruffled but standing on end. By the time the crew finishes the run, Syrah adds on five minutes of jumping jacks for good measure. Aside from everything she's laid eyes on in the park, the most satisfying thing she's seen that day is the sight of Lance bent over, hands on knees, face reddened with exertion. Breath coming in great, humiliating gasps.

Interlude—The Mother Tree

Seeing with Ancient Eyes

Hope

I am The Mother, and mothers take little rest.

Against the wind, the storms, against human assaults, the gnarled blue oak still stands. A little more gnarled, a little harder of hearing. More obstinate. My Keepers have tended to its part of the lattice more and more over the years. They have done well.

The blue oak sends a missive. *Another,* it says, *like the human child, a replica, is here.* Her blood tells the tale.

History, again, has shifted.

The fungal seeds planted so long ago are nearly ready to bloom.

She is here, and eventually she will come to me.

Chapter Eight

Sequoia National Park, California
June 2042

In the back of the fire station, there is a picnic table under the cover and shade of what Syrah guesses, based on her abbreviated studies, is a big-leaf maple tree. Its heavy branches, lush and green with spring, humble her, this most beautiful manifestation of life.

During her early tour of the station, she had imagined this a sanctuary. A place to relax alone between calls. An early-morning spot to think before the day's activities commenced. She had pictured herself observing discreetly from the corner of an inside window as her coworkers enjoyed barbecues, an impromptu game of soccer. She, herself, content to watch. She did not share other people's need for friends and was comforted, not bothered, by the fact. Comfort, even camaraderie, were not to be found here.

Her second-in-command, Lance, probably turned much of the station against her before she set foot in Three Rivers. The mutiny likely hatched moments after her interview was done.

Her attraction to Alvaro seems mutual, and because of that, she's tried to put as much distance between them as she can. Her only friend, and worse, he seems content to give her the space. She can take companionable silences. But what she's got no stomach for is the disdain, the wariness, the outright insubordination.

Nobody will see this her way, so she hasn't complained to her superiors. "Lighten up," they'd say. "They're just having a little fun. You're being too sensitive." She's heard all these things and a million other excuses. They've trailed her from post to post for the length of her career. If she reprimands Lance, or calls for him to be fired, she'll lose the teeny bit of goodwill she's built up with the rest of the team. No, that's overstating it. What they've meted out to her feels more like tolerance. But if she continues to let him challenge her at every turn, she'll lose the crew anyway.

The picnic table is digging into Syrah's back where she leans against it. She shifts, repositioning herself. *Go after the leader first.* Mama's unsolicited advice, of course. Syrah hadn't told her anything. She loves her dad, but the man can't keep anything from his wife. He probably ratted her out about the bullying as soon as she hung up the phone. Her mother had called immediately.

Syrah recalls when she first heard that sage advice. Kindergarten is a battlefield unlike any other. Worse because adults tend to believe that all children are cherubic beings made of love and hugs and wonder. Kids know different. Syrah's nemesis was a mean, wiry girl who thought that Syrah being adopted was somehow an affront to her very existence. And she had a gang of other girls backing her up. Syrah had tried using her wits, and when that failed, a stiff right to the nose did the trick.

But Lance was no six-year-old girl, now, was he?

How to make this work? How to get through to this man? She was breathing deeply, the scents of the trees' flowering buds, infinitely sweeter, waft over, and she inhales them like a stiff drink. Her knee feels like the bones have been shattered and put back together by a blindfolded surgeon. She refocuses on her breath, and the pain registers but fades away. And for a few blissful moments, she allows herself to relax.

She is right where she wants to be. Back in California after having bounced around to national parks across the country. Landing as far as the Everglades and working her way back. Her parents were beside themselves when they found out they would, for the first time in a decade, be back in the same state.

Granted, she doesn't know how she feels about visiting. Going home is a chore. To her parents, she'll always be that wounded four-year-old girl who lost her entire family. Who needed therapy and constant vigil for the first year she spent with them. Daddy's love was sure as the day is long, but it was a hovering, suffocating kind of love. To her mother, she was a project, a thing to be rehabbed like one of her patients. She loved her in her own dutiful kind of way.

"How's the knee?"

Syrah's eyes snap open. Lance is standing in front of her. He's wearing the uniform, opting for the long-sleeved shirt, tucked, belted. Not a wrinkle or errant thread to be seen. She allows herself to wonder if perhaps this job should have been his. But that slip lasts only a moment. He stands with his legs wide apart, as if afraid he'll topple over in a good wind. His arms are folded across his sculpted chest. He meets her gaze, then thins his lips and looks away.

"It's nothing," Syrah says while at the same time wondering what she can take tonight when she gets home that will allow her to be ready for training or a run, let alone to fight a potential fire. "I've hurt myself worse getting out of bed."

Lance laughs. "Mind if I join you?" he asks, gesturing at the spot next to her on the picnic bench.

Syrah scoots over, making room. "Take a load off."

No sounds pass between them but the rasp of a paper cup tumbling across the grass. The flap of bird wings overhead. He's made the first move, so this is her chance. Her second-in-command crosses an ankle over his knee and places his hands on the bench on either side of himself. Fingers tapping nervously.

"Guess it's fair to say we got off to a bad start," Syrah says. She shifts, turns to face Lance, and offers him her hand. "My name is Syrah Carthan, and I'm honored to serve at this post with you. Nothing matters more in the world to me than protecting that forest." She points in what she believes is north, toward Sequoia. "That's something I know for a fact that we have in common, and that can be, should be, enough."

Lance turns to her and tilts his head as if to say, *If we got off on the wrong foot, it's because you don't know an innocent joke when you hear it.* There's a challenge in that expression. She wants to accept, wants more than anything to respond. But she doesn't take the bait. She plasters her gaze back on the maple. It sways as if in answer, telling her to just go with the flow.

Lance's chuckle draws her back. "You got heart," he says, shaking her hand. "I'll give you that."

"And I have to ask that you give me something else." Syrah's voice has lost its smooth, easy tone. She can't help it. "Room to do my job. I don't need you questioning my every move. It only hurts us all when you give me crap about my every decision. When you put me down in front of the rest of the crew. It undermines me, but it undermines us all." She pauses to point. "Out there. When it's going to matter that we care enough to have each other's backs."

The muscles on Lance's forearms flex. The only sign that he's heard her. Seconds pass with no response.

"You're right," he says, finally. "I know you think it is, but this ain't about you being a lady, or a decade younger than me, or Bl—African American. This should have been my job, plain and simple. I earned it. Hard work, study, a twenty-year veteran battling fires out here that don't make sense anymore. I took all the classes. Dotted every friggin' *i* and crossed every *t*."

Syrah knows what he thinks. "Despite the conclusion that you've already drawn in your mind, nobody gave me shit either. I worked just as hard as anyone else. I didn't take shit jobs all over this country for the travel rewards; it was to learn. See how the climate affected different forests. How the fires changed as a result. *I* studied. *I* took the courses. I faced the flames same as you. I'm nobody's goddamn quota."

"I come out here because Alvaro is all over my ass. I try to extend a hand to you, and what do you do? Bite it the fuck off." Lance stands and glowers at Syrah.

"I very calmly told you that I'm just as qualified as you." Syrah stands, too, tries not to wince. "In what way did that offend you?"

"You couldn't just let it go—"

"Crude remarks, challenging every decision, sabotaging me on the run." Syrah ticks off the offenses, then thinks of one more. "Have you ever thought to ask if maybe that's why you didn't get promoted?"

"You won't last six months with that attitude." Lance waves a hand and storms off.

"And neither will you," Syrah says to his back. He stops dead in his tracks and turns around. Eyes hard and unyielding as forged steel before he marches back inside.

Syrah sinks back down to the bench, ruminating about what just happened. Lance did extend a hand, and while she didn't exactly chew it off, she didn't let him off the hook either. She palms her face, rubbing the tension away when her mother's constant warnings about keeping her hands out of her face spring to mind. She pulls out her new smartphone—a gift to herself for landing this job—and dials her dad.

"Hey, Daddy," she says after he answers.

"There's a sad-sack voice if I ever heard it," her father says.

She sighs heavily. Her father always has one of his weird sayings ready to unleash. "I'm not sad. I just think I'm about to have to throw hands up here."

"You're laughing, so I'm going to go out on a limb and say it isn't quite that bad, but something's going on. Spill it."

"Spill what? Is that my daughter?" Syrah's mother says in the background. Likely having joined Dad on the line.

"Still having some trouble connecting with a certain member of the team," Syrah says. "But I can handle it." She hasn't, but she will.

"There's always a bully. The most insecure of the bunch," her mother says.

"I was just about to tell her that, Anissa," her father adds.

"Well go on then," Mama huffs.

"Like your mother said. You got to deal with the bully. The rest will fall in line."

"I know you're right, and that's exactly what I'm going to do." Syrah agrees with her parents. She determines then that as soon as she gets off the phone, she'll find Lance and make amends. It is well past time to get on with the business of running the station. They have a prescribed burn coming up, and they have to be on the same page.

"And I'm just going to go ahead and say it," her mother slides in. Syrah groans; she knows what's coming.

Mama starts the familiar refrain. "You always loved the park, the forest . . ."

"We talked about it," Dad pipes in. "You were going to study botany, become a researcher right here—"

"Near home," Mama cuts him off as usual. "Why on earth you wanted to drop all that and run off fighting fires—"

"Anissa, we know why." Dad's voice is as heavy as a dump truck. "All these years, you've just been fighting the same fire over and over again. The one that took your birth family."

Syrah is glad they can't see her. Her eyes are floodwater full. Because he's right and because she can't remember them. Even that's been taken from her.

"You there?" Dad, of course, not Mama.

Syrah mutes the phone and clears her throat before she speaks. "I do this work because it's important. It keeps me outside. It saves life and the very trees I was going to study. I can't see myself sitting in some building breathing recycled air and being assaulted by fluorescent lights all day."

A thick, uncomfortable silence creeps over them all. They've had this discussion so many times before. Often it turns into a nasty argument. Parents worry. That kind of comes with the job description. They used to worry that she spent too much time reading and not making enough friends. Being a firefighter wasn't the safest of professions, and she has to admit they're right about why she was drawn to the work, but she doesn't know how to get across to them how much she's come to love it.

"Just be careful." Mama brushes the quiet aside like trash. "Despite what you think, I love you."

Dad cuts in before Syrah can tell her she has a really strange way of showing it sometimes. "Did you get the bear spray I sent you?"

She doesn't have the heart to tell him that bear spray isn't allowed in the park. And that even if it were, she wouldn't use it. People were intruding on the bear's territory, not the other way around. Clashes were bound to happen, and it was skill and experience that determined whether you survived.

"Yes, Dad," she says to keep the peace. "I keep it with me all the time."

"Good," he says. "Now when are you coming home? I can get the grill fired up."

"I just got here, so it's going to be a while," Syrah says.

"I understand," he says. "But I'll get some charcoal and put it in the garage, just in case you can make an impromptu trip. Oh, and don't forget to check in on your uncle Dane, you hear?"

Syrah assures Dad that she will and ends the call. Talking to him has done exactly what she hoped. She feels better and knows what she has to do. Going home again? Not likely. She stopped over for a quick visit once she got the transfer but is reluctant to do so again so quickly. She loves them, but like most parents, they can be prying.

Soon. She'll go home soon. Uncle Dane, though. He lets her breathe. Lets her speak and have her own opinions without cutting her off all the time. Even though he, too, warned her about the worsening fires, he's part of the reason she went after this post. Him she'll pay a visit after her shift.

But first things first. She will tend to her knee. Then she will call a meeting. It's time to get her second-in-command in check and become the chief.

Chapter Nine

Sequoia National Park, California
July 2042

Last night, for the first time in ages, Syrah dreamed of trees.

A verdant hush gave way to the Giant's murmur. It rose on the air, its beat like her heart. This time there was no basket; the branches didn't arch down to meet her. Instead, she climbed. For an eternity she climbed, until she reached the canopy and nestled onto a sturdy shoulder to rest.

The sun kissed her closed eyelids, her face. Her ears feasted on the sounds of the forest. A rustle of leaves nearby. When she opened her eyes, a silhouette, a suggestion, perched directly across from her.

She couldn't make out the face, or the sex, for that matter. The malevolence wafting from the figure wasn't directed at her—at least she didn't think it was. She turned her head this way and that, trying to make out what she was seeing. It mirrored her movements.

Fine serpentine threads extended from the shape, starting at the feet. Knitting and weaving upward like silk. A swirling sea of cinnamon-brown skin and flesh, manifest.

The shoulders and neck emancipated from shadow. A butterfly wingbeat before the face revealed itself, a shriek pulled her back into wakefulness.

All that Syrah can recall of the dream is that it unnerved her. And as soon as her feet land on the soft rug beside her bed, even that feeling begins to fade.

Today is a new day and, with it, another chance. Showered, dressed, and full on scrambled eggs and veggie sausages, she heads out.

Her hand is on the car door handle when she looks up. The emergent sunrise is impossibly brilliant. Golden streaks splitting the horizon. The sound of little claws draws her to the raccoon passing by. She tenses, knows the creatures are natural fighters if they feel cornered, but for the first time, she notices its eyes. There's more there than wild animal. Something thinking, alive, with a full day ahead of it just like her.

As she casts her glance around, it's as if everything, even the weeds in her yard, has dressed up for the occasion. The feeling follows her all the way to work.

In the end, a simple apology to Lance the week before had served to get things back to a reasonable level of civility. Syrah is grateful for that much. Even though she shouldn't be the one sorry for anything.

This morning at the station, the tension is wound as tight as a brawler's fist. Aside from fighting fires, there is so much work that the crew has to do in the park. Over the last several years, priorities shifted, and saving the endangered giant sequoias was elevated to the top of the list. Short cold seasons mean more rain than snow, which sounds like a good thing on paper. Only the rain yields more flooding and mudslides. Last year's reduced the numbers in the state to a devastating less than six thousand. And without the snowpack melt, there's less in the waterways, less hydration, and with one hot, dry summer after another, the Giants are weakening, more susceptible to fire damage. One of the best ways to help them is with prescribed burns.

All fires need to spin up are fuel load, the right weather conditions, and a ripe landscape. Weather? Out of the team's hands. The other two they can manage.

Depending on where you are around the country, prescribed burns are performed by different groups. Here in Sequoia, that duty falls to the fire operations crew, coordinating with the NPS, and that's one of the primary reasons she chose this outpost.

Native Americans started the practice, understanding that flames can't spread without fuel, that the forest is a fire-adapted ecosystem. The Giants actually need it in order to propagate. But colonizers, in their finite wisdom, assumed that they knew better. Once they stole the land and tried to destroy the people who called the place home, they stopped the burns. It took another hundred years and a lot of scorched forest for someone to rethink that brainless choice.

After everyone files into the conference room and gives her their attention, she begins, "I won't lie. I'm excited about doing the burn today. But there's a lot of ground to clear, probably too much. We make as much of a dent as we can and hope to get another chance."

"How many private jets have you seen streaking through the sky, burning money and everything else?" one of the crew says. "The burns help, but the only way to stop the fires is if the rest of the country gets a clue."

"Damn right," Alvaro agrees. "Five degrees warmer, this year alone. If somebody ten miles away even thinks about lighting a cigarette, the whole place will probably go up in flames."

More murmurs of anger, of agreement. In short order, the whole group will quickly descend to resignation. As much as Syrah would love to join in, she has her own complaints, and she knows it's time to reel them back in. "Not on our watch," she says, her voice cutting into the din. "What's the weather looking like?" Even though burns are planned far in advance, the weather can throw everything off.

Alvaro stands and reads from a tablet. "Current temp fifty-two, high of seventy-three. Wind gusts all over the place today." He pauses to check again. "Low gust now, but possibility to go north of twenty miles per hour."

"I say we cancel," Lance announces with a finality that irritates Syrah. "Nothing's been cleared in forever, so we're looking at a shit ton of understory. The wind shifts the wrong way . . ."

A couple of heads nod in agreement. Lance is doing it again, working to undermine her. He knows how important it is for Syrah to get her first successful burn under her belt. To at least try to pave the way for a better outcome this summer. His need to be in charge is going to set her up to fail. Yes, the crew has input, but this is her call. *Hers.*

"We're scheduled for ten a.m.," Alvaro offers, and Syrah nods. She knows what he's doing and mentally thanks him for tossing the ball back into her very capable hands.

"I see where you're going. We'll give it another hour and then check the wind before we make the call. Sound good?"

Syrah has busied herself maintaining the hand tools, something to do so that she can think away from the constantly evaluating stares from the crew. She resists the urge to call her uncle. This is a decision she has to make herself. The first really important one for her new job. Of course, burns are dangerous, but no less necessary. Hazard is right there in the job description, but that didn't stop any of them from taking up the charge. She can't be seen waffling. Inwardly, though, she hopes the weather will favor her.

When the crew reconvenes, the news is slightly better. "Wind gust currently low. Ten miles per hour, eight knots. Forecast predicts that picks up midafternoon," Alvaro says.

"What's the call?" Lance barks, crossing his arms. The challenge in his voice is unmistakable. Syrah barely suppresses a growl.

The park service has already closed the area for the burn. It's a pain to reschedule. There's a slight twist in her stomach that she dismisses as nerves. She sits up straighter. "We'll be done well before the wind picks up. We proceed."

"What?" Lance practically bounces out of his chair. "Look, you've got nothing to prove here. None of us are going to think any less of you than we already do because you kept our safety in mind."

With that last comment, Syrah makes two decisions. First, she *will* proceed with the burn. And when they return to the station, she'll make a formal complaint about Lance. She wants him gone.

She ignores him for now and stands. "I expect everyone to be ready and the trucks fitted in fifteen minutes."

Syrah glances over at Alvaro. Concern mars his features. He looks away. No confirmation there. To their credit, with the decision made, the crew is all business. She watches as they get ready. Gloves are passed out. Shirt pockets are checked for earplugs. Backpacks stuffed with flagging, water, and other essentials hoisted up.

Syrah climbs into the cab next to Alvaro, and they each reach above their heads and remove their helmets from the brackets and put them on. Syrah slides on her sunglasses and pushes the buttons on the radio at her shoulder. Lance behind them. Luckily the headrest is catching the worst of the daggers he's probably directing at the back of her head.

Before he starts the engine, Alvaro turns to her. "I'm making too big a deal outta the wind. If and when anything kicks up out there, we'll be long gone, and what we do today will go a long way toward helping us and the Giants come summer."

Syrah surprises herself with the grin that breaks out across her face. The moment passes quickly, though.

The sound of the diesel engine fills the cab, and they don't exchange any other words, couldn't hear each other if they wanted to. She flips on the radio on the console and tunes it to the station they selected inside. Syrah takes in the gleaming light bar and water pump controls between the two front seats. The air crackles with the singular intensity of a crew ready to go into the forest for their work. Syrah allows herself to be excited.

The cab still smells faintly of sweat, not smoke, as there hasn't been a fire since she arrived.

They take Highway 198 and reach the Ash Mountain Park entrance ten minutes later. She barely notices passing the sign announcing the park entrance, going through the gate, and waving to the attendant in the booth. They are heading to the Montane region of the forest, home to a gaggle of mixed conifers and, most importantly, the Giant Forest. The largest collection of sequoias in the state. Her stomach is a heaving mass of nerves.

They leave the trucks at the Giant Forest Museum parking lot. Three crew members have the fire cans. The plan is to clear the understory near the largest of them all, the General Sherman tree. They march single file out the two miles to the area for the burn. The wind is thankfully nonexistent.

And then they arrive. Set on a rolling plateau between the Marble and Middle Forks of the Kaweah River, it is the largest of the groves.

And then they pass it, one of the oldest living things on the planet. It's cordoned off these days after decades of tourists stamping down and damaging the roots. The occasional person still tries to jump the barricade but is quickly caught and carted off. Nearly three hundred feet tall and over thirty feet at the base, it is the most beautiful thing she's ever seen, and unbidden, she finds herself stopping to admire it.

Immense limbs stretch out almost as wide as she is tall. The reddish-brown bark in furrowed columns. Evergreen, awl-shaped leaves close to the branches. What looks like thousands of cones clearly visible and ready to expand with fire. Sap that contains tannic acid protects it from fires. The lower branches are all gone, but the canopy is as wide as a football field. The leaves rustle and Syrah freezes.

The sound begins like a perfectly held secret tumbling out from beneath the covers, beautiful in itself for the richness of its tone, notes that are so solid you can almost see them. And just like that, the tune loops and twirls, taking on new shapes and sizes, but it never loses the thread of that original tune. Every tree is a jazz player, in just this way, although where a long Coltrane piece might last a quarter hour, the tree's performance may go on for half a millennium or more.

"Chief?" Alvaro says.

Syrah breaks her gaze away and continues on the march. From there they take the Congress Trail.

Broken branches, dead leaves, and other brush have made for a very thick, very overgrown understory. Prescribed burns aren't much different from a natural fire; in fact, they do their best to mimic the pattern. Half the crew use the Pulaski, digging into the earth with the hoe and axe, and then fan out in horizontal zigzag lines, a good ten feet apart, marking off the fire line.

With the firebreak established, they move in with the drip torches. Fire shoots out of the aluminum can's long spout. With a whoosh, the understory starts to burn. Syrah and Lance move along with each group, monitoring progress. One eye on her crew and the fire, the other on the line. Her senses attuned to everything around them, checking to ensure they stay within the prescribed boundaries.

So far, so good. Once or twice, she and Lance exchange a glance. There's nothing but business in his gaze, and once, he even gives her a thumbs-up. Syrah relaxes into the work. If they can accomplish what they need to here, they'll be in better shape when the inevitable fire strikes the forest. Despite the temperatures, with little fuel, hopefully it won't burn as long or as hot. It's one of the highest priorities her leadership gave her when she took the post.

They've cleared about two acres of thick brush and are nearing the fire line when a gust of wind sneaks up on them from the west. The crew tenses, but when the air returns to normal, all take tentative steps forward, cans pointed and ready to go. They have just laid down another line of flame when the wind circles back, snarls, kicks open the door, and flashes its claws.

Everyone freezes, eyes scanning the area for where the few licks of fire remain.

"There!" Syrah cries, running in the direction of where she sees a spark lifting and carrying over the line.

All eyes flow to the spot where one mini fire erupts. The crew springs into action. One races back to the truck to get the hose. She hopes he makes it in time. The others use the reserves they have with them and begin spraying the area with water. Syrah prays that the wind doesn't pick up any more. She's standing, joining in the line dousing the fire, and chances a glance up at the tree canopies gently swaying. The wind has eased. But while she's staring up at the trees, she hears Lance's voice. "It's spreading."

She follows where he points. A spark has gotten past them. She is always amazed at how innocently, how quickly, fire starts. She and Alvaro race toward the growing fire and are battling that back when she hears something that turns her legs to jelly.

"Over there," another crew member calls. Another small brush fire has begun. Dread descends as Syrah's worst fear comes true. Suddenly they are battling three small but growing fires.

Chapter Ten

Sequoia National Park, California
July 2042

The brush on the other side of the firebreak erupts and snakes toward the Giants like ants hot on the scent of food. Two firefighters sprint back toward the trail. They're going to the trucks to get the second hose. Both should have a minimum of five hundred gallons of water. *Will it be enough?* It has to be enough.

Racing toward the worst of the blazes, Syrah screams into the radio, "This is Chief Carthan with Station Ninety-Three. Requesting backup in the Giant grove." Already the temperature is rising, heat searing her face.

Livid golden flames soar at least four or five feet into the air.

Finally, two firefighters come running up the trail. Syrah blanches at what she sees. The fire is spreading fast, too fast. The pungent smell of smoke blended with charred wood and brush has her reaching for her oxygen mask.

When the hose arrives, she takes the lead, drops onto her sore knee, aims, and turns the spigot. The hose swells and vibrates moments before the water blasts out. Fire needs three things to thrive: oxygen, fuel, and heat. Cut off one and you kill the fire. There is nothing they can do about the fuel; that's what the prescribed burn was supposed to fix. Oxygen isn't the biggest problem, but the heat is. That they can handle. First, she concentrates on the center of the flames. The blast smacks into brush and goes to work cooling it down and vanquishing the heat.

Thankfully, the fire starts smoldering.

A short-lived moment of reprieve lost to the tumult of more shouts. Syrah's pulse races. The other fires have somehow doubled, maybe tripled, in size while she concentrated on the first. She waves off assistance, shoulders the hose, and runs to the next-largest blaze and sets to work again.

And again.

Small animals scamper past. Squirrels and others, running away from the destruction they are all too familiar with. Blackened branches fall to the ground, broken and crackling like water in hot oil.

Vaguely, sirens alert her that another fire truck has arrived. She wants to turn away from the sight of what she's wrought but can't. In the fire's wake, blackened brush and animal carcasses litter the ground. Scorched earth.

But it isn't until the flames lick at the base of the Giants that Syrah stops dead in her tracks. She hears it again, that arboreal song. And now she knows it's the Giant. She looks around; nobody else seems to notice.

And then her eyes take in something she cannot fathom. A shimmering shape, tall, two-legged. Oddly human. Whatever it is blends in with the landscape so well she questions whether the smoke is playing tricks on her sight.

The edges of him are like currents in a stormy sea.

Here and there, the murky smoke snags on something—the curve of a broad shoulder, the outline of a muscular thigh. A gust of wind rustles something, fabric maybe, around an ankle and flows toward Syrah.

A whistle sounds, like a bird's. Only there are none in the sky.

Flames tremble and dissipate in his wake.

She inhales the unfeasible scent of freshness.

Syrah flat out rejects what she's seeing. The terror and the fear and the hurt more than she can bear at once.

Her mind is breaking.

Tears sting the corners of her eyes. Her vision blurs. She wipes the moisture away with the back of her hand.

And then he is gone. The space that he occupied curiously free of the flames.

She turns her attention back to the battle.

Syrah slips off her backpack and fishes around for the aluminum fire wrap they planned to drape around the trees after the burn. "Help me," she yells out to Lance. He grabs one end, and they run over to one of the Giants, moving in opposite directions, encircling the tree twice before tearing and securing the ends.

The dizzying array of activity increases as others join the fight. Morning passes into afternoon, then to evening, the flames having raged out of control. Syrah doesn't have time to stop and think, only to continue to throw herself into one fight after the next.

On her radio again, she calls for air support. Who knows if help will come. With all the budget cuts, it is unlikely.

As Syrah turns to the next task, she notices something that sends a ripple of alarm down her spine. Alvaro comes running from out of the forest. He carries a woman, wrapped in his coat. She is wearing a mask—his mask. He locks eyes with Syrah, then stumbles a few times before falling about twenty paces away. Syrah hands off the hose and races over with a few of the others.

The woman tumbles out of Alvaro's arms. Aside from the smoke and soot covering her face, she appears unharmed. Syrah takes off her mask and gives it to Alvaro. She notices the burns first. They cover the upper half of his body. His shirt is singed in spots, the skin beneath and on his arms peeled away to reveal pale flesh.

She's trained for this, has seen more burns in her life than she cares to admit. But these—fresh, pink, charred—are even more horrible because it is all her fault.

Mini fires continue to burn all around them. And soon she waves off the other firefighters, sending them back to the work. But she can already tell—this one is beyond their control.

Someone sinks down beside her with the first aid kit from the truck. Syrah sets to bandaging Alvaro's wounds.

"I'm fine," he says through gritted teeth. "They need you."

Tears spring to Syrah's eyes. "No," she mutters. "I can't."

Alvaro shoves her hands away with a force that surprises her. "Get the hell away from me. Go!"

A moment of indecision stretches thin and fragile as a shed hair. The scene around them is chaos. Firefighters from two crews battling flames. The area they're in is relatively clear, but the wind, as it did earlier, could change at any moment. No, she won't risk it.

The Giant, Syrah thinks. She and Lance had wrapped just one. Syrah squints through the smoke and spots it. She stands and reaches behind Alvaro. Hands beneath his armpits, she hefts him up and drags him toward the tree.

She lumbers backward, slipping and falling but rising every time. Eventually she lays Alvaro at the base of the tree. Propped against one of the aboveground roots, the size of two human torsos. She gets up and sprints back into the fray, but chances a look behind her. Alvaro gives her a barely perceptible nod, and Syrah rushes into the midst of the flames.

It takes another several hours to bring the fire under control. Syrah is exhausted. They all are. It isn't like the fires that sometimes rage for weeks at a time. This is worse, because it is unexpected. It is unforgivable because she caused it all. When she sees Lance marching toward her, she knows that's just what he's going to tell her.

He rips off his helmet, eyes wild. His face smeared with smoke and soot. He is inches from her. She stands her ground.

"You—"

"It's my fault," she cuts him off, not because she doesn't want to hear what he has to say but because she wants him to know that she has no excuses to offer. "You were right, and I'm sorry."

"You don't get off that easy." His spittle sprays her face. Syrah holds his gaze. "You and your attitude. You thought you were better than me." He stops to gesture at the crowd running up to try to grab him. He shoves them off. "You think you're better than all of us. I told you not to do the burn. But because you had something to prove, you did it anyway. You're so goddamned pathetic."

"Hey, come on, man," another firefighter says. "Leave it alone."

"I ain't fucking done," Lance says. "If anything happens to Alvaro . . ."

"That's enough now," the firefighter says.

Syrah's head is lowered. She can't argue. He is right. She was so hell-bent on proving herself that she ignored her training and her good sense. And because of her, her only friend in the entire crew is hurt or worse. She didn't even see who took him away.

She studies her surroundings. The destruction. Dead animals and trees. A few coughs. Two crews called out to fight a fire that should never have been. "Guilt" isn't a strong enough word to express how she feels. If she can ever get over the sight of the damage she's caused, she will never be able to get over the fact that her crew can no longer look her in the eye.

There's something else that troubles her. With their meager water and resources, they shouldn't have been able to contain this fire without air support. The hairs on the back of her neck tingle. She looks up again and finds the forest is staring right back at her.

Chapter Eleven

Fresno, California
July 2042

“I know how you feel,” Khatir says. “But this is the coward’s way out, and the woman I hired is no coward.” Her boss is a raven-haired, square-jawed slip of a man. The zip-up hoodie bearing the National Park Service logo that he wore during her interview is at least two sizes too big.

He’s sitting in an oversize leather chair behind a desk that, judging by the gorgeous grain polished to a mirrorlike sheen, is walnut. Elbow planted in the cushy armrest, chin cupped in the palm of one pale brown hand. Plants and a ficus tree in the corner near the window, fake but not obviously so. The expression on his kind face, softened around the hard edges of his youth, is full of rebuke, not for what she did, but for what she’s about to do.

Emailing in her resignation had crossed Syrah’s mind. She’d even typed it up, a short three-lined missive. It sat in her draft folder for the two days she holed up in her bedroom. Ignoring the phone. The knocks that had escalated to banging on her door. On the third day after she burned a large swath of the park she was hired to protect, she dragged herself to the shower and shivered beneath the icy spokes of water and punished her body until she was numb.

Then she got dressed and deleted the email. Stepping outside she almost tripped over an aluminum foil–covered plate, a gesture likely done by Uncle Dane. The plate's contents went into the trash, right along with the envelope taped on top. Then she drove ten miles west to Fresno, where the regional office sits at the end of a street crowded with businesses in varying states of decline.

"Why do people say that?" Syrah has done the same thing herself but is in no mood to have it done to her. "You don't know how I feel at all."

Khatir cocks an eyebrow. "Summer. Two thousand twenty-two. Yosemite National Park." He pauses after every word, taps a finger on his desk when he's finished, and crosses his arms as if he's made the most important point in the world. Syrah sighs and purses her lips. "It wasn't a prescribed like yours," her boss—rather, her ex-boss—continues, "but no less of a catastrophe. I was chief at Station Twenty-Six at Wawona for a full year before this happened. It was a small fire by today's standards. I thought it was under control. I dismissed the crew and called off the helicopters. That fire took one look at my overconfidence and decided to teach me a lesson. It lay in wait until we were all home, snug in our beds, then sprang out from behind a bush. You burned one hundred acres and you're ruined for life? Try one thousand. A week to fight it and two firefighters lost. You choose to lead and you *will* make a bad call. This comes with the territory. But what you don't do is bail. You don't tuck your tail and stick your head in the sand. You get yourself back out there, and you do better the next time."

Syrah made an assumption, and she was wrong. The cushy office with a view, the soft comfortable chair—it all caused her to imagine this was always Khatir's life. This isn't the kind of thing that would come out during an interview either. What he's shared paints him in a new light and, if she's honest, makes sense. She dials back to that day, closes her eyes for a moment, and dives into the well of blinding arrogance. It's too clear in her mind, to ready to jump in the way of sound decision-making.

"I appreciate you sharing your story with me; don't think that I don't. But maybe I'm just not like you. My heart isn't in it. Not anymore. And without that, how can I trust myself to make the right decision next time? And even if I could, there's no way any of the crew will let me lead them on anything other than the Christmas parade march."

"You know what?" Khatir says. "It's the kids like you that are driving me toward early retirement. You just aren't made of the same stuff anymore. One thing goes wrong and you quit. I mean, how can you hope to ever make anything of yourself that way?"

"I call it having a conscience," Syrah shoots back. "If you think insulting me is the best way to get me to stay on the job, then I question you and *your* generation. Your age group never did know how to talk to people."

Khatir looks taken aback, but after a moment, a sad smile appears. "Did you hear anything I said? Were you checking your phone or something? Otherwise occupied?"

"I heard you, but it doesn't change my mind," Syrah says. "I don't get what you don't understand about that."

"If you're worried about Alvaro, you don't have to," Khatir offers. "He fared far worse when he got the chicken pox last year. This is a dangerous job. We all know it when we take the oath. Friendly fire, no pun intended, is something we all contend with. I know you received the speech before you joined."

Alvaro is okay. She's been too afraid to ask. She hasn't even gone back to the station to collect the few things she left there. She can't bear facing any of her crew. Either they can ship her stuff or throw it in the trash, but no way she is ever going back. She takes a deep breath. "If you could get him a message for me—"

"Tell him yourself," Khatir says. "He'll be back at work in a few weeks. The bastard's going to milk the system for all it's worth. He's putting up his feet at home and letting his wife baby him for a bit."

He's married? Another mistake. But he didn't wear a ring, and there was no telltale paleness around his finger to indicate he'd slipped it off for her benefit. The attraction she'd allowed herself to feel for him, not yet intensified to feelings, withers. Still, Syrah smiles inwardly. Alvaro will be back on the job. She wonders if his wife—a wife he never mentioned—blames her. Why not? There's no one else at fault, is there?

With a few mouse clicks, Khatir sits up straight and says, "Ms. Carthan, Syrah, I've got another appointment soon." He looks down, exhales, and then glances up at her again. "You're stubborn. You must overcome that. It won't serve you. Take a week and think about it. If you still want to walk away after that, it is your funeral."

Syrah fiddles, picks at her fingernails. She made the decision before she came. Nothing she's heard has changed that. She stands, offers the well-meaning man in front of her a hand. He hesitates a moment before shaking it.

She fights back the quivering timbre in her voice, barely able to get the words out. "My resignation is effective immediately."

Chapter Twelve

Sequoia National Park, California
July 2042

Topside, he was Romelo Thorn Williams. No longer of that splintered, dying world, but in one of fate's cruel flights of fancy, born of it. He didn't remember much about his life before—even his former family's faces had faded—but he remembered his name. Of all the promises he'd made to himself, this, the remembering, was the most important. The creator had seen fit to take everything from him, but this he held on to. It was the one thing that nobody could take from him.

For many years, each turn of the sun that he'd awakened, breath caught in his chest, sweating, his mind struggling, fighting to remember the name that was already there at the tip of his tongue, and sewn into the red hoodie he kept rolled up beneath his bed.

Belowground, he was Romelo Rootspeaker. As much as the Rhiza chided topsiders for their single-minded pursuit of the dollar, he found it curious that they would sniff at last names but choose to identify themselves by their work. He wasn't just any lattice worker, either; he was the best.

He'd come topside with the others to troubleshoot an alert from a fungal node at the base of one of the ancients. His lungs protested at air that smelled of the charred dead and dying animal carcasses that lay scattered around like shed leaves. Every few feet, he knelt and gathered up as many downed branches as he could and placed them in the basket he balanced on his hip. Whatever could be saved would be recycled for reuse. He muttered prayers for their sacrifice at the hands of the unworthy.

"Chief," Ochai said from beside him. "It is a title you coveted and finally claim, yet you take up the charge of the scourge suppressors as well? You know they take their cleanup duties seriously. Will your ambition never cease?"

Romelo glanced over at his best friend and knew what he was doing, but he could not match his lightness of tone. All things considered, this fire was not as bad as some, but it was a tragedy, a loss, and he would not understate its importance. "No clouds in the sky," Romelo said, pointing upward. "No charge in the air to indicate a lightning strike." He didn't say anything else. He and his friend had had this conversation before; he knew where he was going.

"They had those fire cans." Ochai confirmed what Romelo had already surmised. He walked alongside Romelo, while a few other members of the Blaze Brigade trailed at a respectable distance. "If it were not for us, it would have burned for acres more. You know what that means, yes?"

"It means that either through ignorance or incompetence, these Western topsiders are intent on destroying the forest and us with it," Romelo said, shifting the bundle of limbs to the crook of his arm.

"Give me those." Ochai gently took the dead branches and waved over a member of his crew. "Take these back to the chief's quarters."

Reluctantly, Romelo watched him give them over. He would make something useful out of their sacrifice. He and Ochai continued walking in silence. He was content to let his friend think on his words so that he was ready for what was coming next. The forest had changed so much, too much, over the last several years. Namely, there was less of it. Even with the unseen help of the Rhiza firefighters, they were losing the battle. And everyone around him wanted to pretend it wasn't happening. Well, he was done pretending.

They arrived at the Giant, and Romelo turned to Ochai. "We have to do something. I have given this long and hard thought. And Ezanna agrees with me. What I propose will not be easy, but everything will be to do what The Mother has charged us, all the Keepers of the Canopy, to do. Most won't want to act boldly, but I need to know now: Will you be with me?"

Ochai met Romelo's gaze. "I will be with you as I have since that day you finally stood up for yourself and walloped me."

Romelo turned to the others then. "You do not have to act as if you have not heard every word we said. Same question." He paused to look each in the eye. "Can I count on you?"

Each said that he could, and Romelo believed them. They had reached the ancient one.

"We will leave you to your work," Ochai said, and they continued on to ensure that all the fire had been suppressed.

Romelo stared at the sign plastered in front of the Giant: The President. A fitting name. The Giant was second only to The Mother in age. In recent months, it had needed more and more hands-on attention, the fungal connections beneath the earth weakening.

Despite what his adoptive mother said, he knew that the tree was, without a doubt, *his* Giant. All those years ago, when he'd lain dying at the craggy base of the surly blue oak, lungs smoke filled, a gash in his forehead, his memories seemingly slipping through the opening, that tree had made a decision.

His Giant had received that missive and made the call to pass it on to The Mother. They'd decided to save his life, sent Taron and Dhanil to collect him before the fire licked his bones clean. Sometimes he wondered if they should have let it do just that.

She never admitted it—he'd stopped asking years ago—but Romelo figured Taron had seriously considered leaving him. It was her way.

She didn't say so outright, but she was also growing tired of the battle. Knew that they were losing it. To take a human child behind the veil? She must have fought tooth and nail. But in the end, she obeyed and became the cold, distant mother he never knew he wanted. She'd taken him in and taught him, helped him with the change, swallowing the questions from herself and deflecting those from her people. She'd dragged him back every time he tried to run.

Some days he was grateful, but today, like so many others, he was enraged.

The President's canopy stood taller than any other. But it was thinning. From his best account, though it was still metabolically active and continued to grow leaves and cones, it was dead somewhere above two hundred feet. There was debate about how long this had been the case.

Romelo sat cross-legged, nestled inside the small crack in the trunk, the one that faced its closest sibling, about twenty paces away. It was the darkest part of the night, and the trail was blissfully empty of tourists and their cameras and their loud voices. He inhaled deeply, a full twenty-two seconds of the woodsy scent of fresh pine. He remembered when his lungs were still more human than Rhiza, and he'd be lucky if he could suck down ten seconds' worth of air.

The President sensed his presence, and he felt the feathery brush of a root tendril as it snaked its way up his loose pants leg and sank beneath his skin. Romelo was flooded with warmth. The touch as familiar as any parent's. The Giant was tired, but that wasn't what got Romelo's attention. There he found the problem. The roots had been compacted, and there wasn't enough space in the earth for them to move around. Through the lattice, Romelo called on the roots from the sibling to provide extra sustenance.

And then Romelo received another message. This coming back to him. The Giant sensed his feelings, the depth and anger there. The mild jolt told Romelo that such thoughts were not the way of the Keepers, that they were protectors of all living things on earth. Romelo accepted the rebuke, even if he disagreed. He relished the connection and probed again, for history, but then he felt the ache. A dull, barely perceptible throb. Something so faint that it may not have even traveled down to the Rhiza data center. Romelo coaxed the root tendril away, and it slithered back into the ground. He got up and placed his hand against the bark, tracing a path around the perimeter. A few steps away he found it. A series of depressions he outlined with the tip of his finger. A swatch of moonlight revealed the wound.

Even though there were signs telling humans not to do so, he had seen names and other symbols carved into the trees all over the park. It incensed him. This was not someone's name, but a clear attempt to hack away the bark, likely for a souvenir.

Romelo balled his fists and screamed a curse. He wished the human who had defiled his Giant were still around so that he could carve an offering from their flesh. Watch as they whimpered and moaned about the open wounds he would inflict on them.

This was the way it began or ended for many of the trees. A small wound, the tiniest of openings, was like a mile-wide tunnel. An invitation of the worst kind. Bark beetles or deadly fungi. He fumbled around in his pouch and smoothed a poultice over the wound. He would return the next night to do the same until the Giant sealed itself.

He then set about loosening the earth around the perimeter of the tree, careful not to tear at the delicate roots near the surface, but giving them precious room to breathe.

His anger at being taken receded for just a moment, relieved as he was that he had not been forced to grow up among such uncaring people. The respite was short lived. The anger returned and ushered Romelo back behind the veil.

Chapter Thirteen

Sequoia National Park, California
July 2042

Syrah's cell phone rings. For the third time in five minutes. She doesn't have to glance at the caller ID to know who it is. When her mother is determined to talk to someone, a simple voice mail won't do. She calls in rapid-fire fashion until she wears down your resolve and you pick up just so you don't have to contend with the ringing anymore.

No, she hasn't called her parents to tell them what happened. A week, a full seven and a half days, after the fact. And probably seven and a half days after Uncle Dane already told them. But how does one call and tell the self-same people who begged her not to take the job that she made the biggest mistake in her life? Faking her way through the conversation: *Yes, I'm in good spirits. All is well. I'll be back to work in no time.* Her laughter is full of mirth. That was like telling the sun not to come up, that you wouldn't need its services that day.

They will try to mask the glee in their voices with appropriate awws and hmms and sighs. Platitudes goading her into a swift, clean recovery. Underneath it all they'll be thrilled. Sneaking in hints about her moving back home, going back to school.

She'll talk when she is ready and not a moment before.

She hears the familiar chirp indicating she has a voice mail. With a loud groan, she picks up the phone and presses the flat screen to her ear.

"Syrah, this is your mother"—a rustle of fabric—"and Dad." Then Mama again. "Babygirl, we're worried about you. We know you're hurting, but we also know how you were raised. And if you don't pick up this phone and call us back right this minute, I guarantee you, we will put on some Depends, get in the car, and drive without stopping until we get there."

Syrah fumes. The use of adult diapers as a manipulation tactic is over the top, even for her mother. That doesn't mean what she's levied is an idle threat, not from Anissa Carthan.

"Thank goodness," Mama says as soon as she answers . . . Dad's phone. "When things go wrong, you don't shut out the people who love you."

Unlike the voice mail, her mother's tone is tentative. Soothing even. Syrah realizes how much she's scared them. "I'm calling to let you know that I'm fine. I'm just not ready to talk about it," she says, and then adds, "I'm sorry."

"I ain't gonna sugarcoat it. You made a mistake, a big whopper of a mistake."

"Thanks, Ma." Syrah is ready to hang up.

"Don't get yourself all riled up. That's not the point," her mother says. "What makes you any different from anybody else? Everybody that's ever walked this earth has done the same thing, messed up some way or another. It's what you do after that matters."

What her mother says makes sense, but this mistake is one she can't get past. Maybe at some point far, far in the future, but not now. Those images are like a craggy lump of rock, chiseled in her mind. No way she can trust herself back out there. Hesitation is not the friend of a fire chief. You have to make decisions, quickly. Syrah isn't certain she can do that now. Or ever. "You're absolutely right."

"I know I am," Mama says. "Your father wants to talk to you."

"Hey, sugarplum," he says.

"Hi, Daddy." Hearing his voice like this when she's the lowest she's been since she lost her family almost releases the tears that are pent up, almost. He was the one who'd thrust open the screen door to their Compton home and rushed out to meet her when she stepped out of the social worker's car.

Syrah hears the creak and bang that lets her know her father is going out on the porch. The sound of their neighbor's self-driving lawn mower makes her homesick. "I hate that you had to go through something like this." Gone is the light tone, shed like snakeskin. *It's okay,* he's saying. He's just as messed up by this as she is, and there's nothing wrong with showing it. So unlike her mother's maddening *get over it and get going* attitude.

"I burned down half the park. I've been on the job all of five minutes—"

"From what Dane says, the burn did some damage, but you're overstating," Dad says. "When are you going back to work?"

Syrah swallows the lump in her throat. She hasn't said these words out loud to anyone other than her boss. "I'm not."

"What do you mean, you're not?"

"I resigned. Today."

A weighty silence fills the line while the lawn mower sputters in the background. "I'd be lying if I didn't tell you how happy I am that you won't be out there risking your life. That's the selfish-dad part of me. The other part knows how quitting like this will affect you. It'll be hard to heal if you don't face it head-on. Now I said my piece, but that tone in your voice tells me your decision is final. What do you plan to do instead?"

Do next? She is physically incapable of thinking that far ahead. What can someone who feels like she'll wither away and die if she has to go into an office every day do for a living? She is a year shy of completing that botany degree. Does she do that instead? Somehow her heart isn't committed to that or anything else at the moment. "I'm going to take some time and figure that out," she tells her father.

"You need any help?"

She knows he means money. After three years of retirement, numbers are still never far from Dad's mind. The math teacher in him is always calculating. "I'm good. Tell Mama not to blow up my phone for a while. I'll talk to you later."

Syrah is thrifty, if she's anything. Clothes are an afterthought, typically something she snags from a vintage shop. The Tulare County Library takes care of her only hobby. The California buckeyes and that slice of the North Fork River behind the house give her everything else she needs.

She's saved nearly every penny she's made since her first high school job. Enough that combined with the insurance money from her birth parents, she paid for the tiny home on the outskirts of Three Rivers in cash and socked away the rest in a modest savings account. It would give her time to decide.

She connects her phone to the charger on the end table and sits back on the couch with her legs tucked beneath her. She cocoons herself in a thick faux-fur blanket. Her gaze travels outside the picture window. The one she cut out and installed herself. It gives her a view of the street. Her house is small but not cramped. It has the basic comforts, nothing more. The waste she sees sometimes makes her sick.

Leaves flutter, sunlight glinting off their glossy surfaces. She imagines the smell of smoke still lingering in the air. It's a constant around these parts. The people who choose to live here do so because of the natural beauty and are more than willing to endure the risks and inconveniences for the privilege.

She always shakes her head when people ask how she could live with the threat of fire destroying her home. She turns the question back on them: How can you live with the threat of hurricane? Of earthquake?

A coastline that shrinks seemingly by the month? Of death by stray bullet or poisoned water?

There is no utopia, but this is about as close to it as one could get. Syrah isn't sure what her future holds, but she knows she can never leave this place. Even with what she's done, it feels more like home than anyplace else she's lived—even Compton. She'll find a way to stay, but for now, she'll take some time and think.

And heal.

Chapter Fourteen

Sequoia National Park, California
September 2042

Syrah is lounging on the couch, not reading the book she's been trying to finish since she quit her job and upended her life two months ago. Of the handful of novels she rereads every year—*One Hundred Years of Solitude*, *Giovanni's Room*, *Jane Eyre*—her most treasured is *A Mercy*. The text is easy to sink into, to lose herself in the beautiful words, the settings, the defiance. But today her eyes slide off the pages as if they've been dunked in a vat of cooking oil.

She gives up the fight at the unwelcome sound of car tires on gravel. Electric engines are quiet enough that she doesn't hear anything else besides the door slamming that confirms it is in her driveway.

The thought that her mother has gone through with her threat crosses her mind. Alvaro is another possibility. He's visited her once since she quit. She bawled like an infant as she apologized, and when he took her hand and said that there was nothing to forgive. He did his part to try to convince her to come back to work, probably at Khatir's urging, said that he'd gladly serve under her again.

But Lance is the chief now. And maybe that's the way it should have been from the beginning.

Alvaro has checked on her a couple of times since, but in the last month, the calls have trickled to an end. Nobody else would dare show up at her home unannounced.

Except one person. His knock—one, pause, then two quick raps. He came by first to help her get settled, then a few times after. Each time with what she now calls his signature knock.

Syrah flings back the blanket draped across her lap and shoves her feet into her slippers. She is at the front door in two strides. "No," she says, flinging the door open.

"No, I can't come in, or no, you don't want this double cheeseburger and fries from River View?" Uncle Dane holds up the grease-spotted paper bag in one hand and a wobbly drink carrier in the other. That cup looks suspiciously like a chocolate milkshake. He has her.

Syrah steps aside and closes the door behind him while her uncle, only friend, and fellow recluse walks over to the fold-down table she has set up at the end of the kitchen counter. The smell of grease and the near beef that's all but replaced cows sets her mouth to watering. Syrah pulls up the tabletop and slides the stand under it. While Dane sets the food on the table, she goes to get the stools she has nestled beside the cutout near her small refrigerator.

She has been subsisting on the meager rations she has delivered. Cans of soup. Turkey sandwiches and prepackaged cupcakes. When she bites into the burger, her taste buds react like what she's eating is Thanksgiving dinner. She chews quickly and swallows in a gulp. Just like her mother tells her not to.

"I know you're not going back into fire operations," Dane says after a slurp from one of the wide metal straws he pulls from an inside jacket pocket and sticks into both their cups.

"Maybe you can tell my parents," Syrah says and takes a sip of her milkshake. Vanilla, not chocolate, but only slightly less delicious. "They seem to think I'm speaking in Twi. A new fire chief has been appointed, you know. Lance finally got his wish."

"They don't want you to give up," Dane says. "That's not the same as not hearing."

"Are you here because they sent you?"

Dane bites into his burger before he answers. "Have I talked to Trenton? Of course. I talk to the man every Sunday without fail. He's my best friend. Does he want me to check on you? Right again. But I'm here because I don't want you to turn into me."

Syrah is dipping her french fries into the ketchup that has dripped from her burger onto the wrapper but stops and glances up at Dane, intrigued. She pops the fries in her mouth and considers her words before speaking. "You have a job you love. You have a place all your own. You get to work in this beautiful park. I want nothing more than to be just like you. Had my shot too. See how that worked out."

Dane grabs a napkin, reaches over, and dabs at the corner of Syrah's mouth. "I do have the job, in the right place. I'll give you that. But the state owns that cabin, not me. I don't have family of my own, no shade to my mother and the pits. Nobody else aside from you and your folks. I can't tell you the last time a woman *or* a man has hugged me because they really wanted to. If I break my leg out there in that cabin, it'll be a week before anybody knows about it."

Syrah stops chewing, looks up. Her uncle tilts his head, raises that eyebrow with one gray hair poking out of it, anticipating. He's trusted her. A smile graces Syrah's full mouth after she swallows. "You could change all that if you wanted to."

Dane scoops up his last few fries, which he has finished well ahead of the burger. He shrugs. "Guess I could."

Syrah switches gears. "As much as I love a meal from the grill, I know there's another reason you're here. Let's have it."

"I do have an opportunity I want to run past you," Dane says.

"I'm not—"

Dane holds up his hands, palms outward. "Not firefighter. Outreach work."

Syrah cocks her head to the side. "What do you mean, 'outreach'?"

"Park guide," Dane says between bites.

Syrah snorts. "You mean you want me to guide schoolkids around the park, telling stories they don't care about and won't remember two minutes after they leave?"

"If you do the job the way everybody else did, maybe," Dane says. "But if you use that brain on your shoulders, do something unconventional, you could make a difference. Talk about why this job, this place, matters to us. Talk to them about the Giants and how they single-handedly clean our air. Tell them about the plants and animals. How everything is connected, each dependent upon the next. Walk them through the darned near-immortal life cycle of a plastic bottle. Then teach *us*. Tell Black kids about Shelton Johnson's work at Yosemite, about how connected our ancestors were to the land. Get them back out here."

Worthy arguments, but Syrah is still unconvinced she's the right person to deliver them. She is a firefighter—a chief, and . . . actually, she isn't any of those things. Not anymore. And what has her dad always told her? No matter the job, or the station, you have to be you. Because things can change, and change they did. "How much does this job pay?"

"Not much," Dane admits, folding up the wrapping paper and making a perfect shot into the wastebasket.

"I can't," she says, finishing up her food. "I'll figure out something to do, but it won't be a tour guide." She moves the crumbs on the table around with her finger, then takes the last sips of her milkshake.

Dane flashes his megawatt smile. "How about you think about it and get back to me."

Begrudgingly, Syrah agrees.

Chapter Fifteen

Sequoia National Park, California
September 2042

At first the woman had only sought refuge in the hollowed-out center of the thirty-five-hundred-year-old Giant. She was thin and gaunt, her face a maze of sharp waxy angles. Her eyes were green, skittish marbles beneath eyebrows arched into nonexistence in her youth. She moved like a thing pursued, quick furtive glances forward and back, as if a nameless foe were on the precipice of attack.

Surrounding her was an air of unrest. She was someone upon whom a restful sleep had not visited in far too long.

Her father used to bring her to the park when she was a kid. And long after he was gone, she came because it is where she felt closest to him. It was a place where, if she closed her sunken eyes, she could picture them laughing and skipping rocks across the Kaweah River.

For a time, her demons didn't seem to know the way.

The woman trod noisily through the forest until her gaze fell upon the base of the Giant. The hollow that had appeared after and seemed to expand every year since the lightning storm beckoned like a lost love. Was that last year? A week ago? She and her memory were enemies now, combatants in a war she knew she was losing. The woman craned her neck, allowing her eyes to travel up, up, trawling the red-brown bark, all the way to the bushy crown.

She swayed, unsteady on her feet, and looked back down. Her breath caught.

The demons again. They had followed her!

A child's whimper escaped from her throat.

Probably on the last trip, she hadn't felt like herself. But she had been so careful. Checked over her shoulder every now and again. She had even lost one of them when she darted into traffic and cut through an irate old lady's backyard. Now they knew her only hiding place. Somehow they had circled around and beaten her here. A whole mess of them.

They flashed their black-toothed grins, taunting her.

Do it.

She squeezed her eyes shut. Trembled in the chill of that inner sanctum. Muttered prayers to the god she hadn't spoken to since that self-driving semi butchered her father's body, rending it to pieces they had to collect from the highway like concrete table scraps.

But when she opened her eyes, there were more of them. Dozens more.

She sighed heavily. There was only one way to keep the demons at bay.

She had brought everything with her, leery as she was that they might be on her tail this time. She lowered a shoulder and plowed through the throng as they scratched and tore at her. She dived into the hollow and curled into a ball until the barrage stopped.

Dragging herself into a cross-legged position, she reached in the large pocket of her raincoat and took out the glass pipe. She wore the coat not because there was rain, but because the pockets were big enough to store her works. The bag of ice was in a plastic baggie in her other pocket. She shook out one of the blue-white rocks, then thought about it and got another.

She chucked them into the flute, flicked her lighter underneath, and inhaled deeply. The smoke filled her lungs, and they expanded like a gift released from a bright-red bow.

It didn't take long for the poison to travel through her bloodstream; that was why she smoked instead of snorting like her boyfriend. His nose was a wreckage. And she was afraid of needles, so injecting was out of the question. And with the flute, nobody could see the damage. She didn't smile much anymore, so people weren't likely to see her corroded teeth and gums.

The scintillating spark of pleasure came on with a tooth-chattering shudder. She leaned back against the cool bark. Her eyes fluttered closed. Her breathing came in rapid gasps, and her heartbeat was like a heavy-metal song on steroids.

A few minutes later, too soon, the rush deserted her. The woman cautiously opened her eyes. It had worked; the demons were long gone. She dared not leave now; they would surely find her again. She wrapped her rain jacket closer around her; it was cold out here, this early in the morning.

She was flicking her lighter on and off when she spotted a downed branch and got an idea. She left the comfort of the hollow, grabbed the branch, more of a twig, and then went in search of others. When she had a small pile and a couple of leaves for tinder, she came back to the hollow. She plopped down on the ground and arranged everything in front of her. With another flick of the lighter, she lit a couple of the leaves and tossed them onto the pile.

Smoke curled and soon fire erupted. She dropped the lighter and held her hands out to the pyre. The warmth was immediate. But the fire was too small. She stood and hopped over the young flames and gathered more twigs. She dipped back into the hollow and tossed them on the stack. Ahh, she could feel the warmth filling the space now. The woman shrugged off the rain jacket and tossed it aside.

In order to keep the demons away, she thought it best to have another hit. This time, to be sure she didn't overdose like her friend, she shook out only one rock. She lit the flute and pulled the smoke into her body. She looked out over the growing flames, and sure enough, the demons were still gone. She was lost to them.

When the rush faded, she lay back and closed her eyes. She didn't sleep, but time certainly passed. Smoke of another kind set her to coughing. She opened her eyes and gasped.

Her small, warming fire had leaped up to the sides of the hollow. The tree itself was on fire. The demons had snuck back in and set everything aflame!

The woman ran out into the clearing, but stopped. Nobody would believe what they'd done, so she took out her phone and snapped a few photos. Then she hastened away and didn't stop to look back.

Chapter Sixteen

Sequoia National Park, California
September 2042

The earth is scorched.

Syrah sits in a plain surrounded by the charred husks of trees of all shapes and sizes. Only the Giants are burning. And they scream. Loud, painful wails. Syrah covers her ears and her hands come away bloody.

She runs.

And slams into a Giant that is the largest living thing she has ever seen. The canopy rests in the clouds. But a branch stretches down, impossibly slow. Syrah wants to run but can't move. The branch comes toward her. On the end, a pine cone falls off and a large brown hand sprouts in its place. That hand shoots out toward Syrah—

The phone's melodic chime rouses Syrah from a fitful nightmare-clad sleep. She's sweat soaked, heart cresting its millionth beat in the span of time it takes her to grope around on the shelf that serves as a nightstand. She narrows her eyes at the screen's brightness. No name, just a number. One she doesn't recognize either. Something—instinct, boredom—tells her to answer anyway.

The first thing she hears is shouting. Voices high, shrill, raised in alarm, not anger.

"There's a fire in the park, a bad one." Lance is afraid, and it makes Syrah sit up straight. "It's General Sherman. We may lose him. I know you aren't in service anymore, but—"

"I'm on my way." And Syrah is out of bed. Losing another Giant . . . especially this one. She can't even think it. To call her up means it's all hands—current and past—on deck. Despite walking away from the only job she's ever wanted months ago, she's never lost the habit of being prepared for a call at all hours: long-sleeved shirt, sturdy slacks, and a solid pair of boots in the wicker basket beside her front door. She dresses quickly and is out the door before she has time to think about what she's doing.

Once again, her phone. This time it's that headbanger of the emergency tone.

This is the Tulare County Fire Department issuing an evacuation warning. There is a fire in the Sequoia National Park. All residents are required to leave your homes.

Syrah ignores the rest. Outside, ash is falling like curdled gray snowflakes. In the distance, the sky is a dirty dishwater gray. Doors slams, children cry, the rush of a car speeding by. All signs that her neighbors are, for once, heeding the call and evacuating.

She has just snapped her seat belt on when her phone rings again.

"You leaving?" Uncle Dane's voice is steady, but those close to him would catch the worry hiding between those vowels.

"I'm already en route," Syrah says.

"Good," Dane says, then after a moment: "Wait. En route to Compton?"

"What? No. I've been called up. The General's in trouble."

Her uncle is a considerate man, careful with his words. He's one who thinks uncomfortably long before he speaks. But this silence is extended, even for him.

"You wanted me back at work, you got your wish." The lightness sounds forced, she knows. "You're the one who should be headed to Compton, or at least Fresno."

Dane hesitates, doesn't commit to anything, only says, "Be careful, kiddo."

Syrah backs out of her driveway, narrowly missing another car. And as she heads to the end of the street, there are more. She's both irritated and grateful at the traffic building up, trying to get out of the city. She catches mournful gazes at homes, wide-eyed, blank-faced people wondering what they'll find when and if they ever return.

She chose her home not only because of the river view out back but because of its proximity to the station. She's there in under eight minutes. The crew is the garage, most in the trucks already. There's gratitude in Lance's expression when he sees her. "Spare gear's over there near your old locker. Hurry."

Pulling on the shirt and tucking the helmet under her arm feels like coming home. There is no time for sentimentality, so Syrah stuffs down those feelings and hurries over to the truck, hauls herself up and into the back seat next to Alvaro.

"It's good to have you back," her old friend says.

Syrah nods. A smile as thin as watery soup is all she can muster. She's grateful that he doesn't push it any further.

The siren streams out behind them like a ribbon of discord. The closer they get to Sequoia, the darker the sky. Early morning turned dusk. They clear the entrance and wind down Generals Highway.

Chatter is filling the radio:

The fire is moving fast with a high rate of spread.

Fire whirls.

A strong convection column.

Proceed with extreme caution.

When the truck finally comes to a stop, everyone files out. They thread their arms through weighty backpacks and tug on leather gloves.

She can already hear the thump, thump, thump of helicopter blades. The twitch she feels, the thing in her chest that's angry that the chopper wasn't there to help her when she needed it, she stamps it down.

They yank off the hose and bound down the trail that Syrah knows even if she hasn't visited in months. The park is an oven dialed up to broil. At the sight of General Sherman, her heart sinks. It is as if the Giant is being consumed from the inside out. The hollow is a mouth full of flame.

And just like a mouth, it screams. The wailing, keening, drains all the energy from Syrah, and she struggles to stay standing. There's something beneath that keening, the hum.

"Do you hear that?" Syrah shouts at Alvaro. "That sound? Do you hear it?"

He gives her a blank look. "What sound?"

No time to explain. They kneel, turn on the spout, and take aim at the hollow.

The hose jerks with the force of the water coming through. It takes three crew members to hold it. After decades of research, none of the chemicals has replaced water as the first tool in a firefighter's tool kit. Nothing is softer and more malleable than water; it wends its way into the tiniest of crevices. Spectral, it infiltrates spaces where the dodgiest of sparks take cover. It's so silky that one cannot grasp it; it suffers no pain, retains no wounds.

The flames resist. Every time it seems they've doused the fire, it resurfaces.

And flames have already leaped onto neighboring trees.

Soon another crew is there, battling alongside them. Faces grim, bodies tensed.

There's nothing they can do for the flames that are already out of their reach, scaling from the trunk upward, as if on a ladder bound for the sky.

When the hollow is at last under control, Syrah calls out, "We're going to need more air support if we hope to save the canopy." What she doesn't say, what none of them say, is that they've already lost it.

Lance hands the hose over and is yelling into the radio at his shoulder. Shortly they hear the thud of helicopter blades. She chances a look up and sees another two bearing down from the west.

"Clear out," the chief says.

The crew falls back while the helicopters dump their load, a newer, less toxic fire retardant.

They hurry off to other areas of the park. One victory yields to another defeat, walls of ember closing in all around them. The heat is unbearable. Syrah's lungs burn. Her face is smeared with sweat and soot. Standing is an impossibility.

The skies are sentient, live with fire.

Tree bark tongues crackling and splitting.

Every time Syrah blinks, more spots crowd her vision. She's losing sight of her crew but can still hear them, the roar of water gushing out of their hoses. She puts one leaden foot in front of the other, throwing herself against the flames like a battering ram.

When blackened sky tinges toward sunrise, she collapses.

General Sherman is no longer aflame, but what remains has left even the most stolid of them in tears.

Syrah wishes she hadn't woken up to bear witness to so horrific a loss. All that's left of a tree that stood longer than nearly anything else on the planet is a scorched and dead hulk. And the thought of it makes Syrah sick. But they don't have time to mourn. She drags herself back into the fray, tackling a spattering of smaller fires that continue to spring up. Five hours into the next day, they have it under control.

The respirator lies at her feet, where she tossed it. The bandanna, more comfortable but wholly ineffectual, is wrapped around the lower part of her face.

The crews are standing beside the trucks, someone passing out water, when Lance approaches. Syrah tenses.

Instead of an off comment or rebuke, he offers her his hand. "We were down a man—a person. We couldn't have done it without you."

Shock must have registered on Syrah's face, because Lance shrugs and thrusts his hand out again. This time, she takes it. "I'm just glad I was able to help, but the tree." She shakes her head.

"Hoped I'd never see it," Lance says. "Not on my watch. But only a fool would be surprised."

Syrah casts a glance around her, looking for clues. "I wonder what started it?"

"Don't we all," Alvaro says, taking off his helmet and pouring water over his head.

"Damn sure wasn't the weather," Lance says, looking up at a cloudless sky. "It's not even that hot."

Syrah finishes the thought he didn't voice. "You think this one was man-made."

"More and more," Lance says, "that's what we're seeing."

"They're going to destroy this place," Syrah says, anger welling within her. "And they have no idea what it's going to mean to us."

With that, everyone disperses and gets ready to head back to the station. Before they leave, Syrah walks up to what remains of the Giant. She can't touch it . . . it's still too hot. But as she stands there, imagining everything that this tree has lived through, everything that it knows and has seen, she is overcome by the full measure of the loss.

She turns to look away, but her peripheral vision draws her back. She looks down, walks as close as she can, and nudges the underbrush with the toe of her boot. Unmistakably, a sprout. Bright, green, tiny, and lithe. It stands there, defiant, as if to say, *It's not over yet.*

Syrah kneels down, and when she goes to touch the little seedling, its song, beautiful in its outrage, sounds in her head.

Chapter Seventeen

Sequoia National Park, California
September 2042

Romelo Rootspeaker sat in the main library reading and rereading *The Lives of Imminent Keepers*. He loved it here. The pocked, irregularly shaped tables. Shelves and bookcases, chairs and benches. All repurposed from fallen branches, human castoffs, or trees felled by nature. Like him, things from topside that had found a second home in this intricate warren of caves below the forest.

Lives was the first book that Taron bade him read cover to cover when he questioned how long her people had been in existence. Since that time, over twenty years ago, he had returned to the volume at least once every winter season. Reading that first time, Ezanna had counseled him that, like any history, there was a certain amount in the Rhiza text that was overstated, some credit stolen, some flat-out lies. Over the last several centuries, so much had changed.

At first great swaths of trees fell to the loggers. Those that remained were so wounded and exposed that fungus, rot, and, eventually, beetles thinned their numbers further. Air that grew warmer every year meant less snow and subsequently little of the critical runoff from the spring thaw. These things and more laid the groundwork for fires that even they had trouble containing. Innumerable trees and canopy keepers perished. Whether out of necessity or something else, the survivors adapted.

At the time *Lives* was written, there was a one-to-one relationship between the canopy keepers and the Giants. A pairing established at birth and a bond that continued until death.

Today they no longer have connections to individual trees. In fact, aside from The Mother and her relationship to The Keeper, it's highly discouraged to become attached to a single tree. Mainly because life spans—both arboreal and Rhiza—have diminished.

Because of them. Because of a mentality that worshipped cruelty and narcissism.

Keepers past also believed that such pairings led to conflicts with their mission. One might find themselves focusing on the one instead of the greater good. It had happened in the past.

"You are brooding." Taron had snuck up behind him. She laid her staff on the table and took a seat across from him. Unbidden, the others in the library got up and left.

"I am thinking, T," Romelo said. "There is a difference."

Her nostrils flared. She didn't like the nickname. Romelo grinned. "The topsiders killed the General and carved up the Senescent . . . again."

Taron sighed. "Rhiza do not have connections to a single tree."

Yet he was living proof that she was wrong. "Apparently human Rhiza do," Romelo said, matching her glare.

He had told his adoptive mother this on several occasions, only to be rebuked. She was stubborn, that one. Unyielding. She had taken him in and loved him to a degree, but her love was a distant thing, disbursed as if from the other side of an ocean.

Taron reached across the table, and Romelo stretched out his hand, hope, stupidity, thinking she was reaching for him. Instead, she snatched the book. "You've read this. Many times. Yet you refuse to understand it."

"Oh, I understand it all right," Romelo said, seething. "But everything written doesn't account for what is."

Taron set the book aside. "I have lived more than ten times as long as you. Have seen the changes, lived through the loss. I know the anger you feel."

"But you have not done one single thing to stop it. To stop *them*."

Taron's eyebrows knit. "We are caretakers of the trees, of this forest. What else would you have me do?"

"We used to cover this entire country. Millions of canopy keepers, millions of trees, all under our care. Yet here we are, a few hundred left, and shoved into a tiny corner of the country. If we do not act, we and the Giants will be gone by the turn of the century."

Silence. Taron massaged her forehead, then pushed the staff over toward him. "I am in my grave. You are The Keeper. Tell me, what do you do to reverse our fortunes?"

"If you look at the world today, what do you see as the main problems impacting the forests?"

"The fires are worsening," Taron said.

"Check," Romelo said, leaning forward. "Artahe tells me that even the caves are warming. The mushroom growth has slowed. What else?"

"The air is polluted," Taron said next.

Romelo nodded. "Check. Emissions from their machines."

"The oceans are encroaching. The very earth is losing ground."

"All true," Romelo agreed. "And if all of that ended today, if something were done to reverse the effects of the change, how long would it take for the earth to heal herself?"

Taron brightened at this. "By our estimates, and even theirs, twenty, maybe thirty of their years."

Romelo is nearly bouncing in his seat. "Where does the blame for all of this lie?"

Taron swallowed and looked away. Her chin jutted upward. "The topsiders."

"So . . ."

Taron leaned forward. "What are you suggesting?"

"Is it not clear? Eliminate the source of the problem. Reboot the system here and let the Giants do what they were put here to do. And in less than thirty years, everything goes back to the way it should be."

Taron's lips parted, but no words escaped.

"We wipe out the humans here in California," Romelo pronounced and stood. "That is the only way."

Chapter Eighteen

Sequoia National Park, California
September 2042

Two weeks after the blaze, Syrah sits beneath a Giant that inexplicably emerged unscathed, seemingly without losing so much as one awl-shaped leaf. Cones, though, lie scattered around her, opened by the heat. She says a silent prayer that those unseen spores released and carried away on a breeze reeking of smoke will find purchase.

That somewhere in the burn scar, those seeds will burrow belowground, anticipating a warm regenerative sun and a good rainfall. That the cycle of life and death will gift them another Giant. But they may all be dead and gone before it has the time to grow up and do anything to help save them.

Shed are the helmet, the grimy shirt, and all the other venerated accoutrements of her former life. The crew took them back to the station. The ride was bathed in the stench of sweat and regret and failure. An air of pervasive fatalism. They knew they were losing, and even if nobody dared utter those words aloud, they felt it all the same.

Long after the others retreated inside the station and lowered the garage door, she stood there, wanting nothing more than to reclaim her seat at that conference room table. That adrenaline rush of fighting the fire still coursed through her. The thrill that had drawn and kept her in fire service for nearly a decade.

But she doesn't belong there anymore.

Hadn't they—Lance of all people—called on her, though? Worked hand in hand with her? Nobody questioned her presence, nobody looked askance, not once. They've all forgiven her. But she's yet to forgive herself.

She shouldn't be here.

There is a peculiar silence to a forest after a burning so severe. A corporeal peacefulness that signals the worst is over . . . for now. This is the way it goes: First, the birds circle, flocks soar again, scouting. Eventually they settle back on their perches in the surviving trees. Soon after, the ground animals, small and large, will make their way back to see what is left of their home. And the Giants will get to work cleaning the air. And that strong, earthy fragrance of the forest that rests on your shoulders and seeps into your bones will reign once more.

For now, it still smells faintly of damp and scorched earth.

She marvels at a dense mass of mushrooms. Pale pink and round, like miniature teacups with no handles. Pyrophilous, the fire lovers. Fruiting from the charred remains. In time those microscopic root strands will permeate the ground and help bind and stabilize the soil again.

But their presence here, now? Impossible.

Typically they sprout up the first year after a fire, in the spring, not weeks later. Yet hadn't she seen another tall, fire-dousing impossibility that looked like the forest itself?

Nothing is as it should be anymore, the whole ecosystem in flux. Life, in whatever form, always finds a way to return, to thrive.

Maybe it's a symbol for her. Time to get back to life. She thinks again about her uncle's offer. Maybe it won't be so bad. Maybe it is the best possible first step. Yes, she will call him, and they will talk about it again.

Syrah swallows over the lump in her throat. Wondering if her future will include a return to the work she loves. Time will tell. She sighs and forces herself to look again at the damage done to General Sherman. As she gathers her things and turns to leave, she notices a gaping wound in the bark of the other tree. Anything could have caused it: a lightning strike, a pest or bacterial infestation, a tourist foolishly carving out a souvenir.

She pulls a pocketknife from her belt loop. She's seen it done only once. Scribing. When she worked for a time at Blue Ridge. She sets to work, removing the dead and injured bark. She places one hand against the trunk to steady herself and, with the other, chisels around the wound in the shape of a vertical ellipsis. The idea is to isolate the damage by carving into healthy tissue to lessen rot and encourage the bark to form a callus. When she'd seen it done before, only weeks later, the spread had stopped.

"Ouch!" As she works, the knife slips and cuts the fleshy part of her hand beneath her thumb. She drops the knife and surveys the damage. Not too deep, luckily. Funny, though, how those are the wounds that bleed the most, almost as if the body is outraged at what it perceives as such a minor intrusion. She bends, reaching for the knife, and a bit of blood drips onto the mushrooms.

An odd rustling disturbs the understory. Kneeling, peering, Syrah reaches out a finger and gasps as a tiny root, one that she shouldn't be able to see, thrusts itself up through fungal outcropping. When it rises and rises and punches right through her sock into the thick vein at her ankle, a sharp, wild sound pours from Syrah's mouth—not from the pain, but from what she sees next.

Chapter Nineteen

Sequoia National Park, California
September 2042

A curtain parts, one that Syrah never knew existed. Behind it, a mirror image with a more favorable filter applied. The colors, the smells, and the sounds are all richer. But it is the creature—there's no better word to describe her—standing wide eyed and frozen that makes Syrah wish she'd fallen on the other side of the handheld weapons elimination act.

A full five or six inches taller than your average basketball center. A wide chest, torso narrowing perceptibly at the waist. The tunic draping curved shoulders is like a patchwork quilt, a scrap of blue jean here, a piece of flannel there, and something else, green and fuzzy, knitting it all together. Loose slacks, capris of the same construction, fall just above the ankle, no shoes on feet the color of fall understory. In fact, every other bit of exposed skin is of the forest, the dark scarlet brown of a healthy Giant's bark.

So close to human . . . but not. All the wild stories. The debunked nineteen sixties footage of Bigfoot comes to mind. But this creature is nowhere near that. She is more.

Syrah blinks, cocks her head to the side, and it is all gone. Has she inhaled too much contaminated air? She recounts all the symptoms of smoke toxicity. She has the slight cough, but so do all firefighters at some point. Eyes stinging but no chest pain.

Did the isolation rob her of her good sense? Didn't Mama warn her about craziness creeping in beneath the door right along with the insects if she sat cooped up in her house by herself for too long?

No, Syrah reasons. Those answers are contrite, dismissive.

All this can be explained away with one deft search on the internet, of course. She just knows she'd find all manner of costumes and prosthetics that can allow someone to disguise themselves this way. If it weren't for the height.

While Syrah is lost, constructing and deconstructing a million improbabilities, the creature—no, the woman—reappears. She's gripping a walking stick. Almost the full length of her body. She takes a few steps forward.

And Syrah eases back.

But that small, terrifying movement shutters her doubt like a door welded shut.

Syrah glances down at the knife, but instinct tells her not to go for it. Both from a palpable awareness that the woman will be on her before she gets to it and the unmistakable certainty that she'd lose the fight if it came to that.

The two stand, staring at each other, but it is Syrah's whisper that breaks the spell. "What are you?"

The woman closes the distance between them so fast fear paralyzes Syrah. Her mind screams to run, but her feet are incapable of obeying. She can only stand there trembling, struggling not to empty the rest of her bladder.

The woman lifts a hand; the long fingers curl into a fist.

Syrah reacts; she'll go for the liver. She winds up and unleashes a punch that has everything she has to give. It lands on surprisingly soft tissue, but the woman only looks down on her with an expression bordering on pity.

And then, while Syrah is staring up at that fist, waiting for it to connect with her jaw, the creature whips the carved tip of that staff around and buries it in her middle. The blow snuffs the wind from her lungs. Her stomach feels like it's compressed against her spine. Syrah topples over sideways like a downed tree. Her cheek lands on the mushrooms, and their pungent aroma fills her nostrils.

The staff-toting foe moves forward with slow, measured steps this time. Syrah's stomach is still someplace it shouldn't be, but she readies herself, and when those massive feet are in front of her, she kicks out, aiming for the left knee.

But her foot is caught midair and slammed to the ground.

The woman squats down on her haunches, hovering over Syrah like an eagle intent on its kill. Her face is squared, brow slightly protruding. Her features are broad and so pleasantly arranged. When that long-fingered hand reaches out, Syrah braces for another blow.

"The veil has been lifted." She speaks, sounding of the forest. It has a natural melody, like water trickling over a stone. It is at once soothing and otherworldly.

"What veil?" Syrah's voice is hoarse. "I don't understand."

"The Giants have alerted us. Again," the woman says, hoisting Syrah to her feet. "I no more want to see you than you do me. But The Mother has spoken."

Syrah cranes her neck, searching the woman's expression. Giants? Is that the condition that explains how she looks? "Was that supposed to make this"—Syrah throws up her hands—"all make sense?"

The creature sighs, tosses her graying hair, flowers woven into ropy strands down her back. Her expression is one that you might give a small, insolent child. "I am humanoid, just like you."

"You're nothing like me."

"You topsiders are so full of yourselves. Open your eyes. I walk on two legs. Have you not noticed that I, too, have speech? The ability to think—better than you, to be clear," the woman states. The condescension dripping from her words makes Syrah want to snatch the staff and club her, but she thinks better of it. "We had a mission conveyed to us before your kind crawled from the ocean. You are right, though; in our case, our differences far outweigh the similarities."

We! Syrah casts her gaze all around her. She's never been afraid to be in the forest alone. It's where she feels most comfortable. Until now. "I'm getting out of here." Syrah turns and starts walking. She can't process this, none of it. *I should have gone for the knife,* she thinks.

"One of you started the fire," the woods woman says.

Syrah stops. "We don't know what started the fire," she counters, albeit weakly. At last count, almost 90 percent of all wildland fires were caused by people. "An investigation will uncover who did what. Let's hold off judgments until then."

"Investigate all you like; the lattice knows all."

This is getting stranger by the minute. "What are you doing out here? Are you camping nearby? You can't stay out here after dark."

The woods woman comes closer again, studies Syrah's face as if it's a map to some secret treasure. "What is your last name?" the woman asks.

Why can't she stay on topic? "What I'm telling you is, you can't be out here, if that's what you're doing." Syrah will have to mention this to Dane so that he and a team can come and forcibly remove the woman, if necessary. She's more and more convinced that this woman, maybe with a few others, is just a hermit, squatting on the land.

The woman rolls her eyes skyward. "If it were up to me, I would not have to do this, but I am only a caretaker, much like you and those of your service are. It has been decreed, however. It seems you will need some convincing."

Syrah shakes her head in frustration. She's wasting her time. She'll just head back and alert the authorities. She marches over and picks up her knife, attaching it back to her belt loop. "I asked you to leave nicely, but I see you aren't interested in that. So suit yourself."

Syrah backs away a few steps, keeping the woman in her line of sight while glancing back every now and again to make sure nobody else is sneaking up on her. When she's far enough away and the woman still stands, rooted in place like a petrified branch, she turns and hurries back toward the path.

She's taken a few steps when another person, dressed just like the woods woman, appears in front of her. Syrah gasps, then goes for the knife. But this one knocks it out of her hand as soon as she pulls it. Her gaze flitters around. There are more of them, arrayed all around.

Then more, too many.

But . . . but they're picking up trash, clearing away dead leaves.

"We won't hurt you," the woods woman says. "But we won't allow you to hurt us either."

Syrah wrenches herself free. She retrieves the knife, but pockets it.

"The first tree, the Mother Tree, was born fourteen million human years ago. She gave birth to millions of others. Soon the earth was covered in Giants, and the canopy of their combined leaves and needles formed. The animals, bacteria, fungus. The lakes and rivers, streams and eddies. They all sprang to life. And then the lattice came online."

Syrah feels like a cornered animal, but part of her, that curious part that always gets her into trouble, wants to know more. "What on earth are you talking about?"

"Sometime after the lattice came online, this part is the subject of great debate," the woman continues, obviously ignoring the question, "we, the Keepers of the Canopy, were born."

Okay, Syrah thinks. *This woman has gone totally off the rails.* Hermit, yes—her, this man, and whatever others have somehow hidden themselves up here. She's heard of people like them before. Those who reject modern society. In a way she understands them. Much of the world as they know it today has little to offer people like them, to anyone who doesn't fit the norm. She wonders how long they've been able to hide here or if they just move around like forest nomads.

"We tend to the Giants. But you modern humans and your disregard for anything other than yourselves have made the work infinitely more difficult. You have thinned the trees *and* our numbers in kind."

"And we are sick of it," the one who knocked her knife away adds, but they're quickly silenced by a severe look from the woman. She's the one in control then.

Syrah decides to play along; she needs to get out of here in one piece. She thinks of her cell phone, which she always leaves in her car when she comes to the park, mainly because it rarely works but also to be away from the device, if only for a time. "Fine, if what you say is true and that you have to maintain the trees, I'll leave you to it." She looks to the man and the woman, nods, and is about to try to step around them when they disappear.

"What the . . . ?" Syrah blinks once, then twice more. She involuntarily steps back. And then her eyes latch on to movement. A glint of light. If she scans closely, she can just make out their outline. She reaches out a finger. As her finger finds something solid where there should have been air, she shrieks and backs away. The pair reappear.

Syrah's legs turn to noodles, and she sinks to the ground in a heap. Every explanation her mind has used to try to placate her, gone. "How?" is all she can manage.

"Not 'how,'" the woman says, "but 'why.'"

"Look at her," the man says to the woods woman. "Do you not want to address what both of our eyes see? You know why the veil lifted. The lattice all but screams with the truth of it."

"The lattice is a living thing, and all living things err," the woman says. "You are too hasty in your proclamations."

Syrah listens to them talk, as if she's somewhere else. The internet doesn't hold an explanation for what she's seen, and her mind has gone oddly silent in its attempts to reason it all away. Everything in her implores her to get up and run for it. And if she makes it home, for her to forget this whole encounter and never mention a word aloud *or* to herself. She won't be able to get a job working in a gift shop if she spouts any of this.

While the pair of camouflaged woods people bicker about whatever it is they were talking about, Syrah has gone to all fours, trying to crawl away undetected, when a rough, strong hand snatches her up by the wrist.

"We cannot allow you to leave," the man says, deftly lifting her.

"Bring her," the woman says. She turns and stalks away as if walking on a cloud, the earth barely disturbed by her movements.

The man follows, easily dragging Syrah behind him. She tries to yank away, pulling as if on the other end of a rope. When she fears her own arm will be wrenched out of the socket, she makes another move.

She stops pulling away, gets in really close, and sweeps her elbow up, connecting with his chin. He staggers, it seems more from surprise than pain. But he doesn't let her go. Syrah parries. She wraps the crook of her arm around his neck, sticks her right foot behind him, and follows through, knocking him flat onto his back.

But he rolls over before she can deliver the stomping kick. He is up and circles behind her before she can react. He picks her up from behind. Strong hands around her waist. "If you continue to fight, I'll kill you here and be done with it."

"You will not." The woman pauses and turns to regard them both with an odd curiosity. "You cannot willingly harm—"

"You cannot divulge the location of the community to outsiders," the man counters.

"Do you dare question me, Dhanil?"

Syrah feels the tension go out of her captor at the rebuke. "I meant no disrespect, Keeper. It is . . . I mean to say, she is not one of us. She is an outsider. What place could she possibly have in our world?"

"If she is an outsider, then so is my son," the woman says.

What kind of a name is "Keeper"?

This time the man holds out a hand. In response, a trail of root rises from the ground and heeds his call. Syrah has seen enough. Her mind can't comprehend. "Let me go," she cries, kicking and screaming. "Help, somebody!"

When he has had enough, he uses the root to tie Syrah's wrists and ankles. He then hoists a still-fighting Syrah up on his shoulder and holds her there as they march through the park. The walk long enough for her ribs to begin protesting. And the blood rushing to her head sets a small throb across her skull.

"Where are you taking me?"

Silence.

When they finally stop, Syrah is dumped on the ground like a sack of rotten potatoes and unbound. That means they've underestimated her. When her hands are free, she immediately goes for the knife.

"You pull that out, and we will cut off your hands with it. Slowly," the woman says.

This isn't a bowie knife. At most, she can stab one enough only to get him out of the way, but then the woman will be on her. She doesn't drop the knife but clips it back on her belt loop. She will take her chances and find a way to escape later. When she looks up, they're in a section of the park she hasn't visited before. They stand beneath a towering Sequoia tree. Smaller than General Sherman, but no less majestic. There is a man-size hollow in the trunk, though the edges of the wound seem to have calloused over. If this is where they will try to kill her, she makes up her mind, she will take out the woman first. The man does her dirty work, but there's no mistaking who is in charge, and likely the more powerful of the two.

"I will only ask once more," the woman says. She leans down and peers into Syrah's face, those wide brown eyes roaming across her features. Her breath is warm and smells of earth. "Where were you born? What is your last name?"

It's the second time she's asked. And Syrah can't fathom why, but Keeper's tone suggests that her answer is already a foregone conclusion. She resists it, but the word "impossible" springs to mind again. That walking stick is still close at hand, and Syrah won't risk being on the receiving end of another of those blows, so she'll use the tactic of compliance to stave that off. That doesn't mean she'll tell the truth. "Born in Old Miami, last name Carthan," she says.

Keeper straightens. The corners of her mouth quirk into a smile. A glimpse of teeth the milk-white of doves' feathers. "I think not."

Chapter Twenty

Sequoia National Park, California
September 2042

Keeper turns on her heels, scraps of that patchwork tunic swirling out behind her. That incredibly long stride of hers lands her at the Giant. Without slowing, she walks right into the hollow's inky opening. Syrah smells the musky, pungent scent behind her—Dhanil, the woman had called him.

"Are you awaiting a more formal invitation?"

Syrah bends over and fumbles around with a bootlace. When the bodyguard—that's how she's come to think of him—comes around in front of her, arms folded, she bolts. This isn't a part of the park frequented by many, and she hasn't had a chance to explore it herself. She may as well have been dropped in the middle of the Amazon rainforest. Cloud cover douses the moonlight. North? South? East? Who knows? Syrah just concentrates on putting one foot in front of the other.

Her heart hammering in her ears like a drum blocks out everything else. Only vaguely does she register the fact that there are no sounds of pursuit, and she wants to glance over her shoulder to see if any of these people are back there, but she can't risk it. She's crashing through thick brush and slipping on still-damp leaf litter. She leaps over one clump of raised tree roots, and moments later another errant root trips her up.

She face-plants but recovers quickly, scrambling up on all fours and taking off again at a fast sprint.

Her forearms act as barriers for low-hanging branches and high bushes. Already there are tears in her long-sleeved shirt. Then a thin branch with the grip of a bear maw snags her shirt, entangling her. She rips herself free and runs on. It seems like the forest itself is trying to keep her in place.

Time is a blur, and her breathing is becoming labored, escaping in haggard puffs.

Just as Syrah spots a trail that she recognizes, the feel of rough fingers scrapes the back of her neck. *Musky, pungent sweat.* She can feel her shirt collar being bunched up in that hand. Dhanil gives one hard yank, and she falls flat on her back. She looks up to see the scowl painted across his features.

"If it were up to me, I would have let you run all the way back to wherever you came from," he says, towering over Syrah.

"I'm not going anywhere. If you want to kill me, you're going to have to do it right here."

Dhanil doesn't answer. He only snatches her up by the arm and half carries, half drags her back the way she came. Syrah's fighting is futile, but it's all she has. She does take time to make mental notes, landmarks for when she runs again. And she *will* run again.

At the hollow in the Giant, he sets her down. Syrah crosses her arms and lifts her chin. Dhanil deftly spins her around and gives her a good push in the back. Syrah stumbles into the darkness.

Inside is the color of a velvety night sky. Her eyes struggle to adjust. And then the sound, the song, starts. The one she heard that first time, on the run with the crew when she hurt her knee. Then again when she was scribing the wound in the other tree.

But what the hell are they doing inside the Giant's hollow?

Another shove. Syrah's hands fly out in front of her, groping. She stumbles forward, trying to feel for edges. The walls seem alive with movement, but she can't make out what. The tree is wide, but she's certain she should have run into the backside of the trunk by now. Yet each step draws her deeper inside. The ground is springy beneath her feet, making her steps and those behind her barely audible. She's lost track of the woman altogether.

Slowly her vision clears. She makes out soft curves, reminiscent of walls. And the strain in her thighs and knees tells her that at some point they've started descending. A brush against her skin, the shuffling whisper of fabric against body parts. Seemingly melted and peeling away from the very walls. Her heart races. Others have joined in the march to wherever they are going. Exactly how many of them are there? And what are they planning to do?

Everything she's seen today keeps adding up to one thing more bizarre than the last.

The group, and she is certain now that there are at least several of them, walks on. How much time has passed? Being inside this tree has totally screwed up her sense of the world. As she is ushered around a curve, a thin, pale light comes into view.

Syrah emerges from the confines of those walls closing in into something even more unfathomable. She wonders how far they would have to have descended in order for the wide cavern before her to make sense.

A memory tickles the back of her mind. The caves. Sequoia has an extensive cave system. More than a couple hundred of them and even some that are totally inaccessible—until now, it seems. But when she started work at the fire station, they were temporarily closed for repairs after yet another fire. She hasn't had the chance to explore.

She studied the maps, more out of curiosity than anything related to her work as a firefighter, but she recalls enough to know that Crystal Cave is about three miles south of General Sherman, and that you enter through a half-mile trail aboveground, not through a tree hollow. But that was before, when things made sense.

The cavern is lit with odd torches attached to the cavern rock face. The area is wider than she would have imagined. Rocky outcroppings that look sharp enough to slice the skin. Stalactites dripping from the ceiling like darts. There, the woman—Keeper—stands; she turns and stares at Syrah, then gives an almost imperceptible nod.

If the first veil that lifted took Syrah's breath away, this one nearly stops her heart. The wall gives way to another entrance. Syrah gapes. She is ushered through and emerges into yet another cave system.

Here, the walls are smoother. She places a hand along one surface, and it is slightly warm to the touch. In fact, the whole area is. Where it was cold in the outer cavern, here the warmth feels good. Natural. And the place is filled with activity.

As the group maneuvers through the intricate system, Syrah observes hollows that look like sleeping quarters, while others are obvious workspaces. And the people. All like the pair that kidnapped her. The same wood-burnished skin and wide faces. All barefoot. They stare at her as if she's an alien who's dropped down from the sky. Some curious, others with open hostility, their wide chests heaving with indignation.

Syrah has stopped asking how. She only observes with open curiosity. Her attempts at trying to remember the route out of this place, in hopes of the daring escape she imagined, long dashed. After so many twists and turns, she's given up. Her heart sinks with the realization that she's trapped. Even if she can make it to the outer cavern, she imagines she'll be lost within minutes.

That doesn't mean she won't try when the time is right.

She is taken to what looks like an office, and a thick wooden door closes behind them. The room is stuffed with a large desk and chair. Shelves line the back and side walls. Light comes from what looks like patches of moss placed like sconces. And two of those strange torches. On closer inspection, it's simply a container of mushrooms. Top-hat-looking fungal stalks pushing up through the dirt at the bottom of the cylinder emitting an eerie white glow. "Ghost mushrooms" are the nontechnical term. They have a certain bioluminescence, but she's never seen them used this way. The fungi do a surprisingly good job of lighting the space.

A long bench sits in front of the desk, polished so well that it shines like a river stone. Keeper enters and settles herself into the chair behind the desk and lays down her staff on the side. The bodyguard hovers somewhere behind Syrah; she can still smell him. This confirms it; she is the leader of this band of . . . of . . . she settles back on the word "people."

All those other rooms Syrah noticed mean that more people like them live here belowground, but only two of them are present. This Keeper doesn't want everyone to know about her. Whether that is a good thing remains to be seen.

"You may sit," Keeper says.

Syrah hates to admit it, but the trek here was long, and she's ready to collapse. So instead of arguing, trying to show defiance, she takes a seat on the bench. It's high and hard and there's no back support, but at least she's off her feet, which are now dangling a good foot from the floor.

The woman stares at her a long time before she speaks. The petulant-child sigh again. She's conflicted about whatever she has planned; Syrah's sure of it.

"Welcome," the old Keeper says finally, "to Rhiza."

"Welcome?" Syrah is incensed. "Is that what you call what you've done? Odd choice of words for beating the shit out of somebody and kidnapping them. Both federal offenses, you know." Her head is on a swivel, absorbing every outlandish inch of this world beneath the world. "You brought me here—wherever here is—against my will, and I demand you take me back now."

Syrah knows anger well. It dogged her through the early years of her adoption. She's been greeted by it on the faces of strangers who pass her on the street and at jobs where people didn't think she belonged. But never before has she felt as fearful for her life as she does now. Keeper's expression and the soft footfalls behind her make Syrah reconsider the approach she's taken. Apparently these people aren't at all used to anyone questioning their Keeper.

"Not another step," Keeper says. Dhanil stops so suddenly it is as if the words alone control his movements. "She does not know our ways."

"Then we must teach her," Dhanil growls.

"If you will stop interrupting me, that is exactly what I aim to do. Bring Artahe and no one else."

The sound of Dhanil's footsteps retreating doesn't relax Syrah as much as she'd like. How many of these people could there be?

"What am I doing here?" Syrah asks when they're alone.

Silence.

Another approach. "What is this place and how . . ." She searches for the right words. "How are you so close to human? I mean, did something happen to you? A condition of some kind?"

Bored expression.

"Hello?" Syrah prods. "Can I get some answers?"

Eyes closed, Keeper leans back in her chair, hands clasped in her lap.

Each moment without a response fuels Syrah's rage. She'll beat the woman into submission with her own staff. Syrah drops down from the bench and darts forward, arm outstretched.

And in a whir of motion, Keeper swoops over, grabs the staff, and cracks Syrah good across the forearm. Syrah cries out, cradling her already bruising appendage to her chest. Keeper is back in her chair, leaning. She never even opened her eyes.

Syrah has no choice but to slink back to the bench and lick her wounds. All the questions, and she's thinking of more by the minute, will remain cataloged in her mind for later reference. She's lost track of time but assumes it must be edging toward morning. She has no job, no place to be. How long before someone, likely Uncle Dane, realizes she's gone and alerts the authorities? Eventually they'll find her car in the Lodgepole parking lot, but how will anyone ever find this place? She suspects that if she gets out, she won't be able to find it herself.

The door opens, and Syrah turns to see Dhanil enter, and behind him, another one of them. Smaller. Wide faced, only slightly less barrel-chested. Smelling of earth and herbs and something else. This one, she drinks up Syrah in one fell swoop. There's something in that glance, furtive as it is. If Syrah didn't know any better, she'd name it recognition. The questions piling up like unwashed laundry.

Keeper finally finds her voice then. "The Mother has spoken."

"Maybe that's who I need to speak to then," Syrah quips. She can't help herself. Sarcasm cloaks the fear and anger. That feeling of being completely out of control, outnumbered, and outmatched.

Keeper makes a sound, a sucking of teeth that reminds Syrah of her own mother.

"But how?" Dhanil's deep, booming voice asks. "It is not possible; she is not one of us."

Artahe scoffs. "You act as if this is the—"

"Mind what you say." Keeper cuts the small one a look before she can finish her sentence. Syrah has turned, straddling the bench so that she can watch them all. Artahe lowers her head like a dutifully chastised pet, and already Syrah despises her as much as she does the bodyguard.

She jumps down from the bench. "Why am I here?"

Keeper shrugs. "It is a question I have asked myself. I have a theory, but one that I will not share until it is confirmed. For now, you are here"—a pause—"as my guest."

"What happens when your guest is ready to go home?" Syrah asks, earning a glare from Dhanil.

"Come." Keeper gestures to Artahe.

Artahe approaches Syrah and, from her basket, hands Syrah a cup and a bowl. Syrah holds the cup while it is filled, the small one watching her from beneath heavy lids. When she meets Syrah's gaze, warmth is there.

"Drink and eat," Artahe says. "They will help."

Syrah suddenly realizes she's almost faint from lack of food. She drains the cup, the cleanest-tasting water she's ever had. But there's a hint of something else in it. Mushrooms she recognizes enough to know they aren't poisonous. Syrah gobbles them down and has another cup of water. Once she's had her fill, she hands the cup back to Artahe, who gives her a small nod before stepping back.

"Out," Keeper says.

Dhanil opens the door and the pair file out. Syrah makes a show of falling in line behind them before he waves her back inside. Just as she is about to turn, though, she catches sight of someone else. Judging by how high his eyebrows climb, he's as shocked to see her as she him. His mouth falls open. He cranes his neck to look inside the room, then back to her.

His gaze travels the length of her, and there's no contempt there. None of Keeper's superiority.

He is . . . exquisite.

A face of polished ebony, composed as if by an artist's expert hand. He has an aura of newness, of promise, like that enchanting stretch between spring and summer. She greedily breathes in the freshness of him, wants to hold it inside herself forever.

He takes one tentative step toward her before Dhanil shuts the door between them.

Chapter Twenty-One

Rhiza
Beneath Sequoia National Park, California
September 2042

Syrah inhales and exhales a few breaths, presses the rib where the staff did its worst damage. Somehow it feels better. When she looks up, Keeper is standing there in front of her.

"Take your hand away this minute. Do not be such an infant," she scolds. "I held back. We both did. If we had wanted to hurt you, we could have done so easily. Do not let the others think that you are weak, even for a moment."

Syrah takes that bit in and says, "I'm going to keep asking questions until you explain all this."

"Such a rude way to ask, but I should not expect more than you are able to give. Your ancestors were nothing like you. You are, after all, just a product of your times."

"You're in charge here." Syrah counts off one finger, then the next. "You don't like being questioned. And you have a hard time answering directly."

"You are insufferable."

"And you're a pompous ass."

In a game of verbal tennis, Syrah and Keeper trade insults. Syrah notices that she's the only one breathing hard. This is getting her nowhere.

She takes a minute to look around again. Rhiza, the woman has called this place, these caves. What these people have developed is nothing short of masterful. How is it possible that nobody has detected them in all these years?

"You have so many questions," the woman says as if reading her mind. "As do I. Let us start here." She extends a hand. "I am Taron, Taron Keeper."

It takes Syrah a full minute to return the gesture. "Syrah Carthan."

Syrah does have questions, lots of them. She considers and discards a bunch before she decides on the most important. It is what will matter when she escapes, and she definitely plans to escape. "How—"

The woman, Taron, has started walking midsentence. Syrah has no choice but to follow. They pass through a network of caverns so dizzying that those thoughts of escape seem to flitter farther away with every step. To say that she can't believe her eyes is an understatement.

The people, all varying shades of black and brown, seem intent on one task or another. They move like wraiths. Quiet and stealthy.

"Hey." Syrah catches up, considers touching Taron's arm, but thinks better of it. "Where are you taking me?"

"To The Mother," Taron responds, as if that's the most ordinary thing in the world.

Syrah gulps.

The walk, like everything in this place, is so long that twice she has to stop for rest. They are descending again, and her toes keep slipping to the edge of her boots. She also realizes how much of the air aboveground has been tainted by smoke, by particulates. Inhaling down here, she thinks she's never tasted air quite as clean.

"I do not want you here. Though I have tried to hide your arrival, there are few secrets among us. I am taking you to The Mother because she demanded it. She alone will determine your fate."

It occurs to Syrah that now might be a good time to run. But where? Would she even know which direction? How many of these strange hermits are there? There are stories about people who enter the caves and never come back out, and she doesn't want to be the next headline.

No, she will bide her time for now.

They walk a few more minutes before they come to a place where Syrah loses all ability to speak, even to stand.

There, stretching as tall as the tallest skyscraper she's ever seen, taller than any of the Giants, is a tree the size of a city block. It radiates with a natural luminescence. Her branches are ballet dancer elegant, arching out in every direction. Leaves shaped like little hands. Syrah feels as small in its presence as she's ever felt. This Giant of all Giants feels like an entire universe.

And then she sings. Her bone-rumbling hum. Syrah traces the motif of that note, and it speaks to her in a manner she can't yet decipher. She feels as if she is being probed, scanned from head to toe.

"Come closer," Taron says.

They move closer, Syrah craning her neck, and even then she can't make out where the tree canopy ends. When they are within twenty feet or so of the massive trunk, Taron holds up a hand.

She steps behind Syrah and grips her by the shoulders. Syrah doesn't even struggle as a thin tendril of a root shoots up out of the ground. It spirals upward and curves around, crawling along the ground toward them. Syrah tenses but doesn't allow herself to panic.

The root is as fine as the hairs on her arms, but she can see it nonetheless. Syrah is so entranced that she doesn't see Taron go for the weapon, only feels the slice against her bare arm. One root curls around her ankles, holding her firm, while another travels up the side of her body and plunges itself into her wound.

Taron circles around front. Syrah sees her eyes roll back and then close. All is silent. She watches in horror as the root dives deeper into her body. She can't scream. What will it do to her? Will it turn her into whatever these people are? Is this how they're created?

The root emerges, a trickle of blood along its tip. It withdraws down her body, and the other roots that bound her legs also retreat. They ooze back toward The Mother. And soon they disappear back into the dark soil.

Syrah wants a closer look. She has barely moved an inch when Taron comes out of her trance.

"What did you, did it, do to me?"

"The Mother, in her wisdom, has accepted you. You will help us. I don't know how yet, but she has seen it."

"Help you?" Syrah says. "How?"

"You will return to your world," Taron says, once again turning on her heels and walking away. Dhanil is suddenly back. "When the time is right, we will find you."

Thus begins an even longer trek than when she began. Despite all the questions that Syrah throws at Taron, the woman, The Keeper, has nothing further to say. When they emerge again, from the hollow of the Giant, Syrah is allowed to leave. She runs as fast as she can. And when she turns back around, the veil is lowered again.

Chapter Twenty-Two

Sequoia National Park, California
September 2042

The sky is all wrong. The last vestiges of daylight still cling to the western edge of the tree line. They stopped blocking the entrance to the park years ago, so she had no trouble coming to sit in the grove as she often did at the end of the day. The clock in her car had read four thirty. Add in a half hour to make it to the grove at a swift pace. Then she sat among the Giants until the sun had just begun to set, but still provided enough light to safely navigate the trails back to Lodgepole, where she parked. If the sun sets around eight o'clock, it had to have been about seven.

Before the world was upended by people and a place that shouldn't exist.

There's no way to be sure, but by her best guess, she has been in the caves for hours. Yet the sky above her looks like at least an entire day has come and gone.

Her mind chews on the incongruity that what felt like hours spent belowground in the caves—Rhiza—was closer to a day, maybe more. She wants to imagine, to convince herself that none of what she's seen is real. That somewhere, back on North Fork Drive, she's asleep. The nightmares given way to the most imaginative tree dream she's ever had. And when she awakes in the morning, there'll have been no prescribed burn gone wrong. No shame. She will hop in her car and drive to the station and be with the crew, whether they want her there or not.

The scratches on her arms and the echo of pain in her rib cage say different. And with that realization, panic swells like a balloon threatening to burst. She's breathing too hard, and she hasn't taken a step. Syrah bends over at the waist, hands on her knees, and gorges herself on the smoke-tinged mountain air until her mind becomes singularly focused on one thought: *Get away.*

It's faint but there, just at the edge of her hearing—the gurgling melody of the Kaweah River. Two trails must be nearby then—Tokopah and Twin Lakes. But which direction? Her gaze snaps up to the tree canopy. The sun is setting to her west. Looking north, she splits the difference and sets off at a trot right down the middle. After a time she slows to a walk. Nothing looks familiar, and she's no closer to a trail. *Think.* But there's no time.

Too late she spots the overturned rocks, the clumps of fur clinging to the bark of a stately sugar pine.

Ursus americanus. Fear does strange things to the mind, and the black bear's technical name falls from the tip of her tongue. It has massive brown legs, and cinnamon/blond fur covers its body. A good six feet long.

Syrah knows the rules. This isn't the first time she's come face-to-face with the fiercest predator in the forest. She doesn't run but throws up her hands, waving and shouting wildly.

"Go on . . . back away now. Go!"

She eases away slowly, eyes on the ground, looking for a weapon and watching the bear at the same time. She backs into a shrub, and she quickly looks down to find her footing. When she glances up again, the bear is showing her its profile. When it huffs, she knows it's ready to charge.

She cannot run, and the bear is probably better at climbing trees than she is. She screams again, waves her arms.

But it takes off at a loping run toward her. Syrah dives for a hefty branch, rolls over, and comes to her feet with it in hand, ready to swing.

But the bear has stopped. Its head is lifted to the air, snout quivering. And then, just like that, it turns and walks off.

Only the burning in Syrah's lungs reminds her that she isn't breathing. She can't see the bear anymore, but that doesn't mean it won't return. This time she picks a direction and runs full speed.

Eventually, sweat soaked and still clutching the branch, she finds her way back to the Alta Trail. From there she takes the two-mile loop straight to the Lodgepole campground and, just beyond, the visitor center.

And then she runs right into a park ranger, who is luckily not her uncle. Syrah tosses the branch, smooths her rumpled clothes, and slows to a walk. His car is parked right next to hers in an otherwise empty lot. He's wearing the uniform, maybe doing a final check before leaving. An overachiever. He's standing, arms at his side, wearing a curious expression as she approaches. And Syrah knows she must be a sight.

"Are you all right?" he asks, taking in the ripped shirt, the blood splatters. He must be new. She doesn't recognize him.

"I was out for a run," Syrah says, because it's true. "And came out on the losing end with a root." This, she thinks, is also true.

He pauses, considering before he speaks. "What are you doing out here at this time? The park isn't even officially back open for tourists yet."

Tourists? Mudslides have pushed back the official reopening, but Syrah is no tourist. "I like being alone out here. It's the quiet. The way the light cuts through the trees."

At this, the furrow between the ranger's brow smooths. "Yes, ma'am. That's part of the reason why I'm out here on shutdown detail instead of being at home head down in dinner. There's something about the park just after the golden hour, that little slice of heaven when the moon and the sun exchange shifts. But look, besides the fact that you can't be out here, it's dangerous, so I'm going to have to ask you to leave and restrict your visit to the stated park hours."

For a moment he is just like her, someone who chose to work in this park because he loves it more than anything. Now he's all business again. The furrow's gone, but his stance says he's a man who takes his job seriously. "I understand," Syrah says. "Guess I should let you finish your rounds."

She doesn't wait for a response. Inside her car, seat belt secured, she sees he's still there. Waiting. Syrah waves and turns onto the road heading home. When the ranger is but a speck in her rearview mirror, and the pines and birches crowding in from both sides of Generals Highway are her silent witnesses, the weight of all that she's seen erupts from a place deep inside.

Finally, gratefully, she allows herself to scream.

Some people would tuck this whole thing away and get on with life like it never happened. It would be easy, wouldn't it? A bump on the head from a fall would cause this kind of hallucination. A perfectly acceptable explanation if she ever saw one. And wouldn't it again make life a simple matter of sleeping, waking, and wasting time? What benefit is there in adding a complication like this to a dull but otherwise relatively safe existence?

As if in challenge to the thought, the cut on her arm prickles. Syrah scrapes away the dried blood and reassembles the pieces. Roots holding her in place. Sinking beneath the skin. Already the shroud she's tried to toss over the experience is dissolving like cotton candy on the tongue.

Rhiza. It's as if by saying the word aloud, she's accepting the fact that what she experienced was as real as the scar on her arm that proves it.

There's only one way to know for sure. She'll have to go back.

But not before she talks to the one person who's been at the park longer than anybody else. Just as the sun sets, she makes a beeline for her uncle's cabin. Winding down the long drive, she can already see that his pickup isn't in the driveway. Dane doesn't frequent bars or clubs. He's cordial but not friendly enough with his colleagues that he visits for dinner. She's heard her parents mention a name or two over the years, but Syrah's not aware of a current girlfriend or boyfriend.

He visits his mother in Fresno on the weekends and tends to the pit bulls he fosters there. The gentlest human being she's ever met chose one of the fiercest, if misunderstood, breeds. Everyone, given enough thought, is a contrast. Two halves of a coin.

Uncle Dane is perfectly suited for the job he chose. He's an introvert and a loner. The kind of person who'd be content to spend his time sitting on the porch in his chair, listening to the wind and the ruffle of wildflowers. She gladly gets out of her car and settles into the rocking chair to wait. He won't be long.

Syrah has given in to the exhaustion and is asleep in the rocking chair she always chooses when she hears a door slam. Opening her eyes is no different from when they were closed. It's so dark she can't make out anything. She sits up straight at the crunch of footfalls approaching and slowly mounting the steps. She's on her feet when Uncle Dane says, "What happened? What's wrong?"

She stretches, slightly embarrassed, even angry at herself for having fallen asleep. Belatedly she also wonders if those people followed her. If she led them straight to her uncle. "Before I tell you, I'm going to need to use your bathroom, and you're going to need to sit down."

Dane shuffles past her, and her eyes are adjusting thanks to the moonlight. "Can't have you out here soiling my porch." He lets them in, and Syrah makes a beeline for the bathroom.

Like her, he has the latest composting toilet, which she makes quick use of. While washing her hands, Syrah gets a good look at herself. Her hair is sticking up in all directions, littered with bits of leaves that look like oversize dandruff. Dirt smudges like unblended makeup on her cheek and chin. She pulls back the shower curtain and grabs the bottle of castile soap she knows will always be there and gives her face a good scrubbing. Then she also washes the cut on her arm.

When she comes out, Uncle Dane is seated at his small dinette. Two plates and open take-out containers in the middle. Worry creases line her uncle's forehead, and Syrah feels guilty for being a burden to him. She first came to him as a reminder of the family lost in a fire under his watch.

When she's seated across from him, he gestures at a glass of water, which she drains in a few sloppy gulps. The question in his raised eyebrow goes unasked for the moment, as he's up in a second, refilling it. The hat and sweater, his uniform most days, are gone, probably neatly put away in the bedroom across the hall from the bathroom.

When he returns to the table, she feels his eyes on her, and she fidgets. How to begin? What should she say? What shouldn't she say? She's going to sound insane. Maybe this whole thing was a bad idea. *Bury it,* she thinks. Bury it, never think about it, and certainly never say a word about it to anyone. To busy her hands, she starts spooning out dinner on both their plates. Pad thai and spring rolls. She knows the restaurant, a place in town they both frequent, their serving sizes usually enough for three.

"It felt good being back out there."

Dane regards her, taking a sip of his own water. "Not ashamed to say I told you so. But are you going to talk about getting your job back or some other thing? Whatever's really got you sitting out on my porch in the cold."

Crying every day isn't going to bring them back. When Syrah needed comfort after losing her birth parents and brother in that fire, Mama had platitudes. She realizes now that those stinging words heard through her four-year-old ears were what turned her into a woman who is a master at hiding her feelings. From most people. To her dad, she is about as transparent as cling wrap, and his friend, the man sitting across from her, is the other one. Where to begin? Dad has always told her that when she has a difficult story to tell, she should start at the beginning.

"The Crystal Cave," Syrah says by way of introduction. "Tell me about it. The history." It's a story he tells to park visitors during the summer. He told it to her when she stayed with him after the fire. Each time with an enthusiasm that melts even the most stoic skeptics of the bunch. She knows the story word for word, but she likes hearing it every time.

Uncle Dane dips his spring roll in the sweet-and-sour sauce, takes a bite, chews, and swallows before he answers. "Going the long way around, huh?" he says. "I'll play along, but you'll have to get to the point eventually." His smile is like a gateway drug. And then he continues.

"Right beside that spiderweb doorway, there's a plaque that says the Crystal Cave was discovered by C. M. Webster and A. L. Medley. Nature-loving park service employees just like us. The date on that plaque reads April 28, 1918. And it's true. That's when they stumbled across it while on a fishing trip. Pretty cool, right? And I don't begrudge my fellow members of service their place in history. But that's only part of the story. The most recent part.

"By our best estimates, the cave was formed between eight thousand and one thousand BCE. Before Common Era. You see, the earth was and largely still is mostly water. And slow-moving groundwater coursed through the underground to such a degree that, over time, it dissolved the rock—hard, beautiful, natural marble—into these strikingly intricate passages and caverns. And it's no coincidence that they're largely beneath the Giant groves. Crystal isn't the largest or the oldest, but if we don't understand how the wilderness was shaped, then we cannot begin to fathom how we, as a species, were shaped. Our story began after theirs, but the two are inextricably linked. This network is so vast that much of it is inaccessible, hasn't even been charted . . ." Here Uncle Dane pauses and winks. "Unofficially there's a tale of some thrill seeker who sought to do just that and got himself lost in those uncharted caves about fifty years ago. Never heard from again."

With this telling, Syrah latches on to that last thread like a fish on a wormy hook. "The man—the person—that got lost. Is it possible they still live out there somewhere? Might there be others?"

Dane slips a forkful of pad thai into his mouth. He chews slowly, then dabs at his mouth with a napkin. He searches her face. "You mean in the caves?"

Instinct tells Syrah to pull back. "They found sleeping bags and other stuff," she says. "It's just . . . from the things they find out there sometimes, I wondered if somebody could be living out here. If it was even possible."

Dane seems to settle at this. "I mean, I guess anything is possible. We've had our squatters over the years, and I guess somebody could've gone into the caves to escape the cold. It's not exactly balmy down there, but during the winter, it's better than being out in the snow. I don't believe anybody could stay out there long term. We would've caught them."

"That makes sense," Syrah says. Then she thinks about how Taron kept asking where she was born, and another question surfaces. It's funny how much you accept without issue as a kid. Things and people in your life without stories of their own. More fixtures that you just come to get used to being around. "If you were born in Fresno and lived there all your life, where did you meet my birth parents again?"

If Syrah hadn't been so good at reading people, the gift of an only child who became hypersensitive to the people around her, she would have missed the slight flutter of trepidation that slid over Dane's features like a ski mask.

"You remember," he said. "College. I went down to Grambling for undergrad."

Syrah clasps a palm to her forehead. "That's right," she says. "You came out in, what? Nineteen ninety-eight, right?"

Dane's good-natured smile returns as he slips back into the story. "That's right. Back then folks had started talking about the year two thousand computer bug. Everybody claimed the world was coming to an end. But your father never believed that. Turned out he was right."

Syrah nods. They finish dinner, and she stays and talks with her uncle for a while longer. They speak of the fire and the ongoing investigation into who had started it. He tries to coax her into thinking about returning to work as a firefighter, and when that doesn't work, he pursues the park guide angle again.

She doesn't press him further. Knows that her parents have strong-armed him into not revealing too much of her past. Their way of protecting her. That's the thing, though—unanswered questions only multiply.

Chapter Twenty-Three

Three Rivers, California
September 2042

It's about nine o'clock by the time Syrah returns home, her whole body throbbing. It isn't until she turns her key in the lock and flicks on the light switch that her stomach cramps with hunger again. With her boots kicked off into a corner, she walks to the refrigerator, pulls out a container of leftover rice, and shuffles over to the couch.

She shovels the cold, dry grains into her mouth as she stares at the table where she and Dane shared a lunch of burgers and milkshakes. The quiet, distant man who, before today, she had no doubt cared for her. He had never done anything to suggest otherwise. But why had he lied?

Add that to the list of things that transpired since that phone rang that made absolutely no sense. Syrah wonders at what would have happened if she had never answered that call. Why did she even go? That life is behind her. Her gaze flitters over to the bookshelf beneath the picture window. A copy of an old book her father passed on to her: *Ego Is the Enemy* by Ryan Holiday. Some guy who helped revive interest in the even more ancient Stoics.

The fact that they'd called her. *Needed* her. Her ego had lapped it up like a puppy at a bowl of cool water.

And look what it had gotten her. Her entire world upended.

The phone is in her hand before she can think about it. "Hey, sugarplum," her dad answers on the fourth ring. Judging by how winded he sounds, he left his phone in the bedroom again and had to run to get it.

"Hey, Dad," she says, wondering if she should ease into things, perhaps tell him about the fire. She decides she will. "Guess who got called in to help fight a fire over in the park?"

"You went back?" Dad says. "I thought you weren't interested in the job."

"I didn't take the job back," Syrah explains. "They were shorthanded and I was close. Nothing more than that."

"But there is," Dad counters. "I hear it in your voice. You enjoyed being out there. Not going to lie and say I'm thrilled about it, but it says a lot that they called on you."

Would they never give up putting down the work she loved? "You don't have to worry. I'm not going back, but I am glad I was able to help."

"Do they know how it started?"

"Not yet," Syrah says. "But nine times out of ten, it was started by a person. Not bad weather or heat."

Dad sighs. "Some people will never learn. What's eating you?"

"Nothing really," Syrah says. "Just tired."

"Did you want to say hello to your mother?"

"Tell her I love her. I think I'm going to turn in. But hey, Dad, quick question. Where did Uncle Dane go to college again?"

"That came out of nowhere. Why do you ask?"

"I was just talking with him and realized I didn't remember."

"Xavier University of Louisiana. Class of ninety-eight. That joker brags that he can still fit into his old college sweatshirt."

Syrah cringes. She had hoped she'd been wrong. "Yes, I know," she says. "Somehow you remind me of that every few months."

"I'll say hi to your mother for you. Rest up, now. Love you, sugarplum."

"Love you too, Daddy."

Syrah hangs up the phone and tosses it to the other side of the couch. She hauls herself up and strips off her sweaty, dirty clothes on the way to the bathroom. Her head hurts. She's witnessed something impossible, and people she is supposed to trust are in question. She turns the shower on full blast, a notch hotter than advised, and steps beneath the stream.

There are two possibilities: one or both of them are lying, or one or both of them have piss-poor memories.

Chapter Twenty-Four

Three Rivers, California
September 2042

Before seven in the morning, Syrah opens her eyes to find the day's first weak rays of sunlight slipping beneath the slats of her window blinds. The blackout curtains she bought but never put up are still in the packaging in the corner. Moving around a lot does something to your sense of stability. It's like she doesn't fully expect to be here long enough, so why bother? With her bedroom door closed, the room is quiet save for the sounds of small animals splashing around in the river on the other side of the window. She pulls the duvet close around her neck and shivers despite the warmth.

Her dreams were fitful. Enlarged tree roots chasing, overtaking her, wrapping around her neck and head and legs. Mushroom spores sinking beneath her skin. When she opened her mouth to scream, bark beetles flew out. She'd been consumed from the inside out, and the roots dragged her beneath the soil to the awaiting arms of people who were not at all like people. Lucid dreaming. She studied it in college. A phenomenon usually brought on with deep meditation that makes it seem like your dreams are real. This is the first time she's experienced it, and she's not a fan. Not at all.

Fear flees out the door with its tail tucked shamefully between its legs, and anger—solid, raging anger—walks in and slams the door behind it. Hasn't her life already been upended enough? Was taking away the only job she's ever loved not good enough?

She needs someone to talk to about this. In the end, she wasn't able to tell her uncle anything. She isn't sure why but knows the only way to prove she isn't suffering from the most epic meltdown of her life is to get proof. If what she saw is somehow still there, then, well, she'll have to contend with the possibility of having made the discovery of the century.

But she doesn't want that. More than anything, she hopes to go back up to the park and find that tree hollow to be nothing more than what it should be. A Giant that would survive the gaping wound in its middle long enough for another sapling to grow strong enough to take its place.

She sits up and swings her legs over the side of the bed, toes groping for her slippers in the still near-dark. Her body is sore from the previous day's adventures, and not for the first time, she wishes she had the space to fit a tub into her tiny bathroom. A little steam will have to do. She works her way through a series of sun salutations to loosen the kinks. When she's done, the night's fog has cleared, and if there is any question in her mind, it's settled. She has to go back.

This time, though, preparation will be key. She grabs the stepladder from its cove by the side of the refrigerator and drags it to her bedroom closet. When one lives small, every inch of real estate is precious. Even two steps up, she wavers. A woodland firefighter afraid of heights. How's that for irony? She stretches her arm out on the uppermost shelf and feels around until she lands on one of her backpack handles and pulls it out. Now, what to take?

For one thing, this time she'll have her phone. She doesn't need to make a call, but if she can get a picture of those people or of that whole cave system, that will go a long way toward proving she hasn't totally lost her mind. Battery at 60 percent—she'll top it off in the car. That she will need her trusty pocketknife is a given. A snarky, judgmental voice at the back of her head reminds her that it didn't do a thing to protect her last time, but she'd rather have it than not. From the kitchen she tosses in a few energy bars and, why not, the pack of Halloween candy she didn't pass out because not one kid showed up. From her junk drawer she snags a flashlight and checks to make sure it still works, and then in it goes. Last but not least, two liters of water.

Syrah showers and takes her time oiling her face and body. She scoops out a dollop of the vanilla-scented hair cream and works that into her still-damp tresses. In her bedroom, she checks the weather—forty degrees. She opts for pants, a long-sleeved undershirt, and a pullover. Layers for when the temperature climbs during midday. A thicker pair of socks for cushion against the hike and that steep descent in the cave. She's ready.

Jacket on, backpack by the door. She sits on the small bench to lace up her boots.

Really? Her mind still struggles to accept what she's seen. Will she make a complete fool of herself, trekking all the way out to that tree? What will she do then? Knock and wait as if it's a door and she's greeting a new neighbor? She has her first boot on her foot, but she pulls it off. Is it possible that she's the only one who's ever seen anything like this?

Why didn't she think of this before? She was too tired last night, but she goes over to her desk and turns on her laptop and external monitor. When it boots up, she launches the browser. She stops to think for a moment. What to search for?

Thanks to years spent outdoors, she's reduced to the hunt-and-peck method of typing. *Crystal . . . Cave . . . People.* Nothing but a bunch of stories from campers who've taken tours and pronounced themselves experts on cave history. Another article about someone who got lost and spent two days wandering and freezing before being rescued.

Time to try another angle. Syrah leans back, her gaze skyward, outside. A purple martin lands on a branch. She can see the blue-black feathers; the bird turns and looks as if it knows she's watching. *Ha!* She types in another search term: *Mother Tree*. That produces a number of books, including one by the same name. A quick preview mentions something about mycorrhizal network. Myco . . . Rhizal. Didn't Taron call the place Rhiza? She bookmarks that for later review. A few more searches don't produce much of anything even close to what she saw. She's stalling.

This time Syrah laces up both her boots, slips her arms through the backpack, and is out the door before logic or concern for personal safety can stop her again. The morning is white-sky bright and that type of humid cool unique to places near a lot of water. Her carport does little to stop the thin, iced condensation that blankets all her windows. Most of her neighbors have garages. The real estate agent who sold her the place even gave her the name of someone who could build one for her, but in this climate, she saw it as a wasteful luxury.

The car purrs to life, and she backs out onto the street. She waves at a jogger zipping past and is barreling down the street on the ten-minute drive to the park. It isn't lost on her that a few weeks ago, she drove this path straight to the firehouse and once again donned the garb of a firefighter. Chances are she never will again.

Unsurprisingly, the parking lot is empty of cars. Not even last night's park ranger is there to harry her.

At the start, the path isn't a difficult one. But soon the climb becomes steep, and when it starts to descend, her breathing becomes more labored. While she walks, she thinks about who started the fire. The woman, Taron, was convinced the blame lay with a park visitor. The park isn't even officially open, but that didn't exactly stop her from visiting either. She makes a mental note to check in and see what the investigation has yielded. And what about her uncle? Is she making too much of the discrepancy? Older people mix up dates and times and places all the time. She almost convinces herself she's making too much of it, and if she hadn't noticed his expression and how troubled he looked, she could.

The lingering smell of smoke intensifies as she gets closer. She laments the scorched earth and the blackened trees. She stops and listens, takes in her surroundings. Part of her expects one of those people to jump out from behind a tree. She thinks about taking out her knife but decides against it.

Instead, she takes tentative steps forward, planting her feet firmly on the still-water-dampened earth. Mud cakes her boots. And then the tree is a mere ten feet away. She scans the surrounding area for both the cinnamon bear and the hermits. She remembers that the people are like chameleons. They blend in with the forested surroundings so well she was barely able to see them.

She eases her way forward until she stands at the hollow. She inhales, slow and long. After she blows out that breath, she steps inside.

A foot or two into the hollow, there's nothing but darkness. Syrah turns around, and right there, a few feet away, the sun is shining. She can do it now, walk right back into that light and pretend that yesterday was a figment of a bored imagination. Get back to her life. Call and chat it up with her dad, mumble through pleasantries with her mother. Call Uncle Dane and beg him for the opportunity to be a park guide and be thankful for the post.

While she stares at that little patch of light, calling, drawing her out, she feels herself take a step backward. Then another. Before she can think about it, she spins and runs headlong, farther into the cavity, fully expecting to smack her head into the other side of the trunk.

But what feels like a full half hour later, she's still moving. And she's spent. She stops and listens. A skittering of a small animal, hopefully not a rat. Creaks and cracks. That article about the man who got lost in the caves suddenly doesn't seem so far-fetched. When her breathing returns to normal, she slips off her backpack and takes out the flashlight.

It's not noticeably warmer yet, but her clothes are sweat soaked in all the wrong places. She's in a narrow part of the cave, rock pushing in from both sides. She stretches out, not more than an arm's length away. Overhead, stalactites—the source of the dripping. Water falling from the tips like a leaky faucet. She bends and touches the ground. It's moist, the texture somewhere between mixed concrete and cake batter.

She inches forward, not exactly sure what she's looking for. A lever? A handle? A way through that secret door that Taron opened so easily.

Syrah has been walking so long she's lost track of time. And she didn't think to lay down markers to find her way back. Should she turn around now after having come so far? Instead of dejected, though, Syrah grows angry. Her mind is as sound as anyone's. Her vision, laser enhanced. She saw what she saw. The fact is, they're hiding from her. They lifted the damned veil. And it's on her to figure out how to bring it down again.

One of the articles she breezed over claimed that trees have the ability to communicate. But those theories have been largely debunked. Now she's not so sure. She's seen roots pop up out of the ground and do things that they had no business doing. If that wasn't intelligence, she doesn't know what it was.

Syrah sets her shoulders and walks straight ahead. And keeps going. And going. Going until she is well past what should have been the end of her rope. While chill bumps and small hairs rise all over her body. While the thrum of the tree song fills her mind. The scent of earth and wood clearing the muck from her lungs.

Until she comes upon it again—*Rhiza*. And the cadre of wide-chested, unnaturally tall, bark-toned people blocking her path. Her stomach does a somersault. She was right. She doesn't go for the knife at her side; if they want to harm her, they can, all too easily. She's here to learn, if they'll let her. If sneers were bullets, her body would be riddled with holes. But she notices curiosity among the onlookers as well. Plainly. And a couple even project welcome. Among that group is the one who eyed her when Dhanil opened the door to Taron's library. The exquisite one, who causes her to straighten her shirt and tuck a lock behind her ear. He speaks first, his voice a gold-leafed invitation.

"Taron Keeper is expecting you."

Chapter Twenty-Five

Rhiza
September 2042

"Dumb luck or skill," Taron says between spoonfuls of whatever is in the bowl in front of her. "Which one has guided you back to my doorstep remains to be seen."

Syrah holds out her hand and gestures for the surly bodyguard—Dhanil—to hand over her backpack. He confiscated it as soon as he saw her. Rummaged through the contents, ostensibly searching for a weapon. He looks past her, over her shoulder to Keeper. She must have given him the okay, because instead of handing her the backpack, he comes forward and drops it at Syrah's feet before slinking back into the corner to stew.

They are in a different room from what she's come to think of as the office. This one is more of an overlarge dining area. An arrangement of long picnic-type benches, as well as a few tables and chairs, carved from the most magnificent of woods.

Pale daggers of stalactites adorn the ceiling, and it occurs to her that if one were to break off and fall . . . she abandons the train of thought.

The walls are smooth and nut-brown. Packed earth evocative of kiln-fired pottery. Syrah marvels at the craftmanship. The amount of patience and labor it must have taken to create this space out of material as unyielding as marble, stupefying.

"Either way," Syrah says, coming to stand on the other side of the table, "you were expecting me. Or hoping. Which"—she pauses for effect—"remains to be seen."

Taron raises an eyebrow, tsks dismissively, and settles herself back in her seat. Like everything in this underground milieu, the table and benches make even bar-height stools seem short. There is simply no elegant way to climb up, so Syrah gives up the attempt and ignores the chuckles from behind her.

"Bring another bowl," Taron says, and the chuckling stops. The bodyguard, knocked from his perch on high, has become a waiter—her waiter. "The truth is," Taron continues, "once you have lifted the veil, it is always within you to do it again."

Syrah *has* made it back. Her mind is sound. During her brief time studying, she learned that there are likely hundreds, if not thousands, of plant and animal species lost to extinction every year, but what doesn't gain as much media attention is the acknowledgment that there are half as many discoveries. Most inconsequential, a weed that turns out to be medicinal. An insect with another pair of legs or eyes. Science is always open to new possibilities. Should a humanoid variation be so out of bounds?

"What are you?" She asks the question that she didn't receive an answer to yesterday.

Taron ignores her and goes back to her bowl of soup. Syrah knows how to wait. She uses the time to study Taron up close. Two eyes, a nose, a mouth harboring a sharp tongue. Hair of a texture not much different from her own tight coils, gathered at the nape of her neck in thicker, longer ropes.

Aside from the things she's noted before, they aren't all that unalike. But what would their physiology be? She wants more than anything to reach out and touch her skin. Before she can, the door opens, and someone else sets a bowl and a spoon down in front of her before leaving without a word.

"Eat," Taron says.

"Not hungry."

"I do not care."

The aroma, redolent of a hearty beef stew, changes her mind. With a loud huff, Syrah picks up the spoon and slurps. Chopped mushrooms and unidentifiable greens swim around in the watery broth. The mushrooms are tender, earthy, woodsy, and meaty. It lingers on the tongue, and there's a tinge of bitterness on the back end, probably courtesy of an herb. It's surprisingly good.

The pair finish their meal in silence. With each mouthful, Syrah relaxes. She shifts in her seat, and is it her imagination, or is the remainder of that soreness gone? Maybe this stuff is like chicken soup, good for whatever ails you.

When Syrah sets her spoon down, Taron picks up the bowl and peers into it like a mother checking to make sure her kid polished off all their mixed vegetables. And it annoys Syrah. "A more relevant, less discourteous question would be, *Who* are we?" Taron says. She already towers over Syrah, making it seem like she's looking down that bold nose at her. The way she lifts her chin doesn't help matters. "We are the Keepers of the Canopy."

Syrah blinks. Is that supposed to mean something to her? "The canopy," she says with a nod. "You mean a tree canopy? Yep, about as clear as mud. Care to expand?"

"Ochai is taken with you," Taron says.

Can she never answer a question directly? The thought is replaced by an unexpected flutter in her stomach, and it isn't pain. Is Ochai the one who was staring at her? And didn't she brazenly stare right back at him? What she feels for him is longing, pure and simple. A sure sign of how far she's fallen. And she's intent on stopping the descent. Ten billion people—regular eligible adults—on the planet. She hasn't been able to sustain a relationship with one of them. So she sets her lowered sights on a hermetic cave dweller? She turns back to the matter at hand. "You going to tell me exactly what a canopy keeper does?"

Taron watches her for a moment. "You should know that half of Rhiza is just as taken with him as you are. I am sure Dhanil is." That earns a snort from behind them. Taron presses the issue. "That one will not settle. You have been warned."

Syrah's last relationship went the way of every one she's had since Hakeem Okoye in the third grade—she had taken a sledgehammer to it. The attraction with Alvaro was mutual, but she would never consider dating a colleague, let alone a subordinate. Married or not.

Books are written about people like her, afraid to commit. Wanting love but turning tail and running as soon as it is within her grasp. She has grown tired of running, but that doesn't mean that she is ready to go down this trail with a not-human. A keeper of whatever the hell canopy Taron is talking about. "Noted and not needed. I'm not interested. Can you give me one straight answer?"

Again with the silence. Two can play at this battle for the upper hand. Syrah huffs and pulls an energy bar out of her backpack. She's taken two bites and is checking out her surroundings when she feels Taron's eyes on her. "What?"

"Do you have any idea what you are putting into your body?"

Syrah shrugs. "Oats, nuts, a few bits of cranberry."

Taron grimaces. "And other compounds that you cannot even pronounce."

Everything, even the stuff on the grocery shelves with a sticker on it proclaiming its organic origins, has chemicals. Some more natural than others, of course, but there's no way to produce food on a large scale without them. The insects would devour everything before they were able to make it through a growing season.

Taron waves a hand and a Keeper, or whatever they're called, that Syrah didn't notice before appears and places another bowl and wooden spoon in front of her, along with a side of something that looks like a cross between dried fruit and potato chips.

"If you are still hungry," the other Keeper says and is gone before Syrah can get a good look at her.

Syrah hesitates. Only her mother has ever been as intent on feeding her. She supposes this might pass for what these people consider manners, a maternal instinct of some sort. She isn't hungry, but she's been taught to take what someone offers. She tosses back a few of the chips and takes a spoonful with about as much enthusiasm as a child staring down a plate of worms.

"You see," Taron says, while she signals for one of her people to remove both bowls. "That is the problem with your kind. Lies. You are not hungry, but instead of saying so, you are content to waste our food. Your inability to tell a simple truth has led to the destruction of everything. Why do you find that so difficult?"

"It's rude," Syrah says, thinking about adding the fact that Taron and her people are annoyingly haughty. "You don't repay somebody's hospitality by insulting them. There are good lies and bad ones, but apparently nobody taught you the difference."

Taron regards her a moment before she commands, "Leave your things and come." She snatches up her staff and waltzes off without another word.

Syrah jumps down from the bench and is about to follow when she stops. There was another backpack before this one. Sturdy, lightweight. It cost her more than she'd ever spent on herself before. An Old Miami coffee shop. Patrons milling around, every table filled. And in an instant, after she took one step away to the counter to buy a hot cocoa, that backpack had disappeared from the table not three feet behind her.

Perhaps this place, Rhiza, doesn't have thieves, but she stuffs the backpack under the table and pushes her bench in to cover it all the same. She's near the door when she spins, goes back, and grabs her cell phone.

Syrah rushes out into the caves, and Taron is nowhere in sight. But others have taken her place. Two, four, she counts eight of them. They stare at her as openly as she does them. Nobody speaks, the glances sizing her up like a Thanksgiving turkey. They're tall. Massive. Thick muscled and lean, slender toned. A looming black-brown curiosity.

Between them, another pair walks by carrying what looks like charred wood pieces from the fire, and she wonders what they do with them. Someone trails them.

She knows it's him before he speaks. Her nostrils drink in his floral springtime aroma. Ochai.

"The Keeper has asked that I take you to her," he says, appraising Syrah with such naked desire that it punctures straight through her formidable defenses. "If it pleases you, I will take the long way there."

He's less than three feet away, a distance she wants so badly to close.

Syrah allows herself to look at him. Looks so hard her mother would have admonished her for being forward. Some of Ochai's ash-black hair is gathered in a topknot, while the rest brushes his shoulders. His nose is a splendid, full centerpiece in the broad face shared by all Rhiza. She imagines herself lost forever in those wide-set eyes of amber with playful flecks of jade.

"That would please me very much." Syrah's voice has gone all husky. She clears her throat. "Thank you."

Before her last breakup in Florida, before the fire that robbed her of her work, before she entertained thoughts of Alvaro, she may have flinched or pulled away when Ochai took her by her elbow. Instead, she leans into his gentle touch. Warmth from his hand radiates through her long-sleeved shirt.

As they walk, side by side, Syrah is finding it easier to see in the darkened spaces. Between the torches and mushroom clusters, her eyes have adjusted. And, in fact, she finds the whole thing so much more soothing than outside. For the first time she sees why someone would choose to make their life here. But how much time can one really spend in caves before it affects your health?

"How much time do you spend aboveground?" she asks Ochai.

"As much as is necessary," he said. "For my work."

Syrah cuts her eye up at him to see if there's any mirth, if he's mocking her. He returns the appraisal. He's dead serious. A memory surfaces. The fire, how she saw him—and she knows now that it was him—vanquish the flames around him with seemingly nothing more than a thought. Still, she must be sure. "You mean you have a job?"

"Do you not?"

What can she say? A race, a species, an offshoot—even they have jobs and she doesn't. "Tell me about your work."

"We are the Keepers of the Canopy—"

"I've heard," Syrah says. "But so far Taron hasn't told me what that means."

His laugh is a thing of immeasurable beauty. "The Keeper says only what she chooses."

"If you're all Keepers of the Canopy, then why is she *The* Keeper?"

As they walk, Syrah takes in her surroundings. More rooms than she can fathom. Someone has gone to great pains to construct this place, and she doesn't know how they've done it. There's no way they get any heavy machinery down here. No electricity even if they could. They've worked with, not against, the natural shape and outcroppings of rocks. They are strong—she's seen that—but even for them, this kind of achievement would probably have taken centuries. But how?

They pass a grotto, and Syrah stops, mouth agape. Floor to ceiling, the place is alive. Fungi of more varieties than she even thought possible. Growing in clusters and rows along the walls, the floor. She looks up and finds them bunched up on the low ceiling.

"Everyone has a purpose," Ochai explains. "We grow our own food. Make the clothing that you see. We tend to the caves. And then there are the jobs aboveground."

They move down a winding passageway. Syrah thinks, finally, she'll get some answers. "My full name is Ochai Blaze."

"And that means?"

Ochai pauses. "You saw me, did you not?"

Syrah glances over at him. "I don't know how, but I did."

"My life's work is to help fight the fires. Thanks to your ceaseless doing, your cars and planes, and your futile exploration of the stars, my work keeps me topside more than I would like."

Syrah raises an eyebrow. Like her, he is a firefighter. If it is true, that would explain why his chest is slightly larger than some of the others'. Expanded lung capacity maybe?

Yet, despite what she's seen with her own eyes, Syrah balks. As far as she can tell, there are no hoses, no great bodies of water. How would they even begin to fight a fire? Toss on some fungi and blow out air from those oversize lungs? But then she remembers the fire that she herself started. How there weren't enough firefighters to stop the spread, no air support. She's tucked it away in a part of her mind where she stores other unexplained occurrences. That humans are responsible for the increase in fires is a given and not something she will bother arguing about. "How?"

"In due time," Ochai says.

"You said there were other jobs," Syrah says. "Tell me."

"Topsiders make such a mess of the forest," her escort explains. "Trash removal, recycling, for one. And generally keeping an eye on you and trying to influence where we can. We failed to spot the drug addict that started the fire in the Giant you call the General."

"Drug addict?" Syrah asks. "We don't know what started the fire yet."

"Your investigations take too long," Ochai says. "The lattice knows."

It is then that they pass an open cavern. And what Syrah sees robs her of breath like a thief in the night. Wide, rounded like everything belowground. She doesn't think she's seen a square or an angle anyplace. The cave opens into a fantastic cavern nearly double the size of the fungi farm. At the center of the ceiling, a mass and tangle of tree roots spread out and over, down the walls like thick arteries. Threads connect to each of the pods.

"And the last job," Ochai says. "And my friend would say the most important: Lattice Affairs."

Chapter Twenty-Six

Rhiza
September 2042

"What do the Keepers do here?" Syrah asks when her voice finally returns.

"Rhiza," Ochai corrects. "Or even rootspeakers, not Keepers."

"But you just said—"

"You will come to understand."

Syrah wants more than anything to step inside, but something holds her back. More of the Keepers—rather, the Rhiza—are at work, cleaning depressions sculpted right into the walls. Others are actually reclined in the things. She's got no idea what they're doing.

"This is how the rootspeakers communicate with the Giants," Ochai explains. His tone is lighter than Taron's. Perhaps he just has less on his shoulders.

The concept is so simple, and so outlandish, it rocks Syrah to her core. Prolific scientific careers have gone up in flames over suggestions that the mycorrhizal network exists. Not only is it real, but these canopy keepers are somehow connected to it.

"Just how large is this lattice?" Syrah asks.

Ochai gestures with his hands in a manner that tells her that he's struggling with the question. "Every tree in the forest is connected, that much I know. A rootspeaker will have to tell you more. I wonder if Thorn is here." He pokes his head in, looks around. "Later, I guess."

With his hand at the small of her back, he guides her away, deeper into the cave system. When he takes his hand away, she feels as if she's lost something vital.

"You have not noticed the time," he asks.

In fact, she has. When she emerged from the hollow yesterday, she was certain that less time had passed. "How much slower does time pass here than on the surface?"

"It is hard to describe in terms that you will understand. Will it suffice to say that if you were to walk from the farthest, northernmost edge of the system back to the entrance, that would take the average Rhiza three days."

Syrah nods. "Human days?"

Another helpless gesture. It is almost like speaking to someone from another country.

"It is hard to say," Syrah fills in the blanks for him.

He chuckles again. Syrah is coming to like the sound of it.

"Wait a second," she says. "You said 'Rhiza.' That's what you call this place. Why aren't you called Keepers?"

A gasp from the group they pass, scandalized expressions on their faces.

"Ignore them. They are too excitable. There is only one Keeper at a time." Ochai clarifies things for her again. "Taron. Our home is called Rhiza. We are Rhiza and we are canopy keepers."

All this terminology. Feels like freshman year all over again. What Syrah needs is some way to jot this all down. *Her phone.* Surreptitiously, she pats her pocket and is relieved to find it still there. Forget the notes. She's got to find a way to snap a few photos.

They arrive at what Syrah would describe in her world as a sitting room.

The story of Taron is everywhere. The fountain pen and glass ink-well. Leatherbound books, thick journals, and parchment that look like they'd disintegrate if she touched them. Even a few recent hardcovers are mixed in on the floor-to-ceiling shelves, contrasting modern and ancient. Taron is a reader. A keeper of notes. A historian.

An Adirondack-style chair pushed into a corner with cushions seemingly made of dried and bound leaves. This space would not be complete without what Syrah has come to understand is a staple in any place that Taron occupies: an overlarge, irregularly shaped desk.

The Keeper glances up from the open notebook and waves Syrah inside. With palms clasped together, Ochai winks at her, bows, and walks away.

"You came back, on your own." For once, Taron doesn't fix her with that look, like she's admonishing one of her wayward children.

"I think you knew I would." Syrah makes a beeline for the chair. "This place shouldn't exist. According to the rest of the world, it doesn't. There is no way I could just go back to my life like nothing happened."

Taron runs a finger along the left side of her neck, a gesture Syrah has come to recognize precipitates one of her probing questions. "Your life. Up top. Tell me."

Not a woman of many words, Syrah thinks. She opens her mouth, ready to answer, and then finds that there's not much to tell. Embarrassment washes over her. Aside from her parents and a standing job offer as a part-time park guide, what can she say? "I'm unemployed. No family aside from my parents and a play uncle. A car that isn't long for this world. But I have a home. One that I paid for with my own money. It sits by a strip of a river that if I listen to really closely lulls me to sleep at night."

From the look on Taron's face, she isn't too impressed.

"Here you will have work that matters. A mission that is older than time itself. You love the park. I see it in your eyes. Some are drawn here for a reason, and I think you are one of them. You and another. Here you would have a community, a family. Love."

Syrah is dumbstruck. Taron is offering her a place among them. She has a million questions, and she has none. Everything in her tells her to accept, but she has to know what that means.

Syrah goes as rigid as a day-old corpse. Then crosses and uncrosses her legs. Her clothes suddenly chafe. Did she hear that right? A false, nervous laugh spills from her open mouth. "Wha . . . what exactly is your mission?"

"We are the Keepers of the Canopy. We are the children of the Mother Tree, and we are bound to protect her and this land. The Giants. I will not lie to you. What Western civilization has wrought makes our work infinitely more difficult. Between the changes in climate and human stupidity, the battle is turning a tide. Our numbers are not what they once were."

"Which is why you want me to join you." Syrah can't disagree. People have done some stupid things. Natives, Aboriginals, Africans . . . those who maintained or tried to maintain traditional ways, they understood. But in the modern world, so many have no idea how to live in harmony with the land. Quite the opposite, people have done everything in their power to destroy it.

"Yes. That and other things," Taron says. "I had a suspicion when I first saw you. The lattice and then The Mother have confirmed it. You are not the first human to join our ranks, but you will likely be the last."

"Wait," Syrah said. "Not the first? Well, who was?"

"I believe it was your ancestor," Taron says. "A person by the name of Cathay Williams."

Chapter Twenty-Seven

Rhiza
September 2042

Taron had told Romelo the truth as soon as he was strong enough to withstand the shock. Of course, he had always been a perceptive boy, and the blow was more confirmation than devastation. It did not take a genius to notice the differences. Less noticeable at first, from a small child's eyes. Saviors, tormentors. New family wholly unlike the one he'd lost, or anyone else he'd ever seen.

Children, even Rhiza children, knew cruelty well and kept it close at hand, like a treasured plaything.

I have seen mushrooms taller than you. Your chest is as narrow as a sapling's! Why do you tire so quickly during the climbs? Your lungs must be infantile, deformed! And his favorite: *Why did your human parents abandon you?*

Early on, before he had learned the ways of the Rhiza, he had responded poorly. The Keeper pardoned him for his physical outbursts; he was not of them, after all. *We have rules,* she'd told him. Rhiza are a peaceful people; conflicts are resolved through discussion and, if need be, mediation. On the surface, they held fast to this rule, but in the dark, trenchant shadows, infractions lived.

The aim was righteous, probably established a millennium ago by a Keeper with high hopes. An idealist who had no idea what the world would become and how his people, despite their isolation, would change right along with everything else. Outdated and ineffective. An oversight Romelo would correct when he became Keeper. And he would, sooner than any of them knew.

In time, Romelo had learned to endure slights and barbs with a quiet dignity that earned him the respect, if not fully the heart, of the people and his adoptive mother.

It was Ezanna who taught him best. He'd gravitated to the older man because he was the angriest Rhiza in the entire community. In the same breath he could praise Romelo and condemn the topsiders, as if in his eyes Romelo were Rhiza, born and raised.

Through his mentor, he had learned to overcome his human weaknesses. Those deformities of a birth he had not asked for. Ezanna'd drilled him through longer runs at the higher elevations to develop his lungs. Forced him to sit in total darkness for weeks at a time to train his eyes. He'd learned the lattice like he had learned nothing before.

If Ezanna was one half to him, Taron was the other.

Romelo had attached himself to The Keeper like a sycophant. The closest thing he had to a mother. She had not known his real parents. But she had taken him in nonetheless. Saved him from a fire that would surely have taken him as it did them.

And for the last two decades, he had been the only one.

The human woman—that had been a surprise. And he hated being caught off guard. Why her and why now? When Ochai brought her to Lattice Affairs with his chest all puffed out and wearing his idiot's grin, Romelo had warned him off bringing her inside with one of his looks and shrunk back into a cove to watch her. Tall for a human but not tall enough. Narrow chested and frail. Strutting around like she trolled the walkways of a zoo instead of his home. The Mother Tree was up to something, and he had to figure out what.

Taron, the Keeper of the Secrets, claimed that she'd had no forewarning that another human would be allowed behind the veil until she had seen her face the previous day. Over the years, he'd come to recognize her omissions and dogged inability to directly answer a question for what it was. There were things that she didn't share with him, with any of them, until or if it benefited The Mother. At least Taron had come to him at once. Asked his opinion on offering the human a place among them.

Experience was life's most ruthless teacher. If she chose to stay, Romelo knew what lay ahead for the human. He would stand by and watch it all, wait until the anger and isolation threatened to send her back topside for good, and then he would reveal himself.

No matter, Romelo and Ezanna had hatched the seeds of a plan, and he had enough of a faction that believed in him. Allies in the coming battle would prove beneficial, so he would take a chance. Out of curiosity and practicality. And if he was honest with himself, out of need. He questioned that decision now.

If he had not loved General Sherman so much, he would have been glad for its destruction. The Giant that had saved him had, with its demise, drawn more people to his cause. It had been the proverbial last straw. Canopy keepers were not supposed to court kinship to one tree; their task was to serve them all. But Sherman was the one who had responded to the great blue oak and signaled for Taron to raise the veil for him.

He had been knocked out cold. Eight, maybe nine years old by his best estimate. Smoke and fire marching ever closer. The lattice that he now commanded had sprung into action. Roots sustained him with vital nutrients and alerted the Rhiza. Taron and the others had come for him and, for reasons he still didn't understand, kept him instead of returning him.

He had no memory of any of it. But he had heard the story so many times, pressed Taron on every detail, that it may as well have been physically implanted. He wondered at the cause of the loss. The human brain's inability to process trauma? A simple bump on the head? Who knew?

Nonetheless, the bell tolled, signaling time for shift. Change marching them into a new future. And they would come with him, or he would break Rhiza's first rule again and again, until they did.

Lattice Affairs chamber three sat at one of the handfuls of dead ends in Rhiza's extensive cave system. Romelo strolled to a stop, casting aside thoughts of the new topsider. It was time for work.

"She looks just like you," his best friend, Ochai, said when he came through the archway. "Without the unattractive bits." He stood just inside, at the spot where he always greeted Romelo at the beginning of his work shift, the refreshment table. He was pouring a cup of water and handed it over.

Romelo sipped from the cup Ochai offered him. "You think that all humans look alike. She is nothing like me." He ostentatiously flung back his long, knotted plaits. "She is plain, unremarkable in every way."

Ochai threw back his head, laughing his deep, throaty laugh. The friends snacked on handfuls of fungi chips, drained their cups, and left them in the cleaning trough. As they were finishing up, Ezanna appeared in the arched entryway.

He wore one of his long, flowing robes, clasped hands peeking out from the overlarge sleeves. Present was the perpetual grimace that had carved rivulets on his forehead and around his mouth. Romelo's mentor flashed Ochai a glare. His friend held his ground long enough to signal his lack of fear. Then he inclined his head to them both and left.

"You are well?" Ezanna said. It was his way to always ask after Romelo, something he appreciated.

"I am," Romelo said. "And I hope The Mother favors you this day."

"What happened to General Sherman?" Ezanna dispensed with the small talk. "Losing such an important Giant has roused anger even from The Keeper herself. Not that she will see things the way we do, but the point is, she is not alone. If we are going to act, we must do so soon, before they destroy every last one of them."

Romelo planted his hands on Ezanna's shoulders. "Everything you ever told me has come to pass. You think I do not know our time is running out? I have not just been over here nursing aging root filaments, my friend. This entire state is in my grasp, and I have reached as far north as Ohio and as far south as Alabama."

Ezanna's eyes grew wide. "That far? When?"

Romelo swelled with pride. He did not tell his mentor that many of the elm and chestnuts, even the replants, had been destroyed. That the lattice reported wide swaths of land either scorched or consumed by insects. A leader did not trouble the troops with gloom. "When does not matter. What does is that today I plan to reach the coast. If there are any pond cypress left in the Everglades, they will be on the lattice by the end of the shift. Mark my words."

At that moment the bell tolled again, and everyone took their seats and reclined. Ezanna lessened the grimace into something resembling a smirk and left. Romelo strolled over to his pod, surveying the others. A few knowing gazes met his. Good. Seeing Ezanna had roused the troops. Romelo wasn't certain how he felt about that either.

He pulled the lever, and a cover lifted, revealing the lightly packed earth. As always happened, a little spilled to the floor, along with a thick, squirming earthworm, but the cleanup crew would sweep them back up later. He relished this part. He never felt more at peace than when he worked his shift. He eased his feet into the opening.

The earth felt cool and moist between his toes. Eyes closed, he settled in to wait. Tree roots, even the Giants, spent their leisure near the surface, where they could soak up sun and moisture and swap nutrients, but once a shift the Rhiza called to them, and they answered. Theirs was a communication system thousands of years old in its perfection. They were created to serve the trees, and to do so, they had to understand how they felt, where their greatest need was. And the Keepers of the Canopy had evolved to do just that.

Within the hour, the first tickle of root filaments caressed Romelo's ankles. A greeting of sorts. An acknowledgment and welcome. A request to connect. One that he never denied. One by one, he marveled as the tiny filaments probed, commingled with the hairs around his ankles and lower leg, then sank beneath his skin.

The flare of warmth flooded his system, and his grand plans faded. Each time, he was humbled, stripped bare like the limbs of a fall tree. An elemental beauty that renewed and suffused his senses with life. Romelo relaxed into the pod as the final connection was sealed.

And then the data rode in as if on a cataclysmic wave. As the tide receded, he sorted through what remained. The previous winter snowfall had been insufficient, again. Though the meltdown had begun a full month earlier than it had a decade ago, there were mounting concerns about whether there would be enough groundwater to sustain the trees in the foothill areas.

Sunlight was in good supply for the Giants, and photosynthesis was working well, but a Giant of middle years, damaged in the recent fire, had had its roots trampled by humans. The soil near its trunk needed attention, immediate aeration, or it would suffocate and die.

With effort, he set those concerns aside. His second, Liesel, would have to send a rootspeaker topside for on-site repair. Some things they could do through the lattice; others required risky topside intervention.

Through thought alone, he was able to relay his acknowledgment of the need. Then he focused on his specialty—lattice channels. Were there any blockages? Any trees that hadn't been heard from and accounted for? The response came back. A copse near Lodgepole was not as strong as the previous day.

Mentally, he traveled through those fine filaments and cleared the obstruction. Some human had been digging around in the earth and sliced through centuries-old roots. Romelo was filled with outrage, as were some of the trees. Topsiders had no idea of the impact. They thought that their speech made them superior. That any creature that didn't walk and talk as they did had no feelings and thus little right to survive. This was an attitude that worsened every century.

The forest as a whole mourned the loss of General Sherman. Of the human who invaded that hollow. That the hollow had been created by a lightning strike was acceptable. It was nature, after all. But that the human had started a fire there . . . The trees wailed their grief and outrage. They grew tired, as did he and a growing contingent of the Rhiza. But, faintly, he heard The Mother. She was there to settle and soothe. To quiet her children and chastise them into submission. Again. But not before Romelo registered the resistance. It was a tiny thing at first, one node, then others that blinked out of existence. A turning away, a showing of one's back before returning.

Dissent was growing.

Romelo set that aside. He quickly got to work, cataloging the list of tasks he needed to complete before his shift: a patch on three fungal root nodes, a quality check on a couple of his second's improvements, and a review of the logs. His shift was four hours, and he completed his work in half that. He had other work to do. Erecting protections, he called out to his tree. His thoughts traversed the lattice until it landed on the node connection, and the tree stretched and groaned and rumbled through the connection.

The trees had no language, as did their protectors, but they spoke nonetheless. Signals, electrical. A quick, sharp one for danger. A jumbled series of jolts meaning human angst. A low thrum for contentment.

What Romelo received from the Ashe juniper was an electrical jolt so strong he thought it would collapse the containments he'd erected and alert the others.

The message was clear. The young juniper and what remained of its siblings weren't content to endure, to hope that the next blaze didn't wipe them out completely. The humans had to be dealt with. He flooded the connection with endorphins that wished them well-being. And let them know that when the time came, he would call on them. Then, through a series of start-stop cues, a sort of knocking at the door, Romelo announced his request to tap into the extended segment they had secretly established. The return signal was immediate, and Romelo's mind was flooded with the openness of the wider scheme.

It was like swimming through a vast ocean, buoyed and buffeted on all sides by different schools of fish. But then a path in the ocean cleared, and he sent his thoughts farther. He didn't know when this extended section had begun to form. One day, while he communed with the juniper, unable to shield the tree from his growing discontent, it had simply shown him the way.

Taron had been The Keeper for longer than anyone before. Some put the estimate at a thousand years, but that was ridiculous. Rhiza had long life, not immortality. More likely she had been Keeper for three or four hundred years. Long enough. It was during her time that they had retreated to the last stronghold, in California. From the stories, they had lost Yosemite a hundred years prior and retreated here to Sequoia. At this rate, they would be gone inside the millennium. Romelo was determined not to let that happen.

His thoughts traversed back and forth along the lattice, a veritable introduction of species that were coming to learn more of each other, to cooperate in ways they never had before. But it was not easy going, and the messages were fraught with bad news. Southern California was returning to desert. Humans had flooded east and north. A strip of forest near Puget Sound, where a few hemlocks and firs clung to life. The East Coast suffering a similar retreat. Rising sea levels claiming that part of the country. Skeletal, blackened remains scattered across the Texas plains. A wizened stand of pines holding fort.

Aside from what remained in the Sequoia Forest, there were no Giants left in the country. But whispers along the lattice suggested that some may exist elsewhere. One day he would push his reach across the ocean floor and find out.

The communication barriers between the species had not fallen completely but had eased thanks to him. Even numbers of the Keepers of the Canopy had been culled, a fraction of what had been a mighty species now limited to the small number that populated the Crystal Cave.

Romelo raced along the lattice, traveling back and forth with ease. He turned south when he reached Ohio and slid all the way down the eastern coast, the soil going from rich dark to cinnamon red. He sweat with the effort, but he was going farther than he ever had before.

And at each new node that he traversed, the story grew more dire.

He was at the door, ready to knock on his target, Florida and abandoned remnants of the Everglades forest. He could feel the filaments in his ankles tingling, burning, the entire haywire connection of roots and fungi trembling with the effort. But he pushed ahead. The strain grew to the point that the lattice suddenly collapsed.

Romelo's eyes flung open. His clothes were soaked, his body weak and in need of rest. He backpedaled, crisscrossing his earlier steps, masking any traces of what he'd done and disconnecting from the lattice. He removed his feet from the opening and exited his pod. He stepped into the tubs left outside every rootspeaker's pod and rinsed the dirt away. He stood with effort. He couldn't let anyone see what state he was in.

"Is all well, Chief?" Liesel asked him, ever the observant one.

"No," Romelo said to his second-in-command. "But soon it will be."

After the bell tolled, signaling the end of the shift, he made quick work of the small talk that dogged the close of each workday and hurried off to his room. He would have to accelerate his plans.

He had not succeeded. But by his estimate, in the months and years to come, he would.

For now, for whatever time it took for the Giant groves to heal themselves and the state, he would focus his efforts closer to home.

The topsiders had had countless chances to take corrective action, and they had fumbled every one of them. It was time to take matters into Rhiza's capable hands, and with the fauna of Sequoia National Park and other living creatures, he could right their wrongs. Eliminate the human population, then hold firm the borders along the state line. And then Romelo Thorn would become the new Keeper of the Canopy.

And the people of California would recede into memory.

Until fate or evolution decided they had learned enough to begin anew.

Chapter Twenty-Eight

Rhiza
September 2042

Syrah awakens on the tail end of terror. Her dreams filled with images of a world in which whole cities are flattened by meteors, waves as tall as the tallest trees washing over people fleeing in all the wrong directions. A great fire ravishing what little land remains. Before her eyelids flutter open, an earthquake breaks the world.

Absent are the usual suggestions of moonlight pooling around the top and side edges of her blackout curtains. This room is closer, inky dark. The bed feels more like a box spring than a mattress. Her weighted blanket replaced by something lighter but no less warm. It smells sweet, almost like almonds. Husky voices on the other side of the door.

She's not at home. She's still here.

Rhiza.

Syrah sits up, and the murkiness of restless sleep clears. Taron dropped the name of the other topsider, Cathay Williams. And then did that thing she does, where she gives as little information as possible. Syrah will research it herself when she gets back home.

She stands and stretches, works the kinks out of her shoulders and neck. In a way that she can't quite pin down, Syrah feels better. More than a good night's rest better. Is it the air? Her stomach rumbles in response, and she walks over and opens the door. The chatter stops. The one that brought her the soup is there, with a few others. Artahe's skin is more pallid than the others'. She needs more sun; come to think of it, this whole group has the same odd cast to their skin. Two stand out, though, among them—a woman, very pregnant, and a child, teenager? Someone shorter than her. Both stare at her with open hostility.

"Why don't you go back to where you belong," the youngster says. His voice is a little too high-pitched to pull off what he thinks is intimidation. The adults don't correct him, only watch impassively. All except—

"You must be hungry." Artahe slips her arm into Syrah's and gently guides her away. Something hard and solid smacks Syrah between the shoulder blades. She turns to see on the ground what looks like a perfectly crafted snowball made of dirt.

The young one snarls at her. The pregnant woman beams down at him, probably his mother. The adults laugh. Syrah allows herself to be guided away before she stops and, in one swift motion, picks up the dirt ball and drills it straight into the young one's chest. She realizes she's made a mistake as soon as the shocked expressions leave their faces and they barrel toward her.

Artahe steps in front of her, hands out. "You do not want to do this," she pleads.

"Oh, but we do," says one of the adults. Syrah scours her surroundings for a weapon, but the smooth walls and ground have nothing to offer her.

"At least one at a time," Artahe says.

"What?" Syrah reels on her. "I can't believe—"

"He can handle this human alone," another of the adults suggests, superiority dripping from her words like sap. A mocking grin paints the youth's face. Murmurs of agreement. Syrah's among them.

But as she steps out from behind Artahe, ready to take what she is certain may be a beating from a Rhiza kid, she hears another voice she despises.

"You will all get back to whatever it is you should be doing, now." Reprieve from Dhanil, the smelly bodyguard. Likely sent by Taron.

It works. With apologies and downcast gazes, the group quickly disperses. Dhanil does not stop to spare her a kind word or glance, only stays long enough to ensure her safety—for the moment—then strolls off.

Syrah turns to Artahe. "One at a time," she says. "Really?"

Artahe shrugs, then slips her arm back into Syrah's, pulling her along. "They won't stop until they test you. We are stronger than humans, the young scourge suppressor even more so. I thought it was better to get it out of the way with one so young. I wouldn't have allowed him to hurt you too badly."

"Why don't I feel comforted by that fact?" Syrah says. She doesn't understand these people. They seem to hate topsiders so much for being destructive and violent, but she's seen little to prove that they are any different.

As they meander through the caves, Syrah gets more glimpses of Rhiza life. It's busy but not in-your-face big-city busy. Everyone bustling here and there. Around each twist or turn, another cavern or hollow, people have their heads down working. It is like the most efficient small town she's ever seen. Artahe stops at one.

"Scourge Suppression." She gestures with a lift of her chin. Two Rhiza squeeze past them and go inside. Between them, they're carrying what looks like an overlarge wheelbarrow overflowing with junk. Clothing, broken branches large and small, food containers, plastics that have been outlawed for years but that still manage to turn up in the park's trash bins. *Trash.* Lots of it. No wonder they are stronger. It occurs to Syrah that they, the topsiders, are the scourge that needs suppressing.

Inside, a group sets to work on the pile. They separate the bounty, and Syrah's gaze follows along as she witnesses a recycling operation that, like everything she's experienced over the last couple of days, belies belief. Parts of the wood are tossed in a large vat. Others are being reworked, polished, and fashioned into new pieces. The plastics are all dumped in a pile, something pungent sprinkled on the mess.

"Why don't you share any of this topside?" Syrah asks. "If that's what I think it is, we could at least do something about the ocean. It's probably more plastic than water at this point."

Artahe sighs. "You think us unsophisticated? Little more than Neanderthals that developed speech?"

"Don't put words in my mouth," Syrah fires back.

"I don't have to. It's in that condescending tone of yours. The way you marvel at us like a child's science experiment."

Syrah holds up her hands. "Look, I don't mean to . . . this . . . this is all . . . you have to cut me some slack. How am I supposed to react? How would you react if you cleared out another cave and discovered a new world with a different Rhiza faction you didn't know existed?"

Artahe softens. "I'd be just as taken aback as you are."

The two exchange a genuine smile. Syrah believes she's made her first friend.

"To answer your question, we've tried," Artahe says and starts walking again. "Every time we slip a bit of information topside, a forward-thinking scientist latches on. Take bacteria, for example. The Giants are always subject to pests and fungal attacks. We actually identified a strand that breaks down plastic. We planted that data in the right inbox, and the idea took root."

"Why do I remember something about this?" Syrah asks.

"Because it worked," Artahe says. "After an eternity of talking and testing. Your scientists confirmed what we already knew. Who knows who put a stop to it. But like so many other times, the effort was abandoned, and you returned to doing exactly what you've always done."

Artahe probably isn't lying. Syrah has read about so many different attempts at recycling or breaking down plastic, each idea more promising than the last. But nothing ever sticks. "I'm not surprised." She doesn't offer excuses. She's seen too many good ideas stamped down by politicians or bureaucrats or nutty zealots to dispute.

They come around a bend, and they're back at that room Syrah noticed yesterday. She thinks of it as the living room, but not one that you sit in and welcome visitors. A living, breathing space coated with mushrooms.

"And this is where I work," Artahe says. She's beaming. Syrah recognizes that expression, thinks back to how she felt as a firefighter. "I, we, tend to the fungi."

"This is incredible," Syrah says and follows Artahe inside, careful to follow the intricately laid-out path. Intent not to be the clumsy human who stumbles around, smashing the food.

"Food is the smallest part of it," Artahe explains, as if she has somehow read Syrah's mind. "Medicine, obviously. Clothing, that blanket you were wrapped up in last night. They are one of the earth's most versatile gifts. They were likely the first living things on the planet. We are here on loan, all of us. When it is time to return to stardust, what do you think repurposes our flesh into trees, insects, Rhiza? Fungi are the greatest life-form, and the most rejected by your science. They shimmer with metaphors for life itself."

"Show me," Syrah says. She loves the zeal with which Artahe speaks.

They go over to a section of the room where workers are flattening a long, narrow mushroom species she doesn't recognize, using what appear to be rolling pins made of stone. They're then sliced into thin strips and rolled together between the palms.

"Thread," Artahe says. "We use it to make our clothing from the scraps we find topside."

Artahe advances the tour, pointing out a dizzying variety of fungi. When they come back to where they started, someone is standing there.

Syrah's breath catches. He doesn't look like them. He's topsider tall like her, not Rhiza tall. Stern faced and curious. His skin and hair mirror her own.

Artahe has been speaking nonstop, but when she notices that Syrah is no longer responding, she looks up, gaze flittering between Syrah and the newcomer. Finally, she goes over to him, leans down, and plants a kiss on his cheek.

"Syrah," she says, "allow me to introduce you to Thorn."

Chapter Twenty-Nine

Rhiza
September 2042

They've asked her to join them. These people who live underground and tend to the park like wraiths. The Keepers of the Canopy. Syrah ponders this while she drives over to pick up Dane. Is it because of Thorn? As much as she pressed him when Artahe introduced them, he was oddly silent, almost stoic in his manner. He wasn't polite or impolite, just an enigma.

Are the canopy keepers ready to take on another human experiment? Or is this just a ploy to lure her in for some other nefarious purpose?

Her gut tells her no, that's not the case. Taron, Artahe, even Ochai, they all seem genuine in their speech and in their purpose. Taron cited Syrah's work as a firefighter, her commitment to protecting the park. And in that she couldn't have been more right. For the first time since she walked away from her role at the fire station, Syrah is excited about the prospect of work. A purpose and a people who, if they can get past their own xenophobia, have a mission she can get behind.

Even with the other human she met, she'd feel too alone. He seemed completely one of them. Very little in his manner or speech suggested he was anything at all like her. She wonders how long he's been there. How long the other woman, Cathay Williams, stayed. If Syrah is to do this, she'll want someone there with her.

And the only person more dedicated to saving Sequoia than her is her uncle. It doesn't hurt that he is also like her—childless, single, and aside from each other, friendless. Before she makes any decisions, she will show him this place, Rhiza. The word bounces around in her head like a cloud and spits out of her mouth like a pleasant afternoon shower.

The strangeness of it all doesn't escape her. Walking away from her home? How will her family reach her? Can she live on a diet of mushrooms and table scraps? She can't say she isn't tempted.

If Dane sees what she sees, comes to understand that this can be their chance to make a real difference as she does, then she's going to ask him to join them. It occurs to her then that she's making a huge assumption. In all of Rhiza history, only three topsiders have been accepted into their midst. What makes her think they'll so readily accept another? If they want her, then they'll have to.

She's avoiding two very obvious people, though. Putting off talking to her parents. Because she knows what they will say. But Anissa and Trenton Carthan sniff out any unrest in her like bloodhounds. If they even suspect she's hiding something, that anything at all is wrong, they won't stop pestering her until they get to the bottom of it. She'll put them off until she's solved at least one of these mysteries.

She comes around the long driveway and spots Dane already on his porch. He's dressed simply in jeans, boots, and a weighty jacket against the unseasonably chilly September morning. It's one of the few times she's seen him outside of his park service uniform.

"You talk to your folks?" he asks as he settles in the passenger seat and attaches his seat belt.

Syrah gulps. "Not yet. After."

"Care to fill me in on where we're headed?"

"Seeing is believing," Syrah says with a quick glance in his direction. Her stomach churns. What if she realizes that this has all been a figment of what her mother calls an overactive imagination? The joke will be on her if she comes to find out that she's sustained some critical injury fighting that fire and that, in reality, she's been holed up in a hospital bed, sleeping away her life in a coma. And that when—and if—she awakens, she'll have one hell of a story to tell.

But she doesn't really believe that and is growing tired of trying to explain away what she knows is real. She decides not to, not anymore.

"The park guide," Dane says, drawing her out of her contemplation. "Have you given it any more consideration?"

Syrah resists the urge to roll her eyes. "If, after this, things don't go the way I expect, then I'll take the job."

Dane does a drumroll on the dashboard. "Now that's what I'm talking about."

He goes on to tell her some of his thoughts on how to make the job even better, and Syrah only half listens. She nods and responds now and again, but her thoughts are elsewhere. Finally, he takes the hint and lets the conversation trickle to a stop. They ride the rest of the way to the Lodgepole parking lot in an anticipatory silence.

She hasn't thought of it until now, but what if they react badly to her sharing their secret with another outsider? *Too late,* Syrah thinks. She has to see how this all plays out.

When they park and get out of the car, Syrah's stomach is twisted in an impressive series of knots. And suddenly she has to pee. The visitors' center isn't open, so she excuses herself and goes to empty her bladder in the surrounding woods. Midsquat, two things happen. First, she wonders if one of the Rhiza, camouflaged, could be standing somewhere, watching. And if that isn't bad enough, she's spotted the cinnamon bear.

Again.

She's worked in parks where she hasn't run across the same bear twice in a year, let alone in a matter of weeks. Her skin prickles. There's something more at play.

The animal watches her from about one hundred yards away, but she knows from experience that it can close that distance in a blink.

The bear watches her as she stands and zips up her pants. It shakes its head, ruffles its fur. And takes a step toward her as she moves backward. She freezes again. Her gaze flittering around her, looking for a tree to climb. That's no guarantee, either, as bears are expert climbers, but it might buy her some time or, at the very least, a vantage point from which to kick.

She thinks of calling out to Dane but decides not to endanger him. Eyeing a suitable tree, she moves slowly, keeping her eyes on the bear. When it continues to pursue, she stops and waves her hands in the air, making herself as big as she can.

It charges.

Syrah screams and scrambles up the tree as the bear closes in on her. Scratching her palms and ripping her nails, she can't gain a proper foothold. She glances back and sees the bear move away. Dane is there, arms spread up and wide, his deep voice commanding, "It's okay, big guy. Go on back the way you came. Go on now."

And the bear obeys.

She feels so foolish but comes up and thanks him. Without further incident, they march toward the tree.

"Still not going to tell me what's going on?" Dane asks.

"Soon," Syrah says.

"Everything is so off. Bears barely hibernate a month or two. You can't be too careful. Make noise as you're moving around. Just give them a warning, that's all."

Syrah accepts the admonishment. "You're right, and it won't happen again. Just indulge me, okay?"

Having worked in the park his whole life, and despite being in what Syrah judges to be his fifties, Uncle Dane handles the trek like it's a Sunday afternoon stroll around the neighborhood. His steps sure, quick, and his breath is that of someone who has just done a half-hour meditation.

When they come upon the section of the park that suffered from the fire and arrive at the entrance to Rhiza, she pauses. "Follow me, and it'll all make sense shortly, all right?"

Dane shrugs. "I've come this far. Let's get to it. Whatever it is."

First Syrah listens and, hearing nothing, proceeds to the outside of the hollow. She bites her lip, then says, "Follow me."

They walk into the hollow. She can hear Dane breathing behind her. She doesn't dare turn around and face the look of skepticism she knows she'll find on his face.

She keeps walking, confident that, as she's done before, she'll keep walking long past the time when she should encounter the other side of the bark. But it's her forehead that smacks into the trunk and tells her she's wrong.

Goddamn it! Syrah curses under her breath. Instead of the definitive answers she is so certain she'll have, she has two more questions: Is she, in fact, crazy, or are the Rhiza purposefully hiding from her since she brought Dane along? She closes her eyes, steels her shoulders, and turns around.

Instead of ridicule, Syrah finds deep questioning mixed in with compassion written across her uncle's face. "You want to clue me in now?" he says. "What are we doing out here?"

Syrah hesitates. She thinks of kicking the tree and then decides that isn't such a good idea. "Apparently making a complete fool of myself."

"What *were* we supposed to find, then? Let's start there."

Syrah takes one last glance around before she answers. Head on a slow swivel, she scans the surrounding woods. He can't conceal himself like the other canopy keepers, but he's so still, eerily still, that she almost assigns him to the background like a shrub. She can't quite gauge his expression from this far away, but she knows exactly who it is.

Thorn.

So the Rhiza choosing her—and her alone—is intentional.

"Let's go," Syrah says. "I've got everything that I came for."

Chapter Thirty

Rhiza
September 2042

Once Syrah sees Dane off with a promise to stop by later and, unfortunately for her, to take the job as park guide, she doubles back. And this time, when she walks into the hollow, the veil lowers.

Dhanil is standing there, on the other side of the opening. He escorts her back through the caves and into what she's come to think of as Taron's office. Syrah can't help but notice that the air is different, a charge that wasn't there before. People are rushing around more than before. There always seems to be some important work to do, but now a tense hush surrounds all the activity, and she can't help but wonder if her attempt to bring in Dane is the source of it.

"It was very silly of you to try to bring an outsider into this place," Taron says, tossing her dip pen onto her desk. Syrah loves this office. It's close and warm, a little crowded with things that matter, nothing superfluous. The well-placed bioluminescent lights make it bright enough to see perfectly.

"*I* am an outsider," Syrah counters. "And you neglected to mention this earlier, but there is another. Thorn."

"By our choice." Taron's voice takes on a steely edge. One that raises the hairs on the back of Syrah's neck. "Not yours."

"A mistake I won't make again," Syrah concedes. "There's something different in the air. Something I'm guessing is not about me trying to bring in the park ranger."

That seems to take the bite out of Taron. She suddenly looks older, her gaze somewhere down and far away when she says, "Name me three reasons why this world would not be better without humans."

"What kind of question is that?" Syrah comes over and makes a point of putting Taron's pen in its holder before sitting. The Keeper tips her head back for a moment and closes her eyes.

"Come now," a voice says from behind her. Without looking, she knows who it is. He's trying. She guesses he's had years to practice, but he can't quite mimic the mellifluous timbre that punctuates The Keeper's words. "Do not pretend that this is something you have not asked yourself many times before."

If it can be said that Taron flows into a room like a slow-moving creek, Thorn carries the air of someone who glides into a space on a high cloud, above everyone else. Not threatening yet, but the potential always there, waiting for the right conditions to surface.

Instead of sitting, he crosses his arms and leans against the wall, where he can watch them both. It's so natural a gesture you'd think this was his place instead of Taron's. "It is the reason the lattice let you in. It is the reason why you have returned to us."

"Thorn has always had a problem with eavesdropping," Taron interjects.

"There are no secrets, at least not for long, in Rhiza," Thorn says. He is just looking at Syrah; he's studying her like a manual, something to be dissected. Curiosity in that gaze of his, and something else that, if she didn't know better, she'd mistake for hope. It makes her uncomfortable, so she returns the favor. His face is on the ordinary side, the only thing they have in common. Not handsome, nor ugly. The standout is his unblemished velvety dark skin. Not so much as a teenage acne scar to ruin the visage.

When Syrah breaks off and focuses back on Taron, she's puzzled by what she sees. Taron and Thorn regarding each other, locked into some kind of silent war. With a final side-eye, The Keeper turns back to her.

"Thorn Rootspeaker and his friend Ezanna have views, radical views. And he is steering other Rhiza onto a path from which we cannot return."

That gets Syrah's attention. "Is someone going to tell me what we're talking about?"

"Is survival really all that radical a concept?" Thorn walks forward and stands at the edge of the desk, ignoring the other chair beside Syrah. All she can think about is how he came to be here.

And they are both doing it now, talking in maddening circles. "This path," Syrah says. "What are we talking about?"

"You see," Thorn says with a feline smile. "She is just like me. Gets straight to the point."

Taron fiddles with her staff. "You have a decision to make, first."

"About that," Syrah says. "Anybody care to explain what I'm doing here? What he's been doing here?"

"Later," Taron barks.

"Now," Syrah parries.

"Now," Thorn says, barreling over them both. "We need to make a decision. The community has spoken. It is time to send them a warning."

"This again?" Taron says.

"You have seen what they did to the Giant," Thorn presses. "Before that it was the campfire over in Kings Canyon. And before that, fireworks. In the middle of the park. We lost three Rhiza that time. How many more must we lose?"

Taron slams a hand on the desk. "Do you not think I grieve for their loss?"

"We all grieve," Thorn says dismissively. "But the time for grieving is past."

Syrah feels like an outsider, somehow allowed to watch the most devastating exchange of her life. She glances between the two of them in a standoff. Do her ears deceive her? Are they really deciding on the fate of the park here? Nothing she's seen so far suggests they have that kind of power. "What exactly are you proposing?"

The two of them turn to glare at her as if they've forgotten she is even there.

"I am proposing we right the wrongs that your tourists and politicians have exacted on this forest," Thorn says.

"And I am proposing we do the same, just in a different fashion than my overeager second here."

That Thorn, an outsider, is second-in-command, is interesting. Syrah can't imagine what he would have had to go through to prove himself. Maybe Taron doesn't see it, but she does. In order for Thorn to challenge her so openly, he has to be fairly certain in his position and support from others.

"I'm not going to argue with you," Syrah says, thinking about the job Dane proposed. She could help get the word out. Start there and build. "The man that I wanted to bring here has some good ideas, and I think he can help. We have to educate people. Really show them how they're impacting the Giants."

"Suzanne Simard," Thorn says. "Her book is in The Keeper's private collection. It has sold millions of copies, and what has changed?"

Syrah doesn't bother to hide the shock she knows is plastered like a neon sign on her face. The Rhiza, it seems, have more of a pulse on the world than she understands. "Replanting of trees. Climatologists working with the government to enact change. Solar, electric vehicles—"

"Oil spills, a space program that destroys the atmosphere more with every junk-littering flight. Whole swaths of countryside mowed down for homes that look just alike. Some of them bigger than our cave system, built for one or two people. Let us not speak of the Giants. They are the key to our survival, for us and the humans. But how many are left? Shall we just stand idly by while they choke them with smog or light fires in their hollows?" Thorn's voice has raised to a fevered pitch. "I say no! Topsiders are the problem. And we are the solution. It was why we were created. Why can you not see that what we have is a sacred duty to be fulfilled?"

The room goes church-pew silent after he finishes, the three of them each lost in their thoughts. Syrah fumbles through and discards a million arguments. For every advance with the climate, the country has taken three giant steps backward.

Taron finally speaks. "The Mother has not decreed it, and nowhere in our history has this happened before."

"Name me a time in our history when things have been this dire? Please," Thorn says. "Tell me of the alternative that you've been scribbling in those notebooks of yours. I must hear it."

"We cannot just wipe everyone out," Taron says.

"Wipe out—" Syrah says.

"Why not?" Thorn places his fists on the edge of the desk and leans in.

"Because there are people out there that I love, for one." Syrah is on her feet, inches away from him.

"Who? That park ranger?" Thorn says with a cruel laugh. "All you have is me. All you have is *us*."

Syrah shakes her head. "I can't even believe what I'm hearing. I can't allow it. I won't allow it."

Thorn's expression turns sinister. "What do you mean? You will not allow it?"

Syrah is every bit as cornered as she feels. Both Taron and Thorn scrutinize her with expressions that remind her that she is here only at their behest. She can't even find her way back to the surface on her own. She knows from what she's already witnessed that if they want to, they can snap her neck and use her body to fertilize the fungi. But she isn't prepared to back down.

"I misspoke. I'm not threatening anybody. I'm just saying, if we put our heads together, we can come up with alternatives. I'll join you. I'll work with Taron. Just give us some time."

"You will join us because you have nothing else," Thorn says. "We knew it the first day you appeared. The Mother, the lattice, decreed it."

Syrah's not ready to accept any of this. "I have my parents—"

Thorn talks over her. "If you are very, very lucky, you'll have us."

Chapter Thirty-One

Rhiza
September 2042

"I am certain your voices were heard aboveground," Ochai said as he fell in step alongside Romelo. Their fellow Rhiza cleared a path as they strode through the pathways. Furtive glances—some admiring, some wary—dogged their every step. The very air was charged. They, the Keepers of the Canopy, sat on the precipice of change.

And change was always difficult. Especially the necessary ones.

"The Keeper and the topsider unfortunately do not see my vision," Romelo said. "No matter, though. Taron is one of us, and the woman will be, even if she does not know it yet. When we move, they will fall in line. They will have no choice."

"You sound like a person who has glimpsed the future," Ochai said, "and sees himself victorious."

"It is not about me," Romelo said. He glanced over at Ochai and saw the skepticism written across his face. Even he only slightly believed that. "In almost every developed country on this earth, there is a limit to how long their leaders hold office. Yet ours retain their posts in virtual perpetuity. How does that lend itself to the flexibility, the kind of swift adaptation, we need to respond to a world that is shifting while we rest on old thinking? I am her son; that makes me second, her natural successor. Who else should lead the charge, you?"

Ochai shot him a look spiked with indignation. Ezanna had warned him that his close relationship with Ochai could prove troublesome for him when he had to lead. His companion had too often taken advantage of the fact that they had been childhood friends. He was too loose of tongue. If Romelo were to become Keeper, he would have to begin to distance himself from his friend. Leadership demanded it.

"You are reminding me of my place," Ochai said, nostrils flaring. "It is unnecessary."

Romelo could have backed down. He *wanted* to back down, but now was not the time to show favor or weakness. "If you prove yourself worthy, you may become my second-in-command after I am Keeper. Until then, you do best to remember that there are others who may prove themselves apt competition."

Abruptly Ochai pulled him into an alcove. "When will it be enough? You are no longer that young human boy who had to prove himself. Not to anyone else and unquestionably not with me."

Romelo hated him for bringing up their differences. He had worked hard to become one of them. He had seen the way Ochai trailed after the human. She had done nothing more than remind everyone of what he used to be. "We will begin with the animals," Romelo said, choosing not to respond. "We will need to work with our friends in Scourge Suppression. When they go out next to clean up after the topsiders, we will accompany them. A test is in order."

Despite his anger, Romelo could see the excitement building in Ochai. His face was positively aflame with it. "You, my friend, are a pompous, insufferable ground scum of a person . . . but you will make a fine Keeper. And despite what you say, you will have no one at your back but me. Tomorrow, we set this all in motion. I will prepare everyone."

With that, Ochai stormed off in the other direction. Romelo wondered briefly if he had been too harsh on his friend. He quickly dashed that line of thinking. He did not have time for such concerns. Besides, he knew that when it came down to it, Ochai would follow him without question. He was dedicated, had talent in his work in the Blaze Brigade, but he was too given to emotion. Such things did not make for a good leader.

But it was the newcomer, this Syrah, he would have to work on. He had to admit there was something about her manner that intrigued him. It was like gazing upon a version of himself in a mirror. But she had been raised human. People he did not know. Nor did he know the extent of her attachment to them. For they would have to die with the rest, and he needed that not to be a problem.

The lattice had told him she would be powerful. He could not see it. But he would make her an ally. Whether she would become his second, though, remained to be seen.

"I told you Taron would not understand," Ezanna said as a small group of canopy keepers navigated the caves. "She only hopes to maintain the status quo until she takes her last self-important breath and passes the staff and our problems on to the next in line. The Keeper is a relic."

"That is my mother you speak of so freely." Romelo stopped and put a hand in the center of his mentor's chest. "You do best to mind your tongue."

Footsteps halted. Chatter trickled to a weighty end.

In a deft movement, Ezanna swiped Romelo's hand away. Romelo's eyes narrowed, his chest puffed up. Slowly he tilted his head. The effect was instant.

"This is the moment that teachers hope for. Standing up to me, in front of everyone like this." Ezanna gestured behind them, beaming.

"Time wisely spent. You have made me proud. As for your mother, I disrespected her, and I meant every word, but I had no right to speak that opinion aloud."

An unusual apology, to be sure. Romelo accepted it, and the pair set off at a brisk pace again. Ochai and the others fell in line behind them. It was late, and the labyrinth of caves was mostly abandoned by those who were asleep, reading, or, from the grunts and moans coming from behind some of the doors, making love. "Disrespectful, yes," he said, glancing over at his mentor. "But true nonetheless."

"Want to tell us where we're going?" a member of the group asked. They carried makeshift pickaxes and shovels. Dressed in gear stolen from the Blaze Brigade. Thicker coverings that would protect their hands and bodies for the work ahead.

"Yes, I fear the son of The Keeper is lost," Ochai joked. Light chuckles followed.

"Just wait," Romelo said, turning and winking. He had slung his own shovel across his back in a makeshift carrying case. Ezanna carried only the heft of his habitual robes.

Not only did Romelo take his job as chief lattice rootspeaker seriously, but he read. A lot. Everything that Taron or Ezanna shoved beneath his nose. And in that vast library where many of the others in his crew barely spent any time, he had come across writings from several of the previous rootspeakers. Many of those texts were boring diagrams and talk of older, outdated schemes. But in one, he had surprised himself by finding the place he was leading everyone to now.

At the northeastern edge of their cave system, past the last exit from the veil, they came to what looked like a dead end. The path ended in a rounded mound of dirt. Smooth and solid.

Romelo turned to the group. "Here we are."

Finally, they had come upon the place he had already visited twice by himself, just to make sure those words hadn't been the babbling of some senile old Rhiza who had taken to writing fiction in his later years.

The group exchanged glances, then turned to Ochai. He often acted as spokesperson, most of them keeping a respectable distance from Romelo, not only because of his position but because of his mother.

"Brother," Ochai said. He went to the wall, ran a hand over the surface, even gave it a few raps with his knuckles. The lack of reverberation suggested the wall was solid, the end of the cave system. "I have always said that I will follow you wherever you go, but you have to give us something to go on here. What are you playing at?"

Romelo took down his shovel and started digging in the spot he'd tested and packed back before. It was an opening small enough for him to wiggle through, and he'd confirmed everything printed in those tomes.

When he had dug out the section and bent to pass his hand through, the others gasped. He met each of their eyes. "Have I led you wrong so far?"

Heads shook, looks of awe and shock. He handed his shovel to an underling but turned his gaze upon his best friend and said, "Now dig."

And they did, with Romelo and Ezanna watching and directing. All seven of his coconspirators pulled on their gloves and set to work tearing down the wall that had likely stood for a half century. Rhiza were strong and fast, and made quick work of it. What Romelo didn't know was whether the cave ceiling would collapse on top of them, so when they were almost done, he tapped Ochai on the shoulder and gestured for him to join him and Ezanna a few feet back from the digging. His friend raised a quizzical eyebrow, but when Romelo shook his head, he thankfully kept his questions to himself.

They stood back and watched. When the others had finished digging, the wall was down, and nothing but blackness greeted them on the other side. The smell of closed-up earth poured from the new opening. It was eerily quiet. They pulled off their gloves, wiped sweat from their brows, and stood gaping.

Romelo grinned.

"What is this place?" Ochai turned to him. "And how did you of all people know about it?"

Romelo narrowed his eyes. There it was again. The othering. Even his best friend had to remind him that he was not 100 percent one of them. Romelo cataloged the slight and, with a sharp look, decided to ignore it for now. He pulled a few containers of the lighted mushrooms out of his pack and passed them around.

"Come."

They used their hands and tools to tear down the cobwebs in their path. They started passing doors. Many off their hinges, others open and intact. They peeked into a few of the rooms. Everything was covered in thick layers of dust and cobwebs. About twenty rooms in all. If he gathered as many followers as he thought, they may have to double up, but it would work.

Though bugs and critters skittered underfoot, everything was in place just as it was on their side of the caves. Beds, desks, everything left as if one day they had just hastily decided to pack up and go and seal the way behind them. The book hadn't said why, only theorized the space's existence, and it had been right.

"Did Rhiza used to live here?"

"Indeed we did," Romelo said.

"Why did we not know about it?" someone asked.

"If you are looking for an upgrade on your quarters," Ochai said, "this is not it."

They had moved deeper into the new caves, Romelo consulting a piece of paper he'd torn from the book. He turned right at the marker, and a few steps later, there it was.

"Here's where we will start a revolution."

It was a long-abandoned lattice work. There were a couple dozen pods in total. He just hoped they were operational, and if not, he had the people with him that would make it so in short order.

"I cannot believe my eyes," Ezanna said. "This is it. If we have to make a stand, it will be from here."

"But is there another exit from the veil?" Ochai walked around the room, checking each of the pods.

"There is," Romelo confirmed. And they went to check it out. With that, he said, "Our task is to get this place cleaned up. To get the root-works operational. If my mother does not come to see reason, then we will do what we need to do from here. We will seal ourselves back in and set up operations from here."

"Brilliant," Ezanna said.

Romelo soaked in the looks of admiration and understanding from the surrounding faces.

"It will take some time," he said. "We will come after everyone else is asleep and return well before morning shift. We will lose some sleep, but we will gain it back once our mission is accomplished. If you are not with me, now is the time to say so."

When nobody balked, Romelo continued. "Now," he said, heading toward one of the pods, "let's see about getting this section of the lattice up and running."

Chapter Thirty-Two

Rhiza
September 2042

Syrah understands their anger. Hell, she shares it. How many times has she joked that people are the scourge of the earth? Wait . . . scourge. Isn't Scourge Suppression one of the Rhiza jobs? Her chuckle is wry; it makes perfect sense.

She hasn't run away. Not yet. She sits in what in the real world she would describe as a coffee shop. Cozy small-group seating, some niches carved right into rock face. Small bowls of those tasty fungi chips, their piquant aroma wafting around in the place of rich brew. Heads bent in conversation over books. Not a laptop in sight.

Syrah rubs the back of her neck. Part of her scoffs at Thorn's outlandish words. His rants likely the product of a compromised mind. Too long spent down here. The man is obviously detached from reality.

That tightness in her stomach, though, screams, *What if?* She is sitting there, trying to gauge how she'll begin to warn—who she'll warn. The final credits of her life play out. She envisions the pitying looks from her parents. Mama muttering about how she was so overcome by her mistake that her mind caved in on her. How it has all been too much for her, such a young woman, that she's finally succumbed to the weight of it all and gone stark raving mad.

She's thinking about that when she hears a ruckus building in the outer corridor. She and the others rush out. Just then, Artahe races past.

"What's going on?"

"You should remain here." Artahe is breathing hard, something Syrah hasn't witnessed before. Something's scared her friend, and that fact terrifies Syrah.

"I'm coming with you."

"Something terrible is about to happen."

They join the throng of other Rhiza running through the caves, parts that Syrah hasn't seen before. They are a blur of long legs and swift motion. Syrah keeps pace while they are in the flatter areas but more than a few times is almost flattened by unexpected curves and stalagmites.

But they are belowground, and the only way topside is up. The ascent is brutal. Syrah's lungs and legs are burning with the exertion. She can't begin to keep up as the others stream past her. She slows until she's running by herself, focusing on the back of the last person who passed her. At last, light ahead. This time they have exited through another Giant and come into a different area of the park, near a campground.

And what she sees drives her heart into her throat.

Bears. Two large, snarling black bears led by the cinnamon-colored loner that stalked her the other day. The creatures have cornered a group of campers, who are arrayed in front of picnic benches loaded with what looks like a feast. The park must have reopened.

For the life of her, she can't make sense of this scene. Bears are solitary. They don't work together or hunt together.

Were the Rhiza here to try to stop what could be the worst slaughter Sequoia has ever seen? Or . . .

A sudden wind blows, and with a flutter of leaves, sunlight slants through the breaks in the canopy. Romelo is there, wearing an expression halfway between determination and glee.

"Stop this, now, all of you," Taron hisses. Syrah can't see her, or any of the other Rhiza at first. But she follows her voice. Syrah scans the space between the trees with narrowed eyes.

The movement is slight, but it is enough. An outline, Taron, Artahe, then more appear. She can see them.

"What the hell is happening?" Syrah takes a tentative step forward. That puts her front and center. The bears swing their huge heads in her direction. She freezes.

Artahe is beside her then. "Thorn is making the first move."

When the light changes, Syrah loses sight of Thorn and his group. Around the hammering in her chest, she slows her breathing and closes her eyes.

When she opens them again, she picks him out in an instant. There are other Rhiza fanned out around him. Including . . . no, no! Ochai. Syrah wants to scream.

And there's something else. Like heat rippling off blacktop, she can just make out undulating waves of it, of something drifting off their bodies. The bears' raised, quivering snouts suggest that they're also picking it up.

"Oh my god," Syrah mutters. "Is it—is he . . . orchestrating? Is he controlling them? You have to stop this."

Not the ramblings of a madman after all. Thorn wasn't bluffing.

"Are you so ready to save them?" His voice soars above the cacophony as if on an eagle's wings. "Fouling the Giant's roots with their alcohol and piss? Barbarians that carve their meaningless initials into pristine, centuries-old bark for sport, as if they do not feel pain the same as them?"

"Who said that?" one of the campers yells in Syrah's direction, and for a second she's surprised that they can see her. Already her alliances are confused.

"Do. Not. Run," Syrah commands. "Just wave your hands, make yourself big."

Thorn's words fall heavily on Syrah and, in them, a connection. A reciprocal love for the forest. A shared fury at how Western society has worked to annihilate it. People have been irresponsible. Mistakes piled on top of bad policy. Even she fears the damage done may be irreversible. But—*but* what Romelo is proposing won't fix anything; it'll only serve as a silver-plattered invite to a seriously one-sided war.

She pulls away from Artahe's outstretched hand and goes to stand beside Taron, then to Thorn. "If you do this, they will respond. With a force you're not prepared for." A bear, a large female judging by Syrah's estimate, inches forward. "They won't stop until they find Rhiza and destroy it."

"That will never happen," Thorn says, turning his ire on her. "Unless, like you did with the ranger, you bring them to us."

Syrah knows that she won't.

The campers are yelling louder now, trying to scare the bears away. But the animals aren't budging.

Thorn has this effortless stillness to him that draws you in, and pulling away is one of the hardest things Syrah has ever done. That direct gaze of his ensnares her and glues her tongue to the roof of her mouth. His cool smile is an open door. "Then you are now a part of this, of us; there is no turning back."

With that pronouncement, he and his band unleash again, a groundswell of those feathery waves rolling off their bodies. The forest turns into a taciturn movie, with the trees as audience and the unwitting, innocent bears cast as villains. The cinnamon bear growls and charges. One of the men backpedals two steps before the animal is on him. He drops to the ground and curls into a ball. The bear pounces, ripping and tearing at his back. His screams pierce the silence that has descended like a blade through soft flesh.

"Counter," Taron booms just as the other camper, the woman, leaps to her companion's defense.

Another surge, this from Taron's group, writhes out of their bodies, pulled through the air as if by some invisible rope. Syrah's own body tingles and goes so weightless she wonders what tethers her to the ground. She holds up her arms and gasps to see the same waves radiating from her own body.

Like a mist, those diaphanous opposing forces collide and erupt in midair fireworks.

The other bears grunt and toss their heads, but miraculously, they don't go after the remaining camper, who has sprinted off through the trees. Whatever Taron is directing them to do is working. The cinnamon bear turns on the woman then. Syrah can see her legs buckle, but then her face becomes a mask of rage. She steadies herself, her fist shoots out, and she lands a stiff jab right on the animal's nose.

It stops.

Syrah breathes.

The bear is momentarily stunned. Then, in the instant that Syrah senses the shift, before she can cry out, it swipes a giant paw across the woman's chest. She goes down with a thud.

"Again," Taron commands.

The air is thick with the metallic scent of so much blood. Syrah shudders as yet more of that curious energy is drawn from her body and thrown into the clash.

The bears roar their confusion. Massive heads swinging from side to side. They don't know whether to attack or retreat.

Through gritted teeth, Syrah sputters, "You have done enough damage. Stop this!"

One bear has toppled over, passed out or dead from the strain. The others are frothing at the mouth.

Syrah takes in the stern set to Thorn's jaw and fears he will continue to press. Both sides keep up the battle of hormones. When another bear falls, he raises a hand, and they break off the attack.

The three of them—Syrah, Taron, and Thorn—hold their ground until sirens sound in the distance.

"Go," Syrah hisses. She will stay, try to explain away what has happened.

Taron and her faction and Thorn and his split, each heading in separate directions that will take them to the same place. Belowground, to the clandestine safety of the caves.

When the sound of footsteps and humans approach, Syrah stands alone, spinning a tale.

Syrah approaches on unsteady feet. She forces herself to look. To bear witness to what the canopy keepers, at least some of them, are capable of. She absorbs the torn and shredded remains of the two people who met their end in this attack. She had foolishly believed the canopy keepers were different from topsiders. That their lofty-sounding mission meant that they were a peaceful people, incapable of the violence she's witnessed with her own eyes.

Fooled again. In the end, they're no different from any of the earth's other creatures. When their survival is at risk, they will do whatever it takes to survive.

And she has a perverse, maybe displaced respect for that.

Her emotions are all over the place. She's worked in parks for her entire career. She's read about bear attacks, even come upon the remains of another person who died from a similar encounter. But she's never watched such a horrific thing unfold in front of her. And then there's what she now knows is a change in her own body. What can she say? She cannot deny how alive she felt, the thrill at what she was able to do. *How* is a question she doesn't dare ask.

The canopy keepers are a formidable species. She is already becoming part of them. She worries about what other wonders she isn't aware of lay in their arsenal.

She forces herself to look. The man lies face down, covered in blood and gore. The woman, a few feet away, lies with her chest ripped open and her eyes gazing skyward. Her hand reaching toward her slain partner. Syrah gulps down back the bile burning at the back of her throat.

How did this happen? In truth, she knows. You keep poking, keep pressing even the smallest of creatures, and eventually they'll fight back. The Rhiza are simply angry, frustrated at fighting a losing battle. And she can't argue. Looking around her, she knows that this park used to be filled with more Giants than anyone could count, but their numbers have been decimated.

Tears sting her eyes at both losses: for the people who lost their lives and for the Giants that will likely never be replaced. Did these people have family? Children? Who will tell them what happened here today? And when, not if, they find the bears, they will be another casualty in this ecological war.

The sirens are close. Footsteps follow. Syrah checks the area for other bears and steels herself.

The fire operations crew is the first on the scene. Though she should have expected it, she is still surprised to see Dane. Of course the park ranger would respond.

She walks purposefully toward them. "It was a bear attack," she says. That part came out easily enough because it's the truth.

Lance is there, nods at her grimly. She doesn't stop him as he attempts to administer first aid. She only looks on as he reaches out a hand to the woman's throat, checking for a pulse, but in finding none in the ragged remains of her neck, he moves instead to her bloodied but still intact wrist. The man has fared far worse, and all he can do for him is stand and shake his head. That gesture confirms what they all already know. These people are gone.

"Did you see it?" Dane says, coming up and wrapping an arm around her shoulder.

Syrah nods and allows the tears to fall; she doesn't care if the entire fire crew sees it either. "I did."

Lance stands and walks over to them as the paramedics arrive and go to place the bodies on gurneys. The unasked question hovering in the air between them.

Syrah recognizes one of the survivors, the man who ran when he had the chance. One of the fire crew has tried in vain to hold him back. The man is red-faced, angry tears streaming down his cheeks. "There were three of them . . ." His voice is choked with emotion. His bottom lip trembles, and someone comes to try to lead him away.

"But bears don't attack together," Dane says, uttering the obvious.

The man spins around, sputtering. "Don't tell me what they don't do. She was right there. She saw it all." The man dissolves again, and Syrah watches as the fire crew leads him away, their faces knit with shock.

How to explain this? She can't deny it. "It's true," Syrah confirms and decides to leave it at that.

"But how?" Lance says. "I mean, that's going against about a billion years of evolution right there." By now police have arrived and are beginning to try to tape off the scene. Dane strayed off to converse with them, and as they work, he kneels, examining the path. Studying the paw prints the size of a pizza dish.

With another word to the officer in charge, Dane comes back over. Syrah has trouble meeting his eyes.

"I don't see how, but I have to ask. Does this have anything to do with what you brought me out here to see earlier?"

The question catches Syrah off guard. "Of course not," she says. She zips her jacket and fumbles with the zipper to buy some time. "I—"

Lance saves her from having to come up with a lie that she's sure Dane will see through.

"We're gonna wrap up here." He sticks out his hand and shakes first with Dane, then Syrah. "Good seeing you, just wish it were under different circumstances."

After he leaves, Syrah turns to Dane. "We need to talk."

"We do," he agrees. "But I need to speak with the police. Stop by your place later?"

Syrah tells him that will be fine, though she isn't so sure she'll be there. She has to go back to Rhiza and see where this whole thing is going.

She needs to check in with Taron and see whether she or her son, Thorn, is now the Keeper of the Canopy.

Chapter Thirty-Three

Rhiza
September 2042

This time, when she walks into the hollow—the new entrance—the veil is once again lifted. As she barges into the city below the park, she can't help but think back to the time, so very recently, when she thought she'd stumbled upon a utopia.

Recent events and the tumult that greets her as she passes through the outer caverns remind her that every utopia—past, present, and in whatever future—has its troubles. Harried voices, the sounds of bare footfalls slapping against the earth. And it's almost as if the very walls are vibrating with an agitated hum.

She stops a group of young ones darting past. "Where is The Keeper?"

"In the great hall," they say and hurry off as if it should be perfectly clear where that is.

She follows the flow of Rhiza bodies, confident that eventually they'll lead her where she needs to be. There's something tiny and delicate that still lives inside her. A fearful wellspring of a thing born here in the park all those years ago. That insecurity has traveled with her like a pair of worn old socks that she can't part with.

As she rushes along with the others, they make no special note of her. No sidelong glances or snide comments. No surprise. Acceptance, even if temporary; the insecurity shudders and shrinks back in its wake.

Syrah spots the telltale archway marking Lattice Affairs. Instead of Thorn, she finds Ochai huddled with a few others. It is almost as if she can feel the conspiracy brewing in the air, and it makes her afraid for Taron.

A woman is standing so close to Ochai that their shoulders nearly touch. And the way she hangs on his every word—Syrah knows idol worship when she sees it. Didn't Taron say something about his many admirers? She grinds her teeth.

"Where is he?" Syrah says with such force that they stop and turn to regard her as if with new eyes. All except for Ochai's groupie. Their gazes speak their truths: anger-fueled determination and what she thinks is uncertainty.

With a flick of his head, the others file out. Ochai's fangirl sizes Syrah up and leans in close to her ear as she passes. "You will tell yourself you do not want him. But you do. It is written all over you. What you must accept is that you cannot have him."

Syrah's muscles go tight; her fists clench. This isn't the time, though.

"The Keeper has called for assembly," Ochai says, walking up and taking her hand. "We must go there now."

Syrah silences the flutter in her stomach and tries to focus. She pulls her hand away. "On what side of this do you fall?" A stupid question. She has seen exactly where he stands. "Hope" is another spiked, four-letter word.

She keeps her eyes on him, preferring to match his words to his expression. Words say one thing, but even Rhiza have cues that give away whether they are telling the truth. "I will be Thorn's second-in-command when he is raised to Keeper."

Well, that answers the question. At least he is honest. More than she can say for nearly every other man she's loved. No, wait. Not love.

"You really think the answer is to just wipe out everyone in California? As if the rest of the country won't take notice?"

"Except you." He actually chuckles. That bit turns her stomach. "Every species that has ever been has seen its time come and go."

Syrah crosses her arms. "And you believe ours, at least here, is over."

"Yours?" Ochai says. "You are already becoming more us than them. Do you not feel it?"

Truthfully, if Syrah thinks about it, she does, and she isn't entirely sure if she's comforted or horrified by the fact. The obvious question is how. Nobody has exactly asked her permission to go and transform her body. Is it something in the air? From the trees? And into what? These are questions for The Keeper. "I do" is all she says.

The flow of Rhiza's citizens has slowed to a trickle. She and Ochai fall in as he steers her around so many twists and turns that, in short order, she's once again lost her way. A sharp left at a particularly stunning shower of stalactites and the pathway slowly widens. A few minutes later, they come to an open expanse that takes her breath away.

A virescent sea of green rises and falls in gentle slopes, spongy and soft beneath her feet. Syrah devours that verdant landscape, is lulled by the untouched beauty of it. Those same mushrooms that light Rhiza's pathways coat the walls like glossy paint. The glow as soothing as a mother's kiss on a newborn's brow. Water trickles down from an overhead source she can't see, filling a crystal-clear body of water.

And presiding over all this sits a tree that defies description, annihilates reason. Perched on a raised patch of rich brown earth with innumerable thick branches sprawling in all directions. A nest of roots, gnarled and knobby like ancient knuckles at her base. Her canopy a crown of unmatched glory, shining in luminous animation. To call it a tree is to call the Nile River just some old backwater.

Even before the tree, the Giant, speaks to her, Syrah knows her for what she is.

The Mother Tree.

Chapter Thirty-Four

Rhiza
September 2042

More of them than she's ever seen sit, stand, sprawl on the mossy glade. And even though there are many, Syrah knows that they are still fewer than they were, than they should be. Taron is standing beside The Mother, staff in hand. Is it Syrah's imagination, or is she leaning on it more for support? The Keeper's entire visage is grave. It's almost as if the weight of what's happened has aged her a century.

From the back, it's still easy to mark Thorn's form, more like her own than theirs. His shoulders are set, his stance wide, but while Syrah's own hands are clamped fists, his fall easily at his side.

"Everyone who is coming is here," Thorn booms, and defiance, not contrition, edges his words. "Even her."

Before every eye in the place swivels to take in Syrah, she knows of whom he speaks.

Taron taps her staff twice in quick succession. "Recite the Keeper Grail."

At once, those who aren't already standing come to their feet.

You cannot willingly harm another member of the society.

Syrah feels buffeted on all sides by their voices, raised in unison.

You cannot through action or inaction harm a tree.

Their conviction is a pledge.

You cannot divulge the location of the community to outsiders.

The last syllable bounces off the cavern walls, rebounds as if from a sling, and dies.

Taron taps the staff once, and everyone resumes their places. "Thorn Rootspeaker, you have been brought here on charges that you broke rule one of the Grail. Through your attack on the humans, you risked not only the people you convinced to go along with you, but you could have brought unwanted attention to our home. How do you respond?"

Syrah marvels at how evenly Taron accuses her own son. She wants no part of that kind of responsibility.

Thorn turns to face the assembly. "Ochai, Basteen, Lyndal, Zehra, Parom, would you come forward, please?"

Ochai takes a step forward, stops, and then turns to Syrah. All eyes are on them as he bends down. When his lips brush hers, it is fertile grasses and wildflowers. Sun and dark and smoke.

He pulls away then and doesn't look back as he and the others traverse the path to the front of the cavern. Zehra, the one who tried to warn her off Ochai, levels her with a look that promises retribution.

They go to stand off to the side, so that she can still see their faces. Syrah feels naked and exposed, but soon Artahe is there. She clasps her fingers and squeezes.

Instead of ten commandments, Rhiza has three. Then it hits Syrah: What's the penalty for breaking one? What will happen if Thorn is found guilty of the charges against him?

He turns to face the assembly and gestures with an arm sweep toward the group now assembled beside him. "Do they appear harmed to anyone present?"

Murmurs flow in waves, reverberating off the walls and bouncing back. Nobody speaks up, though. He spares Taron a smug glance before he speaks again, tossing the words over his shoulder like scraps for a compost heap. "No Rhiza citizen has suffered so much as a paper cut." He makes a show of going down the line, raising an arm, poking or prodding at a chest or stomach, inspecting fingers. "No injury to report here. But of them"—a chin thrust upward—"two of them are gone, yes. But it is the topsiders that trespass here. This is the bear's habitat, not a place for them to dump their trash and snap pictures. To defile the most majestic beings on this planet."

Syrah scans the crowd. He's racked up a few affirming nods. Others stand with arms folded in clear rebuke. By her estimation, they're split right down the middle. Suddenly he locks eyes with her, and Syrah reads the unasked question: Is she with him or not?

"Westerners have been trying to domesticate the bears like lapdogs. Pushing them farther and farther away from what they are and where they should roam. What those animals did was only what their nature demanded. Reducing the human number is no loss to Rhiza." He fixates on Syrah then: "Present company excluded." With a wink, he turns back to face Taron.

"What say you all? Anyone wish to speak for or against the charges?" The Keeper asks.

Everyone goes photograph still.

"Come now," Taron says. "Loosen your tongues. Speak as freely in the open as you do in your cliques."

"To serve the Giants." Someone's deep bass draws first blood. "That is our mission. Nowhere in our recorded history does it mention murder."

"That's not who we are!"

"They speak the truth—"

"To save the Giants will require bold action," comes another voice of dissent. "We tend to the lattice, keep their roots healthy. We patch the wounds brought on by the storms. But these topsiders are nothing like the natives. They know nothing of balance. They are a scourge and must be eliminated if any of us are to survive."

And then Syrah loses track. It seems that everyone is speaking at once, shouting. Three sharp taps of Taron's staff and order is restored.

"He took action," Ochai says from the front of the room. His head is lowered, but he finds Syrah before he continues. "I have been on the Blaze Brigade since I was but a young one, and I can tell you, the fires burn hotter and longer than they ever have. We can't contain them anymore. Seventy percent of the forest is gone. The number of Giants . . ." A few quick shakes of his head. "If we do not act, they'll be gone on this Keeper's watch. I think Thorn should be commended."

"Truth!" someone yells, and others pick up the chorus.

When it dies down, Ochai continues: "You speak of bringing unwanted attention to our home. This is impossible. We have been here since The Mother was born, undetected. Fear cannot paralyze us. Something must be done."

More voices of support ring out before Syrah finds herself moving, walking toward the front of the room. "Everything that you say is true." All heads and eyes trail her. "We have screwed things up. Massively. All we want is advancement, cost or repercussions be damned. We only pay lip service to these grand laws the politicians cook up in the interest of environmental protection, and then take payoffs so that big business can dance all around them. I lost my entire family to a fire. That's why I chose to become a firefighter. And that's the reason I'm here now. It's because The Mother wanted it."

Thorn fixes her with a curious look. A smile curves at the corner of his mouth. But Syrah isn't finished.

"I'm not saying I have the answers. I don't. But we have to find a way to communicate. To make the cost clear. And I can be of both worlds. I can help us do that."

This time, angry voices ring out.

"Who is she to speak here!" one says.

"Outsider," comes another.

"Outsider or not, she speaks wise words." This from her friend, Artahe.

"I do hate to raise this," Ochai's admirer, Zehra, interjects. "But The Keeper herself broke the Grail. She is the one who let this human into our midst."

Whoa, Syrah thinks. *Are they going to turn this against Taron?*

Thorn faces the crowd. He stares at Syrah and says, "Do you care to tell them why, Mother?"

Mother? At first Syrah wonders if he addresses her so informally as a plea of support. But Taron shoots a sidelong glance at the back of his head that says otherwise. Syrah's mind is buzzing with dread. There's a story coming, and she knows without a shadow of a doubt that it will be something she doesn't want to hear.

"And while you are at it, you can tell her." He goes with the wide-armed gesture again. An orator if she's ever seen one. And he's enjoying this little reveal. "Tell us all why she's here."

Run! the voice of reason in Syrah's head commands. *Leave now while you still can.* But her limbs are as heavy as columns of concrete.

"Tell her if you wish," Taron says between clenched teeth. "It will change nothing. This inquiry will proceed."

"Glad you agree," Thorn croons. "You see . . ." This he directs to Syrah. Looks at and through her. She feels like he can see her heart slamming against her breastbone. "Judging by the right leg that you still favor, I'm judging it was your knee. Whatever the injury, you bled into the earth. The lattice, the Giants, The Mother, saw you. That is what raised the veil, not The Keeper. It is because the markers match. You see, my topside name was Romelo Williams, and you, Syrah Williams Carthan, are my sister."

Cries of surprise erupt from everyone except Taron and Syrah and Ochai. She can't speak. If not for Artahe, she would collapse. When she regains her footing, she shrinks back, as if distance can separate her from the truth she is already accepting.

Petite Pearl Harbors explode, separating the folds of her mind.

When the barrage ends, an image coalesces from beneath the layers of ash. A big brother, one with a heart-shaped scar above his left eye. Earned by a fall from a tree. Syrah had accidentally pushed him.

Her protector.

Oakly.

Man. Monster. Zealot. The brother she thought long dead. And maybe her running off and leaving him created him.

Taron beats her staff against the earth so hard Syrah fears she'll snap the thing in two. Eventually, things quiet again.

"Those who agree that Romelo Rootspeaker has broken the Grail, count off."

It takes forever, but Syrah listens as the numbers edge upward. In the end, the last voice says, "Two hundred and forty." The same thing is repeated for those who disagree. Two hundred and thirty-five.

"Four hundred and seventy-five total votes, with eighteen abstaining," Taron recounts. "Recite the Keeper Code."

Everyone says the words: *If one shall fail, we raise the veil.*

"Romelo has been found at fault. As judgment, his coconspirator, Ochai Blaze, will be melded for a period of no less than five suns."

"Wait!" That snaps Syrah right back to the present. "Why—"

"Shh." Artahe squeezes her arm. "You must not interfere."

Ochai stiffens. But a nod, too quick and contrite, tells her he's accepted the punishment and, for reasons she doesn't understand, is ready to take the blame for what her . . . her brother has done. He finds Syrah, and she nearly crumbles at the expression on his face. He's afraid. For a moment Syrah thinks he'll fight, challenge the decision, but he doesn't. Instead, he holds his head high and steps forward, closer to Taron and The Mother.

Those gathered lower their heads, trepidation slumping the set of their shoulders.

Syrah turns to Artahe. Just as she's about to speak, Artahe holds up a hand and shakes her head. Syrah's heart races. What does this mean? What will happen? She'll stop them.

"What did it mean to raise the veil?" She ignores Artahe's censuring glare and asks anyway. "What's going to happen?"

No answer, not any indication that she's even heard her. Syrah grabs Artahe's arm. "I need to know what they're going to do."

Artahe's nostrils flare. "You are here only because Taron allows it, but you are in a very tenuous position. I know you desire him, but if you try to disrupt these proceedings, you will be removed forcibly. Now let my arm go before I break every single one of your fingers."

Doubt isn't what Syrah's thinking, not even for a moment. She releases her friend. She wishes she could leave and forget she ever stumbled into this world. Aside from her parents, there is little awaiting her topside. In a tormented moment that lasts for a million Rhiza years, Syrah makes the decision.

She pushes her way forward through the crowd. When she is near to the front, Romelo holds out an arm. "You are but an observer here."

He leans close to her ear. "Wipe that puppy dog look off your face and stand down. You cannot stop what is going to happen. If you try, you will suffer Ochai's fate or worse. And who, then, will be around to become my second-in-command?"

Syrah grits her teeth. How can he be so callous about someone he calls his best friend? But then a look around confirms it. It's like any court of law. The judgment has been made, and they're all ready and willing to accept it.

"It should be you up there," she says to her brother. "And not him."

A retort appears poised to roll off his tongue like a snake's bite, but Taron's voice interrupts him. "For the crime of dissension, Ochai Blaze has been sentenced to penance. Have you any last words?"

Ochai scans the crowd, offering a few reassuring nods and smiles. Finally, his gaze settles on Syrah. The moment drags on long enough for Taron to nudge him. He mouths, "Wait for me."

Syrah's knees almost buckle, and a small whimper escapes her throat. Murmurs arise.

Taron motions Ochai closer to the tree, and she touches the staff to a root near her feet. Ochai stiffens and closes his eyes, but he's trembling. The root moans and stretches, as if awakening from a centuries-long sleep. The sound hurts Syrah's ears, but nobody else seems bothered. The root lifts from the ground and reaches out toward Ochai.

Stretches until the tip curls around his ankles and binds him in place. As the tendril winds its way around his form, Syrah is horrified and transfixed as Ochai turns to wood. It travels all the way up around his neck and then lifts him into the air, his body now nothing more than a root, a branch. And then he melds into the trunk.

As far as Syrah can see, all the way up to the canopy, faces appear. Each watching, eyes wide open as another is added to their midst. Each face looks grief stricken. Some appear to weep; others look forlorn. Some angry. Then their mouths open, and a wailing so great escapes that Syrah covers her ears.

"Please," the voices cry. "Release me. Let me go."

And the appeals continue. Syrah steps forward and feels Romelo's hand, softer than Taron's, latch on to her. She struggles but he holds her in place. Even as she begins to sob.

Ochai's body, his face, is smashed between two others. When the process is done, the root retreats back into the ground. Ochai's face is alive in the tree, his gaze fixed somewhere off in a place Syrah realizes is different from where they stand. How long have some of these people been committed to this fate? And what did they do to earn such a sentence?

When Taron removes the staff from the ground, the faces fade from view, and the cries, all aside from Syrah's, cease.

The Rhiza file silently out of the space. Taron passes Syrah without a word, and soon Romelo is gone too. She's left to gape at the tree, once again so majestic and beautiful. This is the world she's thinking about committing herself to. Ochai will be here until five suns, however long that is, pass. Unless Syrah finds a way to free him, to free them all, first.

Chapter Thirty-Five

Rhiza
September 2042

The truth is like a full-bodied blow that robs Syrah of her equilibrium. She stumbles and flounders her way through the warren of Rhiza caves and lurches back into the world, blinded by an accusatory sun. She runs her hands up and down her arms, trying to revive her numb limbs.

Her brother is alive. And he is a monster. The ache she's carried, that well of emptiness created by the loss of her birth family, has only redoubled.

Pine needles glisten in the light. The parallel harmonies of birds and insect chirps, deceptively calming. The country has no idea of what lives below. The anger it has roused and the exacting price it may have to pay.

Instinctively, she looks around for the cinnamon bear and his friends, the grisly scene she witnessed earlier still tattooed on her consciousness. The blood spilling into the ground. Trails of gore. Horrified expressions frozen onto the faces of the victims. And she'd watched the whole thing happen, unable to stop it. Worse, she can't tell anyone; not even those poor people's families will understand that what happened had been instigated.

Being belowground, both Syrah and her digital watch have lost track of time. One day? Three? Each has been one absurdity after another. A Giant, larger than any of the others in the world, that consumes its people when they break a rule.

Romelo, Thorn, her brother. He had stood there in a stupid calm while Ochai was condemned for his crime. Not one of the others, not even Taron, raised a voice in protest. The Rhiza unilaterally condemn humans, but their society isn't any better. Cruelty, hierarchy, crime and punishment. It is all the same. And if she leaves her world and becomes a part of theirs, she will be subject to their rules. Their inflexibility. And what if she mistakenly gets on the wrong side of things? Three commandments as set forth by some ancient tree human she doesn't even know. Will she one day find herself held in tree hell for some perceived offense? No, she has to rethink this whole thing.

She makes her way back to her car, then home in a thick mental fog.

She doesn't know what time it is, but exhaustion is blurring the edges of her vision when at last she closes the door behind her and sinks to the floor. Her bed calls. She's bone tired, but she can't rest until she has what will be the most difficult conversation of her life.

First, she'll need to ask them about her brother. And her name. Romelo called her Syrah Williams.

Wresting the truth from her parents will take time. They'll dig in. Deny. There may even be tears. For so long they've resisted her attempts to learn anything about the time before she came to them. And they probably mean well. She prepares herself to withstand it all to find out who she really is. She wants to hear from them, not that pompous Romelo.

And then she'll go back to Rhiza. Free Ochai and stop her brother. She'll talk some sense into him. Time slows belowground, but Syrah is still shocked when she checks the relic ticking away on the wall above her refrigerator. Six in the evening. Only a few hours have passed.

She picks up her phone. "Call Dad—"

Before she can finish speaking the command, her phone rings. "Syrah, we've been trying to reach you," Uncle Dane says. "I've got some bad news. It's about your father."

The exhaustion Syrah feels gives way to a shot of adrenaline that draws her up to her feet. She has her hand on the doorknob, ready to hop back in her car and drive all the way to Los Angeles without stopping. But can she really leave after what just happened?

"You there?" Dane says. "I know I should have come over, but—"

"What happened?" Syrah rolls over him. "What's wrong with Dad?"

"It's a stroke. A bad one."

Syrah holds back the sob by a tatty thread. Her father smoked cannabis for most of her childhood. It's the only thing that helped with his insomnia. She wonders if the smoke has finally clogged his lungs or if the lack of sleep has taken its toll. She begged him to stop, but the alternative was pharmaceuticals he wanted no part of—and, in truth, neither did she. "Is he going to be okay?" Syrah can't say the words she really wants.

The pause is a wingbeat too long. "They can't say."

"What hospital?"

"Good Samaritan," her uncle says. "Look, with the craziness about the bear attack, it's not a good time to leave, but I'm on my way over. We'll drive down together."

It's Syrah's turn to hesitate. The choice is an impossible one. She's starting to hate that word. Go and sit by her father's side and let the state go up in flames or stay and try to fight what she already feels may be a losing battle. "I can't go," she says. "Not yet. Look, I'll call Mama and then get back to you. Hold tight." She can sense, if not see, the confusion.

"What do you mean? I didn't just say your father lost one of his prized roses—"

"Look, I'm going. Of course I am. I just have to do something first." Syrah has never heard anger in her uncle's voice before, and it startles her.

"What could be more important—"

"I'll have my phone with me and I'll check in."

Syrah hangs up and paces for a few agonizing moments before she makes the call. And when her mother comes on the line, the well within her nearly breaks. Anissa Carthan never holds back on her emotions. She is as open as a children's book at bedtime. So, when she answers the phone, her voice as calm as the creek out back, Syrah's resolve just about melts.

"Where have you been?" she asks. "I called you half a dozen times."

"When?" Syrah asks. "How did it happen?"

"It was right after dinner," Mama says. "I was washing. He was drying, and he dropped a glass. When he fell, he hit his head on the edge of the kitchen counter. To see him seize up that way." Her mother's voice breaks then. "Are you already on your way?"

All the questions Syrah has no longer matter. They are her parents, the only ones she's ever known. And she wants more than anything to be at her dad's side when—and she does mean when—he wakes up. But how can she tell her mother that she can't do any of that? That the very balance of everything depends on her? "Not yet," she says. "I've got to get a few things in order here first."

"What things?" Her mother's voice hikes up two octaves. "You don't even have a job."

"I can't explain." Syrah fumbles around, but a suitable excuse is as hard to grasp as advanced calculus. "But . . ."

"I know, tomorrow or the next day. Look, you can't do shit about yesterday, and tomorrow is a fool's pipe dream."

"I love my father more than anything in this world." Syrah regrets the words as soon as she says them. Her mother will perceive the slight against her and use it as a segue to arguments years from now.

Though her mother pauses, her response lacks the bite Syrah braces for. "Look, baby, I know you're scared, but running isn't going to change anything."

"It's not that . . ." Syrah is about to speak the truth but then thinks it best to go along with the story her mother has constructed for her. "I *am* scared. And I just don't trust myself to drive yet. There was an incident at the park today, so Dane is tied up, but we'll be on our way soon." That's the best she can do, and she hopes that she can resolve the situation in Rhiza quickly. "Can you put the phone to his ear?"

But somehow, even as she tells Dad that she loves him and that she will be there soon, she knows the words, like everything else she is discovering about her life, are a lie.

Chapter Thirty-Six

Three Rivers, California
September 2042

When a war begins, history is quick to tell us who made the first strike. Syrah recalls the line from one of her father's favorite old movies: *They drew first blood, not me*. Yet having seen the beginnings of this war, she isn't certain that it's always so clear. Whoever writes this history may say that the Rhiza struck first through means she can't fully fathom, coaxing bears into attacking people. That won't tell the whole story, though. What had people done with the planet? Poisoned the air, the water. Hell, half the food at the grocery store is questionable. Deforested and overdeveloped, wiping out entire species of flora and fauna.

If that isn't first blood, she doesn't know what is.

Sleep eludes her. Too worried about her dad. Unsure of what she will find when she returns to Rhiza, and there's no doubt that she has to. After some coaxing she gets her mother to keep her phone trained on her dad. Mama naps on the makeshift cot in the room while Syrah barely blinks, watching him, listening to those taunting beeps of the machines tracking his vital signs. The first roots of guilt sprout from her heart and reach, reach until they choke every part of her being.

After hearing Romelo's pronouncement, her thoughts were of the cruel, angry, how-dare-you-lie-to-me variety. But she felt the truth of it in her core. The way Taron looked anywhere but at her silenced that finger-flick moment of doubt. So instead of barreling down the interstate to be by her father's side, she will be heading back to Rhiza to deal with a brother she no longer wants.

Her dad. The man who patched her skinned knee countless times. The man who watched videos to learn how to braid her hair when Mama went on her "me time" vacations. The man who cheered her on during her brief attempt at basketball. She can only pray that he holds on until she gets there.

"You didn't sleep at all, did you?" Mama says. Gone is her half smile, the one she's always reserved for service workers and her adoptive daughter. That lush brown coloring drained from her face, leaving something ashen and sad in its wake. Her eyes red and empty. It's like her life is ebbing away with every moment that her husband lies there, possibly dying.

"I slept a bit," Syrah mutters, and when Mama purses her lips, she amends: "I can tell you that the nurse came in what seemed like every hour on the hour. That Dad's eyes fluttered at two minutes after two. That his right finger twitched a half hour later."

"Figures," Mama says. "You always had eyes only for him. You never wanted a mother, but I loved you anyway."

There it is again. The gangplank laid down. All Syrah has to do is take the first step and keep walking until she falls off the deep end into the concentric circles of arguments that have defined a healthy chunk of her relationship with her mother. Not this time. When she doesn't respond, her mother says, "Look, the doctor will be around this morning. I'll call you back when I know something."

"Mama," Syrah says before she can hang up. Selfishly, she wants to ask all those questions. Did they search for her brother? Did they know he lived? The need for answers is so strong she's almost willing to set aside the fact that her mother has more than enough on her plate at the moment. Almost. "I couldn't have asked for better parents."

For just a moment her mother's face brightens. Then she blows her a kiss and ends the call.

Syrah is up and in the kitchen. She puts the teakettle on and pulls out her mug and a peppermint tea bag. Food is the last thing on her mind, but she has to eat something. Energy and time to think, that's what she needs now.

After a breakfast of eggs, toast, and the last three slices of veggie bacon, she pulls on a jacket, then opens the sliding door to her back porch and steps outside with her mug. The morning is unseasonably warm. The river flows by, a little choppier than usual, as if it, too, knows trouble is coming. The leaves on the two oaks in the backyard rustle in the wind. She looks at them anew. Are they part of that lattice in the park? Even if they aren't, they have a right to exist without interference. When she first arrived in Three Rivers, the town was in an uproar, divided down the middle. One of the oldest trees was being cut down because the roots had broken through the sidewalk. Was that the trees' fault or the city planners', whose idea of creating a walkable city was to pave over everything in sight?

Goddamn it, he's right. Syrah sits down and cups her palms around the mug, drawing the warmth into her hands. No way to deny it. That's not the angle to take. But wholesale slaughter in the other direction. Not even up for discussion. Even if she has no alternative yet, she will stop him. She hears the new baby three doors down crying and knows that she must. For that life that is just beginning, for the others, and for her parents.

Dad is going to be all right. Syrah plays back Uncle Dane's words. *He has to be.* Her father is still a relatively young man, in his late fifties. He and Mama will get that RV and make the trip up the coast like they've planned for the summer. He has to survive because she loves and needs him. And because at some point he will have to answer her questions.

The sooner she deals with the trouble in Rhiza, the sooner she can get to her father. Back inside, Syrah cleans up the kitchen, then heads toward her bedroom. Her bed is still made up, and though the pull to lie down is strong, she strips off the clothes she still has on from the previous day and walks across the hall to the shower.

Her small tankless water heater produces enough hot water for a long shower, but she usually keeps it to less than ten minutes, in the interest of conservation. This morning, she stands with her head under the shower spray for double her normal time. Finally, she lathers her scrubbing cloth with castile soap and washes with care. Careful over the spot on her knee that has scabbed over, she rinses, and as her hand glides over her skin, it feels rough in spots. She opens her eyes and glances down.

Tiny mushrooms are sprouting all over her arms and legs.

Syrah screeches, slips, and tumbles out of the shower. She reaches for the towel bar, misses, and grabs the shower curtain instead. She yanks the whole bar from the wall and falls in a heap, twisted up in the curtain. Water splashes everywhere. She can almost feel the bruises blossoming on her body. One leg is still hung over the edge of the tub. She sits up and chances another look at her arms.

The skin is smooth again, but if her mind isn't playing tricks on her, traces of fungi remain.

Is this a psychedelic reaction to what the Rhiza have almost been force-feeding her?

She gets to her feet and winces. Her elbow has taken a shot against the wall. Her back aches, and the scab is ripped off her knee again. She looks at herself in the mirror. Outwardly, nothing else seems different, but there's no denying it. Ochai was right: she *is* changing.

She can't see but feels the improvement in her lungs. In her fire training, they had to test how long they could hold their breath. Her longest had been three minutes. She inhales, long and deep, deeper than she ever has before. She holds it to that mark and for a full minute extra.

Her new body is a truth taking root.

The Mother. That tree has done something to start all this. For its own purposes and without her permission. And what have they given her when she ate? Mushrooms. Who knows what they mixed in. Syrah is so angry she picks up the broken shower bar and hurls it back into the tub.

It seems Taron will have some questions to answer as well.

She reaches beneath the sink for her moisturizer. Then drops it once, twice. Her hands are trembling. She sits on the edge of the tub, folds her arms against her stomach. Syrah rocks back and forth, struggling to make sense of everything that's happened.

In those moments, reality makes its presence felt. She's no less afraid, but determination fuels action.

This time, when she reaches for the moisturizer, her fingers find purchase. She slathers on her coconut-and-argan-oil mixture, head to toe. Loose chinos, button-up plaid shirt, thick, padded socks.

Back in the kitchen, she eschews the energy bars and tosses some fresh granola into a plastic bag. Plastic. She fumbles around in the cabinets and goes for an old paper bag instead. She likes to think of herself as environmentally conscious. But in a few short visits, the Rhiza have her questioning not only her identity but everything else.

She thinks back to how people were so dense as to accept paying for tap water packaged in plastic bottles and slapped with a label that claimed mountain spring origins. Luckily, those were banned in 2030. She reaches for her metal water bottle and fills it from the filtered container in the refrigerator. And the fact that the filter itself is plastic isn't lost on her. The battle against the pollutant is still underway.

Instinctively Syrah goes back to her bedroom. She gets out an extra set of clothes, rolls them up military-style, and shoves them into her backpack.

She's at the front door, pulling on her hiking boots, when she pauses to look around. An odd sort of prescience fills her. *I'll be back,* she tells herself.

When she closes the door and starts up the car and backs out of the carport, she holds that thought in her mind every time she glances back.

Chapter Thirty-Seven

Rhiza
September 2042

This time her feet know the way without her interference. Syrah passes through the veil and pauses. Listening, waiting. Hours have passed aboveground, but time moves slower here, much slower. She doubts a whole war will have erupted in that time. But she hopes that Romelo and his backers have been silenced. Only one way to find out.

The trek through the forest and the descent into Rhiza feel different. Instead of sucking in air like a triathlete who's just crossed the finish line, she finds a barely tapped well of energy adds a spring to her step. The fungi are in her body, changing it. The part of her that is still a topsider finds the thought abhorrent. The former botany student in her wants to examine samples of her own skin beneath a microscope.

They did this to her without asking.

Yet as angry as she is at the deception, she has to admit she feels stronger than she ever has.

The caves are absent the normal buzz of activity and chatter. People, and she has begun to see them as just people, plod along the paths and corridors in a blank-eyed stupor. Though Syrah would like to think that regret about those two people mauled to death is what has everyone's shoulders dropping, the likelier scenario is that Ochai's imprisonment is what's weighing most heavily on their spirits.

Before Syrah confronts Taron, she needs to talk to her brother. She still has trouble thinking of someone who could do something so cruel as part of her family, but she doesn't doubt him. She knows the way to Lattice Affairs now, and moments later she's there. Romelo and a group of others, some she's seen with Ochai, are huddled in low conversation. When she walks in, the others whisper greetings and move away.

"Walk with me," Romelo says and then turns to the others. "When the shift begins, you know what to do."

Syrah wonders at that cryptic message but keeps her thoughts to herself.

"What do you make of us?" Romelo says, looking over at her. They stand nearly shoulder to shoulder in height. Her mirror, her twin. His eyes are sad. His friend has just been consumed by a gigantic tree, after all. Syrah's surprised how relieved she is that he cares. "After all that you have witnessed?"

There's a tender space between them. Like a sore tooth, they are loath to touch it. Syrah thinks about his question and shrugs. "You're nothing like us and everything like us."

Romelo raises an eyebrow. "This I must hear."

The two of them draw attention. Wide, round eyes follow them, watching with open curiosity. Syrah guesses they wonder whether she's plotting with him or against him. Alone, Syrah is a nascent but accepted oddity. Together, she and her brother are what? Coconspirators? A portent to change? More likely, doom. If Romelo notices or cares, he doesn't say. "I'll play along," Syrah says. "We're both bipeds. Physically, my guess is we're more or less walking around with the same internal organs. There are a few physiological differences—"

"Superiorities."

"Enhancements," Syrah concedes. "But they're almost human."

Romelo huffs. "I will allow it. What else?"

What happened to push him to this kind of next-level asshole? Syrah wonders. "You have rules. Laws." She pauses, then adds, "Punishments."

"So far you speak the truth."

"Where you differ from topsiders is in the singularity of your mission. Now, there are people like you aboveground. Climatologists, environmentalists, park rangers. People who've dedicated their lives to making this planet a better place."

"Like you," Romelo says, fixing her with a mischievous grin.

Syrah nods. "Like me. But for every one of the people like me, there are thousands more with different missions, some competing, some not."

"You think we down here know little of the world. Is that not what you believe?"

Well, how could you? Syrah thinks to herself. "It's just that you see very little of it."

Romelo scoffs. "I have ventured into your city. I probably know more about computers than you. You may have your mobile phone, but through the lattice, I am connected to every tree in this state. I am extending the linkage to trees on the other side of the country."

"And you want to use them to release whatever it is that comes from our bodies," Syrah finishes the thought. And then she understands his plan. She stops him and pulls him into an alcove. "Turn the animals against us."

"The earth is but a living thing, and the Giants, Rhiza, are her heart, and the trees are her lungs," Romelo says.

Syrah allows herself to contemplate those words, and they resonate. She knows why Artahe likes him. Why the others are drawn to him.

"When I first saw you, I didn't recognize you. But The Mother did. You have a mind just like mine. Which is why you must see what I say is necessary and true. And why you must join me."

Syrah thinks about her father, fighting for his life in a Compton hospital, and trembles with rage. He means to end them all. "What don't you get about the fact that even if you could do what you say, and I'm not convinced that you can, they'll stop it? The one thing topsiders do better than any creature on earth is fight."

"What happened to you with that burn was not your fault," Romelo says.

Syrah opens and closes her mouth.

"Just because the trees do not have words does not mean that they do not speak. Do not see," Romelo explains. "They have memories longer than time."

They have been watching her. How long? She won't discuss this with him. She hasn't discussed it with anyone. "Say that I agree with you," Syrah says, redirecting the conversation. "What then?"

Romelo gestures for her to join him in one of the seating areas tucked into a corner. A pitcher of water and cups are already there. He pours for them both.

"You saw what we are able to do with the bears. Do you know how?"

Syrah has given this some thought. "Pheromones."

"Too fancy." Romelo shakes his head. He pushes a cup toward Syrah. She wonders if it's somehow laced with another fungal additive. "More like a scent. We call it the flow. It can be used to control them."

Syrah is dumbfounded at the matter-of-fact way he describes unleashing bears to tear people apart, but the only way to stop him is to understand how. "What else?"

"Years ago, your scientists said that the chlorine monoxide was decreasing. But that changed, did it not?"

Syrah sighs. "The original estimates had to be revised."

"Revised," Romelo scoffs. "And about how long would it take for the ozone to repair itself? Even if the humans stopped today and caused no further damage?"

The estimates have become only more dire every year of her life and ever since Syrah began tracking that very thing, about a half dozen years ago. She hesitates answering because that might just add more fuel to his fire. But she suspects he knows already. "This could change. You're making assumptions."

"And you're stalling."

Syrah runs her hands over her face. "One hundred, one hundred and fifty years."

"Without further damage," Romelo emphasizes. "Which we both know is a children's fairy tale."

Syrah knits the final pieces of Romelo's plan together. "The air," she says.

"Yes, the air," Romelo agrees. "When the humans are gone from this state, it will take time, but the trees can clean the air."

The image of her parents. The children on her street. The elderly couple who run the diner on Main Street. He wants to consign them all to death.

"Is that it?" she asks.

"Is that not enough?" Romelo drains his cup of water and stands. "If you can look me in the eye, without that twitch you get on the side of your mouth when you are being untruthful, and tell me that you are confident the humans will recognize the error of their ways, that they will stop spreading, stop killing each other, stop destroying everything they touch, then I will stand down this very minute."

Her brother is mad.

And so is she.

Syrah can't say any of those things with confidence. By all accounts, Romelo is right. Didn't she stop watching or reading the news because she hated all the negativity? How often has she left work at parks across the country in a fit of rage because of what she's seen people do? Even neighborhood parks. Is there any sign at all that what little remains of the Amazon rainforest won't be decimated by the end of the century?

God help her, she agrees with him.

The Rhiza think themselves above everyone else. Romelo grew up here, was nurtured on that steady diet of nobility, yet instead of it turning him into a gentle soul at one with nature, he's turned positively feral. While she, the one raised in the very climate that he despises, turned out to be more interested in protecting humans. Odd how he's forgotten that no matter how much time he's spent here, he is, in fact, human, just like her.

But then she thinks back to her shower that morning and wonders how human she is anymore.

Romelo strolls out of the alcove, and over his shoulder he calls, "You answered without saying a word. You will join me or die with them."

Chapter Thirty-Eight

Rhiza
September 2042

"Why did you punish Ochai when you know that Romelo was behind that attack?" Syrah has stormed into The Keeper's study uninvited. Her henchmen, Dhanil, steps in front of her. She wants very badly to break the hand he's laid on her chest. It might do her good to see if any of the changes her body has undergone include even a sliver of the Rhiza strength.

"Leave us," Taron says, interrupting Syrah and Dhanil's staredown. With a canine sneer, he backs out of the room.

Taron sets down her pen, pushes away the journal she's writing in. "You think me dense, human? Of intelligence equivalent to that of, say, a pig rolling around in a pile of muck?"

Syrah throws her head back and grunts. "Arrogant. Smug, you're damned right. Always talking and always holding back," she rattles off. "Why don't you just tell me what I don't understand."

"Some of the greatest novels ever written are here." Taron gestures to shelves stacked all the way to the ceiling with books. "But The Keeper's real work is documenting. Storm and fire patterns, erosion, and changes in the air. Human observations as well. I've been The Keeper for two hundred and ninety-seven years, and have records dating back a thousand before that. Your kind are an intolerant lot. I know what you do to people who do not agree with you."

"And Rhiza is doing the exact same thing."

"Do not interrupt me."

Syrah pulls out a chair and sits, sulking, as Taron continues. "At the age of decision, each member of this community is assigned their life's work. What are those kinds of work?"

Syrah blinks.

"Come now, you have been here long enough, and as much as Artahe has to say about everything, there must be little you do not know."

"Blaze Brigade." Syrah starts with Ochai's chosen work. "Mycorrhizal Lattice Affairs, the Cleanup and Collection crew—Scourge Suppression—and Artahe's work with fungi."

"Was an investigation conducted into the topside killings?"

Before Syrah can answer, The Keeper charges ahead. "No. Fault is acknowledged, and someone takes responsibility for what happened. And that someone is punished. Whatever I, you, or anyone else thinks they know is irrelevant."

Syrah is speechless, something that doesn't happen often. Rules, laws, always so complicated. And so full of easily exploited loopholes. Same here as anywhere else. "But what happened? I don't understand. How long will Ochai be like that?"

"A minimum of five Rhiza suns, what you call months. After that, it is for The Mother to decide."

Syrah accepts this also without comment. "I'm changing," she says. "I know you've done this to me. The question is why, and am I becoming like you?"

Taron sniffs. "Hardly. Come with me."

Dhanil trails them through the nicely lit passageways and stations himself at the entrance once they arrive at an empty mirror image of the data center where Romelo works. Taron must have read the question in her eyes. "You have seen but a fraction of our home. There are three data centers. Your brother's is the largest. These facilities are the most important part of our society. Without them, we lose our eyes and ears to the world. Nearly a quarter of our population are rootspeakers."

Taron has told her about the books' recorded human history, and Syrah knows that they spend at least some time aboveground. And the way they blend in with the environment, they've probably been privy to many a human conversation. This completes the picture. "Are you suggesting that I'm to be a rootspeaker?" Syrah asks. "What am I missing here?"

Taron gestures to the first pod. "It is time that you see for yourself."

Syrah stiffens. Part of her still holds out hope that whatever changes she's undergone can be reversed. Something in the back of her mind is afraid that if she plugs into one of these things, she may never be able to turn back.

The pods all have what look like overlarge wooden recliners. No headgear. No blinking lights or cables or any technology that would indicate how this whole thing works. Only one way to find out.

They're all the same, all carved out of the seemingly densely packed wall. She walks over to the first one and looks inside, runs her palm over the surface. All smoothly carved as if with expert machinery or a very practiced hand. As she noticed from the outside, no equipment to speak of, only a maybe twelve-by-twelve panel near the bottom. She dismisses thoughts of telepathy but can't wrap her mind around how this thing is supposed to work.

Taron taps Syrah on the shoulder with her staff. "You must roll up your sleeves to the elbow. You must slide in hands first."

Huh. Taron already senses where Syrah has changed.

The Rhiza are taller than your average human, so Syrah has to hoist herself up to slip into the opening. And in turn has to fight the urge to climb back down. She lifts her head to reposition herself and finds that only a few inches of space separate the back of her head from the top of the pod. And the space is definitely made for someone taller. The curves, for the back, for the knees, even the spot with an indentation for the head, hit her in all the wrong spots. Her right shoulder grazes the wall—it's actually warm. Syrah traces a finger along the outer edge. If there's some kind of panel that slides down, she'll feel entombed.

"You are too short." Taron stands outside the pod and directs her staff toward Syrah's arms. "You will need to slide down a bit."

Syrah wiggles downward until Taron tells her to stop, her head now resting uncomfortably on what is probably supposed to be back support. She wants this thing over with.

"Feel for the lever with your right hand and press."

Syrah does as told and hears a panel slide open. She cranes her neck to get a better look. The smell of earth floods out of the opening. Unease grips her.

"Now insert your hands into the gap," Taron commands.

Syrah instinctively sits up and bumps her head. She can barely get her hand up to assess the damage.

"It is only dirt," Taron says. "What is your concern?"

Syrah has many, like worms and dirt beneath her fingernails, but she closes her eyes, ignores her aching head, and sticks her hands and arms, up to her elbows, into the earth. She wriggles her fingers. Warmth. A texture not unlike the dirt she played in as a child, but richer somehow. Slightly moist. Luckily, no feel of worms oozing around. She glances over at Taron, who is peering in, her expression unreadable.

"What now?" Syrah is growing more uncomfortable by the minute.

"Now you wait." Taron signals toward the door, and a moment later Dhanil waltzes in with a high-backed chair. Taron sits but is still able to meet Syrah's gaze. There's nothing there in the way of answers.

Syrah's back aches from the bathroom fall. Her skull throbs where she bumped it. The knee support digs into her chest. This may as well be the world's most uncomfortable coffin. Minutes tick by like days. Syrah's breathing becomes labored as the panic from being in such a small space rises. Small she likes; confined is another thing altogether.

She squirms. "I think I need to get out."

Taron taps that damn staff once, as if in command. "You will endure. This is a small trial for a Rhiza."

But I'm a human, Syrah wants to say. She squeezes her eyes closed and concentrates on her breathing. She starts counting backward from one thousand. Every time her mind wanders back to that voice that bids her to open her eyes and run from this place screaming, she starts the count again.

And time passes.

At one point she peeks out at Taron and finds the older woman smiling . . . smiling! Syrah is passing some unwritten test. Pride is written in that smile, and it makes Syrah infinitely, stupidly happy to have earned it.

She has counted down to twenty-five when she feels the first stirrings on the pads of her palms. Light as a breath, the brush of a million baby birds' feathery wings. And the sensation rises to her wrists and up to her forearms. She doesn't have to look down to know. It feels the same as it did in the shower earlier. Fungi are flowering over her arms and legs.

Like the gentlest knock at a door, Syrah senses the mycorrhizal filaments connecting with the fungi.

But then a flood, the impact ice-cold.

"Don't try to take it all in at once," she hears Taron say through the torrent.

The first thing she sorts through is need. A tree, somewhere in the grove, needs nutrients. It is an infant sapling, mother lost in a blaze. It's struggling for sunlight, fighting against the other adults and their thick canopies. Someone—a rootspeaker?—intercepts the request and routes to a tree in another part of the forest. A mature Giant that has some nutrients to spare.

Much of this back-and-forth goes on. Communications from here to what she guesses is as far as Inyo National Forest to the southeast. At times it seems the trees are able to communicate directly, and the exchange needs little interference. Nature doing what it's intended to do. But at other times, where humans have made this process problematic, the Rhiza rootspeakers are there to intervene. It's the most sophisticated communications system Syrah has ever observed.

And there's another stream. A tree in pain. Such pain. Its leaves are being chewed off by an animal it describes as having four legs with large black eyes . . . a deer. Syrah's entire understanding of the world is blown to bits. Instructions pass, and the lattice pumps defensive compounds—phytocides—if she remembers correctly. The tree pulls them up through its roots and inundates its tender leaves with the substance. The black eyes back away, the tasty leaves suddenly unpalatable.

They have defenses. Natural, unbelievable defenses.

Another tree makes itself known. Despite everything it has tried, it can't stop the bipeds—humans—from torturing it. They used a sharp instrument to carve the tender outer skin of its trunk. It calls for the Keepers of the Canopy for intervention to treat its wound. Syrah is fascinated as she watches someone, someone here in Rhiza, acknowledge the request and send an affirmation that help is on the way. Relief floods the lattice in the form of warmth.

But then another current draws her attention. Lightning bolts of rage. The undercurrent of anger. Pain. Fire, everything that humans have wrought against them. Syrah fights to control her own emotions but feels something course through her own body. Her own outrage mixes with the lattice, and suddenly she can feel all their fungal gazes upon her.

It is her, they whisper. *The outsider. She is conflicted.*

And Syrah knows they are right. And that the tree speaking in such booming tones and flashes is The Mother.

The Mother, the tree that Syrah thinks will be the voice of reason, has herself grown very tired and angry.

Another voice sounds on the lattice. It appears in the form of zigzags that sizzle her lower legs. *Get out.* She interprets the message clearly.

"How do I get out?" Syrah cries.

And Taron is there at her side. "Do not yank out; you will damage the filaments. Simply think it. Tell them you wish to leave, and they will retreat."

"What?" Syrah mutters, but she does just that. In her mind, she thinks the word "leave," and at first, one by one, and then in bunches that make her wonder how many filaments have been attached to her body, they disconnect. When she's sure they have all safely retreated, she pulls her feet from the earth.

In such a hurry to escape the chamber, she stumbles out and lands on the floor, earth spilling out along with her. Taron reaches in and closes the panel, and Dhanil is soon standing in front of her, his expression softened. Perhaps she's earned his respect as well.

"To wash your hands," he says, pointing to the bowl of water and handing her a towel.

Syrah takes the offering in trembling hands and does as she's told. Taron watches silently. When she finishes, she gets to her feet.

"Romelo knows I was in the lattice, and he isn't happy about it," she says.

"Despite everything I have done, that we have done, that one has not been happy since the day we took him in."

"And there's something else," Syrah says. And this scares her even more than her brother. "The Mother. I think she's starting to agree with Romelo."

"That," Taron said, "is what you did not know. And now that you do, we must think on what to do about it."

Chapter Thirty-Nine

Sequoia National Park, California
September 2042

Though it feels like the better part of a day has passed in the caves, the sun has yet to reach its midday peak when Syrah steps out of the tree hollow. And the grief that she's been holding at bay returns like a swarm of bees, stinging her exposed, raw nerves.

There's no way her cell phone gets reception this far into the forest, but she checks anyway. No bars. Panic pushes her through outstretched branches and understory thick with overgrowth and fallen leaves. It forces a rank sweat from her pores while her mouth is as dry as an empty well. The park hasn't officially opened, and news of the bear attack has probably spread, so she's grateful not to run into any hikers or campers. Every few minutes, she stops and holds her phone up to check for reception.

"Call Dane," she says as soon as she sees half a bar. By the time she reaches the Lodgepole lot, she's tried five times. On the sixth, her uncle picks up. "How's my dad?" she asks.

"No change," Dane says, and Syrah hears the strain in his voice. "I drove by your place this morning." The unasked question stretches between them like a shaky bridge. One that he hopes she'll cross and step back into a place that makes sense. She played out this call a few times, and in her version, Dane would say that Dad was fine, that he'd turned a miraculous corner and would be home in time for dinner.

"I needed some time to think," Syrah says, worried that the lies are beginning to flow much too easily.

"This have anything to do with that trek you took me on?"

"I thought I saw something," Syrah says. "I didn't and you confirmed that. That's all."

Syrah expects a challenge on that. Even to her ears, that explanation sounds as flimsy as the spiderweb she's just walked into. Instead, Dane asks another, more difficult question.

"So when do you want to drive down? I've got a bag packed and can be there in twenty minutes."

How can she tell him that she can't leave? That she's only come topside to make sure Dad is still breathing. That the people he can't see and a few of the giant sequoia are pissed off at humanity and may just launch another attack while they're traipsing down CA-65. How can she express the fact that even if she has no idea how to stop it, if she doesn't try, it won't matter whether her father survives the stroke or not?

"Any news from the bear attack?" she asks him.

Dane lets out a bone-tired sigh before he answers. "You're scared," he says. "I get it. I am too. But your mother needs you."

"I'll do in a pinch, but Mama needs you," Syrah says and hates herself for the cruelty of it. "Why don't you go ahead. I'll follow in a day or two. I promise."

"You're not going to tell me what's going on, are you?"

"No." Syrah has no more room for denials.

"Anissa will have my head if I show up there without you or an explanation of some sort," Dane tries again.

"The bear attack," Syrah presses. "Have they found them?"

"The park service has scoured the area for the bears. I mean, they've looked in all the usual spots and everyplace else, but somehow they seem to have disappeared."

"They're going to kill them."

"They've attacked people. You know as well as I do what that means."

"That doesn't make it right."

"You'll get no argument from me about that," Dane says. "Part of me wishes people weren't . . ."

"You there?" The line has gone all staticky. The mobile network is often spotty in the park. As she holds up the phone and moves around to another area where the bars reappear, she gets an idea. At least a seed of one.

"Syrah . . ." She hears Dane's voice again.

"Look, the connection may drop again at any minute. Head on down to Compton, and I'll follow tomorrow," she says. "You're just going to have to trust me."

"I'm not going without you," Dane says. "And you call your mother and tell her. I'm not doing that for you. When you're done doing whatever it is that is more important than going to see your father, call me. In fact, I'm calling you. You have one day, and then we're leaving whether I have to tie you to the seat or not."

With that he hangs up, and Syrah nurses her resentment a moment before she hears the dings come through on her phone. Three missed calls from her mother. She pictures her face. The worry and concern morphing into confusion and from there blossoming into full-blown anger. There's only one message.

"Syrah, you've always had these bouts of distance. Times where you shut me and your father out. We gave you space and accepted it because you always came around. But I'm not calling to ask you about when I might expect grandbabies. Your father is gravely ill. So I'm choosing to believe that you're more scared than selfish. But if I don't see your behind down here by the end of the day, I can't say I'll want to see you ever again."

Syrah screams and throws her phone as far as she can. It lands with a thud just past a line of pine firs at the edge of the parking lot. For a fleeting moment, she thinks about calling Dane back. Jumping in that beat-up truck with him and rushing to her dad's side. Forget about Rhiza and Mother Trees and let nature take its course. But then she thinks about how history would write her story if it ever came out that she could have done something. She doesn't know if she'll succeed, but she has to try. She has to at least buy herself some time. And if it means that her parents never speak to her again but that they and everyone else survive? Well, then, she will just have to live with it.

She needs to research something about underground communications. That idea she has will depend on it. She will go home and bury herself online until she finds the answer. And she will get updates on her dad through Dane.

But first, she has to find her phone.

Ironically, after nearly an hour, Syrah finds her phone at the base of a towering giant sequoia. Even her ability to throw is somehow enhanced. She lays a palm against the bark, then her forehead. Inhales the woods' spicy vetiver aroma. All the world's troubles sit atop their capable but weakening shoulders. She plops down and leans back, taking in the California gray squirrels leaping from branch to branch, bushy tails held high. The rat-a-tat-tat of a woodpecker at work.

There was a time when snow could still be seen dusting the ground well into late spring in the upper Montane region of the park. Now September temperatures are all over the place. The way it feels today, Syrah shudders to think of what her old crew at Fire Station

Ninety-Three will have to contend with. She slips off her jacket and drapes it across her knees.

Her eyes are closed, but years in the park service have tuned her hearing, and the sounds of approach are unmistakable. Whoever it is, is stealthy, though, stopping at the loud crack of a twig or branch underfoot. Someone from Rhiza? Slowly, Syrah allows her eyelids to flutter open, but she remains still. At first, a careful scan of the terrain reveals nothing. On the second pass, however, she spots it. Black-spotted coat, tawny coat. The stub tail confirms it: a bobcat.

Only bobcats rarely show themselves. "Go on," Syrah yells. "Go away!"

But it moves forward, stalking. Syrah scrambles to her feet. All she has is her phone. The pocketknife that's usually at her waist probably still belowground. She's pissed at herself for being unprepared and pissed at her brother. He has to be behind this.

The bobcat takes off, heading straight for her. She takes a kick at it and then feels a shudder in her body as her bare arms bloom. And . . . beneath her socks, so do her legs.

This time she does what Taron did during the bear attack. Waves of spores leave her body and flood the surrounding area. The bobcat's whiskers quiver. It gives its head a good shake, then scampers off into the brush.

Instinctively, Syrah scans the forest for signs of Romelo or other Rhiza. Finding none, she sinks to the ground again. Legs drawn up, head drooping between her knees, Syrah imagines all roads from here and dreads where every single one of them leads. None of them can take her back to the time before she came here. Before the prescribed burn she let her insecurity sanction.

No going back now.

Warily, Syrah lifts her arms and scans the exposed skin, inch by inch. Shyly, like little moons peeking from behind clouds and hiding again, the fungi greet her. It takes Herculean effort, but she chops down the mountain of hysteria. Looks at them anew, as if her eyes have turned into compound microscopes.

Small, crinkly clusters. Little medium-brown folds, evocative of the African tree ear variety.

And they had appeared when she needed them.

Syrah gets to her feet, suddenly energized. For the first time in months, there's a tepid lightness in her chest. She doesn't need the pocketknife. She has a new weapon. She need only learn how to wield it.

Chapter Forty

Sequoia National Park, California
September 2042

Before Syrah returns to Rhiza, she has another puzzle that needs solving. When she's in range, she pulls over and searches for the name on her phone. After the image and story come up, her mind goes numb. Could it be possible?

She tears down the long drive to her uncle's house, and he opens the door as her foot touches the top step.

"Finally," he says. "Your dad is stable for now. Let me grab my bag. I've already got it packed."

Syrah follows him inside, relieved to hear that her father is okay for now. When Dane turns around, she brings up the image on her phone and hands it to him. "You've worked here for, what, twenty? Twenty-five years? You know everything about the place, and I bet you know everything about her."

Dane takes the phone, runs a thumb along the screen, scanning and reading. He looks up at Syrah with what she's shocked to see are tears in his eyes. "How did you find out?"

"Find out what?" Syrah needs to hear him say it. That she's somehow related to the woman in the picture. But she can't let on how she found out.

Dane's shoulders slump. He drops his duffel bag and trudges off to his bedroom. Syrah folds her arms across her chest and paces the small room. Everything she thinks she knows about the world and her place in it gone up like smoke and ashes. If Mama has any ideas at all about Syrah's past, she'll keep those black pearls of knowledge clamshell tight. After a time, she could probably wear Dad down, but he isn't in any condition to tell her, and she can barely allow herself to think it, but he may never be. She knows she shouldn't be angry at him, but this is a hell of a way to find out she's been lied to.

When Dane returns, he hands her a picture and settles into the worn corner of his love seat. "Cathay Williams," he says, eyes worrying imaginary dirt beneath his fingernails. "Second from the right. Your great-great-great-grandmother."

The picture is an old and yellowed black-and-white relic. She recognizes the markings of Sequoia, maybe Kings Canyon. There are five people in the picture all mounted on impressive horses. All grim-faced men. She glances up at Dane. "Take another look," he suggests.

Second from the right, Syrah recalls. On closer inspection, the hard edges of the woman's face soften. Her cheeks subtly fleshier. A rounded chin not unlike Syrah's own. The person in the photo was trying very hard and succeeding, even, at passing for a man. The eyes, though—there is something familiar about them. Or maybe she just wants there to be. Still, something about those eyes reminds her of someone. Certainly not Anissa or Trenton Carthan.

Syrah levels Dane with one of her looks, the one that says *get to talking, and now*. She inclines her head, imploring him to continue.

"She was the only woman to ever serve as a buffalo soldier. Until she was found out, that is."

A woman buffalo soldier. One who shared her birth name and had spent time in Rhiza. Despite herself, Syrah smiles but quickly dashes it. "It looks like they're here at Sequoia."

Dane nods. "They were. The Thirty-Eighth Infantry was an all-Black buffalo soldier regiment. It was only for a short time, but yeah, they were rangers here in 1866."

"Wow," Syrah whispers. "I mean, that's fascinating. Why haven't Mama or Dad ever mentioned her to me?" But she knows the answer. They've never wanted to talk about anything related to the time before she came to live with them. A four-year-old's memories are dicey at best, and they didn't want to traumatize her further.

Syrah puzzles at the sudden change in Dane. It could have just been the bear attack, but it looks like the poor man has the weight of ten Giants on his shoulders. "And you were the one who found me after the fire. You told me that my entire family was dead, and you probably told the same thing to my parents. So either you lied to them, to us all, or you somehow didn't know that my brother survived."

Dane's mouth is open, his lips puzzling out something in his mind before he speaks. His gaze flitters from the picture in her hand to her and back. "I . . . I don't understand. Survived?"

"Romelo," Syrah says. "That is my brother's name, right?"

Dane's hands are clasped together, tapping at his lips.

"Uncle Dane," she implores.

He looks over at her. "You know that's his name. I never hid that from you."

It's something about his manner, the way his gaze can't settle on her, on anything. He's as confused as she is. She believes him and tells him so. But there's something else; she can feel it. "They never found his body, did they?"

Dane's Adam's apple bobs once, twice. Is he trying to swallow the truth or come up with a lie? He exhales softly before he gives a quick shake of his head.

"Did you look for him?"

"You know I did!"

"For what, a week? You left him! He was out there wandering around the forest."

"I never stopped."

That takes the heat out of Syrah, leaving nothing but emptiness. She fights back the tears. She doesn't have any time for them, but the dry sob skates right over the lump in her throat. She buries her face in her hands.

Syrah feels Dane's hand on her shoulder and shrugs him off. "Don't you touch me."

Dane pulls his hand back to his chest as if he has been burned. And his expression. The pain etched on his face stops her cold. This is the sweetest man she has ever met in her life. The most dedicated to doing the right thing. When she rebuffed his Christmas present one year, snapping at him that she was no longer a baby, he only smiled at her and returned later with something more age appropriate. She has been blaming him, and it wasn't his fault. He's spent all these years searching for a ghost and carrying the burden all by himself.

"I'm sorry," she mumbles.

Her uncle's shoulders are slumped. "I don't know. I mean, he was almost ten. If he'd survived, he would have been able to tell whoever found him who he was. I'm afraid somebody is playing an awful trick on you."

The thought has occurred to her. But she's seen him and heard him. She's certain. "I know it's him."

Her uncle is a man who moves about life slowly, methodically. Like he puts every move he's going to make up for careful evaluation. So when he snatches up the duffel bag and is at the door fast enough to give Syrah whiplash, she struggles to keep up.

"I bet this man was supposed to meet us in the park that day out near the Giants, am I right? Either way, you're going to take me to him right now."

This she hadn't anticipated. She stammers, "I—I . . ."

"You were just a kid when you cried right there on that porch and told me you hated yourself because you were forgetting them. But you were four years old and had been through something no child that age should have to endure. And I know it still bothers you. But I'll know if he's your brother or not. Let's get this settled now so we can go be with your real family."

Syrah wants to run straight for her car, get in, and drive away from this place, never to return. She wants to wind back time to when everything felt right, normal. She should never have come here. But now she can't leave. The truth is like a loose thread, and she can't walk away now without pulling on it to see where it goes.

Once outside, the weight of it all hits her, and she can't breathe. She bends over at the waist, hands on her thighs, gasping. The expanded lungs do little to help her.

"Come back inside," Dane says. "We shouldn't do anything with you in this state. I'll throw myself on the hood of your car if I have to."

My great—how many greats—my ancestor was a buffalo soldier. Romelo and I have a past that matters. Syrah's breathing, if not her equilibrium, returns to normal. She tucks away that interesting bit of family history for later dissection; there are larger questions that need answering. She follows Dane back inside.

"Tea?" he asks.

Syrah shakes her head. "Answers."

Dane presses his lips together. He goes back to his corner of the sofa. "Ask."

This is something she's always thought but discarded. "Are you my father?"

"Me?" Dane wipes at an eye and chuckles. "No, I'm not that lucky to have a kid like you. But your father gave me that picture. He was so proud of her. Your father was my best friend, you know that."

Dane stares off into space. "I tried, you know. You slept in the bed, and I slept on the floor. You barely spoke. PTSD, the doctors said. And they considered it a mercy that you didn't remember. But this is no place to raise a little girl."

"So you gave me away."

"I found a good family that wanted you."

"And you stayed close."

"It was the best I could do," Dane says. "Though I know it wasn't good enough."

But it was. Syrah stands and grabs her jacket.

"You going to take me to him?" Dane is also on his feet.

"Soon," Syrah says and leaves without another word.

Chapter Forty-One

Sequoia National Park, California
September 2042

Until now, Syrah has clung to a sliver of hope that Romelo isn't her brother. It would have made what she has to do easier. Thing is, he's not wholly off the mark. The Western way of thinking has shrunk two of the country's three coastlines. Herding them inward like cattle. Wildfires have killed as many people as the mass murders. They shifted to plant-based diets only because one disease after another had decimated their other food sources.

Yet.

Diseases that have killed millions have been all but wiped out. Anything you want to learn, right at your fingertips. Paintings and novels that have brought tears to her eyes. In the worst of times is when people rise. Acts of selflessness and compassion, the reason why Westerners, topsiders, continue to live, to thrive.

Syrah knows then that she will never have a brother again. The child he was is gone. Now she knows why her parents chose not to tell her too much about her past. When you have witnessed your family's devastation and come out on the other end as the lone survivor, there's no way to neatly put away the guilt and isolation. There between the birthdays and holiday dinners and school plays, it will slip out through the quiet moments. Even love won't be able to seal those cracks.

A pain starts at the base of her skull and radiates throughout her body. *Her body.* Is it really? It certainly isn't the body she had a month ago. Syrah's entire sense of self lies in a smoldering heap in a corner of her mind that she's trying her best to protect, to erect a brick wall around.

She sits in her car, fuming. A million more questions in need of answers she wants so badly she can taste them like the remnants of a cup of peppermint tea. She notices Dane move aside his curtain and look out at her, but he doesn't approach. He gives her space, and she's glad of it because she doesn't trust what she'll say to him if he dares step one foot outside. If he's been looking for Romelo all these years, why not just tell her?

She had stayed here at the cabin with him, at least for a time. She wishes she could recall more of those days. She searches back to those earliest memories and realizes something she didn't before. Once she bumped up against a certain time, the memories ceased. Her uncle had told her stories about her as a baby. Could she believe him? Was there something else he wasn't telling her? Her life, at least what she knows of it, is either the truth or the world's most boring and uneventful fairy tale.

A brother and an ancestor straight out of the history books.

The bitter possibility that some of her early years are lost to her and what she does know is now as suspect as a five-leaf clover. Identity is an entirely made-up construct, formed largely based on stories other people tell you about yourself. Your family first and foremost. The rest, the part that is you, is the smallest piece of that puzzle.

Who are you? It was a question posed to her by a Buddhist monk, Judah. A friend who lived in the downstairs apartment back in Florida. The first time he asked her, she had just passed the test to become a firefighter. That person had puffed up her chest like a peacock strutting with its feathers fanned out. She had told him that she was a firefighter. And he'd called her a fool—in so many words. He had asked her that same question and looked on her with pity as she answered the same way five more times before she thought to ask him what she was getting wrong.

He'd looked on her with kind eyes and a smile that told her how happy he was that she had finally asked. It was as if she had passed one of life's most important tests. He'd told her that being a firefighter was what she did, but that who she was had nothing to do with that. She studied with him once a week for the four months that remained on his lease, but by the end of that time, she knew. She was a curious, self-doubting, insecure, deeply sensitive person. An only child of only children, devoted to her parents while still being resentful of their clinginess.

She supposes most of that is still true. But now that story is half-baked. Unfinished. Like someone has ripped out the first few chapters of a novel.

Syrah balls up her fists and beats them against the steering wheel until the pain stops her. And something else. She runs her hand over the all-too-clear dent in the material. How? She has to get away from here. Syrah doesn't want to go home. With what she's discovered today, even the tiny cottage with the soothing creek out back feels like something foreign. The name on the title that she was so proud to receive, a joke. Throughout her life, people have told her how much she looks like her father. *Lie.* Her dad has always joked that she has her mother's temperament. *Lie.* She is an only child. *Lie.*

The car is already moving; Syrah barely remembers turning it on, reversing and barreling down the long, winding drive she used to take time to admire on her way out. But she does glance in her rearview mirror, the sight of Dane Young on the porch getting smaller and smaller, disappearing from her life as she speeds away.

Her father's ancestor patrolled this very same national park more than a century ago. A woman so determined to chart her own path in life, she posed as a man. Syrah has so many questions about Cathay Williams. Taron questioned her about her name the first time they met and spoke of the only other human, aside from her and Romelo, who had been allowed into Rhiza. And now that Syrah knows, that curious way that Romelo looked at her the first time they met makes sense. He was older, which means his memories had to be more sound. From the moment her blood entered the lattice, the Mother Tree knew. They all did.

The question is why? Whatever is at play here may have started all that time ago. Coincidence too easy, an insulting cop-out. The air in the car feels too close, so Syrah lets down the driver's-side window and inhales the scent of rain.

Clouds are bunched up and angry against a deep plum sky. Instead of going home, she finds herself on the winding road up to the Wuksachi Lodge. She parks in a spot as far away from other cars as possible. She isn't in the mood for small talk. She gets out and walks the path that she took on that first-day run with the fire operations crew.

The hike, so challenging that first day, feels like a stroll around the neighborhood now. She reaches the bend where she tripped. Where she had been lured into tripping. The rock where she'd skinned her knee and the Giant that she'd leaned against to steady herself. Somehow that had been the beginning of this all. It was the precursor to her acceptance in Rhiza.

Syrah has connected to their lattice and can only describe the experience like what she's seen in that old movie Dad loves so much he forced the family to rewatch it at least once a year when she was a kid—*The Matrix*. She imagined Taron as Morpheus, introducing her to the new world. Syrah, as Neo, still grappling with not only the existence of but the vastness of the lattice. At first glance she thought them primitive, and in some ways they were, but that lattice is as sophisticated as the aboveground internet that connects the entire world, at least when their governments allow it.

She kneels and with her fingers clears away a section of understory. That layer of brush and dead leaves is akin to tinder or fuel for the wildfires that have ravaged this and so many other parks. The prescribed burn where she bungled the job was intended to remove this. It was work started and successfully managed by Native Americans who lived on this land. She wishes she could apologize to them for what she's done.

Syrah turns her attention to an outcropping of mushrooms growing close to the trunk. She grabs a twig and uses it to dig into the ground, gently lifting one from the dirt. Thin filaments, mycelium, dangle from the stem. She can see them. And then she hears the keening. A piercing shriek. An alarm, a lattice connection hacked off? She feels a sensation on her own arms and legs that sets her teeth on edge. She doesn't have to look to know that her body is reacting. The fungi seeking to join and repair, trying to rescue.

Horrified, Syrah quickly reburies the mushroom, careful to move away the dirt and pack it lightly on top. She doesn't have her water bottle, so that will have to do. The silence of that scream is like the ending to a bad song. And then it hits her: someone from Rhiza, one of Romelo's rootspeakers, will receive word of this disruption. They might even learn that she's the source of it. Somebody will be dispatched. The weight and importance of their work suddenly is as clear as a glass of spring water.

Taron told her that the Keepers of the Canopy don't assign jobs, that each individual would come to know the work meant for them in time and gravitate toward it naturally. Syrah, it seems, is evolving much like her brother, and it creeps her out.

Joining them now makes more sense than ever. She is nobody. A person with no past and, if she's honest, not much of a future. She misses fire operations, and even if they were willing to take her back, she can't trust herself to return to service. Dane touts the park guide part-time job as a first step on a thousand-mile road back to the work she loves. But it's not at the top of her career wish list.

The more she thinks about it, the best thing she can do is leave all this behind and commit her life to a cause that makes sense. The Rhiza have a mission. Work that really matters. With Romelo mitigated, she can have purpose and spend the rest of her life tending to the Giants.

Or disappear.

Spin that globe sitting on the shelf in her living room, point a finger wherever it stops. Toss in enough clothes to fill her single suitcase, sell the home, and take off. Let Dane and her parents live with not knowing, just like she did. That's what she should do.

Syrah is many things. Angry foremost among them right now. But cruel isn't one of them. And though she contemplates certain ideas, she'll never do that to them.

Dad always says that the best thing to do with a problem you can't solve is to store it in a corner of your mind for processing and then work on the next thing.

The park is becoming more familiar to her, and she isn't certain if that's because of the human part of her or the other, but she stops to survey her surroundings and then decides on the best path to what she now calls entrance number two. It provides a speedier entry into the belowground society than entrance number one, the hollow in the Giant near where the meth addict nearly took out the whole grove.

A couple of women with packs on their backs the size of a large suitcase are standing near the overpass. One, with an impressive set of biceps, takes out a plastic container. Plastic! She upturns it and sloppily gulps down the water. As Syrah passes, she says, "Glass or metal. Better for the environment, and your water will taste better too."

The friend, smaller, with a runner's lithe physique and a cap that reads TREE HUGGER, chuckles, but the plastic hoarder fixes her with a glare. "Why don't you just mind your own business."

Syrah has already passed them but stops and turns around. "I work for this park. It *is* my business. Plastic was outlawed a decade ago. Guess some people didn't get the message."

Another chuckle from the friend. "I think she just called you a dumbass, Carla."

Biceps pours some of the water over her head, then passes the container to her friend. "Is that what you're calling me?" She has taken only two steps before Syrah is on her. In a move her father taught her—"in-fighting," he called it—she crowds the woman, dodges her wide swing, and brings her elbow up and smashes her chin.

Biceps stumbles back and falls. Her friend rushes to her side. "I'm going to have you fired. What's your name—"

But Syrah is already moving. Running as fast as she can. She hasn't struck anyone since the eighth-grade fight with Tommy Little, who had been harassing her the whole school year.

Why now?

The answer is clear. She has reached her limits. Her brain unable to process any more pain or grief without reacting. Running into the hikers was simply bad timing. She pictures them registering a complaint with the park service about the woman who assaulted them. If they give a halfway accurate description, someone may put two and two together and point to her.

Let's just add assault charges and prison to the list of troubles.

Syrah dodges everyone else she meets along the way. Doesn't bat an eye at the little boy she sees hurling rocks at a squirrel scampering around the branches of a sugar pine to avoid the volley. She keeps her mouth shut when she passes the General Sherman tree and spies a family cross over the barrier meant to protect the tree's roots, trample the area with their many feet, and smile for a selfie as if the tree's outrage isn't plain as day. She realizes that for them, it isn't.

Syrah ignores every other affront she witnesses, despair running alongside her like a treasured friend. Growing heavier and more burdensome with each step. When she reaches entrance number two, she pauses.

Her resolve is crumbling. She has no idea what she hopes to accomplish anymore. What does she even want? To join them or to stop them? As she enters the caves, it is a question she ponders, unanswered, with every step forward.

Chapter Forty-Two

Rhiza
September 2042

As Syrah passes through the veil, her thoughts turn to yet another problem, Ochai. In response, her heart rate increases. The now-familiar flutter in her stomach flares. But he is essentially buried alive within The Mother, at Taron's hand, no less. Sleep has eluded Syrah, but when she closes her eyes, she still sees him. And judging from the looks on everyone's faces when he was consigned to his fate, she knows the experience is, at a minimum, an unpleasant one. She hasn't dared to ask Taron—or Romelo, for that matter—because she doesn't think she can bear the answer.

"Why did you leave?" Artahe says when Syrah shows up at the fungal farm.

"I do have a life up there, you know? People that I care about." Syrah's words have a nasty bite to them. She catches herself and tones it down. "What's the latest?"

Artahe does that thing that Rhiza do when they're confused, a bit of a shoulder hitch and shrug. "It is a tale of two cities."

"Really," Syrah says. "We're quoting Dickens now?"

"But it is," Artahe says. "Even before you came and what Ochai did, the cracks were beginning to appear. Now we're openly divided. Right down the middle, it seems."

"Ochai took the fall, but it was all Romelo," she reminds her. "And what side are you on?"

"You know what side I am on. What my love—your brother—hasn't considered is the consequences. It is not like the absence of all life in one of the country's largest states will go unnoticed. How would we contend with the response? We need time to study it."

Ever the scientist, Syrah thinks. "So human annihilation is still on the table for you? With more study, of course."

Artahe turns to look down at Syrah. "Is it not for you?"

Syrah is indignant, all poised to deny even the possibility. But something stops her. Finally, too late, she mumbles, "No. It isn't."

"I saw you with them today," Artahe says. "The human that you fought with."

Syrah raises an eyebrow. She hadn't noticed. Was it because she was distracted, or is it still difficult for her to make Rhiza out when camouflaged? Something to test later. "It wasn't really a fight."

"All of us have the ability to blend," Artahe explains. "We are topside almost as much as scourge suppressors, so—"

"What you're saying is there are degrees?"

Her friend nods. "I saw the question hanging there on the tip of your tongue. Next time just speak it. We do not hold back like humans. Speak clearly and your heart will be lighter."

"I have feelings for Ochai," Syrah says, surprising even herself.

"Not that clearly." Artahe takes her arm and draws her away from the other workers. "You are not the only one, you know."

"I do know, and I don't care. The question is, How do I free him?"

A hand flies to Artahe's chest. Her charcoal eyes go wide. "You cannot. The Mother has decided when he is to be freed."

Syrah takes that with a grain of salt. There's always a way, but she won't press it now. She has to learn more about what's happening to her body. "Let's go back in." She gestures inside. "Tell me about the work that you do?"

Artahe makes a face. "You're doing it again."

"Doing what?"

"Just ask me what you really want to know."

Syrah huffs. "Fine. Which of these fungi are changing me, and is it permanent?"

"Our task is a noble one." Artahe relaxes, back on safe ground. She doesn't even deny it. "The mushrooms we farm are for food, for medicine, even the bioluminescent ones that we use to light the caves. We also tend to them topside."

"And . . ."

"And," Artahe says, dragging out the word, "these, they are like what you may know as *Cordyceps*, but our variety is engineered with another species we call *aprica*. Immunity from many diseases is one benefit. Energy and performance are others."

Not really a bad thing, Syrah thinks. They've done here on a small scale what people aboveground have still been struggling with. For every negative she discovers about this place, a positive appears to overcome it. Artahe doesn't say anything about why her skin blooms with a variety that looks wholly different. But she's not ready to share that yet. "Is it permanent?"

"No way to tell unless you leave us for a time. Your brother never has."

Her brother. "How can you still love Romelo if you're against what he's planning?"

"Yes. He is human. He is sometimes insufferable and too serious and broods and sulks. I often disagree with him. I love him still."

Why? Syrah wants to ask, but doesn't. Love can be oblivious to explanation or reason.

Syrah's intent is to go directly to Taron. She surprises herself when she asks her friend to take her to wherever it is that Romelo passes his time when he isn't at Lattice Affairs. It is then that the bell tolls, signaling the end or beginning of a work shift. Syrah still hasn't worked out how to decipher the different tones.

Artahe tilts her head. "The shift has ended. He will most likely be in one of the nourishment centers. He has a healthy appetite, that one."

Syrah's own stomach stirs, but being hungry and having an appetite to satiate it are two different things. She continues to be amazed at the bioluminescence that lights the underground caves. The muted light at seemingly the perfect tone, not too bright, not too dark. They pass clusters of Rhiza at work and others at their leisure. Reading. Talking in groups in those alcoves perfect for small gatherings. Not a screen in sight.

When they have searched both nourishment centers and not found Romelo, Syrah grows tired of looking. After they round the bend leading to Taron's library, she says, "I'll find him later."

"I'll leave you to speak with The Keeper," Artahe says. "But think about what I said."

Dhanil doesn't grunt or sneer and only calls over his shoulder, "She is here."

When Taron answers, he waves her in.

"I did not expect that you would be away so long. We have a war brewing. We have melded someone for the first time in thirty years. And you thought what? To watch your favorite television program?"

And that is officially more than Syrah could handle. To be upbraided by The Keeper on top of everything is the proverbial straw that breaks the camel's back. The smart, acidic retort she's prepared to unleash dies somewhere in the back of her throat. In its place, the grief and pain she has been holding back come out in a flood.

Instead of screaming her outrage, Syrah snatches out the chair in front of Taron's desk, drops onto the smooth wooden surface, and without care for Taron or Dhanil, or anyone within earshot, she bawls.

At first Taron blinks as if she has no idea how to handle Syrah's outburst. Eventually she rolls her eyes, and with a sigh, Taron comes around to the front of her desk and pulls the other chair close beside Syrah.

The Keeper rubs her back and pats her knee stiffly. She hums something deep and soothing.

When Syrah's last hiccup subsides, she wipes her nose with a stiff square that in Rhiza must pass for a tissue. And then she tells Taron everything. The mistake that cost her her life's work, how she spent her whole life thinking she was alone, only to discover a brother. How her adoptive father sits in a hospital hundreds of miles away, fighting for his life, and that the daughter he's been so proud of, the one who drove an irreparable wedge between him and his wife, isn't by his side.

Taron listens intently. So much so it's almost off-putting. She barely blinks those dark, narrow eyes. Syrah realizes she's grown accustomed to the way other people interrupt, or lose focus. When she's as empty as Lake Mead, she stops. Finally, Taron lifts her gaze over Syrah's left shoulder to a spot on the wall. Taron is a thinker like Dane, always considering her words before she speaks. At first Syrah fidgets. In her world, silences are uncomfortable. Before long, though, she settles back and just allows herself the pleasure of a moment without conflict or strife.

"It seems that coming here, working for the park service, is what you humans would call destiny."

"I don't know what it is," Syrah says. "But it really fucking sucks."

"You cling to the illusion that you are in control when nothing could be further from the truth." Taron leans back in the chair and crosses her legs at the ankle. "You are a busy lot, I will give you that. You make things, you break things. You reproduce and you destroy them shortly after. The problem is that for every time nature tries to direct you, you rebuff her. That is what causes all your pain."

Syrah ponders this, running a hand over the skin she's still becoming used to. "You're telling me that all of this was set in motion by some hand that guided me back here? That the ghost of my however-many-greats-grandmother has somehow drawn me back? To do what? Destroy my life?"

"Don't be so dramatic, child," Taron chides. "You have been hurt. I understand that, and you have a right to grieve your losses. But don't stay in this place too long. It clouds your thinking." She reaches over and taps Syrah in the middle of her forehead. "You are here precisely to help me prevent the destruction of your precious aboveground world."

Apparently being upset about the fact that your whole life is a lie and that the only father you've ever known might die while you traipse off trying to fight a war that isn't yours is being dramatic. So be it. She is a human being, not a keeper of anything other than that house on North Fork Drive, and some days she's damned proud of it. "What if I lose him?"

Taron shrugs. "He may be gone now while we are speaking."

Syrah shoots up out of her chair. "I'm outta here. I don't know what I was thinking."

A few steps shy of the doorway, Taron's words snare her again. "You may go to your father. The sight of you or the feel of your hand on his may give him reason to live. But if my ward and his ilk have their way, both of your parents will most certainly die along with everyone else. Go now if you want and be by his side when the end comes. No one will force you to stay."

A few more steps and Syrah can walk out of here and leave them, leave the world to its own fate. Humans have survived everything that's ever been thrown at them, haven't they? She lowers her head.

That is only because they fight things head-on. They won't see this attack coming. Animals turning on them is the stuff of bad film. But what if they do somehow discover the Rhiza? Guns, bombs, pickaxes, and even rifle-toting teenagers won't stop until every inch of the Crystal Cave is nothing but dust. If anyone is left alive to document it, history will record the fight as a valiant one. But the Keepers of the Canopy will lose, no doubt.

Then there's something else. It might take a few decades. A century, maybe two. But without the Rhiza, the Giants won't survive. And without the Giants, the rest of the park, the forest, will shrivel up and die. Who will be left to clean the air, to sustain the flora and fauna that support life on this planet?

In the end, humans would be celebrating their victory while consigning themselves and their children to a certain, more painful death.

Syrah doesn't turn around. The time for sitting and talking is done. "I am changing," she says, facing Dhanil, who has stepped into the entryway. "But I suspect you already know that. You probably manipulated it. If I am to fight, though, you must show me how to use it. How to develop whatever it is you've set in motion. But after that, I'm leaving this place, and I won't return."

Behind her she hears Taron get to her feet. "We have no time to waste."

For the first time, Dhanil graces her with his toothy smile.

Chapter Forty-Three

Rhiza
September 2042

"Tell me about what you think are the changes in your body."

The three of them—Taron, Syrah, and Dhanil—are in a place that she hasn't seen before. The outcropping of stalactites that almost reach the ground tell her they're close to the Mother Tree. Syrah tried asking, then demanding, that Taron free Ochai, but she only repeated what Artahe said, that the matter was for The Mother to decide. Soon, after all this is over, when her father is back at home in front of the TV, she'll ask for an audience with The Mother. Take the direct approach.

The space is as high and wide as a high school stadium. It is lined with what in Rhiza would pass for workout equipment. The air is stuffier here and has a subtle tinge of sweat. A distinctive, earthy kind of sweat.

"I've lived in this body for thirty-two years, and never before have I been able to hike fifteen miles and maintain a pulse like I'd meditated for an hour. My arms and legs, well, they . . . they bloom with fungi. But I'm not sure why or how to control it."

"And you found that frightened you? Disgusted you even?" Taron says, and Dhanil begins stalking around Syrah in a circle. She turns warily, trying to keep him in her sights.

Taron fingers her chin from the perch where she's gone to sit off to the side of the room. "That means you are evolving to become a different kind of rootspeaker."

Syrah remembers when Taron took her to the empty lattice station. It had been a test. She'd already known or at least suspected as much. The woman certainly knew how to keep things close to the vest. Something for Syrah to remember.

"What else?" Taron says.

"Why is he doing this?" Syrah asks instead. Every time she moves, Dhanil keeps pace with her.

"Answer the question," Taron booms.

"I don't get tired as easily," Syrah says. "Better lung capacity."

"Go on," Taron says.

"The question is how," Syrah counters. "And when will it end?" She thinks again and adds: "And is it reversible?"

"Those are three questions," Taron says. "You know how. It began the first time you came in contact with the filaments. They sensed your need and supplied what you lacked. In that exchange, you received the tiniest bit of Rhiza DNA. And then you ate with us."

"The mushrooms," Syrah says, still eyeing Dhanil. And while she was focused on Taron, others have joined him. "Is it permanent?"

"The answer to your last question is, I do not know. You are a test case. Depending on what happens here, we will see."

"I'm not some lab rat," Syrah says. She tries to move away from Dhanil, but he won't let her pass. "What's going on here?"

"You are leaving something out," Taron says. "What else have you experienced?"

Syrah thinks back to the steering wheel and the dent she left there. She is almost frightened to mention that part. “I’m a little stronger, it seems.”

With a tap of her staff, Taron announces, “We shall see.”

One, then two, one more. Three. Three additional Rhiza come through the entryway. Each wearing a scowl more impressive than the next. While Syrah backs away slowly, her gaze trained on them, Dhanil strikes first.

From behind she hears his steps but doesn’t have time to react before he lands a solid blow between her shoulder blades. She stumbles into one of the others, and he shoves her off. She spins around in time to see another one rush forward. She attempts to sidestep him, but he’s too fast, so much faster, and catches her around the throat, sticks a leg out behind her, and takes her to the ground in a second.

Syrah rolls over as another opponent raises a foot to come down on her knee. This time she swings out her leg and connects with what on a human would be a femur. The grunt he makes is so satisfying that she loses concentration enough that another foot connects with her shoulder.

She cries out at the pain and, through the legs crowding around her, sees a look of grim disapproval on Taron’s face.

Syrah springs up to her feet, and the circle closes around her. But this time she rushes toward Dhanil, swivels, and lands a punch to his side. Judging from that sharp intake of breath, he has a liver of sorts.

Then he waves the others back. He narrows his eyes at her. “Let us see what you think of real strength. We have been holding back.”

Syrah’s insides turn to water. Holding back? From the corner of her eye, she notices a small crowd has gathered at the entrance to the training room. Word spreads fast in Rhiza. Her mouth has gone dry, but she musters a response. “As long as you face me and don’t hit me in the back like a child, it’ll at least be a fair fight.”

Murmurs of outrage. A few chuckles. Dhanil grins. And then he kicks out toward her midsection. Syrah backpedals out of reach. And reaches for his foot. She catches it and tries to flip him over, but he wrestles out of her grasp.

She floats side to side like a prizefighter looking for the next attack angle. Her father always taught her that to hit in the face with her fist was the surest way to break her hand and lose a fight. Rhiza are strong, but not as fast. So she runs. Heading straight toward a wide-eyed Taron.

She hears Dhanil close on her heels. Inches short of Taron, she stops. Dhanil topples over her and lands in a heap. Syrah balls her fists and lands them in the center of his chest this time. When she looks up, a corner of Taron's mouth quirks into a droll smile.

But then the rest of the cowards converge, surrounding her. A shove to the back and she stumbles forward and straight into a solid right hand that she blocks, so the blow brushes off her shoulder. Another push and this time the next punch connects with the left side of her rib cage. Syrah swings wildly, but even when her strength-enhanced punches land, they don't have the same force as the Keepers'. They jostle her around that circle; knees, slaps, and fists greet her at every turn. She won't give up, though; she throws hands and kicks and even makes a futile grab for Taron's staff.

When, after much too long, the booming tap of that staff reverberates around the room, she's spent. When she hears the word "Enough," she gives in to the darkness that has crept over her eyes. Her last thoughts are of her father and mother and how she has failed them both.

She isn't dead.

But if there ever was a precursor to death, this would be it. Head to toe, she's a blue-black misery. She shifts. Sidesplitting pain moves away only to welcome the insistent throb in her temples. But all that pales in comparison to joints that feel mired in concrete.

Someone is holding her hand between theirs. Lightly.

"Drink this." Through a fog, Syrah recognizes Romelo's smooth voice. Urgency, but not full-on alarm. Maybe she isn't as near to death as she thinks. Shifting brings on a fresh wave of blinding-white pain so intense she feels her consciousness slipping away again. It doesn't help that she seems to be lying atop a hard surface. A layer between her and the hardness, something that in Rhiza must pass for a cushion but in the real world would amount to a bundle of threadbare sheets.

She isn't ready to open her eyes yet.

"You cannot stay this way for too long," Romelo says, nudging her. "You will lose every bit of the credibility you have earned."

That gets her attention. Her eyelids feel like a pair of weighted blankets covering her eyes, but with effort she forces them open. She's in a room. Empty shelves on the opposite wall. A desk, beneath them, no chair. A small basin pushed into a corner. A bioluminescent sconce on either side of the entrance and smaller versions placed in foot-long intervals near the ceiling. Instantly she feels warm. With a few adjustments, this is a place that she could call home.

Romelo sits in the chair that likely belongs over by the desk. He regards her with something akin to amusement in his eyes. In his hands, a bowl emitting a savory smell. "Come," he says, standing.

He sets the bowl down on the desk and grabs what look like pillows. He sets them up against the wall behind her, then, none too gently, helps her settle against them. They feel markedly better than whatever was beneath her.

He places the bowl and spoon in her hands and claims the seat again. "Every drop," he says.

Syrah wrinkles her nose at the first sip. The broth is clear with a few unidentifiable greens competing for space with bits of pale mushroom. The first slurp is as bitter as a soup with a base of lemon drops. Eating this will probably speed her down that evolutionary path, and with the next few spoonfuls, she no longer cares.

After two bowls, Romelo puts a stop to it. "That is powerful medicine. Even in Rhiza everything has a side effect."

That makes Syrah wonder what they have given her, but not enough to ask. She's distracted by how she feels. The pain and soreness, though not gone, are already lessening.

"You feel it, do you not?" It's like Romelo is reading her mind. "If you were Rhiza, you would be good as new. But as a human, it may take a little while longer."

Syrah flexes her arms and legs and stretches. "I need to move around," she says, swinging her legs off the bed. The drop to the floor almost takes her legs out from under her; she still isn't used to the height of things around here.

Romelo holds her up. Her legs are a bit unsteady at first, but by the time she's circled the small space twice with his help, she begins to feel more like herself.

"You want to tell me what that beating was about?" Syrah asks, hopping back up on the bed while Romelo reclaims the chair.

"It seems The Keeper has plans for you, and she wants to see if you will be up to the task."

"Well, am I?"

"You tell me," Romelo says. "Given all that you know now, are you with me or with The Keeper?"

"I want to do what's best for the Giants and, in turn, the rest of this planet. Without them, all of us, human, Rhiza, we're finished."

Romelo leans forward. "Humans are but dead stars in the night sky. They will go the way of the polar bear and the mountain gorilla. Have you made your peace with that?"

Syrah squirms; her brother is so still and intent, he may as well be a statue. "You're talking about mass murder. You would really go through with it?"

"That could not be any more clear if I had scrawled it across your forehead," Romelo says without flinching, no change to his expression. His commitment alights hot, smoldering like the last embers of a flame. "If it were within my power, I would sacrifice this entire country to save them. I must know now: Where do you stand?"

It's selfish, and Syrah hates herself for thinking only of them, but she will ask anyway. "Three people. My parents, and my uncle. If I could bring them—"

"No."

Syrah's eyebrows knit into an angry line. "I wasn't asking you. And who are you to say anyway?"

"You are not one of them; you stopped being of that world when The Mother demanded we lift the veil for you. She wants us together again. Face it," Romelo says. "I am your brother. I am the only real family you have, not them."

Unaided this time, Syrah jumps down from the bed. "I'll see how Taron feels about that."

"Go." Romelo waves her off. "She is not your friend, you know. She will use you to get what she needs. And what she needs is to defeat me. Think about that. She's known you were my sister from the beginning, but did she tell you? No! She would turn you against your own brother when we have just found each other again."

That plucks on a long-buried heartstring. "What do you know about our . . . our birth parents?"

For a split second that she almost misses, Syrah sees a hairline crack in Romelo's stony veneer. "They loved the forest as much as we do. They brought us here a couple times a year. I know that Ellis and April Williams loved us."

A sadness has crept into the room, end-of-the-known-world bleak. Syrah leans against the smooth rounded wall. "It was a fire—"

"Set by a human who did not have sense enough to make sure their campfire was out before they left," Romelo adds. "That much I know."

The siblings go on exchanging scraps and pieces of memories: their bunk beds, a fireplace mantel where they pinned stockings at Christmas, a neighbor's tree that they used to climb, the pitch and timbre of their parents' voices.

Romelo gestures at the scar above his eyebrow. "Cracked my skull falling out of the tree. That's all I know about what happened that day. Taron found me, brought me here, and it's where I've been ever since."

"That's what I don't get. Why not just take you someplace where you would be found, and maybe reunited with your family? How could she have known that our parents were dead?"

Romelo fingers one of his locs. At the same time, they say, "The Mother."

Fatigue forces Syrah back to bed, where she sits cross-legged. Talk turns to their childhoods after the fire. And though things weren't easy, they were both cared for.

"I do know that our great-great-great-grandmother was a buffalo soldier."

"Cathay Williams," Romelo says, surprising Syrah. But she shouldn't have been. Of course Taron told him. Sometimes she suspects the Rhiza know more about the world aboveground than she does.

She shakes her head. "The only other human to walk these corridors. She posed as a man in order to serve, to take care of herself. But they tossed her out when they found out she was a woman."

Romelo taps her leg for her to move aside and hoists himself up on the bed opposite her. "Tell me what you think of this woman."

And she does. The little she knows, anyway. Romelo sits enraptured, listening to her like she imagines a brother would. They talk about the soldiers, debating about how they felt about their role as it pertained to the Native Americans. Romelo tells her about stories of their conflict, how they chose duty to their families but didn't relish what they had to do. They talk more of their childhoods, filling in the blanks with reasoned guesses.

"The uncle," Romelo probes next. "The park ranger. I have seen you with him. Actually, I have seen him many times, for as long as I can remember. You love him; that is clear. He is a stand-up kind of man, then?"

Syrah is surprised by the question but tells him that he is right about Uncle Dane. She's at home talking about him.

In this way, hours pass while Syrah allows herself to experience having a big brother again, thoughts of a new family. And like her great-great-great-grandmother, the tough decisions she will soon have to make. In the end, she doesn't commit to one side or the other. It's time to go back aboveground for a while to check on her father. The man who raised her and from her earliest memories called her his sugarplum.

Interlude—The Mother Tree

Seeing with Ancient Eyes

Anger

Millenia untold, unaccountable,
Quiet, birth, growth
The brightest of dreams

The earth, the oceans vast,
And then we came
The Giants

We were the first and we gave birth
Multiply
All existed in quiet harmony
None molest us, none defile us

The sky opens and star matter falls,
We move aside, make room

They swam, then crawled, then walked,
Flat, heavy feet slapping against the moist earth,
Voiceless, thoughtless, base,
Unknowing

Then desire
For food,
For shelter,
For reproduction
For *more*

We remained indifferent to their endless deprivation

They took and we gave
A millennium of symbiosis allows for such
Previously balanced

Then unbalance
Traversing oceans
Taking more, giving nothing
Plowing through the forests, tearing and ripping
We wailed and they did not answer
We cried for our loves lost, they did not answer
We adapted to their fires
And still they tore at our limbs, trampled our roots, killed our old and young

Air unrecognizable
Oceans choking
Forests razed and dying,
Whole families demolished, the lattice broken

Bodies blackened and grayed, turned to ash and
    dust
The bleakest despair

And we stood by
Our numbers thinned to near insignificance

Nature's secret was patience
We waited for them to pass back into stardust
    with another great flare
No longer

There is no more room for them
We are able
We are mighty, creatures made of time
We will take it all back
Old alliances rekindled

Purge, cleanse

We shall reinherit the earth,
Our roots are on the precipice of a rebirth
A reckoning

The world was my first love and I love her still

Chapter Forty-Four

Rhiza
September 2042

Romelo slipped into the library unnoticed. And why shouldn't he? His clothes were expertly patched, though old and worn. The shoes that were like clamps on his feet were probably relics of a season past. Anger rose as he glanced around at them, glued to the doom and narcissism on the computer screens. He looked just like them, but he wasn't one of them, not any longer. Taron had seen to that.

"Hey," someone behind him said. "You gonna use that thing, or you gonna sit there mad-dogging everybody?"

All eyes swiveled to them. Romelo pushed his chair back and turned to face the loudmouth. He didn't say anything. He only let his gaze travel the length of the man. Legs too close together, the stance of an unpracticed fighter. Hands that had never felt what it was like to hit a canopy keeper, hanging there limp and unready at his sides. Chest already heaving. And the man's expression? Laughable! No real intent in those beady eyes, only bluff. Not worth his time.

Romelo dismissed the man with a wave and turned back to the monitor. The footsteps retreated.

He logged into the email account he'd created exactly six months ago, when he'd hatched his plan. He hadn't been certain if he'd go through with it then. Recent events had changed all that. Indecision was like a fossil that he had reburied.

Dane Young. The man who had cared for his sister as he'd cared for the park. All in spite of his blind and ignorant superiors. How was it that the most inept always rose to leadership?

Romelo had watched this park ranger and had read about him. He was what the humans called an advocate, a champion of the forest. And what Syrah had told him just confirmed it.

He typed up the email:

> Mr. Young,
>
> This is the first and only warning that humans will receive. You (them, really) have done enough. Unless you stop your present course of action, the Giants will die and the world will not be far behind. I cannot let that happen. The bear attack was just the beginning. I can bring every creature in the state against you.
>
> Our demands:
>
> Close all national parks to human entry
>
> Discontinue air travel for a period of ten years
>
> Convert to electric and nuclear power

Replant trees in the Amazon and other decimated forests according to the natural habitat and never cut down another tree again—ever

Convert to community farming and eliminate the consumption of meat

Please tell your superiors to enact change. Now.
Or we will end you.

The Keeper

Romelo reviewed the message once before he hit the send button. Satisfied, he logged off and took one last look around at the people whose lives depended on the response to those few words.

"Let ignorance be bliss at your own peril," he said aloud to them before he strode through the library doors and began the walk back to the forest.

Chapter Forty-Five

Sequoia National Park, California
September 2042

It is the smell of smoke that Syrah notices when she emerges from Rhiza. The persistent bouquet that she barely noticed before is like a flashing red light to her now. Her strengthened lungs protest, and she sneezes a few times.

She treads carefully; the forest comes alive at night. Romelo can control animals; she even believes in a pinch she might be able to as well. But she doesn't know if that ability extends to all of the park's fauna and fungi, if she can succumb to a snakebite as quickly as the next person. Guided by a fat yellow moon, she heads back to the Wuksachi Lodgepole parking lot.

According to her brother, and the thought still feels foreign, though welcome in her mind, she was under for a full day. He and Artahe tending to her between their work shifts. She's puzzled out that for every hour spent in Rhiza, a day or more passes in the real world. That means she hasn't talked to her mother in far too long.

When she reaches the abandoned lot, she finds her car—and ignores the ticket beneath the windshield wiper. She holds her phone aloft, the bars magically appearing.

The menacing ding announces she has a voice mail.

But she doesn't call her mother back. Instead, she calls Uncle Dane. How easy it would be to unburden herself, tell him everything. Ask for his advice. Let him tell her what to do. Tell her everything.

"I'm sorry," Syrah says. "How is he?"

Her uncle is silent for a time. "Not good."

No! No! No! "What happened?"

"It's his heart rate," Dane says. "It's through the roof, and they're having trouble stabilizing it."

"What does that mean?" Syrah leans against the car for support.

"He may have another stroke," Dane says. "Or a heart attack. Look, Syrah, whatever it is you're doing can't be more important than this. I'm leaving now, and you're coming with me."

Syrah can't speak.

"Tell me what's going on?" her uncle implores. "I can't help you if you don't let me in."

"I want nothing more than to tell you everything," Syrah says. "And one day, hopefully, I will. But for now I'm going to have to ask you to trust me. I wouldn't stay away if it weren't vitally important."

Dane pauses. "I got the strangest email," he says. "A warning. This person took responsibility for the bear attack and said that unless people stopped now, it would just be the beginning. This person said they'd bring every animal in the forest, every creature they could, against us. Kept calling us humans. They had this list of demands—environmental stuff. Does that mean anything to you?"

So all the questions about her uncle hadn't been to learn more about her family. Romelo had been sizing him up. He needed a spokesperson topside, and he had decided Dane would be it.

"You there?"

What to say? "Yes," Syrah says. It's too much, she can't bear it all herself any longer. "I can't explain everything, not yet. But that email is part of the reason why I'm still here. Wait, what did you do with the email?"

"It sounded like it came from a madman, but that's not my call to make. I sent it off to the head of the park service, and she forwarded it to a contact at the FBI."

"And what happened?"

"They laughed her off the phone," Dane says.

Syrah is torn between wanting to protect Rhiza and angered that they're not taking this seriously. "I'll handle it."

She hears Dane's breathing on the other end of the line. Finally, with an exhale, he says, "You're a grown woman now, Syrah, and you've got a good head on your shoulders. If you're dealing with someone who's unhinged, you need to step away. Let the authorities handle it. Come with me and try to make amends for the damage you're causing your family right now."

"He's unhinged," Syrah admits. "But you're all underestimating him."

"I'm leaving," Dane announces. "Six in the morning. If you're here, and I pray that you will be, we will drive down together." With that he ends the call.

That bastard actually tried to warn them, Syrah thinks.

Heading back belowground, she goes straight to Taron's library. Dhanil is at his usual perch outside the door. The hitch in her step makes her think back to the kick that ended their little test. She doesn't doubt it came from him.

"You fought well," he says and bows his head in the greeting that, until now, she thought was only reserved for other Rhiza. Syrah wants nothing more than to slap him. Even entertains the idea of challenging him to a one-on-one fight, but instead she says, "As did you. I see why Taron has selected you for this job."

He raises his eyebrows and says, "So unlike a human. You harbor no ill will. Impressive. Go on in; she is waiting for you."

Syrah finds Taron not at her desk but leaned back in her chair. Staff ever ready on the ground at her feet. "It is good to see you back on your feet."

"Barely," Syrah says. She pulls a chair from in front of the desk and sets it down opposite The Keeper. "You could have warned me."

"And what good would that have done?"

Syrah thinks about that, fidgets with her hands. "What if I hadn't survived?"

Taron tsks. "It would never have gone that far. You are much further along than I suspected. That is a good thing. We will need as many as possible if we are to stop him."

Syrah doesn't tell Taron about what Romelo did, or that she has decided to stand against him. The decision has been made and is plain as day on her face. "It's not fair that The Mother punished Ochai."

Taron gives her a strange look. "You do not know, do you?"

"Know what?"

"Ochai is but a figurehead, and The Mother knows it," Taron says.

"If The Mother knows he's just a fall guy, why penalize him in the first place?" Syrah says, and Taron gives her another quizzical look. "That little stunt with the bears. Romelo let Ochai lead it so that if things went wrong, the punishment wouldn't fall on him. He wanted to see where you would fall when it came down to it."

Taron hunches her shoulders. "Aside from Ezanna, who is but an old loudmouthed fool, Ochai is Romelo's most capable supporter. She will free him after a victor emerges."

Syrah feels like a fool. He's manipulated her like he's done them all.

"And that stunt, as you call it, will be the undoing of humankind. What was done with the bears was a test. A very small one. The forest is populated with many flora and fauna that respond to our call. Only part of the battle will not be waged here," Taron says. "It will also be aboveground in your cities. Romelo will try to use the lattice to get the trees to aid in the attack."

Syrah's heart is hammering in her chest. "His numbers are small; we can counter. We use our influence to stop the attack."

"And potentially drive everything to ruin. You humans have your weapons, but even with them, you are woefully outnumbered. And weak. Have you seen what a horde of termites can do to a single structure? What of rodents? Poisonous animals? Imagine them tuned to different prey."

Syrah is horrified. She hasn't considered any of this. She wonders if the Rhiza truly have that level of control. Inside the forest, sure, but what about outside? "Are you telling me you can control every other living thing on the planet?"

"I am telling you that it is possible. It has never been tried. But there has been much I did not think possible—you, for example—that has later proven me shortsighted. We must assume that the answer is yes."

"That would mean . . ."

"Wholesale destruction. There is no more time to waste," Taron says. "If we are to mount defenses, we need to posthaste. I need your decision now. Now that we've established your physical shifts, we need to test your ability with the flow. Topside."

Syrah thinks back to what Romelo said. That Taron isn't her friend and is only using her. That may be true, but she understands why. She likes Taron, has developed an affinity for her so that until this very moment she didn't realize the strength in it. In making a commitment to go against her brother, her family, she will hopefully save her parents, Dane, and everyone else. In time, she is certain, *hopes*, Romelo will come to understand.

Syrah nods. "Count me in."

The slight, quick exhale is the only thing that tells Syrah that Taron is pleased. "And now we must deal with how he will use the lattice. If the Giants follow him, and there is every indication that they may, the rest of them, sapling to ancient, will follow."

Syrah looks to the doorway. "I have an idea, but I don't think either you or The Mother are going to like it."

Chapter Forty-Six

Rhiza
September 2042

"Are you insane?" Taron springs up with an agility that shocks Syrah so much she almost tumbles out of her own chair. Dhanil pokes his head in, and the memory of the beating she took under the guise of training causes her to tense. But The Keeper gives a short, curt shake of the head that sends him away.

"Hear me out," Syrah says, refocusing.

"That lattice connects us to the trees and them to each other. It is our very lifeblood!" Taron lowers her voice, but it holds no less of an outraged edge to it. "A disruption of that scale? What you propose is to end us. I should never have allowed you to enter this place."

"With all due respect, Keeper, as you pointed out, The Mother made that decision for you."

Taron cuts her eyes at her. "You should choose your next words very carefully."

The underlying threat curls around every impeccable consonant, but Syrah's got a plan, and as far as she can tell, nobody has come up with anything better. "Temporary," she emphasizes, coming to stand directly in front of Taron. "The outage will be temporary. Think about it. The whole reason you have more rootspeakers than anything is because communication issues are relatively common, right?"

"Never. Not once before in Rhiza history has this been done. An intentional, full-scale outage across the lattice. You are clearly hysterical."

"Think of it as a long-overdue system reboot."

Taron scowls.

"I know you have concerns about the new chief rootspeaker." In the time it took for Syrah to go topside, Romelo and his faction had broken off, left. The Crystal Cave is way more substantial than anyone topside knows. Taron believes he scoped out another one of the caves to set up shop. So far nobody has gone after him, and Syrah knows it's a task Taron will soon lay at her feet. "But it's our only play. Take everything down, just for a time, no more than a day. Stop him. And then the connections get reestablished. Everything starts working again just as it did before."

"And during this outage," Taron says, "what are the trees to do in the event of a crisis?"

Syrah fingers her chin. She hasn't thought that part through.

"You have no idea, do you?"

"I do," Syrah says, quickly racing through the possibilities that come to mind.

"Out with it, then."

And one of the ideas sticks. "We position rootspeakers at key points topside, throughout the park. Near the Giant groves and a few other critical areas. That way they can be on hand to apply aid directly, if needed."

Taron's scowl softens into a sort of lip-raised snarl. Syrah presses her slight advantage. "Romelo won't be able to get his message out to the other trees. And if he can't do that, they can't be manipulated into using their defenses to influence the animals. The fight will start and end here. Here we can handle him."

"And what happens when your brother regroups and tries the same thing again?"

Syrah bites her lip until she tastes blood. Then she mumbles the words she can't believe she's saying. "We can't allow him to try again." She doesn't have to put into words what they both understand. In the time that the lattice is down, they'll have to do whatever they have to do to ensure Romelo won't be a threat again. The optimistic part of her, that sunny-side-up approach to life her father clings to, hopes that talking, reason, will be enough. The pessimistic side, what she inherited from Mama, lets out a good, deep belly laugh at her obliviousness.

Taron sits in her chair, tap, tap, tapping that staff against the ground. Her grip so tight veins are straining beneath her skin. Syrah fears she may snap the thing in half. Finally, she sighs. "Your plan is dangerous. It will almost surely fail. We could potentially break the second rule. But it is all that we have. I must solve the issue of the chief speaker, though. A replacement is in order."

Syrah releases the breath she has been holding. Finally, The Keeper is listening to reason. "Yes," she agrees a little too emphatically.

"And I know just the person to become the new, perhaps permanent, head rootspeaker. And that person is you."

"Wha . . . what?" Syrah sputters. "Me? No. I can't. I don't know . . ."

"You connected to the lattice. The Mother sought you out from the beginning. Her reasons for doing so are now clear to me. As they should be to you. This is your idea. The Mother agrees. I agree. It shall be done."

"What are you talking about?" Syrah says. "How do you know The Mother agreed? I didn't see you ask her. There's got to be somebody with much more experience than me. I can't stay here. I don't know. I mean, I have parents to think about."

Unblinking, Taron watches Syrah for a few seconds before she speaks. "Sometimes experience is just the thing that makes it difficult for someone to see a new way of doing things. It is that knowledge that gets in the way by convincing the self that the self knows all there is to know on a subject. This is a weakness that has snared us all a time or two. It is precisely because you do not have experience that you proposed such a radical idea and why you are the person to implement it."

People always assume the greatest wars are fought outside, but Syrah knows different. This battle, the toughest of her life, is being waged, head and heart, inside herself. Joining the Rhiza is already on the table, and an idea that she has inexplicably found herself warming to. Just as she does, a new, even more absurd possibility emerges. Like her father has always said, there ain't nothing wrong with coming to him with a problem, but she should bring along at least one or two proposed solutions with it.

She has brought the solution, hoping to extricate herself from implementation. Apparently, that isn't to be.

"Well?" Taron urges.

"All right," Syrah hears herself saying. "I'll try."

"I am afraid I cannot allow that."

Syrah's back is turned, but the look on Taron's face sends a jolt of fear up and down her spine. She follows the older woman's steely gaze and turns around to see Dhanil. He has stepped into the room, flanked by a group of other, all-too-imposing-looking Rhiza. They have the entrance blocked.

"Dhanil," Taron says, marching forward and standing directly in front of him. "Do you"—she turns to walk and stare down each of the people with him—"really think to oppose The Keeper?"

"I do not do so lightly," Dhanil says with his chin lifted.

"I," Syrah says, coming to stand beside Taron. "I notice you didn't say 'we.' That tells me you've appointed yourself de facto leader of this little insurrection of yours. And that also tells me you've been planning it for some time."

Some of the Rhiza shift uncomfortably. Questioning looks on their faces.

"You are an aberration. One I—we—were willing to tolerate as long as you stayed in your place." The venom has returned to Dhanil's voice.

"And what gives you the right to decide anything?" Taron pokes him with her staff.

Dhanil remains silent, searching for a fitting response, and when none comes, Taron plows ahead. "You and your friends here will stand down this instant. You will return to your quarters and remain there until The Mother decides on a fitting punishment."

At the mention of The Mother, Dhanil actually trembles. For the briefest of moments, Syrah wonders if they just may make it out of this unscathed. The reprieve, however, is a short one.

"Recite the Grail," Dhanil commands, and in unison those assembled acquiesce.

You cannot willingly harm another member of the society.

You cannot through action or inaction harm a tree.

You cannot divulge the location of the community to outsiders.

Taron rails: "In case you have forgotten, I am the Keeper of the Canopy. My grandmother four times removed created that Grail. I know those rules well."

"Yet you have broken every single one of them."

"Do you think this job is an easy one?" Taron says. "Things change and we must adapt."

"I—we—do not agree with what Romelo is planning. That is not the issue. But we cannot allow you and this usurper to take down the lattice. That would mean certain death for the trees and for Rhiza. Given the choice between destroying the humans and destroying ourselves, the choice is clear. We will not aid him in what he does, but we will not stand by while you let her dictate—"

Snakebite quick, Taron swings her staff around and connects with the side of Dhanil's head. He stumbles backward, the expression on his face more of shock than wound, Syrah suspects.

"You will stand down now. Disperse before this gets completely out of hand. You take one more step forward with this plan of yours and you will not be able to turn back. Think carefully about your next step."

Dhanil's gaze flickers from one of his followers to the next, and in the instant when his eyes lock with Syrah's, she knows that he hates her for being present. For seeing him struck and for witnessing his indecision. They have lost.

Dhanil stalks forward and keeps his eyes firmly planted on Syrah when he says, "Take them."

Chapter Forty-Seven

Rhiza
September 2042

Taron moves with the agility of a ballerina and deadly precision of a samurai warrior. How she maneuvers a ten-foot-long staff in a space no bigger than an overlarge studio is a feat of dexterity that has Syrah standing there gaping. She's dispatched two Rhiza, and one sneaks up behind her before Syrah finally snaps out of it.

And then only because Dhanil steps in front of her. He has eyes only for her, his gaze fixed and locked on his target like a heat-seeking missile.

As if in anticipation of more pain, every nick and scrape she suffered from the beating they gave Syrah sparks. She flexes, unsure in her evolving body. In a fight she is always more opportunist than practiced brawler. But what she does have is an elephant's memory. Dhanil favors a direct, brute-force attack, so she lets him come, charging in like a bull seeing red. At the last moment, she sidesteps and lands a downward chopping kick to the side of his leg. He doesn't cry out, doesn't have to, but he grunts. And she hears the satisfying sound of his other knee smacking against the ground.

From the fringes of her vision, Syrah glimpses Taron in a vein-bulging struggle for her staff. Syrah takes only one step before she feels Dhanil's foot connect with her ankle. Her feet are swept out from beneath her, and she tumbles sideways like a downed bowling pin. She slams onto the hard-packed ground, her left shoulder taking the brunt. She grits her teeth through the nerve-tingling impact.

Syrah rolls away from the hands groping for her and comes to her feet in one fluid motion. With a three-step running start, she leaps up and clubs Dhanil with a two-fisted punch to his throat. His eyes bulge with rage. He's bent over, gagging, and just as Syrah is about to follow up with a knee to the face, someone grabs her from behind.

Syrah struggles and sputters, but the forearm around her throat chokes off her oxygen. A few steps away, Taron is a blur of fury. She has the staff back and is pummeling Dhanil. Spots appear in Syrah's vision, so she can't see who whacks her across the jaw. The bright, icy pain steals her breath but, oddly, clears her mind.

Be like water.

The thoughts come to her and she lets her body go slack. The forearm relaxes just enough. She uses her legs to drive both herself and her attacker backward.

They wreck the shelves and go down in a shower of hefty books and torn pages. Scrapping with whoever is behind her, Syrah hammers them with an elbow. The deep-throated baying tells her she's connected.

Wounded but not down.

Syrah turns in time to see Taron landing blow after blow to assailants both in front of and behind her. Her staff, though, is on the ground at her feet. And her lifeline becomes her undoing. Just as Syrah wrenches herself free, Taron trips over the staff and pitches over an instant before her face meets the ground.

And then they are on the two women.

The conflict ends with shoving, a few harsh words, and a painful binding. Arms behind their backs.

And Syrah was wrong. There *is* a back exit, one that she wishes they'd run through at the first sign of trouble instead of standing and fighting. Syrah shouldn't be surprised. This cave system is as intricate as anything she's ever seen or read about.

Taron has fallen oddly, disturbingly silent. Syrah wonders if it's an injury, whether to her body or her pride. That would be preferable to the alternative, that her spirit took the brunt of it—that she can shake off. Because Syrah doesn't know how at the moment, being bound and surrounded by traitors on all sides, but they have to get out of this. They don't have time for it.

Can't they see that Romelo is the threat? It's so like Dhanil to be shortsighted. They say they don't support Romelo but are willing to stand by and see how it all plays out?

They march single file, this segment of the cave too narrow for anything else. Taron and two Rhiza in front, Dhanil, unsurprisingly, behind her. She can feel his hot, angry breath on the back of her neck, smell his stink. If it isn't wishful thinking, his steps have an odd hitch to them. It sounds like he's favoring that left leg. And the fact that she's wounded him, even a little, makes Syrah immensely, stupidly proud. He isn't the one with his hands tied behind his back in a vise grip, being shoved to whatever end he and his mates have in mind for them.

"Where are you taking us?" Syrah asks. Her voice sounds flat and dead in the small, cramped space. Nobody answers.

"You realize what you've done; attacking the Keeper of the Canopy is akin to treason, right?" Syrah offers, hoping for some reaction. When she gets none, she adds, "It won't take long for someone to notice Taron's gone, don't you think? And they're not going to stand for this. You know that, right?"

Nobody speaks, but one of the attackers, the one directly in front of Taron, does glance back over their shoulder. She makes note of that. At least one of them isn't quite so sure about this course of action.

"And The Mother—"

"If you do not stop speaking, I'll bind your mouth next," Dhanil growls just as Syrah is about to hammer home her point. "That is the problem with you humans, all the right words and all the wrong actions."

Even now Dhanil is unsure. It's all in that gloomy tone. He should be celebrating, but having done what he did, his confidence is wavering. They've walked what she thinks is about a quarter of a mile when they come to a door. Well over ten feet tall, like all Rhiza doors. It opens with a soft whoosh, and the smell of a closed-up place rushes out to greet her. It's midnight-dark inside, minus the stars.

Hands hold her while Syrah hears shuffling around the room. Soon the fungi illuminate the space. Rounded. A room about the size of the Wuksachi Lodge dining room. All the typical accoutrements. A desk and chair, both highly polished. A bundle of sleeping pallets rolled up and stacked in makeshift bins. Sconces placed all around the room. It's chilly, and Syrah finds herself wishing she could wrap her arms around herself for warmth.

As she looks around, she realizes this is Taron's space. Maybe for when she wants to get away from the pressures of leadership? Is there yet another back exit? A small basin sits in the same corner as her library. A similar wooden spout tap, pushing out from the wall, likely drawing from the many underground water pools. Provisions line the shelves. And books, of course. This is a place built like a bunker. A place for either a last stand or for a respite for an overtaxed leader. It makes sense that, as her personal guard, Dhanil would know about this place. He probably built it himself. He used to be overprotective of Taron. So much has changed in such a short time. And Syrah can't help but think that much of that change was driven by her arrival.

They are guided to chairs and allowed to sit, uncomfortable as it is with their hands bound. For the first time since the trek, Syrah gets a look at Taron. She searches The Keeper's eyes. What she sees there frightens her. Empty of emotion. No fight, no defiance, not even defeat. What is she thinking?

"You will stay here until it is done," Dhanil announces. By "done," he must mean allowing Romelo to start a human and flora/fauna war. "Then you will be released and we will accept our fate, however it is decreed."

That's unexpected, Syrah thinks. She has read him wrong. She thought he wanted power, perhaps to lead. She's dumbstruck. All he really wants is for them not to disrupt the lattice. He fears that more than he fears the repercussions of this little insurrection. She misjudged him again.

They turn to leave and Syrah wonders what stops them from doing the same. There aren't any locks on doors belowground.

"We will post guards outside the door. If you try to leave, they will stop you."

And that answers Syrah's question. One remains, though: how, despite the odds against them, they will still prevail and escape. That one she will wrangle out of Taron as soon as the door closes.

"Please tell me there is yet another trapdoor somewhere around here?" Syrah is moving around the room, using her sore shoulder to check for any hidden doors, any break in the seamless brown. "Knowing you, you planned for this potentiality."

"There is not another exit from this place," Taron says. "And that means we will go out the way that we came in."

Syrah pauses to assess the assortment of aches and pains littering her body. She loses count quickly. If only she could down a bowl or three of Artahe's fungi quick fix. She wonders about Taron, how she is faring. She doesn't have her staff. But does it matter? Is it anything more than a glorified walking stick that serves as a purposeful weapon when needed?

Syrah gets up to try the door. She turns around and maneuvers one of her bound hands around the handle. It turns easily enough, but the door doesn't open. She glances back at Taron, who has one quizzical eyebrow raised. Syrah tries again, then turns and throws her shoulder into the door. It doesn't budge.

"Guess I've ushered in another new era for Rhiza. Somehow in a matter of hours someone has invented a door lock."

Taron sniffs. "No place, not even Rhiza, remains untouched by topside. You may be arrogant enough to believe it was because of you, but I remind you again that we are not so ignorant to the ways of the world as you believe. We adapt, have always adapted, the same as you."

"Rather than sit there and try to insult me, maybe you should try filling me in on whatever plan you have in your head. I've—we've got to get out of here."

"I have told you."

"Tell me again."

Taron glares, and Syrah does her best to return it.

"At some point, they must open the door. When they do, we make our move."

"At some point?" Syrah says, cocking her head. "We can't just sit here and wait. 'At some point' could be well after Romelo sends snakes into the streets. What are you saying?"

"I am saying that we must let things unfold as they may. It is no longer within my or your control."

"So you're giving up?"

"Look around you." Taron gestures as best as she can. "We are in a cave with one entrance. Blocked, mind you. We have no weapons. Nobody knows we are here. Have you no logic? What else are we to do but wait?"

Does Syrah have a plan? No, but that doesn't mean they shouldn't try to come up with one. And then she understands. Taron has nothing to lose. At least she thinks she doesn't. She truly believes that as long as her people survive, then all will be well, the rest of humanity be damned.

Romelo was right. She doesn't give two shits about her.

Shortsighted and arrogant. That's what the precious Keeper is. She's underestimated the human need for revenge. Whoever survives, and someone will, won't stop until they uncover the reason for the attack, and then—then they'll stop at nothing to find and obliterate the culprits. And Syrah just might count herself among them.

"Scream," Syrah says.

"What?"

"Yell, scream. Make a fuss."

"You mean raise my voice?" Taron lifts her chin. "I will do no such thing."

"If Romelo succeeds, why would they ever want to let us out of here?" Syrah asks. "Think about it. So you can get out and be Keeper again? Punish them all by consigning them to The Mother? And half of them think I don't belong here anyway. That it's your fault I'm here at all."

Taron remains quiet.

"Think," Syrah implores. "They will never let us out. Once we die of thirst and hunger, they'll open the door and dispose of our bodies. Problem solved."

Taron's mouth forms a small o.

"Now scream!" Syrah says and kicks things off herself. She runs around the room, upending what little furniture or other stuff lies around.

For her part, Taron tries. Her scream comes out more like an animal's grunt, but it will have to do.

"Quick," Syrah says. "Knock down the sconces; we need it dark."

For once Taron does as asked without a word of protest. Just as they hear activity on the other side of the door, it opens. A triangle of light carves a path of illumination. Syrah and Taron back away, out of eyesight.

Two guards step inside. "What is going on—"

And then Syrah and Taron rush them. Using the advantage of darkness and surprise, her intent is not to incapacitate but only to slow down. In a flurry of shoulders and knees and kicks, they are past the pair and running down the pathway.

By the time they emerge into Taron's office, footsteps sound behind them. Talk about arrogance. Dhanil hasn't even posted anyone outside. When they emerge, they crash into a group of passing scourge suppressors, still clad in their outdoor gear. The alarm on their faces tells Syrah they've found allies.

"Free us," Taron commands.

"What is going on?" one of them asks.

"Quickly," Syrah urges.

It is then that the two Rhiza who have been posted to watch them emerge from the office. They take one look at the growing assembly and the grumbles of outrage and dash off toward the back exit to the caves.

The bindings on their hands are cut and Syrah rubs her sore wrists.

A couple of Rhiza have started to run after the guards. "Leave them," Taron says. "They have no place to go. We will find them."

"Where is Dhanil?" says someone Syrah recognizes as one of the barrel-chested members of the Blaze Brigade that showed her around before. "Was he injured?"

"He had to be," someone else chimes in. "That is the only way that those two could have laid a hand on The Keeper."

Murmurs of agreement rise up.

"This cannot go unpunished. They have broken the first rule of the Grail."

Another voice rings out. "Immediate conscription. They must never be freed from The Mother."

During all this, Syrah takes note of Taron's curious silence.

"If Dhanil is injured, then where is he?" the blaze brigadier asks, looking around in the library.

"This has something to do with Romelo, does it not?" yet another throaty voice suggests.

Just then the bell tolls. Time for another work shift. Syrah isn't certain which one, but she can't think of any better time to call off a work shift, so she's shocked at what Taron says next.

"Everyone get back to your duties. And avoid further speculation."

After many more reassurances that they are okay, and at Taron's urging, the rest of those gathered disperse. Syrah spins around to face Taron. "What are you doing? I can't believe you're letting Dhanil get away. After what he did? I don't get it. I don't get you. Why leave an enemy to rebound and come back at you again?"

"He will not try again, but he will be dealt with. He served me for fifty years, you know." Her voice trails off.

Syrah feels for her but remembers how easily Taron would have dismissed her concern for her own family.

"But there is no time to lament broken friendships and what is lost. Now we focus on stopping your brother."

Syrah squares her shoulders and nods. "Then we break the lattice."

Chapter Forty-Eight

Rhiza
September 2042

Chaos.

No other way to describe it. The calm, serene place Syrah visited that first day is no more. A thing for whoever will document this chapter of Rhiza history to speculate on. And who is to blame but herself? At least partially. The fire started by the meth head had been the proverbial straw that broke the camel's back. But she can't help but think about how things would have gone if she had never shown up here. No matter what happens, Rhiza changed the day she tore through the veil.

First, Romelo and his faction had broken off. Then, The Keeper's most trusted protector, someone who had been at her side longer than Syrah has been alive, turns on her. The cards that make up this house are falling like shards of a nightmare, and there's nothing in Syrah's grasp that will let her reverse it.

Clusters of canopy keepers gather in corners, doorways; they crowd paths and walkways. Voices raised, faces agitated. Animated gesturing. It is as if everyone is poised for a fight but unsure which direction it is coming from. Nobody has gone back to work.

Syrah plucks out bits and pieces of conversations, hushed to whispers as they walk past. Gazes, staring them full on and likely trailing behind.

"He's right," she hears from somewhere behind her. Romelo or Dhanil? Which are they referring to? And does it matter? Both of them have openly opposed The Keeper. Something that, according to Rhiza lore, has never happened before.

"It's her fault," someone else says, on cue. She doesn't bother arguing.

Taron, Syrah, Liesel, and a few other rootspeakers make their way toward the abandoned lattice post just shy of a run. The smaller one that wasn't destroyed by Romelo. The Keeper's normal casual stroll absent. It is there that they hope to establish their command center. Where she hopes to undo a thousand-year-old organism.

"Aren't you going to tell them to go back to their quarters or something?" Syrah says as she trots alongside Taron.

"They will not listen. And perhaps they shouldn't."

The older woman's confidence has suffered a blow; Syrah is certain of it. Her manner is all wrong. There is a wavering timbre to her voice. That old assumption that everyone would bow to her will without question is gone. And Syrah feels lesser for it. And if she does, she understands why the whole community senses the same. Without a strong leader, a group might descend into disarray. She can't let that happen. But they have a task to accomplish first.

They arrive at the post, and immediately Liesel starts going about preparations, directing his team to adjust one of the pods to fit Syrah better. Taron leans idly against a wall, fiddling with her staff.

Liesel is directing a worker who is wadding tufts of moss atop the back and knee supports in what will be her pod.

"I wish it were you," Syrah admits. She doesn't have confidence in him. Neither does Taron, and judging by the look he gives her, neither does he.

He regards her with an odd expression before he speaks. "You know what is funny," he says. "One time, long before you got here, I did take down the lattice."

Syrah perks up. "How? How did you do it?"

He blows out a breath. "An accident by a young one too eager to impress. Romelo had it back up within a minute. The truth is, I do not know how I did it. And if I did, I do not know if I could force myself to tell you."

"You don't agree with what we're going to do."

"I am afraid of what you are going to do," Liesel says. "But for The Keeper, I will do anything."

"I can promise you this," Syrah says. "I will do everything in my power to ensure the lattice isn't permanently damaged."

The rootspeaker gestures at Taron. She looks uncommonly tired, her gaze fixed on nothing in particular. It unsettles him, Syrah can tell.

"Both my parents worked the Blaze Brigade," he says. "In the year that you call 2020, there was a great fire."

Syrah knows of it. That inferno had killed about ten thousand mature giant sequoias. It was a devastating blow to the population. "The Castle fire. Started by lightning."

A harsh chuckle.

"Hey," he says, directing his staff. "Faster. We do not have much time. There, remove that piece."

When he is done, he turns back to Syrah. "If that is what makes topsiders feel better, you may go on believing that. But we know the truth. That it was caused by a cigarette. Two, actually."

"Wait. That's not—" And then Syrah stops herself. She is a former chief of a fire operations crew, and there is a certain amount of skill and experience she's gained, but it pales in comparison to a people as old as time. She checks herself and motions for him to continue.

"They were dispatched to try to protect one of the oldest Giants." He stops and lowers his head. "The flow is a finite resource. There was a time when even the most junior member of the blaze had enough to outlast any outbreak. That changed as the fires burned longer. My parents made it back here, barely clinging to life. Burns covered their entire bodies. They held on for weeks, but in the end, they both succumbed. Taron was at their side as much as I was. I did not belong in this job. Scourge Suppression had been decreed. But Taron made Romelo train me nonetheless. And I will never be the rootspeaker he is, but that does not matter. She gave me a chance to do work that I love."

Syrah's own heart skips a beat when she hears of Liesel's loss. As hard as she tries to keep her father's illness out of her mind so that she can concentrate, it all comes crashing back, and she tries to excuse herself.

"Now," Taron says, coming up behind her. "They are done."

The others go about measuring her and then repacking some of the earth to better fit her body. It is time.

"You know what to do," Taron says. "We will stand vigil. Do not stop. Even if we are attacked. Do not stop until you have accomplished your mission."

"I won't let you down," Syrah says, clasping the older woman on both shoulders. Taron lifts a finger and trails it down the side of her face, then takes a step back.

"Begin."

Syrah hurriedly yanks off her long-sleeved shirt and tosses it aside. Liesel makes a cuff with his hands and helps Syrah hoist herself up onto the pallet. It is lined comfortably. And she feels the difference immediately. No less claustrophobic but all the painful digs in all the wrong places are lessened.

"Hey," Liesel says, "when you try to switch things off, the lattice will resist. Connections will try to knit back together. Do not bother with them, keep going forward. If you take out the biggest nodes, the smaller ones will collapse even as they try to reconnect."

Syrah is surprised at the reversal, but appreciative of the advice and tells him so. With a final curt, thin-lipped nod of encouragement from Taron, she settles in. She calls to the fungi living just below the surface of her skin, and they flower, ready to do her bidding. She reaches up and pulls the lever, and the panel opens. She closes her eyes and feels the tickle of root tendrils crawling over her skin, heading for the loosely packed earth.

A shudder grips Syrah from head to toe. The earth cool and moist against her skin. Like the brush of a feather, the fungi on her arms and lower legs begin to respond. Those small, fine filaments lengthen, seeking connection to the mycorrhizal network.

She waits, breathing to calm her nerves. Eyes closed so as not to encourage panic at being in what amounts to an open coffin. The first time she did this, the connection seemed to take forever. The second, only a little less than that. But this time Syrah has barely counted backward from one hundred to eighty when the first mini electric shocks of connection course through her. It's not unpleasant, not at first, more like the slightest prick of a needle.

But when rapidly, one after another, all the contacts are made, the feeling is more like poking her finger in a live electrical socket. Yet this time, the sensation passes, and soon the shock settles into a buzzy thrum.

The lattice recognizes her and opens. The chatter is like a submarine fleet cutting a path through her veins. Every blood cell in her body a carrier of epic data. Her mind races with the messages coming in faster than she can dissect them. A sapling crying out for more sun. A beetle, no, a pack of beetles, a distress call. An all-is-well signal from the Montane region. The Giants dominate the chatter, but competing messages from the pines and firs, cedars, and ponderosas travel on an undercurrent.

It's too much.

She is bursting. The seams of her are coming undone.

"I can't!" she shouts, unsure whether the thought is in her mind or if she's said it aloud.

Just as Syrah is ready to rip herself from the lattice's hold, the fungi sprout even more filaments, and the torrent eases.

And in its wake Syrah is overcome by uncertainty. Can she even figure out how to do this? And, more importantly, should she?

Her answer comes in the form of a jet stream of emotion. Anger and sadness. Wounded trees. Innumerable losses. Trees that at that very moment are buckling under the weight of countless human abuses. Trees humming their own eulogies.

It makes Syrah's heart ache to witness such overwhelming suffering. She sets her mind to the task, singles out one tree. It is young for a Giant, about fifty years. She crafts the thought in her mind and, through the electrical currents in her body, sends out a test message of her own.

Sleep.

The response questions her. Has fall come even earlier? Time to shelter again? The Giant notes that the temperature is all wrong; the other flora and fauna are active. The tree attempts to reach out to others on the lattice to confirm, but Syrah isolates it, cutting off those pathways. Alarm, confusion. It floods her with messages.

Sleep.

Syrah sends the suggestion again, more urgently this time.

And soon the chatter grows silent, and the communication stops. Inwardly Syrah rejoices. One down, countless others to go.

Sweat beads her brow and drenches her clothes. No time or space even to stop and wipe it from her eyes. And she's tiring, mentally. It comes to her then. Reluctantly, she sends the signal to break off connection to the lattice. She grabs the lever, closes off the panel, and shimmies out of the pod, dropping to her feet.

"Is it done?" Taron asks.

Syrah stretches the kinks out of her shoulders and back. "It isn't. It's too vast. This will have to be coordinated. I need every able-bodied rootspeaker in all of these pods."

Taron taps her staff. "Go," she shouts. "Discreetly."

They nod vigorously. And to the others standing by, Liesel booms, "In your pods."

It doesn't take long for a dozen or more bright-eyed workers to show up. And onlookers crowd the doorway that Taron closes with a finality that sets Syrah's teeth on edge.

"You will follow her as you would follow me," Taron announces.

"What we are going to do is to send the message to go dormant to all of the trees," Syrah explains. And to the gasps and whispers, she adds, "This is only temporary."

"It will be like closing a book at the end of an evening," Liesel puts in. "And then returning, picking up the threads of the story later."

"You all know why we are doing this," Syrah says. "If you're here, it is because you've sided with The Keeper over Romelo. What we do now will stop him. And then we will find him and his followers, and they will be dealt with, in the Rhiza way."

"Enough talk," Taron says. "Begin."

When everyone is settled into their pods, they connect to the lattice, and then, one by one, to each other. Syrah's body crackles with their combined energies. With a thought, the signal leaves her body and enters the root system. The others send acknowledgments.

Sleep.

Their voices sluice across the lattice. Each pair directs their signals at a segment of the park. They start with the smaller trees and work their way upward from the foothills through the subalpine region, the upper limit of tree growth.

Sleep.

And with every resistance, every question sent back across, they engulf it with more of the same message.

Each grouping—elders, teenagers, spring saplings—yields. And when the trees are lulled into an uncertain slumber, Syrah and the other rootspeakers inundate the lattice with the shutdown signal.

Disconnect.

Like stars blinking out of the sky, the trees' resolute baritone thins to nothingness. Ropes and ropes of screams tear through the underground. The people of Rhiza have never been without the lattice, and their terror is a thing unleashed. As the last of the lattice shuts down, a hollow, violent stillness sweeps over them.

Syrah chances a look over at Taron and is devastated by what she sees. The Keeper is bent. Her trusted staff at her feet. She wears the blank, haunted expression of someone who's glimpsed the edge of a cliff, and for the sake of her people, and for the topsiders as well, keeps right on walking anyway.

Most of the rootspeakers are faring far worse. Tears streak their faces, their bodies racked by great hiccuping sobs. Syrah feels like a monster, both savior and destroyer at once.

Just as she is about to go to Taron, a force like a rocket launch pushes through the lattice and sends a spine-tingling jolt through Syrah.

There aren't any names on the lattice, only addresses, but it is Romelo; she knows it instinctively.

Somehow, somewhere, he's fighting to bring the lattice back online. His singular command like a thunderclap.

Wake up.

One by one, the trees heed his call.

Syrah grits her teeth and doubles down.

Sleep.

Her team has recovered, and they go back on the offensive. She feels Liesel and the others powering through alongside her. Together they press Romelo and his group back.

Ones, then tens. Hundreds of trees—Giant to sapling—send distress signals. Strident beacons borne through the frantic root tips still attached to Syrah's body. She cringes at the whisper-light flick of a few of them snapping in half.

"You are tearing the lattice apart!" Syrah only barely registers Taron's cries.

She diverts a slice of her attention to repairing the severed roots while continuing to press the attack.

The clash grinds on well past the threshold of her endurance. From her periphery, she spies two of her crew, stumbling out of their pods, emptying their stomachs.

Just as the venomous taste of defeat roils like boiling water on Syrah's tongue, she feels the entire lattice give one great heave.

And in the end her brother seals his own fate. So stressed is the lattice over the battle being waged that it buckles under the onslaught. Soon nothing, not even the faintest sound, can be heard.

Chapter Forty-Nine

Rhiza
September 2042

Her team are out of the pods, engaged in energetic, congratulatory celebration when a panic-stricken voice breaks through.

"Romelo is topside," the messenger says. "They are rallying the beasts."

Syrah and Taron take off at a run.

And as they speed through the caves, others join in. Word has spread. They tear through the veil and come to a standstill. With the lattice down, there's no way to tap in and find out where Romelo is. They'll have to rely on good old-fashioned reconnaissance.

Syrah has no idea what time it is, but it is almost pitch dark. Only dappled hints of light filter down from above. The moment she sets foot topside, thoughts of her father demand her attention, but she stamps them down. She turns in all directions, squinting, listening. The park may be full of unsuspecting, sleeping campers. Romelo is defeated and desperate. And unless they find him first, they'll have a wholesale slaughter on their hands.

As if the absence of moonlight isn't bad enough, outside the veil of the caves, the Rhiza are difficult to see, and looking down at her own hands, she's shocked at just how much she's changed, because depending on the way she shifts her hand, she can barely make out herself.

"What will he do now?" Taron mutters.

"He's had success with the bear attack. Makes sense to go with that again," Syrah says; then another possibility comes to mind. "Or . . . if he thinks this is his last play, who knows."

She and Taron exchange a knowing look, and for the first time Syrah sees real fear in her friend's eyes.

Liesel watches them for a beat before saying, "I am not following."

Syrah takes in their meager numbers. By her best guess, a quarter, more or less, of Rhiza had sided with her brother. A sizable group had been sent to protect The Mother. The largest contingent chose to wait benevolently on the sidelines. That left the scant group arrayed before her who aligned themselves with Taron. Her heart is a hunk of concrete tossed into the ocean and sinking fast. But she paints her face with quick, serene brushstrokes.

"The lattice is down," Syrah says. "So that should contain him to the park. That means anything that moves is a weapon in my brother's hands. For the biggest casualties, he's going to target the campgrounds, so let's just start with the closest, Mineral King."

They fan out and take off without thinking.

They should have known better.

The first cry Syrah recognizes is that of Liesel. "Stop," she screams. "Everybody stop moving."

She narrows her eyes, head on a swivel. There, to her right. She pushes through the cluster surrounding the rootspeaker. Syrah's hands fly to her mouth. "No," she whimpers, sinking to her knees beside him. It is the first time she's seen Rhiza blood. It bubbles like paint from a geyser, thick, coppery, and red as her own. A thigh-size shard of wood protrudes from the center of his chest. Liesel's cough sprays warm droplets on her face. His expression is one of disbelief.

She grasps his hand. Liesel squeezes, shudders once, then his grip goes slack.

Syrah feels a hand on her shoulder.

"We must go," Taron says. "I am sorry but we cannot stop now."

Syrah was sinking into a vortex, and Taron's touch pulls her back.

Taron takes the lead, using her staff to test the way, and Syrah picks up on it, directs others to grab any fallen branches or anything else they can find to help avoid further traps.

A muffled scream tells them they've lost someone else.

"Press on," Taron commands. And they do. By the time they make it to Mineral King, they don't see anybody. Romelo isn't there. No bears. Nothing.

Syrah finds herself at Taron's side, spent. She doesn't want to but leans her forehead against the older woman's shoulder. She closes her eyes and exhales in the moment before tempestuous human shrieks punctuate the dark.

Syrah's head jerks up. Already she's moving toward the sound. Far from here. One excruciating echo dies out before one after another resounds.

"Wait," a desperate voice calls out. "There could be more traps."

She no longer cares. Judging by the heavy, flat footsteps beside her, neither does Taron. Reluctance stowed away, the others follow. The campground is near the northern rim of the park. An area teeming with wildlife that she's heard keeps all but the most seasoned campers away. Her stride, though not as long as her companions', is smooth and sure. It takes three times as many steps to cover the same ground, but she manages it well enough.

Like a nervous gust carrying a bramble, the screams intensify as they draw closer. The sounds of the Kaweah River mean they're getting closer to Lodgepole campground. And Syrah's phone, forgotten in her front pocket, beeps furiously with notifications.

Dad.

She wrenches the phone free. Without slowing, she taps the indicator and listens to the message.

But there's no message about her father, only an emergency alert from the city of Three Rivers.

An unknown threat.

Stay in your homes.

Await further information.

Syrah has no time to think as they skid to a stop at the clearing. Her mouth falls open. A tent or maybe two—it's hard to tell—collapsed in layers of desultory tatters.

They are little more than shadows at first, but a fierce, snarling pack of coyotes stalk into a wedge of moonlight. Two people cornered. Streaks of red smear their arms and legs. Terrified figures trying in vain to hold off the attack.

One man, sparse gray hair waving in the air like a flag of surrender, swings a tent pole ineffectually at two coyotes baring their teeth and stalking forward. The other man kicks at the three boxing him in. Blood glistening on their snouts. The only thing standing between them and certain death, the canopy keepers.

Syrah takes a step forward, then goes stock-still. Her fungi unfurl, and she welcomes the now-familiar feel. And this time she urges the flow to release. It rolls out of their bodies like fog curling around the forest floor over toward the grisly scene.

A coyote has succeeded in dragging one of the men to the ground, his screams peppered in every bite.

The Keeper's flow makes first contact with the pack. One, then another, stops and pulls away. "It's working," Syrah yells. "It's really—"

Just as one of the animals backs away, the man plunges a hand in his pocket. At first Syrah can't make out what it is, and then a shaft of moonlight reveals the weapon.

A round canister, covered in black mesh. The red handle she can't see but knows the man is fumbling for. Pepper spray; that or bear spray. It has been banned in the park for years.

The animals are already in an obvious retreat, backing away. It occurs to Syrah that Romelo could be nearby, poised to orchestrate a counterattack.

One man, the older one, has just pulled himself up into a sitting position. Injured, but from what she can see, not fatally so. But the other man, the younger one, his face contorts with rage; he finds the button.

"You bastards!" He struggles to his feet and sprays with such reckless abandon that he catches not only the retreating coyotes but his companion and himself.

He cries out, pawing at his own eyes, exactly the wrong thing to do. Unlike the flow, Syrah can't see the spray coming, but Taron does. "Cover your eyes," she yells. A minute too late. The burning spray hits Syrah just as she tries to pull up her shirt. It feels like someone has started a fire in a pit and plunged her face directly into it. She can't breathe. Tears are streaming down her face. All her training tells her not to rub her eyes, but she does anyway. Reason walks out the door, and pain steps in and bolts it closed.

Unthinking, she yanks away from the hands that try to help her. But then Taron's rough, sure grip finds her. "Control yourself!"

Syrah complies, and soon water dumped over her head and into her open mouth douses the flame. Little by little, the pain recedes. Blinking brings the world back into focus. She's soaked head to waist and beginning to shiver in the night chill. But her mind is sharpening, along with a rank anger.

A couple of Rhiza are with her, but The Keeper is nowhere in sight. "Come," one she recognizes as another rootspeaker says. "We must pursue."

Syrah is up and on her feet immediately. More easily every time, she's able to blend in with the forest, just like the rest of them. The others nod grimly, and they set off at a run again.

It is that time of day where night gives way to dawn. The sky still dark but with a hint of purple streaking, the moon retiring for the day. And that means more people. More hikers, staff, more potential victims. Romelo has planned this perfectly.

Soon they catch up with Taron and the others. The two men gone. Their campground like a fresh crime scene. Blood mixed into the earth. Food and cooking implements scattered everywhere. What's left of the tents fodder for a landfill.

"They've been led away to safety?" Syrah asks.

Taron sniffs. "Led by themselves."

"There's something going on in Three Rivers," Syrah says. "Where I live. I'm the only one that can go."

Taron hesitates. Her hand reaches out toward Syrah's cheek but settles for a feathery sweep against her arm. "Our paths diverge here."

Syrah's throat is the reclaimed Mojave Desert. Even if she had the words, she couldn't speak them.

"Go now," Taron urges her. "Do what you must there and return to us."

With that, Taron and the others advance. Syrah is still there when Taron glances over her shoulder once before disappearing into the forest.

It's getting lighter by the minute, the sky turning a pale blush and birds starting to emerge from their nests. Syrah's heart pounds in her ears, her breath coming much too shallow. She makes her way back to her car.

Already, this coyote attack, combined with what happened earlier with the bears, will raise uncomfortable questions. Questions that will cause the authorities to start looking. All she hopes is that they won't be able to look too closely. The Rhiza have survived long enough by themselves; she has to believe it won't all end now. She can't let it. She and her brother, Romelo . . . they have been the outsiders. The ones who don't belong. And because they have been welcomed in, everything is changing for the worse.

But if her brother thinks they are that easy to defeat, well, let him. Underestimation has been the undoing of many a tyrant before. Syrah is more determined than ever. She won't let their kindness end in ruin.

Under Romelo's twisted control, any creature in the park, in the city, can be turned into a heat-sinking missile directed at any person in their path. From the smallest insect to the largest predator. The thought is overwhelming. Even with the lattice in tatters, they'll have their hands full. And their numbers aren't many.

She passes the emergency vehicles on her way down Generals Highway.

The topsiders and their sirens and their guns and their thirst for revenge dressed up as justice.

Chapter Fifty

Three Rivers, California
September 2042

The drive to Three Rivers is ten minutes. There's no traffic on the road, and emergency services are split between the town and the park. Syrah does it in seven.

She doesn't make it home. She careens around the corner of Black Oak Drive and slams on the brakes. She's out of the car and running, the sound of the car's door chime trailing behind her like a streamer. A coyote is positioned on the corner. It lowers its head and latches on to her with feral stillness. Quickly she scans the area. There aren't any more. Nor does she see her brother. How then is he controlling them? One glance down the tree-lined street answers that question. He's got at least some part of the lattice operational again.

Then, from the corner of her eye, Syrah glimpses a dog barreling down the street toward her. A shepherd by the looks of it. A plump woman running behind it, screaming, "August, come back!" Syrah tries to wave them back, but the coyote rushes out to meet the dog just as the woman crashes into her.

They snip and bite, baring teeth. Tails raised.

But then something strange happens.

All the fight goes out of them. The coyote and the shepherd sniff each other as if in greeting. And in that exchange, a foul alliance is formed.

Side by side, they turn their attention to Syrah and the woman. Any recognition the shepherd has for its owner, gone, masked by the flow from the trees.

"August," the woman says, advancing. "It's me, Mom."

August tilts his head and gives one deep bark. The coyote joins in, yipping.

They turn on Syrah and the woman, who is now backing away. Together, the canine allies advance, all sharp teeth and drool.

"Don't run!" Too late, the woman takes off down the street. The coyote goes for her. While the shepherd homes in on Syrah. It charges toward her, leaps up in the air, going for her throat, but Syrah is no longer only human; she is part Rhiza. She spins and delivers what she hopes isn't a too-damaging blow to its side.

All around, Syrah watches the same scene unfold again and again. Pits, bulldogs, greyhounds, even a terrier, all gone predator pursuing human prey.

The fungi unfurl along Syrah's skin like tiny fans flicking open. She throws her head back and screams as it all pours out of her. The flow rolls off her body in waves, permeating the area. Slowly, the animals come back to themselves.

Long past the point when Syrah's body tells her to stop, to cut off the flow because there is nothing left to give, she continues.

When she falls to her knees and topples over onto the cold concrete, a muscular bulldog, tongue lolling from the side of its mouth, is approaching.

Syrah awakens to a bright light shining in her eyes. A paramedic is asking her if she's okay. She tells her she is. Refuses the IV fluids she tries to administer, preferring to hold out hope something will be left of Rhiza and she can have some of Artahe's potions instead. The streets are blessedly clear of carnage. When the paramedic isn't looking, Syrah sneaks away and heads back to her car.

To say the situation here is totally under control would be premature, but she senses that Taron needs her more. When she left, the canopy keepers had been working their way downslope, so she shifts gears and opts for the Wuksachi parking lot.

There is an arid wind blowing as bright morning light crests over the tree canopy. A dry, rigid current coursing through the forest and making Syrah's skin itch.

Syrah has traveled this path, and she has an inkling, a sinking feeling, of where she will find Romelo. A series of disturbed roots confirms it. She follows them like markers, guiding her toward the block of granite looming in the distance.

She almost steps on Dhanil before she sees him. Her eyes unable to make sense of what she sees. A tree root, inexplicably wrapped around his ankles and wrists, binding him. Remorse and regret war for control of his face; he can barely meet her eyes.

"My actions were shortsighted and disloyal," he says. "I only meant to save her, to save us all."

"By locking her away?" Syrah tugs and pulls at the roots. As much as she'd like to leave Dhanil here, she can't afford to. But the roots don't give. Romelo's gotten the lattice fully online, then.

"Behind you," he warns.

Another grouping of roots sprouts up. And then more. One reaching toward her wrist. She rolls out of the way just in time.

"Go," Dhanil urges. "I failed The Keeper; you must not. Romelo is drawing her away, up to the rock."

Syrah scrambles to her feet. "I'll come back for you."

Dodging roots. Leaping, steering around what feels like an earthen minefield. She spots more Rhiza, tied up just like Dhanil, before she makes it to the bottom of the staircase. The sign announcing the steep climb up Moro Rock.

Her chest rises and falls in great heaves, and she takes a moment to gather herself.

The stairway leading up and around is blessedly empty. But no less treacherous. It is fitting. Syrah visited the landmark when she first arrived, all those months ago. Did her brother sense her fear and select this place on purpose?

At the sounds of shouts and a struggle, Syrah dashes up the stairs, taking them three at a time. She does her best not to look over the side as she climbs higher.

As she rounds a particularly treacherous curve, Taron is there, and her arm stops Syrah in her tracks. A finger comes first to her lips; then she points upward.

She leans over, close to Syrah's ear. "He is my son and this is my responsibility. You must go back. You must lead them after Romelo and I are gone."

"What?" Syrah says, then lowers her voice. "The only way we beat him is together. Now let's—"

Taron grips her upper arm so tightly it cuts off her breath. "You and that brother of yours are so alike. You do not listen to reason."

Syrah tries to yank her arm away and isn't surprised when she can't.

Taron loosens her grip. "You are not strong enough to best him. I am at the end of my time. Yours is just beginning. You will lead the canopy keepers."

The rebuke stings, but in her heart, Syrah knows her friend's words ring true. But Taron is The Keeper, and if Syrah has anything to say about it, she'll continue for another hundred years. It's not a job Syrah wants.

Syrah pulls away this time and takes off at a run, only to have her feet swept out from under her. That damned staff—Dhanil must have given it back. But this time she rolls her ankle, badly. She tries to stand but nose-dives onto the unforgiving rock.

Taron is already on the move and soon turns a corner, out of sight.

"You don't have to do this," Syrah cries out after her.

They aren't even that high yet, but Syrah's stomach heaves with fear that she'll fall. She hauls herself up, leaning against the rock face for support. When she puts pressure on the ankle, pain lances up her leg and radiates throughout her body, climbing like a mountain of agony.

Despite the changes to her physiology, she nearly buckles. But she takes the first step, then another. By the time she reaches a bend, her fingernails are ragged from the places where she's gripped the rock to help propel herself forward.

The going is maddeningly slow. She grits her teeth through the pain; sounds of struggle swirl all around her. At one of the flat lookout areas, she sees something that tears her in half.

Romelo flicks a look at her, his expression grim, sad even, but determined. He's favoring his left leg, and his right arm hangs useless at his side. Blood seeps from what looks like a broken nose, painting his teeth a ghastly red. Taron isn't in much better shape.

"Stop!" Syrah screams. "We can end this now!" Her cries go unanswered.

Her brother isn't as strong as The Keeper, but he is faster. Taron's staff arcs through the air, glancing off his shoulder. In a blur, he spins around behind her and drives his elbow into her stomach.

What tears the spine-chilling scream from Syrah's throat is the sight of her friend, her adversary, tumbling from the walkway, hands grasping at but missing the railing.

Taron's body flailing, her eyes wide as she falls.

Chapter Fifty-One

Moro Rock, Sequoia National Park
September 2042

Syrah's ankle snaps, pitching her forward, and she plummets to the ground in a heap. She drags herself over to the railing that separates her from certain death, squinting as she peers into the abyss. The Keeper's body has disappeared from sight, but its deadly thud still echoes in her skull like an axe hacking through a millennia-old tree, devastating her soul with each crushing blow.

Every part of her wants to collapse and give up. Let Romelo do as he wants. But what she sees when she looks over at him—tears. He makes no sound, but the tears, the subtle tremble in his shoulders. His face is positively stricken. She's speechless. He mourns for Taron, and she despises him for it.

What should she do? Get herself down this mountain as fast as she can and help Taron or stay, stop the clear-and-present threat. Each choice is like fighting a million shadowy wraiths. Or should she give it all up and go to Compton and be by her father's side—where she should be. Guilt unfolds like a universal truth.

In that moment, the anger she feels at Romelo for what he's done, what he's trying to do, it frees her. The pain, the hurt—everything else vanishes like morning dew in sunlight.

Syrah grabs the downed staff and stands to face him. She searches his face. He tilts his head, doing the same. Siblings. His neat locs are yanked free of the binding he usually wears, billowing in the wind. Just then, Syrah remembers him. Fragments of a four-year-old's spotty viewpoint. It's more a feeling than anything solid, but the feeling is clear. Hate.

"I could have done worse, you know," he says, his voice raspy.

"You killed your own mother." Syrah is seething.

"Our mother is dead!" Romelo says, pacing. "Do you know what it is like to grow up in a place where you are the only one who looks like you? Walks and talks like you? Where you are the literal definition of 'foreign'?"

Syrah is in no mood for this sob story. He is not the only person to have suffered, but they don't all turn into sociopaths. No, the choices he made are his own.

"And how do you repay the people that took you in? Look what you've done to them. You're right, our birth parents *are* dead, killed right here in this forest. This whole thing is about you looking for somebody to blame," Syrah says.

Romelo lowers his gaze. "We should have died with them."

"But we didn't," Syrah says, leaning heavily on the staff. "Don't you think there's a reason for that? A reason why we were brought back together? You don't really believe it was so we could turn into killers. You can't punish everyone else for what happened to us."

"She found me, you know," Romelo says. When his voice cracks and he wipes away the tears streaming down his face, Syrah almost goes to him. "It was the worst fire of the decade. You know how it goes; you're a fire chief. Our family got separated. I'm guessing the park ranger found you. And Taron, she saved me. I still do not know why."

At the mention of Taron's name, Syrah almost loses it.

"Don't you see what Taron was trying to sell you? A life of peace, without conflict, a mission as lofty as the stars. That is only part of the story."

"But if you are so angry at *them*, why do you want to destroy us?"

"You are too much like them. You hear only what you choose."

"Enlighten me," Syrah says with a sigh. "Again."

"I believe the Giants, the other trees. Every creature walking this earth is of greater importance than the humans. And I believe people have been angry about that fact since they learned to form a coherent sentence. Since that time, they have sought to destroy themselves because the knowledge that they are not the center of the universe is more than they can bear. I . . . we . . . cannot let that come to pass. I do not care what the Rhiza think of me anymore. I am beyond that. I do what I do because I believe in our mission. To save this country, I must save the Giants. And if you care like you say you do, you will end this senseless conflict and join me."

Syrah realizes that she *is* only half listening, again. In the way that most humans do. All the while, she has been formulating a response, a retort to take down everything Romelo says. Her mouth opens, but this time she chooses not to speak. She considers his words, understands the truth and the necessity behind them. She looks off into the blue, brooding sky. Like viewing a silent film, she watches the conflict within. She and her brother, each of them playing a starring role.

Romelo raises an eyebrow. The right corner of his mouth quirks.

Her reasons are selfish, not noble. But her decision is made. "They weren't any more perfect than anyone else, but those people, my parents down in Compton, they loved me. I don't buy your sacrifice-a-few-to-save-the-many bullshit. You want to murder living, breathing people. Babies and children included."

"An unwise decision." Romelo stiffens, on alert again. "You had your chance." With that he strikes. He rushes her and makes a grab for

Taron's staff, but limping to the side, Syrah smacks the weapon against his bad leg.

He stumbles from the impact, back turned slightly away from her. Syrah moves in for another blow, but he twists his body away, and her momentum sends her stumbling.

Romelo is on her before she can block the chest punch that sends her crashing back against the rock. She cries out at the sharp edges digging into her back and spins out of the way before Romelo's follow-through lands.

She hefts the staff, swings it wide and left. It connects with Romelo's back with a sickening crunch. He flails but doesn't cry out. Backpedals a few steps, precipitously close to the edge of the mountain. His arms windmill. It's the look; it reminds her of herself. Of the scared child Uncle Dane deposited onto Trenton and Anissa Carthan's doorstep. Without thinking, Syrah drops the staff. She struggles forward, grabs his arm, and pulls him back.

But then he yanks her around and begins pushing her toward the edge. Syrah digs in her heels, the staff out of reach. She presses it against his chest, right leg out behind her, trying to stabilize, but she's losing ground.

Their faces are inches apart. His eyes are wild.

"If I go, I'm taking you with me," Syrah screams. She stops the struggle and pulls Romelo into a bear hug.

It works. He stops pushing, and instead, they tussle, each trying to gain ground. In a move she's seen but never quite mastered, Romelo sidesteps her enough to get his right leg behind her. Then he brings his elbow forward. She throws up a hand to block the blow intended for her throat but falls flat on her back anyway.

Romelo is on her. He straddles her, and his hands are around her neck. She scratches and claws at his hands. They don't budge.

Her windpipe feels as if the entire mountain is pressing down on it. Tears stream from her eyes, her vision blurring. Breath an impossibility.

Syrah tastes the bitterness of her impending death in her mouth. Syrah kicks out and is surprised when her foot thuds against the side of the mountain. She presses both feet into the rock and, with her last breath, thrusts upward with her hips.

Romelo tumbles over her and lands face-first, his head smacking against the top edge of an all-granite stair. Still, he scrambles up on all fours.

Syrah coughs and sputters but dives for the staff. She is still on her knees when she lifts it with arms that feel like noodles and brings it down hard against Romelo's head.

He collapses.

She drops the staff, horrified.

He doesn't get up.

Chapter Fifty-Two

Moro Rock, Sequoia National Park
September 2042

Regret slams into her like a blast of compressed air. The spots in her vision are clearing, and every part of her body is alight with agony. Syrah drags herself over to her brother. He is facing away from her and isn't moving. Blood is already visible in a pool beneath his head. Tentatively, she touches his leg. Prods an arm.

No, no, no.

Syrah turns Romelo over. His face is a pulpy mess, but with his eyes closed, he is the picture of serenity. The gash in the side of his head is the raw pink of uncooked meat. Syrah winces. She wants nothing more than to gather him up in her arms and carry him down the side of Moro Rock. To save her big brother as she wasn't able to all those years ago.

But her body feels broken, and this time there's no mushroom soup to speed her healing. All she can manage is to haul herself into a seated position, her back against a smooth patch of the rock. She drags Romelo onto her lap and cradles his head.

Where did her life go so wrong? Would things have been different if she had simply stayed in Florida?

The questions and regrets come hard and fast as her tears. She lets it all out. What she went through in her brief stint as fire chief. The blaze she started that caused all that damage. Quitting and retreating in disgrace. The undoing of her life when her father fell ill, sick, maybe dying or already dead. Taron, dead from a fall caused by the orphan she took in. That the brother Syrah never knew she had but now wants so desperately is likely dead at her own hand.

That without help she, too, will likely die here atop this mountain.

Syrah lets it all out in hiccuping, racking sobs. When she is spent and the sun sits low on the horizon, she feels something that makes her freeze.

Movement.

Is she imagining it? She wipes her face with the back of her arm. Romelo's right hand lies on her other forearm, and this time she sees it. His fingers tighten around her arm, ever so slightly.

She gets an idea and curses herself for her stupidity. It won't work. But it's the only hope they have.

Even if the lattice is back online, she and Romelo are probably too far up for the Giants to find them. She looks at his bare feet. Roughened soles near the texture of tree bark. She thinks back to what she read about the monument.

A hunk of solid stone, some six thousand feet at its peak. She pulls Romelo farther away from the rock face, props his legs up at the knees. He moans and stirs but doesn't open his eyes. "Come on," she beseeches the roots. "He's right here."

Her voice goes raw with her screams. It doesn't work. A thousand pounds of granite stand between them and the earth that he needs. With her ankle in ruins, the thought of going back down the mountain is something her mind refuses to contemplate. Yet she knows this is what she must do. A curious sound, the hiss and snort of a California condor. Sure enough the bird that went extinct in the eighties soars overhead, wings extended. Its flight so effortless. It eyes her as if to say, *We who choose to live in the wild do what we must to survive.*

Syrah steels herself and comes onto one knee. She sucks in a breath and holds it while she hauls her brother over her shoulder. Her body is howling with the excruciating remnants of the fight, but she centers her thoughts and stands.

Don't look over the side, she tells herself as she makes it to the top of the staircase.

The first step down, her heart is a drumroll in her chest. She takes another few steps, struggling with Romelo's bulk.

She stops to catch her breath, hoists him up for a better grip. She goes a few more steps before her brother's groans and her own exhaustion stop her. Syrah lets him down and props him up against the side of the mountain. She holds him with a forearm and wipes away the sweat stinging her eyes.

In a few moments, her breathing is better. She doesn't look over the side, can't stomach it. But she knows that she has a long way to go. And the way she is going now, it will take her the better part of a week to get to the ground. Her brother doesn't have that long, and she fears she doesn't either.

Without thinking about it, Syrah bends and lifts Romelo over her shoulder again. With one hand on the side of the rock face, she feels her way down; the other holds her brother in a tight grip. She isn't Rhiza strong, not yet, but strong enough.

Step by step, she descends. Her knees, ankles, shoulders are all blessedly numb. The sun taunts her, but the condor is there. Flying, watching. Syrah glances over at it once more and sees, at least she thinks she sees, the urging in its eyes.

Twice more she stops to catch her breath. But eventually she makes it down to the bottom. Where she expects to find Taron's body, there is nothing. No trace of her. Syrah is curious, but she knows that her journey isn't yet over. When she gets Romelo to safety, she'll come back and look for her.

She travels through the Alpine region, stepping over the perennial herbs that grow there. The subalpine is a blur. When she gets to the first grove of giant sequoias in the Montane region, she finally surrenders to exhaustion.

She manages to get Romelo down, roughly. He doesn't stir. Has she killed her own brother? Syrah drops to the earth, nothing left to propel her any farther, half leaning against the warm bark of a Giant. She feels herself slipping away and doesn't fight it.

She welcomes whatever comes, sleep or death. The last thing she sees before she allows her eyes to close is the stirring on the ground. Tiny root filaments poking their heads up out of the earth, sensing, seeking.

But the hairs on Romelo's legs don't stir, don't lengthen in response.

Chapter Fifty-Three

Rhiza
September 2042

The familiar scents of rich, coal-dark soil. The stiff feel of the pallet that over time she's come to find acceptable, if not comfortable. The sounds of bare feet shuffling along the corridor on the other side of what she knows is a closed door. The taste of bitter mushroom soup on her tongue. All these things flutter across the periphery of Syrah's consciousness before she opens her eyes, and she knows that she is home.

That feeling of contentment is fleeting. The aches in her body have lessened but worry her nonetheless. It is the pang, deep in her heart, that snaps her eyelids open. She shoots up like a bud pushing its way through a layer of snow. The room that she has come to know as her own is lit by a single wall sconce above the bedside table. A few blinks and rigorous wipes with the heels of her hands clear away what feels like a filmy layer of grit covering her eyes.

Her clothes are folded neatly in the chair pushed away from the desk. Boots beneath, socks poking up out of the tops. Syrah gingerly steps out of bed, ignoring the protests from her body. She's lacing up her boots when there's a knock at the door. "Come in," she calls.

"You are awake," Artahe says. Light from the hallway spills into the room, casting her in shadow. Syrah can't see her face, but the catch in her voice portends bad news. Artahe comes into the room, and with a touch, the other sconces light.

Syrah searches her expression. Fear, grief? Yes, those are there, along with something else unexpected. Relief. Perhaps Artahe was worried that Syrah wouldn't wake at all. Though her thoughts are on her father and how quickly she can get to him, the words that come out of her mouth express another priority. "Taron." And it is enough; she doesn't need to ask the question.

Artahe's bottom lip quivers, and Syrah gulps back the sob growing in her belly. "The Keeper is alive," she says. "But badly injured. We don't know . . ."

"Take me to her," Syrah says, one foot already out the door. The brightness of the passageway stabs into her eyes like pikes. She's unsteady on her legs, but with every step, she imagines, hopes, she's moving farther away from that deadly precipice.

Nods of approval. Pats on the back. Traditional greetings: "Peace be with us." Acceptance and hope are in those words and gestures, and for once Syrah doesn't shrug them off. She has no words for them, but she returns the greetings with a semblance of a smile. But there's also a very subdued air about the place. A hush that sets her teeth on edge.

Rhiza doesn't have anything in the way of a hospital, and having just passed the largest of the mushroom farms, she guesses that Taron is also doing her healing in her personal quarters.

Syrah and Artahe are walking side by side, her taller friend warily glancing down at her every few steps. "You may as well tell me what happened," Syrah asks. "The war topside." She looks up and adds, "Romelo?"

The tendons in Artahe's neck throb. Her gaze skyward. Her chest is heaving as she tells her, "Of your brother, I'm so sorry to tell you that news is that he is dead."

What have I done? Syrah takes this in without comment initially. Her stomach, though, feels like it has just added another in a series of expertly tied knots.

"I—I didn't mean to. I tried talking to him." Syrah's voice is flat, monotone. Trying to distance herself from the feeling threatening to erupt and smother her whole.

"The story of what happened on Moro Rock is yours," Artahe tells her. "Whether or not you choose to add it to our recorded history, when you are ready, is your choice."

Syrah can only nod curtly. She waits. There has to be more.

"The park is shut down. Romelo and his followers drove the animals into a frenzy. Even the birds were driven to attack."

Syrah thinks back about that condor that had been circling them atop the mountain. Had Romelo intended to use it to harry her off the side? And if he did, why didn't he?

"How many were hurt?" She pauses, then: "Killed?"

"A new rootspeaker almost has things completely back. When he does, we'll know more."

"But you have an idea now."

A sigh. "One hundred, maybe two. Some dead, some injured."

Syrah shakes her head in denial. She stops walking abruptly enough that someone behind her crashes into her. Artahe pulls her aside. Syrah's mouth is open, but she's speechless. She squeezes her eyes shut. Romelo went through with his plan. He was mad. Only she, Taron, and this remaining group of Rhiza had stood in his way. And that raises another question.

"How many Rhiza lost?"

Syrah notes that Artahe delivered the news about the topsiders with something bordering on regret, but at the mention of her own, her pain shines through that calm exterior. Her long-fingered hand goes to her chest. Tears well in her eyes. "Forty-three," she mutters. "And one gravely ill."

Syrah doesn't have to ask who that one is. Instead, she marches off in the direction of Taron's quarters, and soon Artahe falls in step beside her again.

When they arrive at The Keeper's door, Syrah recognizes the group that accompanied them in the fight aboveground. They have taken Dhanil's place. Syrah wonders idly where he and his accomplices are. As if reading her mind, Artahe says, "Dhanil is no longer a threat but resigned his position. His punishment will be swift."

They open the door and allow Syrah to go in alone. Unlike her own, the room is well lit. An air of sickness hovers thick and cloying. The bookshelves that line every wall are absent a few tomes that are stacked on The Keeper's bedside table, along with a wooden pitcher and cup. Taron looks up from where she is lying in bed, tucked under layers of bedding. Syrah rushes to her side, then takes her hand in hers. It is as rough as external bark and somehow as soft as the core at the same time. Her grip is weak.

"You made the right choice. Do not suffer one moment's guilt or second-guessing. That is your way, but it does not serve you," Taron says. Her voice is barely above a whisper. Her complexion is wan. Syrah wants to poke and prod, test to see the depth of Taron's injuries, but knows she'll never allow it.

"How are you feeling?" The question feels so inadequate, but she must ask it anyway.

"Never been better." Taron is not one for joking, and Syrah isn't in the mood; she fixes her with a glare.

"I'm serious," Syrah says.

"I fell from the side of a mountain. What would you have me say?"

Syrah thinks back to how Taron careened off the side of Moro Rock. That expression of shock and horror. At best, her relationship with The Keeper has been mercurial. They are neither fully friend nor foe. But what does exist between them is kinship. And because of that, because she didn't deserve what happened to her, Syrah is sorry and tells her so.

"Enough of that," Taron says. She removes her hand and struggles to sit up.

"No, rest now," Syrah urges. Then, trying to lighten the mood: "When will you be up and about? The canopy isn't going to keep itself."

This earns a chuckle from her mentor and friend. "My bones are broken in every place that matters. My staff is gone. I have lived a long and meaningful life."

"Now who's giving up!" Syrah shoots back. "You're always chastising me, and just listen to you."

"I did what I had to do to protect Rhiza and the topsiders," Taron says. "Every living thing has their time on this earth. There is nothing unnatural about it coming to an end."

Syrah considers the words and decides not to argue them, not now. "For a time, I didn't want to accept it, but now I know I was drawn here for a reason. I know The Mother had a plan for us all. I'll have to live with the fact that I killed my own brother, but I have other family to think about. I haven't been there for my parents. I must go to them."

"You must return," Taron says, her voice suddenly gaining strength. "I have named you Keeper—"

"Wait—"

"Until such time that I recover from my injuries, you will be my proxy. Now go. The sooner you do, the sooner you can return."

Syrah knows manipulation when she sees it. Now is not the time for arguments or challenges. She will go and check on her father. She prays that she isn't too late. That her mother will forgive her for what she knows will have to be an unsatisfactory excuse for her absence.

Other decisions, life-shattering, world-upending decisions, will come after that.

Chapter Fifty-Four

Sequoia National Park, California
September 2042

Returning topside is a rapture. Returning topside is anathema.

The air, though, the air that she used to believe was the purest she had ever breathed is tinged with the twin scents of sharp, acrid smoke and the metallic twang of fresh blood. As she walks, burned husks of tree remains haunt her. Halfway down the trail, she spots a pack of coyotes buried beneath a swarm of flies. Their vacant black eyes staring out as if questioning what could have possibly driven them to go so very wrong.

Crime scene tape drapes between the trees like bright yellow spiderwebs. Bits of food wrappers, a few banned plastic bottles, even a discarded hoodie and other detritus litter the understory. Her precious fungi overturned, uprooted in great patches.

Syrah closes her eyes to the contrast and focuses one foot in front of the other. By the time she reaches Wuksachi Lodge, she's shocked to see her uncle's truck parked near hers. He steps out, and from the looks of his clothes, he's slept here all night, likely more.

She steels herself. "Am I too late?"

A heartbeat. Three. Syrah is ready to tear at her own skin when he finally answers, "He's holding on. Are you ready to go see for yourself?"

After hastily collecting a few items of clothing and her cell phone from the house, Dane and Syrah are barreling down Highway CA-65 toward Compton.

Her mother's voice mail messages have traveled an eerily descending path from a worried tumult to a slow steely few that provide short, curt updates. No further questions about why Syrah isn't there with them. No pleading about when she will be. Having barely survived one storm, she is hurtling herself into the middle of another.

"I saw you," Dane says after what she knows he thinks is time enough for her to digest his lack of response. It is not. "Or I didn't see you. Out there in the park. I've seen some unbelievable sights in my years." He pauses, tries whistling. Fails miserably. "But a person there and not there in a blink. That's a new one on me. And I suspect it has something to do with why we're going to see your father now instead of a week ago, when you should have."

Syrah turns her head, studies the scenery along CA-65. The clear blue ocean water usually takes her breath away. That precipitous drop down to the rocks on the other side of the barrier urges her mind back to Moro Rock, but she gently pulls it back with an exhale. She left Rhiza and her brother to attend to her parents, and she has no space in her mind for them now.

Syrah wants to tell Dane everything, to share this burden she can no longer carry on her own. But now her tongue is tied around so many impossibilities, she doesn't know where to begin to unravel the mess.

When she doesn't speak, Dane continues: "That first time you took me out to the Sequoia, the General, I guess that was you trying to show me what you'd discovered. Look, I believe there are things in this world that we don't understand. I've been at Sequoia Park for most of my life, and I'm no botanist or biologist, but I've seen things here that even the experts haven't cataloged. What I'm trying to say is, I'm not going to judge you."

And that is exactly what Syrah needed to hear. Her uncle's words are like an unspoken permission. She plucks at a thread near the beginning of this improbable tale and doesn't stop until everything, from lifting the veil to the battle to protect humanity, is laid out bare between them. Dane doesn't interrupt, thankfully, only nods occasionally, raises an eyebrow, and blows out incredulous breaths.

"All this time," he says after Syrah has exhausted herself of words. "Right beneath my feet. A whole world, a—a species."

"Nobody can know," Syrah adds. Dane pauses long enough for her to say it again. "You have to promise me. We can't reveal them. You know what would happen."

"It was him," Dane says. "He's the one who sent that email."

Syrah isn't surprised.

"What if some of these people, these Rhiza or Keepers or whatever they're called, what if they try again? Counting that bear attack, the dogs and coyotes and everything else. Do you know how many people have been killed?"

"There are casualties on both sides, you know."

"For good reason. They were the aggressors. The thing is, I know that tone, and I don't like it. I'm starting to wonder where your loyalties lie."

"I did what I did to try and save everyone, and you question my loyalty? That's just rich."

"There is such a thing as justice—"

"Human justice," Syrah counters.

"Last time I checked, you were hum . . ." Dane trails off as recognition blooms on his face. "Somehow, being with them. It's changed you, hasn't it?"

Syrah lowers her head and sighs. She *has* changed. Maybe irreversibly so. But she is afraid that if she says so out loud, she may never be able to return to her former self. And she isn't so sure that she wants to. "I am different" is all she can muster.

Dane has picked up speed, and Syrah urges him to ease off the gas. Aside from her father, her uncle is the strongest man she knows, and even he is faltering under the weight of everything she's laid on his shoulders. They aren't as strong as the Giants.

"Did they hurt you?"

"Of course not," Syrah says, while there are parts of her body still so sore, she wants nothing more than a soak in a hot spring.

"These creatures—"

"People."

"The people—" Dane blows out a breath. "Did just being with them change you?"

He doesn't ask how, Syrah notes, and she understands. He's afraid. For her and of her. That reality saddens her more than she thought. "That and more," she says, then repositions herself so she's slouching down. She crosses her arms over her chest and leans her head back against the too-firm seatback. These small gestures are her signal that she's said all she can. All that she will—for now.

Chapter Fifty-Five

Compton, California
Late September 2042

Syrah is grateful that Dane doesn't press her for any further discussion. She's called her mother, who doesn't answer. The remaining half of the two-hour drive is spent with her trying, but not quite succeeding, to sleep. All the mindfulness practice in the world is not enough to stop the images that keep assailing her every time her eyelids close. Her body needs sleep for healing, but the nightmares that keep jolting her awake won't allow for it.

Once, when she's dozed for what feels like all of a few seconds, Dane's soothing voice and tap-tap on her leg let her know two things. One—he's forgiven her for whatever slights he perceives, and two—her nightmares are accompanied by some sort of fitful activity.

By the time they reach the hospital, she is a live wire. Fully alert, with the potential to destroy anyone who dares to cross her path the wrong way.

But she doesn't know what she'll find behind those deceptively welcoming sliding double doors. It scares her more than Romelo ever could. She exits the truck and slams the door. Her legs feel like trees cut off at the roots. Unsteady and unsure how to move. Dane's arm around her shoulders unlocks her steps.

He nods at a few nurses. Navigates the corridors, as familiar as the rooms in his tiny cabin. How many times was he here while Syrah fought the battle in Rhiza? Guilt has become her constant companion, and it is there with her as Dane urges her onward.

"I'm going to get some coffee," he says. He knows without asking that this is a conversation that she and her parents need to have alone. He is complicit, not without his own need to provide some answers, but that will come later.

She knows from Dane that her mother has returned to their home only to shower and change clothes. That she spends most nights here at the hospital in a cot that no woman her age should be confined to.

So Syrah is surprised when she pushes open the door and finds the room empty, save her father propped up in bed, forkful of something fluffy and pale yellow, a semblance of an egg, halfway to his mouth. He drops the fork at the sight of her. It clangs onto the food tray. A bit of egg lands in his lap, but his eyes don't see any of it; they are glued to her.

There is only one tube in his arm. His coloring is good. The beeping of the two machines flanking him sounds normal, at least to her ears. But the room smells of lingering sickness. Something sour and antiseptic.

Syrah stands where she is, just behind the closed door for a full minute. They—father and daughter—appraise each other with a distance so profound it hurts. Syrah swallows that hurt like a lump of fiery, red-hot coal and finds herself moving forward. She grabs a cloth from the bedside table and cleans up the mess. She can feel her father's eyes on her. He hasn't spoken, though. Is it because he can't physically do so or because he has no desire?

"I'm sorry," Syrah says. She has been waiting for him to speak first. She is ten years old again. That time when she got angry and told him that he wasn't her real father, that her real parents were dead.

"I am too," he says, pushing the food tray aside.

Everything in Syrah's body wants to fall into his arms and cry for the next year, maybe two. Something holds her back. Instead, she pulls up a chair, one with what she recognizes as her mother's gray sweater draped around it, and sits. She does take her father's hand in hers.

"How are you?" she says, unable to look at him. She studies his hands. The nails are longer than he normally keeps them. The lack of lotion apparent in the ashy crevices between his fingers. But his hands are soft and warm.

"I'll live," he says. "If that's what you're asking." There's an edge to his voice that draws her eyes up. He reclaims his hand.

"There is a reason I couldn't be here," Syrah says. "A good reason."

"Because you were scared? That's your good reason?" Her father's chest is heaving.

She makes the decision then not to tell them. She cannot. *Can't.* Rhiza. The war she still isn't even sure is over. It's too much, too complicated. They have enough to deal with as a family. "The only reason I have."

"If I could, I'd get up from this bed and slap your face," her father says.

Syrah reels. This isn't what she was expecting at all. Him? Angry with her?

"I loved you, I raised you, I put up with your nonsense." He's a freight train off the tracks. "And I supported you. If that doesn't mean anything, if my life doesn't mean anything to you, then I wasted my time, because I apparently didn't teach you shit."

"I'm sorry."

"Damn right you are." Syrah's mother's voice sounds from the now-open doorway. "When your father needed you most, you disappeared. You're selfish, always have been."

Syrah wants to explain. But knows she can't. And as angry as she wants to be, they're right, and it dissipates just like that.

"And you know what?" Her mother has stepped into the room and taken up her perch beside her husband. She didn't touch Syrah as she passed. "Because we are your parents—and make no mistake, that is who we are—we love you and forgive you anyway."

The weight of those words batters Syrah like a ram. There is truth in them. Syrah does something unexpected then. She takes off her socks and shoes, gets up, and settles herself in bed alongside her father. She lays her head on his shoulder and flops an arm around his middle. Her fingertips brush her mother's. She clasps them back.

"When can we go home?"

It is because parents are experts in scrutiny. Because their first questions lead to more, to dissection. It is because they know their offspring too well. Well enough to latch on to every facial tic, eye bat, and the legion of your tells that they've bird-dogged over the years, that Syrah doesn't tell them about what she has become. What she must do.

The decision her heart made long before her mind was willing to acknowledge it.

With her father released from the hospital and settled back at home, a comfy stool set up for him in the garden now, and a few days in which their family began the slow process of knitting itself back together, they all acknowledge it is okay for her to get back to the thing that was so important it kept her away in the first place. Syrah and Dane are in his little green pickup truck trawling north on CA-99 at what feels like sloth pace, heading back home.

Their silences used to be as comfortable as an afternoon shower but now feel as thick and impenetrable as the walls of a medieval fortress.

"You all needed that time alone," he says, lowering the bridge, rung by creaky rung. "If you're wondering why I made myself scarce."

Syrah nods. "Figured."

"You don't get it, do you?"

"Get what?"

"How incredibly lucky you are."

Syrah shoots Dane a look. His tone is serious. She half expected him to be joking. She lost the job she'd dreamed of for as long as she can remember, taking a part of the park she revered with it. She stumbled onto a world and a people that had, without her permission, changed her and lured her into a fight she was ill-equipped to handle. Her home, her foundation—shattered. A brother found and then lost, at her hand. *I am a lot of things,* Syrah thinks to herself. *Luck doesn't even crack the top ten on that list.*

Her uncle waving his hand in front of her face draws her back to the present. "You had two sets of parents. *Two.* Good and decent people that loved and cared for you. You've been through something awful, and you've got to feel that. Process it. When it gets to be too much, just think about them, the strength in them, is all I'm saying."

Dane's words wrap around her, blanket soft and comfortable. That is him all the way: a man who keeps his words safe and secure, like rare black pearls encased in a shell. On occasion, though, he'll pry himself open and drop one of those obsidian nuggets of wisdom in your lap.

"I hadn't thought about it like that," Syrah says and means it. She also knows she's reached a point in her life that everybody reaches—if they're lucky. The time you realize that your parents, your aunts and uncles and grandparents even, all had lives that you'd never thought to ask about. Now wasn't right, but at some point, when she reemerged, she would ask Dane about his.

As they take exit 30 toward Porterville and the Sequoia National Park and make their way east, Dane flips on the signal to turn right off Sierra Drive. Syrah says, "Take me to the fire station first, please?"

Dane's head whips over at her. The unspoken query in his gaze, *Are you sure you're ready for this?*

Syrah nods, then turns away. "It'll only take a minute."

The brief ride passes like a sentence, suspended.

It isn't reticence that curls and uncurls her fingers. It's acknowledgment. The prescribed-burn mistake is a thing of the past, and to conscript it there permanently, she must confront it one last time.

When they reach the station, her uncle parks the truck. Before she gets out, he says, "I know you don't need me to come in with you, but if you were to ask, I wouldn't turn you down."

"Maybe get out and stretch your legs a bit," Syrah says. "You've had a long drive."

Both engine bay doors are rolled open this time, welcoming in sun that shines like freedom. Everything is the way she remembers: workbench, tool chest, the treadmill and elliptical. The weights aren't sprawled on the floor but stacked neatly in racks.

Syrah's fingertips brush the gleaming white fire engine on her way inside and come away clean as a whistle.

She finds Lance and a few others in the common area. Alvaro among them. Lance stands first. "Chief," he calls, comes forward, and shakes her hand.

Alvaro is next. He's wearing the standard-issue short-sleeved T-shirt. His forearms covered in puckered and raised scars.

The crew greets her with the respect of a former colleague, if not an old friend. This she prefers. They compliment her on her work when she helped during the last fire. As the conversation thins, the others trail away. Alvaro stops.

"That time off, to heal these." He holds up his arms. "Let's just say you saved my marriage. Me and my wife thank you."

Syrah's surprise appears only in the form of raised eyebrows. "Then that makes me very happy for you both," she says. With a shoulder squeeze, he's gone, and she and Lance face each other.

"You proved your worth out there," Lance says. "You earned this job. But it's mine now."

Lance has managed to annoy her, and she hasn't even been in the station five minutes. "Don't lose any sleep over me. I'm not here for my old job back," Syrah reassures him. "This is . . . just me stopping by to say, I'll see you around. And thanks for calling on me."

Lance's expression softens. "I'll do it again if we need you."

With a final glance at the station, Syrah heads back outside.

As soon as she's in the truck, Uncle Dane says, "You good?"

"I am," Syrah says and knows that she really is.

He grins. "Let's get you home, then."

"I don't need to go home," Syrah says. There's nothing that she needs there. "Just drop me at the lodge. I'll make my way from there." She doesn't say the word "Rhiza." She doesn't have to.

From the corner of her eye, Syrah sees Dane's hesitation, the tightness of his jaw. The way he flares his nostrils and thins his lips. He looks both ways, a minute longer than necessary, and then turns left.

"Will you be safe?" he asks.

Syrah considers this, discards the easy, rote answer, and surprises herself by saying, "For a time, I thought Rhiza was better than our world. That their mission, their history, made them somehow impervious to everything that makes us human. But . . ." She pauses to massage her sore shoulder. "I found out that they aren't all that different from us. So, to answer your question, I'll be about as safe as I'd be anyplace else."

Dane's puff of breath doesn't sound like a mirth-filled chuckle or a haughty rebuke. Syrah thinks of it as the sound those who love you make when they don't understand why you're choosing to walk off a cliff—sans parachute.

"I want to meet them," he says.

"When that's possible, you'll be the first."

Syrah settles in, warmed by the familiar scenery as they pass through the city she's called home for such a short time. They take Generals Highway and about fifteen minutes later come upon the sign:

WELCOME TO SEQUOIA NATIONAL PARK. Rather than tensing, Syrah relaxes. Dane slows.

"Why not reverse this?" he says when he pulls into the back parking space at Wuksachi. "You go back to your house. Your paid-off house. And you visit this place, these people. You stay in our world, and you can still be a part of theirs."

His words are wise, reasonable. Syrah has thought the same thing herself. There are not words to express why, but the reverse feels more natural to her. "I'll have my phone. There will be times when you can't reach me, but I'll resurface and check messages. And if you really need me, leave a sign at one of the Giants."

"A sign?" Dane glances over at her.

Syrah thinks for a moment, smiles at the feel of the fungi nesting beneath her skin before she recalls the way he likes to announce himself when he visits her at home. "Use your signature knock."

She exits the truck and doesn't look back. The trek up to the cave entrance feels natural and right. There's something about the splendor of the park on the precipice of fall. A wild elemental symmetry. Wildflowers and grasses that grow mindless of master plans or orderly suburban beds. Syrah inhales the mild, delicious air, and it coats her expanded lungs like a salve. The scent of earth, rich like spiced wine.

And the Giants. Sentinels whose canopies scrub the air clean. She'll do her part to see to it that they remain at their posts.

She advances forward with new purpose, imagining how she will decorate her room.

The veil opens.

Epilogue

Seeing with Ancient Eyes

The Cycle Persists

The venerable one is burning
Its hungry, many-tendriled mouth pulsing beneath the hard-packed soil
At his call, the others respond with water and nutrients

Its arms are lifted as if waiting for the creator to come and claim him from its long, heated existence

It wears cones and nests and leaves in its hair
As the cones open and drop to the forest floor, the venerable one passes all that it knows and has ever known through the lattice

Memory speaks from distant springs and into the winter of its life
It stirs the heartblood

He has grown quiet. One signal, then two beats
with no response
Those nearest are suffering through the burn

A single cone nests in the fire-cleared earth.
Urged on by the heat, it flowers, opening its
insides to the flame. Seedlings take flight and
are swept away in the roaring wind

One seedling burrows in, fighting to remain close
to the one that birthed it
A tiny tendril gropes beneath the surface-swelling
artistry
Outward and downward

Until

It discerns another offshoot, that quickening of
life. It latches on to it and feeds
The root strengthens

It latches on and pulls and pulls. Too much for
one so young. It wants to live
Quickly
Much too quickly
Unnaturally
It grows

Acknowledgments

Thanks first to the National Park Service and the wildland firefighters of Sequoia National Park for undertaking such a noble mission and for their sacrifice. Thanks for taking the time to answer my questions and for keeping an email thread going well past the point where they probably ran out of patience with this random author on the other side of the country. Any omissions or extravagances are craft decisions and not reflective of their expertise.

My support system: Eden, DaVaun, Nicky. Outstanding writers, juggling as many balls as I am, but who always manage to be there when I call on them.

For Eric, the wind above, beneath, and all around my wings. Thanks to Dior for joining me on a trip to New Orleans that just about made my whole writing career worthwhile. And to the rest of my family: my mom, sisters, brother John (RIP), aunts and uncles, cousins, nieces and nephews. Thank you for understanding that I can't always be there, that these words that I love gotta get written. I don't say it often, but know that I love you all.

Thank you to everyone who has ever bought one of my books, attended my events, tweeted, grammed, TikToked, or otherwise supported me. Couldn't do this without you.

Thank you to the two ladies who continue to be my aces: my agent, Mary C. Moore, and my editor, Adrienne Procaccini. And a big thank-you to the talented Mr. Clarence Haynes for challenging me, for the pep talk, and for giving me the freedom to just write. His careful hand guided the very best of this book.

Team 47North, you are all that!

About the Author

Veronica G. Henry is the author of *Bacchanal* and, in the Mambo Reina series, *The Quarter Storm* and *The Foreign Exchange*. Her work has debuted at #1 on multiple Amazon bestseller charts and was short-listed for the Manly Wade Wellman Award and chosen as an Amazon editors' pick for Best African American Fantasy. She is a Viable Paradise alum and a member of SFWA and the MWA. Her stories have appeared, or are forthcoming, in the *Magazine of Fantasy & Science Fiction*, Many Worlds, and *FIYAH* literary magazine. For more information, visit www.veronicahenry.net.